唐詩英譯研究

趙娟 編著

崧燁文化

前言

　　唐詩是中國文化的瑰寶，它以深邃的意境、精巧的思想、雋永的藝術魅力，對後世的文學發展產生著極其深遠的影響。「熟讀唐詩三百首，不會吟詩也會吟。」可見，讀唐詩對提高詩學修養有著不可忽略的作用。因此，古今中外許多翻譯大家都在為唐詩走向世界做著不懈的努力。

　　早在 19 世紀末，英國漢學家翟理斯（Giles）就曾把唐詩譯成韻文，得到評論家的好評。如英國作家斯特萊徹（Strachey）所說：「翟譯唐詩是那個時代最好的詩，在世界文學史上佔有獨一無二的地位。」20 世紀初期英國漢學家韋利（Waley）認為譯詩用韻不能因聲損義，主張把唐詩譯成自由詩或散體。他的譯詩實踐與理論開啓了唐詩翻譯史上的詩體與散體之爭。一般說來，散體譯文重真，詩體譯文重美，所以散體與詩體之爭也可以昇華為真與美的矛盾。唐詩英譯真與美之爭一直延續到了今天。

　　把唐詩翻譯成英文是漢譯英中難度極大的工作之一。不過，「詩雖難譯，但還是可譯的」，隨著時代的發展，語言的交流愈發頻繁，文化的共通空間越來越大，再加上新的翻譯輔助工具的出現，提高了唐詩的

英譯質量，讓西方讀者體會唐詩之美並不是一件不可能的事。近年來，國家愈發重視傳統文化的外譯工作，越來越多的優秀外語人才加入唐詩英譯的盛事之中，唐詩翻譯呈現出一片欣欣向榮的景象。這些不同的譯者有著各自不同的文化背景、不同的人生閱歷，對原詩意境有不同的欣賞角度，產生的譯作也是各有千秋，因此唐詩英譯工作呈現出姹紫嫣紅、異彩紛呈的局面，儼然一幅百花齊放的翻譯春景圖，為唐詩英譯注入了生機和活力，值得我們深入地研究和學習。本書就是在這種時代背景下開展的對唐詩英譯活動的探索，旨在梳理唐詩英譯進程中各個不同時代和譯家的翻譯策略與方法，為後來的研究者提供可資借鑑的方法和文獻資料。

　　本書共分四章。第一章梳理了唐詩的主要派別及主要代表詩人的詩歌風格。第二章對唐詩英譯理論進行了梳理。第三章主要論述唐詩文化詞彙和典故的英譯策略。第四章收集了唐代詩人的部分名作，每首詩歌均選配三篇以上不同譯者的英語譯文，這些譯文均出自西方漢學家之手或是中國現當代翻譯大家筆下。本書對這些譯本的翻譯技巧和方法進行了歸納總結，從對比的角度進行了賞析。一首唐詩配上多首英語譯文符合德裔美國心理學家埃倫菲爾斯（Von Ehrenfels）首創的格式塔心理學所提倡的感知心理特點，即一首原作詩歌被翻譯成多個色彩各異的英語譯文後，我們閱讀這些譯文時仍能辨別出其原作是誰。這樣做還有一個目的，即同一原作被不同譯者翻譯成英語後絕不會完全相同，甚至還會在名家的譯文中發現誤譯、漏譯的現象，個中緣由希望讀者能自己從閱讀和欣賞中體悟出來。

本書條理清晰、觀點明確、論證合理，論據也較充分，對於唐詩英譯有一定的指導性；對於唐詩愛好者提高其鑒賞與翻譯水準也不無裨益。但囿於筆者水準，本書難免存在紕漏與不足，望讀者不吝賜教。

趙娟

2018 年 9 月

目錄

第一章　唐詩說略 / 1

　　第一節　唐詩的主要派別 / 1

　　第二節　唐詩的詩歌風格 / 20

第二章　唐詩英譯理論研究 / 39

　　第一節　翻譯的主體和客體 / 40

　　第二節　直譯與意譯 / 47

　　第三節　歸化與異化 / 52

　　第四節　目的論 / 58

　　第五節　三美論 / 65

　　第六節　生態翻譯學 / 71

第三章　唐詩文化詞彙及典故英譯研究 / 79

　　第一節　中西思維方式對比 / 79

第二節　孫大雨唐詩譯作中民俗文化詞彙的英譯 / 82

第三節　《長干行》中文化詞彙的英譯 / 89

第四節　《清平調》中的典故英譯研究 / 94

第五節　《錦瑟》中的典故英譯研究 / 100

第四章　唐詩不同英譯本賞析 / 107

第一節　李白詩歌英譯賞析 / 108

第二節　杜甫詩歌英譯賞析 / 141

第三節　白居易詩歌英譯賞析 / 166

第四節　王維詩歌英譯賞析 / 193

第五節　孟浩然詩歌英譯賞析 / 201

第六節　李商隱詩歌英譯賞析 / 209

第七節　唐朝諸家詩選譯 / 214

參考文獻 / 233

後記 / 242

第一章　唐詩說略

唐詩泛指創作於唐朝的詩。唐詩是中華民族珍貴的文化遺產之一，是中華文化寶庫中的一顆明珠，同時也對世界上許多民族和國家的文化發展產生了很大影響，對於後人研究唐代的政治、民情、風俗文化等都有重要的參考意義和價值。

第一節　唐詩的主要派別

唐朝是中國詩歌的繁盛時期，詩歌的風格流派千姿百態，絢麗多彩。例如，王維的田園詩恬靜幽美，李白的詩奔放飄逸，杜甫的詩沉鬱頓挫，白居易的詩通俗平易，李商隱的詩精工典麗，等等。詩歌是詩人的性格、氣質、閱歷、素養等方面的寫照。唐代形成了豐富多彩的創作流派，是一個時代文學繁榮昌盛的重要標志。除了李白、杜甫兩座壁立萬仞的高峰以外，還有許多流派和大家。

一、山水田園詩派

山水田園詩，源於南北朝詩人謝靈運和晉代詩人陶淵明，唐代以王維、孟浩然為代表。這類詩以描寫自然風光、農村景物以及安逸恬淡的隱居生活見長。詩境雋永優美，風格恬靜淡雅，語言清麗洗練，多用白描手法。

山水田園派以山水等自然景觀為主要描寫對象，歌咏田園生活，大多以農村的景物和農民、牧人、漁夫的勞作為題材。詩人們以自然山水或農村自然景物、田園生活為吟咏對象，把細膩的筆觸投向靜謐的山林、悠閒的田野，描繪田園牧歌式的生活，借以表達對現實的不滿以及對寧靜平和生活的向往。

（一）主要特點

山水田園詩屬於寫景詩的範疇。這類詩歌的主要特點是「一切景語皆情語」，亦即作者筆下的山水自然景物都融入了作者的主觀情愫，或者借景抒情，或者情景交融。

（二）主要代表人物

山水田園詩派以孟浩然、王維為代表，此外還有儲光羲、常建、祖詠、裴迪、綦毋潛等人。他們繼承陶淵明、謝靈運、謝朓等人的田園詩、山水詩的創作傳統，形成了具有共同題材內容和相近藝術風格的詩歌流派。他們的詩歌描繪自然山水和田園風光，表現返璞歸真、怡情養性的情趣，抒寫隱逸生活的閒情逸致。他們的詩歌風格清新自然，意境淡遠閒適，寫景狀物工致傳神，提高了詩歌表現自然景物的藝術技巧，是唐詩藝苑中的一枝奇葩。

1. 王維

王維是盛唐山水田園詩派的代表作家，具有多方面的文學、藝術才能，精通繪畫、書法、音樂。王維早年立志於功名進取，寫了許多風格雄渾、境界開闊，充滿豪情逸氣的詩作，其中以邊塞和遊俠題材的詩歌居多，如《少年行》《從軍行》《老將行》《隴頭吟》《使至塞上》等。但在唐代詩歌史上奠定其地位和最能標志其詩歌藝術成就的是山水田園詩。他的山水田園詩主要內容是描繪田園隱逸生活、自然山水，如《渭川田家》《山居秋暝》《終南山》《鳥鳴澗》《鹿柴》《竹里館》《辛夷塢》等，或寫田園生活的恬靜閒逸，或寫自然景物的清幽秀美。

（1）王維山水田園詩的藝術特點

王維的山水田園詩是詩情與畫意的高度統一。蘇軾曾評論說：「味摩詰之詩，詩中有畫，觀摩詰之畫，畫中有詩。」（《東坡志林》）王維善於發現和捕捉自然景物的形象特徵和狀態，以畫家的繪畫技巧去構圖和選擇色彩，並將詩人對自然的獨特的情感體驗、審美感受及精神境界融入景物之中，創造出優雅秀美的藝術境界。

王維的一些山水田園詩在幽邃、寂靜、空靈的藝術境界中直接透入了禪宗佛理的觀照，是禪意、禪趣在詩境中的藝術體現。

王維的山水田園詩既有陶淵明詩歌渾然天成的藝術境界，也有謝靈運詩歌細緻精工的刻寫。語言清新明快，潔淨洗練，是樸素平淡與典雅秀美的完美結合。而且詩歌語言具有極強的藝術表現力。

（2）王維山水田園詩代表作

   山居秋暝
空山新雨後，天氣晚來秋。
明月鬆間照，清泉石上流。
竹喧歸浣女，蓮動下漁舟。
隨意春芳歇，王孫自可留。

   終南山
太乙近天都，連山接海隅。
白雲回望合，青靄入看無。
分野中峰變，陰晴眾壑殊。
欲投人處宿，隔水問樵夫。

2. 孟浩然

孟浩然是與王維齊名的唐代山水田園詩派的代表作家，是唐代第一個大量寫作山水田園詩的詩人。他的詩歌以山水詩居多，或寫遊歷所見各地山水景色，或寫家鄉自然風光。其中往往在抒寫孤高的情懷中夾雜著失意的情緒，在以景自娛中融入了旅愁鄉思的情懷，如《宿建德江》《臨洞庭湖贈張丞相》《江上思歸》等。他的田園詩主要是寫隱居生活的高雅情懷和閒情逸致，如《過故人莊》《遊精思觀回，王白雲在後》等。

（1）孟浩然山水田園詩的藝術特點

  孟浩然的山水田園詩的風格大多是平和衝淡，清新自然，不尚雕飾，而又能超凡脫俗。沈德潛評論說：「孟詩勝人處，每無意求工，而清超越俗，正復出人意表。」（《唐詩別裁集》）聞一多說：「淡得看不見詩了，才是真正孟浩然的詩。」（《唐詩雜論》）他的田園詩深受陶淵明的詩風影響，寫得平淡自然、質樸真淳，富有生活氣息，如在《過故人莊》中描繪農家的淳樸生活和鄉村的自然景色，在淡淡的筆墨中都表現得十分自然而親切。但孟浩然的山水詩也有寫得氣象雄渾、境界闊大的，如《望洞庭湖贈張丞相》。

  孟浩然的詩歌語淡而味濃，正如沈德潛所論：「襄陽詩從靜悟得之，故語淡而味終不薄。」（《唐詩別裁集》）他的詩歌善於運用平淡的語言，融入個人的主觀感受和情感意蘊，創造出清遠拔俗的藝術境界，蘊含了濃厚的詩歌情致韻味。

（2）孟浩然山水詩代表作

　　　　過故人莊

故人具雞黍，邀我至田家。
綠樹村邊合，青山郭外斜。
開軒面場圃，把酒話桑麻。
待到重陽日，還來就菊花。

（3）孟浩然詩歌成就

第一，盛唐山水田園詩派的第一人，「興象」創作的先行者。

孟浩然是唐代第一位創作山水詩的詩人，是王維的先行者。他的旅遊詩描寫逼真，《望洞庭湖贈張丞相》寫得氣勢磅礡，格調渾成。

孟浩然的一生經歷比較簡單，他詩歌創作的題材也比較單一。孟詩絕大部分為五言短篇，多寫山水田園和隱居的逸興以及羈旅行役的心情。其中雖不無憤世嫉俗之詞，但是更多的是屬於詩人的自我表現。孟詩不事雕飾，佇興造思，富有超妙自得之趣，而不流於寒儉枯瘠。他善於發掘自然和生活之美，即景會心，能寫出一時真切的感受。如《秋登萬山寄張五》《夏日南亭懷辛大》《過故人莊》《春曉》《宿建德江》《夜歸鹿門歌》等篇，自然渾成，而意境清迥，韻致流溢。

在孟浩然這裡，山水詩中的形象已不再是山水原形的描摹，也不是在其中簡單地加入了自己的情感，而是採用了表現手法，將山水的描繪與自己的思想感情及性情氣質的展現合而為一，因而使其山水詩中形象的刻畫達到了前所未有的高度，使其山水詩中的形象提升為藝術形象的一種高級形態亦即『意象』。可以說在孟浩然之前，還沒有哪位詩人在山水詩中如此深深地打上作者本人性情氣質的個性印記。

第二，清淡自然的詩風。

孟浩然的詩歌主要表達隱居閒適、羈旅愁思，詩風清淡自然，以五言古詩見長。

孟浩然是唐代第一位大力寫作山水詩的詩人。他主要寫山水詩，是山水田園詩派代表之一，他前期主要寫政治詩與邊塞遊俠詩，後期主要寫山水詩。其詩今存二百餘首，大部分是他在漫遊途中寫下的山水行旅詩，也有他在遊覽家鄉一帶的萬山、峴山和鹿門山時所寫的遣興之作，還有少數詩篇是寫田園村居生活的。詩中取材的地域範圍相當廣大。

山水詩在孟浩然筆下又被提升到新的境界，這主要表現在：詩中情和景的關係，不僅是彼此襯托，還是水乳交融般的密合；詩的意境，由於剔除了一切

不必要、不協調的成分，而顯得更加單純明淨；詩的結構也更加完美。孟浩然在旅程中偏愛水行，如他自己所說：「為多山水樂，頻作泛舟行。」（《經七里灘》）他的詩經常寫到漫遊於南國水鄉所見的優美景色和由此引發的情趣，如《耶溪泛舟》。

房日晰在《略談孟浩然詩風的清與淡》一文中指出：「縱觀孟詩，其詩風之淡，大致有三：一為思想感情的淡，沒有激切的情緒的流露；二為詩意表現的淡，沒有濃烈的詩意的展示；三為語言色彩的淡，沒有絢麗色彩的描繪。」

第三，豐富的山水詩歌意境。

孟浩然山水詩的意境，以一種富於生機的恬靜居多。但是他也能夠以宏麗的文筆表現壯偉的江山，如《彭蠡湖中望廬山》。清人潘德輿以此詩和《早發漁浦潭》為例，說孟詩「精力渾健，俯視一切」（《養一齋詩話》），正道出了其意興勃鬱的重要特徵。盛唐著名詩評家殷璠喜用「興象」一詞論詩，在評述孟浩然的兩句詩時，也說「無論興象，兼復故實」（《河嶽英靈集》）。所謂「興象」，是指詩人的情感、精神對物象的統攝，使之和詩人心靈的顫動融為一體，從而獲得生命，具有個性和活力。重「興象」其實也是孟浩然詩普遍的特點。通過對幾首不同的作品進行比較，可以看得更清楚。《望洞庭湖贈張丞相》《宿桐廬江寄廣陵舊遊》《宿建德江》這三首詩都寫了江湖水景，但風格各異。第一首作於孟浩然應聘入張九齡幕府時。他為自己能夠一展抱負而興奮，曾寫下「感激遂彈冠，安能守固窮」（《書懷貽京邑同好》）、「故人今在位，歧路莫遲回」（《送丁大鳳進士赴舉呈張九齡》）之類詩句。正是這種昂奮的情緒，使他寫下了「氣蒸雲夢澤，波撼岳陽城」這樣氣勢磅礡的名句。第二、三首均作於落第後南遊吳越之日，前者以風鳴江急的激越動盪之景寫自己悲涼的內心，後者則以野曠江清的靜景寫寂寞的遊子情懷，它們的神採氣韻是很不相同的。本之以「興」，出之以「象」，突出主要的情緒感受而把兩者統一起來，構築起完整的意境，這是孟浩然寫景詩的重要貢獻。

第四，創造性的詩歌表現。

出入古近的體格，饒有灑脫自在的情致，也是孟詩創造性的表現之一。孟浩然詩歌的語言，不拘奇抉異而又洗脫凡近，「語淡而味終不薄」（沈德潛《唐詩別裁集》）。他的一些詩往往在白描之中見整煉之致，經緯綿密處卻似不經意道出，表現出很高的藝術功力。例如，他的名篇《過故人莊》通篇侃侃敘來，似說家常，和陶淵明的《飲酒》等詩風格相近，但陶詩是古體，這首詩卻是近體。「綠樹村邊合，青山郭外斜」這一聯句，畫龍點睛地勾勒出一個環抱在青山綠樹之中的村落的典型環境。還有那一首婦孺能誦的五絕《春

曉》，也是以天然不覺其巧的語言，寫出微妙的惜春之情。

另外，孟浩然在詩體的運用上往往突破固有程式的局限，讀來別有滋味。例如，《舟中曉望》平仄聲律全合五律格式，但中兩聯不作駢偶，似古似律。胡應麟《詩藪》提及此類詩「自是六朝短古，加以聲律，便覺神韻超然」。又如《夜歸鹿門山歌》，這是一首歌行體的詩，但通篇只是把夜歸的行程一路寫下來，不事鋪張，其篇制規模類似近體，吸收了近體詩語言簡約的特點，而突出歌行體的蟬聯句法，讀來頗有行雲流水之妙。

第五，獨特的詩歌美學觀。

在詩歌創作的藝術形式方面，孟浩然也有其獨特的見解。他主張詩歌要用形象思維，通過詩的語言塑造形象，通過形象顯示詩歌的意旨。讀者「棄象忘言」而得意。他在《本闍黎新亭作》詩中寫道：「棄象玄應悟，忘言理必該。靜中何所得？吟咏也徒哉！」孟浩然借用了佛學和道家哲學中的「棄象忘言」說，提倡詩歌創作的抒情言志、表情達意不必太直露，要有弦外之音、象外之旨。

孟浩然還主張作詩不必受近體格律的束縛，應當「一氣揮灑，妙極自然」。《孟浩然集》有詩267首，其中五言古詩63首，七言古詩6首，五言律詩130首，七言律詩4首，五言排律37首，五言絕句19首，七言絕句8首。從中可以看出，除69首古風外，全是近體詩，而五言律詩又最多。可以說他是盛唐詩人中大量寫作近體詩的第一人。但這些詩大都不能算是嚴格合律的近體詩。如《舟中晚望》《洛下送奚三還揚州》《洞庭湖寄閻九》《都下送辛大之鄂》《與諸子登峴山》等詩，皆與五言律詩的對偶不合。但詩品家對它們的評價卻相當高。嚴羽《滄浪詩話》稱：「皆文從字順，音韻鏗鏘。」

孟浩然五言律詩不合律有其深層次的美學原因。他追求自然美，是對初唐過多追求形式美的矯正。他把古風與近體做了整合，他的近體多為古風化的近體。孟浩然將近體詩的格律精神與古風的自然平和有機地結合起來，從而達到了一種「興象玲瓏」的藝術境界。讀孟浩然的詩，看不到近體格律的束縛，而是有行雲流水般的自然。既接受近體格律，又不被近體格律所累，一切以自然為第一標準。

二、邊塞詩派

邊塞詩派是盛唐詩歌的主要流派之一，其詩以描繪邊塞風光、反應戍邊將士生活為主。漢魏六朝時已有一些邊塞詩，至隋代數量不斷增多，初唐四杰和

陳子昂又將其進一步發展，到盛唐則全面成熟。該派詩人以高適、岑參、李頎、王昌齡最為知名，而高、岑成就最高。其他如王之渙、王翰、崔顥、劉灣、張謂等也較著名。這些詩人大都有邊塞生活體驗，他們從各方面深入表現邊塞生活，藝術上也有所創新。他們不僅描繪了壯闊蒼涼、絢麗多彩的邊塞風光，還抒寫了請纓投筆的豪情壯志以及徵人離婦的思想感情。對戰爭的態度，有歌頌、有批評，也有詛咒和譴責，思想上往往達到一定深度。邊塞詩情辭慷慨、氣氛濃鬱、意境雄渾，多採用七言歌行和七言絕句的形式。傑出作品如高適的《燕歌行》、岑參的《走馬川行奉送出師西徵》等。另外，中唐盧綸、李益也有些格調蒼涼的邊塞絕句。

邊塞詩人是一群具有豪俠氣概的天才型詩人，他們動輒以公侯卿相自許，抒發出了大唐盛世所特有的氣勢，後來只有高適一人在「安史之亂」後因功封侯，其餘諸人多擔任一些微末官吏，但是他們的呼聲卻是任何人都不可以忽視的。

盛唐的邊塞詩具有美學風格，它包含了雄渾、磅礡、豪放、浪漫、悲壯、瑰麗等各個方面。

唐代邊塞詩的代表人物有：高適、岑參、王昌齡、李益、王之渙、李頎。

(一) 主要特點

一方面邊塞詩，以誇張、對比、襯托的手法對殘酷的戰爭、惡劣的環境進行展示，如「戰士軍前半生死」「黃沙百戰穿金甲」「孤城落日鬥兵稀」；另一方面，邊塞詩更凸顯人面對戰爭時奔湧出的巨大精神力量。其中既有不屈的意志和必勝的信念、保家衛國的豪情，還有在戰場上建立功績的壯志，如「不破樓蘭終不還」「願將腰下劍，只為斬樓蘭」「相看白刃血紛紛，死節從來豈顧勳」。這兩個方面既是對立的，又是統一的，這種對立統一所產生的張力使詩句具有永不泯滅的魅力，詩句中洋溢著的崇高感成為中華民族的最強音，千載悠悠。盛唐邊塞詩的特點主要表現以下四個方面：①題材廣闊。題材一方面包括將士建立軍功的壯志、邊地生活的艱辛、戰爭的酷烈場面、將士的思家情緒，另一方面包括邊塞風光、邊疆地理、民族風情、民族交往等內容。其中以前者為主要題材。②意象宏闊，大處落筆，寫奇情壯景。③基調昂揚，氣勢流暢，富有崇高感。④體裁兼善，歌行、律絕皆有佳作。

(二) 代表人物

1. 高適

高適是唐代著名邊塞詩人,高適與岑參並稱「高岑」,與岑參、王昌齡、王之渙合稱「邊塞四詩人」。其詩筆力雄健,氣勢奔放,洋溢著盛唐時期所特有的奮發進取、蓬勃向上的時代精神。

(1) 高適邊塞詩的藝術特點

「雄渾悲壯」是高適邊塞詩的突出特點。其詩歌尚質主理,雄壯而渾厚古樸。高適少孤貧,有遊俠之氣,曾漫遊梁宋,躬耕自給,加之本人豪爽正直的個性,故詩作反應的層面較廣闊,題旨亦深刻。高適的心理結構比較粗放,性格率直,故其詩多直抒胸臆,或夾敘夾議,較少用比興手法。

高適詩歌的注意力在於人而不在於自然景觀,故單純寫景之作很少,常在抒情之時伴有寫景的部分,因此景色描繪中往往帶有詩人個人主觀的印記。《燕歌行》中用「大漠窮秋塞草腓,孤城落日鬥兵稀」勾畫淒涼場面,用大漠、枯草、孤城、落日進行排比,組成富有主觀情感的圖景,把戰士們戰鬥不止的英勇悲壯烘托得更為強烈。高適在語言風格上用詞簡淨,不加雕琢。

(2) 高適邊塞詩代表作

別董大

千里黃雲白日曛,北風吹雁雪紛紛。
莫愁前路無知己,天下誰人不識君。

2. 岑參

岑參對邊塞風光,軍旅生活,以及少數民族的文化風俗有親切的感受,故其邊塞詩尤多佳作。風格與高適相近,後人多並稱「高岑」。岑參是唐代著名的邊塞詩人。岑參的作品,以邊塞詩為主,自出塞以後,在安西、北庭的新天地裡,在鞍馬風塵的戰鬥生活裡,他的詩境空前開擴,愛好新奇事物的特點在他的創作裡有了進一步的發展,雄奇瑰麗的浪漫色彩,成為他邊塞詩詞的主要風格。

(1) 岑參邊塞詩的藝術特點

岑參詩歌的題材涉及述志、贈答、山水、行旅各方面,而以邊塞詩寫得最出色,「雄奇瑰麗」是其突出特點。岑參兩度出塞,寫了七十多首邊塞詩,在盛唐時代,他寫的邊塞詩數量最多,成就最突出。

在岑參筆下,在大唐面前,任何敵人都不能成為真正的對手,所以他並不著重寫士兵們的艱苦戰鬥和不畏犧牲,他要寫的是橫在戰士們面前的另一種偉

大的力量，那就是嚴酷的自然。如《走馬川行奉送出師西征》中，雪夜風吼、飛沙走石，這些邊疆大漠中令人望而生畏的惡劣氣候環境，在詩人印象中卻成了襯托英雄氣概的壯觀景色，是一種值得欣賞的奇偉美景。如果詩人沒有積極進取精神和克服困難的勇氣，是很難產生這種感覺的，只有盛唐詩人，才能有此開朗胸襟和此種藝術感受。

岑參以出奇的熱情和瑰麗的色彩表現塞外之景。在立功邊塞的慷慨豪情的激勵下，將西北荒漠的奇異風光與風物人情，用慷慨豪邁的語調和奇特的藝術手法生動地表現出來，別具一種奇偉壯麗之美。它們突破了以往徵戍詩寫邊地苦寒和士卒勞苦的傳統格局，極大地豐富和拓寬了邊塞詩的題材和內容。

（2）岑參邊塞詩代表作

　　　　白雪歌送武判官歸京

北風卷地白草折，胡天八月即飛雪。
忽如一夜春風來，千樹萬樹梨花開。
散入珠簾濕羅幕，狐裘不暖錦衾薄。
將軍角弓不得控，都護鐵衣冷難著。
瀚海闌干百丈冰，愁雲慘淡萬里凝。
中軍置酒飲歸客，胡琴琵琶與羌笛。
紛紛暮雪下轅門，風掣紅旗凍不翻。
輪臺東門送君去，去時雪滿天山路。
山回路轉不見君，雪上空留馬行處。

三、浪漫詩派

浪漫詩派是中國詩詞四大流派之一。浪漫詩派詩作色彩絢麗，既有奇幻的想像，又有奔放的筆調，融合繼承了楚辭、樂府詩的浪漫傳統，開創了奇險詭麗的藝術風格。他們崇尚自我，注重情感流瀉，發揮想像靈感。

（一）主要代表人物

浪漫詩派的主要代表人物非李白莫屬。李白（公元 701—762 年），字太白，號青蓮居士，又號「謫仙人」，是唐代偉大的浪漫主義詩人，被後人譽為「詩仙」，與杜甫並稱為「李杜」。為了與另兩位詩人李商隱與杜牧即「小李杜」區別，杜甫與李白又合稱「大李杜」。其人爽朗大方，愛飲酒作詩，喜交友。

李白深受黃老列莊思想影響，有《李太白集》傳世，詩作多是醉時寫的，代表作有《望廬山瀑布》《行路難》《蜀道難》《將進酒》《梁甫吟》《早發白帝城》等。

李白所作詩詞，宋人已有傳記（如文瑩《湘山野錄》卷上），就其開創意義及藝術成就而言，「李白詩」享有極為崇高的地位。

(二) 李白詩歌的主要成就

李白的樂府、歌行及絕句成就為最高。其歌行，完全打破詩歌創作的一切固有格式，空無依傍，筆法多端，達到了變幻莫測、搖曳多姿的神奇境界。李白的絕句自然明快，飄逸瀟灑，能以簡潔明快的語言表達出無盡的情思。在盛唐詩人中，王維、孟浩然長於五絕，王昌齡七絕寫得很好，兼長五絕與七絕而且同臻極境的，只有李白一人。

李白的詩雄奇飄逸，藝術成就極高。他謳歌祖國山河與美麗的自然風光，風格雄奇奔放，俊逸清新，富有浪漫主義精神，達到了內容與藝術的完美統一。他被賀知章稱為「謫仙人」，其詩大多以描寫山水和抒發內心的情感為主。李白的詩具有「筆落驚風雨，詩成泣鬼神」的藝術魅力，這也是他的詩歌中最鮮明的藝術特色。李白的詩富於自我表現，主觀抒情色彩十分濃烈，對感情的表達常常具有一種排山倒海、一瀉千里的氣勢。

李白詩中常將想像、誇張、比喻、擬人等手法綜合運用，從而營造神奇異彩、瑰麗動人的意境，這就是李白的浪漫主義詩作豪邁奔放、飄逸若仙的魅力所在。

李白的詩歌對後代產生了極為深遠的影響。中唐的韓愈、孟郊、李賀，宋代的蘇軾、陸遊、辛棄疾，明清的高啓、楊慎、龔自珍等著名詩人，都受到李白詩歌的巨大影響。

(三) 李白詩歌的風格

李白詩作豪邁奔放，清新飄逸，想像豐富，意境奇妙，語言奇妙，立意清晰，浪漫主義氣息深厚。

李白生活在盛唐時期，他性格豪邁，熱愛祖國山河，遊蹤遍及南北各地，寫出大量贊美名山大川的壯麗詩篇。他的詩，豪邁奔放，清新飄逸，想像豐富，意境奇妙，語言輕快，人們稱他為「詩仙」。李白的詩歌不僅具有典型的浪漫主義精神，而且從形象塑造、素材攝取到體裁選擇和各種藝術手法的運用，無不具有典型的浪漫主義藝術特徵。

李白成功地在詩中塑造自我，強烈地表現自我，突出抒發主人公的獨特個性，因而他的詩歌具有鮮明的浪漫主義特色。他喜歡採用雄奇的形象表現自我，在詩中毫不掩飾也不加節制地抒發感情，表現他的喜怒哀樂。對於權豪勢要，他「手持一枝菊，調笑二千石」（《醉後寄崔侍御》二首之一）；看到勞動人民艱辛勞作時，他「心摧淚如雨」。當社稷傾覆、民生涂炭時，他「過江誓流水，志在清中原。拔劍擊前柱，悲歌難重論」（《南奔書懷》），那樣慷慨激昂；與朋友開懷暢飲時，「兩人對酌山花開，一杯一杯復一杯。我醉欲眠卿且去，明朝有意抱琴來」（《山中與幽人對酌》），又是那樣天真率直。總之，他的詩活脫脫地表現了他豪放不羈的性格和倜儻不群的形象。

　　豪放是李白詩歌的主要特徵。除了思想、性格、才情、遭際諸因素外，李白詩歌採用的藝術表現手法和體裁結構也是形成他豪放飄逸風格的重要原因。李白善於憑藉想像，以主觀現客觀是李白詩歌浪漫主義藝術手法的重要特徵。幾乎篇篇有想像，甚至有的通篇運用多種多樣的想像。現實事物、自然景觀、神話傳說、歷史典故、夢中幻境，無不成為他想像的媒介。李白常借助想像，超越時空，將現實與夢境、仙境，將自然界與人類社會交織在一起，再現客觀現實。他筆下的形象不是客觀現實的直接反應，而是其內心主觀世界的外化。

　　李白詩歌的浪漫主義藝術手法之一是把擬人與比喻巧妙地結合起來，移情於物，將物比人。

　　李白詩歌的另一個浪漫主義藝術手法是抓住事情的某一特點，在生活真實的基礎上，加以大膽的想像誇張。他的誇張不僅想像奇特，而且總是與具體事物相結合，誇張得那麼自然，不露痕跡；那麼大膽，又真實可信，起到突出形象、強化感情的作用。有時他還把大膽的誇張與鮮明的對比結合起來，通過加大藝術反差，加強藝術效果。

　　李白最擅長的體裁是七言歌行和絕句。李白的七言歌行採用了大開大合、跳躍宕蕩的結構。詩的開頭常突兀如狂飆驟起，而詩的中間形象轉換倏忽，往往省略過渡照應，似無跡可尋，詩的結尾多在感情高潮處戛然而止。

　　李白的五七言絕句，更多地代表了他的詩歌清新明麗的風格，如《早發白帝城》《送孟浩然之廣陵》《靜夜思》等，妙在「只眼前景、口頭語，而有弦外音、味外味，使人神遠」（《說詩晬語》上）。

　　（四）李白詩歌代表作

　　李白詩歌代表作有《將進酒》《蜀道難》《夢遊天姥吟留別》《靜夜思》《望廬山瀑布》《俠客行》《春思》《秋歌》等。

將進酒

君不見，黃河之水天上來，奔流到海不復回。
君不見，高堂明鏡悲白髮，朝如青絲暮成雪。
人生得意須盡歡，莫使金樽空對月。
天生我材必有用，千金散盡還復來。
烹羊宰牛且為樂，會須一飲三百杯。
岑夫子，丹丘生，將進酒，杯莫停。
與君歌一曲，請君為我傾耳聽。
鐘鼓饌玉不足貴，但願長醉不復醒。
古來聖賢皆寂寞，惟有飲者留其名。
陳王昔時宴平樂，斗酒十千恣歡謔。
主人何為言少錢，徑須沽取對君酌。
五花馬，千金裘，呼兒將出換美酒，與爾同銷萬古愁。

蜀道難

噫吁嚱，危乎高哉！蜀道之難，難於上青天！蠶叢及魚鳧，開國何茫然！爾來四萬八千歲，不與秦塞通人煙。西當太白有鳥道，可以橫絕峨眉巔。地崩山摧壯士死，然後天梯石棧相鉤連。上有六龍回日之高標，下有衝波逆折之回川。黃鶴之飛尚不得過，猿猱欲度愁攀援。青泥何盤盤，百步九折縈岩巒。捫參歷井仰脅息，以手撫膺坐長嘆。

問君西遊何時還？畏途巉岩不可攀。但見悲鳥號古木，雄飛雌從繞林間。又聞子規啼夜月，愁空山。蜀道之難，難於上青天，使人聽此凋朱顏！連峰去天不盈尺，枯松倒掛倚絕壁。飛湍瀑流爭喧豗，砯崖轉石萬壑雷。其險也如此，嗟爾遠道之人胡為乎來哉！

劍閣崢嶸而崔嵬，一夫當關，萬夫莫開。所守或匪親，化為狼與豺。朝避猛虎，夕避長蛇；磨牙吮血，殺人如麻。錦城雖云樂，不如早還家。蜀道之難，難於上青天，側身西望長咨嗟！

四、現實詩派

詩歌藝術風格沉鬱頓挫，多表現憂時傷世、悲天憫人的情懷。

(一) 主要代表人物

現實詩派主要代表人物為杜甫。杜甫（712—770年），字子美，漢族，本

襄陽人，後徙河南鞏縣。杜甫又自號少陵野老，唐代偉大的現實主義詩人，與李白合稱「李杜」。為了與另兩位詩人李商隱與杜牧即「小李杜」區別，杜甫與李白又合稱「大李杜」，杜甫也常被稱為「老杜」。

杜甫在中國古典詩歌中的影響非常深遠，被後人稱為「詩聖」，他的詩被稱為「詩史」。後世稱其杜拾遺、杜工部，也稱他杜少陵、杜草堂。

杜甫創作了《春望》《北徵》「三吏」「三別」等名作。乾元二年（759年）杜甫棄官入川，雖然躲避了戰亂，生活相對安定，但仍然心系蒼生，胸懷國事。雖然杜甫是個現實主義詩人，但他也有狂放不羈的一面，從其名作《飲中八仙歌》不難看出杜甫的豪放氣概。

杜甫的思想核心是儒家的仁政思想，他有「致君堯舜上，再使風俗淳」的宏偉抱負。杜甫雖然在世時名聲並不顯赫，但在後代聲名遠播，對中國文學和日本文學都產生了深遠的影響。杜甫約有 1,500 首詩歌被保留了下來，大多集於《杜工部集》。

(二) 杜甫詩歌的主要成就

杜甫詩「有集六十卷」，早佚。北宋寶元二年（1039 年）王洙輯有 1,405 篇，編為 18 卷，題為《杜工部集》。錢謙益編有《箋註杜工部集》。楊倫說：「自六朝以來，樂府題率多模擬剽竊，陳陳相因，最為可厭。子美出而獨就當時所感觸，上憫國難，下痛民窮，隨意立題，盡脫去前人窠臼。」

在杜甫中年因其詩風沉鬱頓挫，憂國憂民，杜甫的詩被稱為「詩史」。他的詩詞以古體、律詩見長，風格多樣，「沉鬱頓挫」四字準確概括出他自己的作品風格，而以沉鬱為主。杜甫生活在唐朝由盛轉衰的歷史時期，其詩多涉筆社會動盪、政治黑暗、人民疾苦，他的詩反應當時社會矛盾和人民疾苦，他的詩記錄了唐代由盛轉衰的歷史巨變，表達了崇高的儒家仁愛精神和強烈的憂患意識，因而被譽為「詩史」。杜甫憂國憂民，人格高尚，詩藝精湛。杜甫一生寫詩一千五百多首，其中很多是傳頌千古的名篇，比如「三吏」和「三別」；其中「三吏」為《石壕吏》《新安吏》和《潼關吏》，「三別」為《新婚別》《無家別》和《垂老別》。杜甫流傳下來的詩篇是唐詩裡最多最廣泛的，是唐代最傑出的詩人之一，對後世影響深遠。杜甫作品被稱為「世上瘡痍，詩中聖哲；民間疾苦，筆底波瀾」。杜甫詩作是現實主義詩歌的代表作。

律詩在杜詩中佔有極其重要的地位。杜甫律詩的成就，首先在於擴大了律詩的表現範圍。他不僅以律詩寫應酬、詠懷、羈旅、宴遊以及山水，而且用律詩寫時事。用律詩寫時事，字數和格律都受限制，難度更大，而杜甫卻能運用

自如。杜甫把律詩寫得縱橫恣肆，極盡變化之能事，合律而又看不出聲律的束縛，對仗工整而又看不出對仗的痕跡。例如，被楊倫稱為「杜集七言律第一」的《登高》：「風急天高猿嘯哀，渚清沙白鳥飛回。無邊落木蕭蕭下，不盡長江滾滾來。萬里悲秋常作客，百年多病獨登臺。艱難苦恨繁霜鬢，潦倒新停濁酒杯。」全詩在聲律句式上，極其精密、考究。八句皆對，首聯句中也對。《登高》中嚴整的對仗被形象的流動感掩蓋起來了，嚴密且舒暢。

　　杜甫律詩的最高成就，就是杜甫把這種體式寫得渾融流轉，無跡可尋，寫來若不經意，使人忘其為律詩。如《春夜喜雨》：「好雨知時節，當春乃發生。隨風潛入夜，潤物細無聲。野徑雲俱黑，江船火獨明。曉看紅濕處，花重錦官城。」該詩上四句用流水對，把春雨神韻一氣寫下，無聲無息不期然而來，末聯寫一種驟然回首的驚喜，格律嚴謹而渾然一氣。

　　杜甫善於運用古典詩歌的許多體制，並加以創造性地發展。杜甫關心民生疾苦的思想和他在律詩方面所取得的成就直接影響了中唐時期元稹、白居易等人的新樂府創作。他是新樂府詩體的開路人。他的樂府詩，促成了中唐時期新樂府運動的發展。他的五七古長篇，亦詩亦史，展開鋪敘，而又著力於全篇的回旋往復，標誌著中國詩歌藝術的高度成就。社會矛盾重重的宋代更是學習杜甫最興盛的時代，出現了以杜甫為宗的江西詩派。明末清初的顧炎武等人也有明顯的學杜傾向，也像杜甫一樣用律詩反應當時的抗清鬥爭，慷慨激昂。

　　杜詩受到廣泛重視是在宋朝以後。王禹、王安石、蘇軾、黃庭堅、陸遊等人對杜甫推崇備至。近千年來的研究資料，治杜之風不絕。宋代有許多杜詩的編年、分類、集註等專書，如王洙《杜工部集》、郭知達《九家集註杜詩》、徐居仁編輯的《分門集註杜工部詩》等。後世註釋杜集的亦在百種以上，較流行的有錢謙益《箋註杜工部集》、仇兆鰲《杜詩詳註》、楊倫《杜詩鏡銓》、浦起龍《讀杜心解》。《新唐書》《舊唐書》都有杜甫本傳。兩宋以後，詩話筆記中評點、解釋杜詩的文字非常豐富。明末王嗣有《杜臆》、清施鴻保有《讀杜詩說》。中華書局 1964 年出版《古典文學研究資料匯編・杜甫卷》。另外，中華書局還將五四運動以來較重要的論文匯編成《杜甫研究論文集》。關於杜甫的傳記和新的研究專著有馮至《杜甫傳》、蕭滌非《杜甫研究》、傅庚生《杜甫詩論》、朱東潤《杜甫敘論》。較詳實的關於杜甫的年譜有聞一多《少陵先生年譜會箋》和四川文史研究館的《杜甫年譜》。

(三) 杜甫詩歌代表作

石壕吏

暮投石壕村，有吏夜捉人。
老翁逾牆走，老婦出門看。
吏呼一何怒，婦啼一何苦。
聽婦前致詞，三男鄴城戍。
一男附書至，二男新戰死。
存者且偷生，死者長已矣。
室中更無人，惟有乳下孫，
有孫母未去，出入無完裙。
老嫗力雖衰，請從吏夜歸，
急應河陽役，猶得備晨炊。
夜久語聲絕，如聞泣幽咽。
天明登前途，獨與老翁別。

新婚別

兔絲附蓬麻，引蔓故不長。
嫁女與征夫，不如棄路旁。
結髮為君妻，席不暖君床。
暮婚晨告別，無乃太匆忙！
君行雖不遠，守邊赴河陽。
妾身未分明，何以拜姑嫜？
父母養我時，日夜令我藏。
生女有所歸，雞狗亦得將。
君今往死地，沉痛迫中腸。
誓欲隨君去，形勢反蒼黃。
勿為新婚念，努力事戎行！
婦人在軍中，兵氣恐不揚。
自嗟貧家女，久致羅襦裳。
羅襦不復施，對君洗紅妝。
仰視百鳥飛，大小必雙翔。
人事多錯迕，與君永相望。

五、禪詩

禪詩，顧名思義，是指與念佛、參禪相關的詩，是富含禪理、禪意的詩詞作品。禪詩或稱佛教詩歌，是指宣揚佛理或具有禪意、禪趣的詩。

(一) 禪詩的分類

禪詩大體可分為兩部分。

一部分是禪理詩，包括佛理詩以及中國佛教禪宗特有的示法詩、開悟詩和傾古詩等。這部分禪詩的特色是富於哲理和智慧，有深刻的辯證思維。

另一部分則是反應僧人和文人修行悟道生活的詩，諸如山居詩、佛寺詩和遊方詩等。表現空澄靜寂聖潔的禪境和心境是這部分禪詩的主要特色。這些詩多寫佛寺山居，多描寫幽深峭曲、潔淨無塵、超凡脫俗的山林風光勝景，多表現僧人或文人空諸所有、萬慮全消、淡泊寧靜的心境。

唐代禪詩是中國古代詩苑中的瑰寶，具有「禪」與「詩」的兩重性，側重表現禪理、禪趣，語言清新自然，內容富有哲理，充滿空寂的禪意，在陶冶人們思想情操等方面有著極其重要的地位。自十七世紀以來，唐代禪詩逐漸走出國門，迄今在英美國家的譯介已經走過了幾個世紀。英美漢學家如德庇時（John Francis Davis，1795—1890 年）、理雅各（James Legge，1815—1897 年）和翟理思（Herbert A. Giles，1845—1935 年）、龐德（Ezra Pound）、洛威爾（Amy Lowell）、賓納（Witter Bynner）等人對於中國古詩在英語世界的翻譯和接受起到了重要的作用。這些英譯漢詩中包括不少唐代禪詩。自 20 世紀 50 年代以來，先後有幾十位歐美譯者翻譯了中國唐代禪宗詩僧寒山的詩歌，如阿瑟·韋利（Arthur Waley）於 1954 年翻譯了 27 首寒山詩，加里·斯奈德（Gary Snyder）於 1958 年秋在《常春藤》雜誌上發表了 24 首寒山譯詩，伯頓·華茲生（Watson）於 1962 年出版了一本英譯寒山詩，共譯詩 124 首。唐代禪詩在英美國家的譯介成績斐然。有不少學者對唐代禪詩的英譯做了研究，取得了一批研究成果。這些研究成果主要分為兩類：

其一，對唐代禪詩譯本的分析以及翻譯策略與方法的研究。例如，曹陽（2006）在其論文《關聯理論與王維禪詩英譯》中運用關聯理論對王維《鳥鳴澗》的四個譯本進行了分析，指明了各個譯本的優缺點。吳迪（2013）在其論文《框架理論視角下的王維禪詩英譯語義差異辨析》中，運用框架理論探討王維禪詩英譯的策略和方法。段政絲（2014）在其論文《本雅明翻譯理論

下的中國古典禪詩英譯研究——以王維禪譯詩為例》中從以王維的山水禪詩為案例，對中國古典禪詩的英譯問題進行探討，提出與之相關的翻譯原則和翻譯策略。

其二，唐代禪詩譯介對英美文化影響的研究。例如，朱徽（2004）在其論文《唐詩在美國的翻譯與接受》一文中探討了唐詩英譯對現代美國詩學與詩歌創作的影響以及對促進東西方文化交流與對話所起的重要作用。張廣龍（2005）在其論文《寒山詩在美國》一文中運用多元系統理論分析寒山詩在美國的影響。楊鋒兵（2007）的論文《寒山詩在美國的被接受與誤讀》從中美兩種不同文化背景出發，細讀文本，結合美國當時的政治、經濟、文化等狀況，探討寒山詩在美國接受與誤讀的原因。朱徽（2009）在其專著《中國詩歌在英語世界》一書中精選了自19世紀中葉以來的20位代表性英美翻譯家，對他們英譯漢詩的主要成就、譯學思想、翻譯策略、形式技巧、歷史貢獻和誤解誤譯等進行系統的分析評述，並對一個多世紀以來中國詩歌在英語世界的翻譯與傳播做了歷時性的描述。張梅（2012）在其論文《「改寫論」視角下中國古詩在美國的翻譯與接受》中探討了中國古詩英譯對中西文化的交流以及現代美國詩學的發展產生的重要影響。江嵐（2013）在其著作《唐詩西傳史論——以唐詩在英美的傳播為中心》一書中考察了眾位主要譯介者的成果，客觀地評價譯家們對唐詩西漸進程的歷史貢獻，演繹出唐詩西傳的歷史淵源與發展脈絡，並探析其階段性成因與特徵。

國外也有學者對英美國家的禪詩譯介進行了研究。例如，溫伯格（Eliot Weinberger）和帕斯（Octavio Paz, 1987）兩位學者對比分析了王維禪詩《鹿柴》的十七個不同英文譯本。霍克斯（David Hawkes, 1962）對比分析了韋利（Arthur Waley）、華茲生（Burton Watson）、施耐德（G. Snyder）三家的寒山詩譯本，指出華茲生寒山詩譯本的語言特色不如韋利的文雅，施耐德的狂野介於兩個譯本之間。同國內學者一樣，國外學者主要探討了各個不同唐代禪詩譯本的優點和缺點以及唐代禪詩翻譯應採取的策略和方法。

國內外學者對英美國家的唐代禪詩譯介做了研究和探討，取得了一些研究成果。這些研究成果富有開拓性，對後期研究具有較強的啟發意義，但在以下幾個方面存在不足之處：首先，研究存在某種程度的重複研究現象，研究對象仍有拓展的學術空間。當前的研究主要對一些代表性禪詩和一些著名詩人的禪詩展開論述。例如，寒山和王維的禪詩研究頗多，而對其他唐代詩人的禪詩基本上沒有展開研究。其次，當前的大多數禪詩英譯研究將禪詩作為一般詩歌英譯加以研究，沒有突出禪詩的佛禪文化特質，主要揭示了唐詩英譯的普遍翻譯

特質，而沒有突出唐代禪詩英譯的個性特徵。最後，唐代禪詩在英美國家譯介的歷時梳理、整體性研究還有待加強。當前的研究成果針對個體性詩人如王維、寒山等人的研究居多，而系統整體地梳理唐代禪詩英譯的成果不多。

(二) 禪詩代表作

　　過香積寺（王維）
不知香積寺，數里入雲峰。
古木無人徑，深山何處鐘。
泉聲咽危石，日色冷青松。
薄暮空潭曲，安禪制毒龍。

夏日過青龍寺謁操禪師（王維）
龍鐘一老翁，徐步謁禪宮。
欲問義心義，遙知空病空。
山河天眼裡，世界法身中。
莫怪銷炎熱，能生大地風。

　　神秀偈（神秀）
身是菩提樹，心如明鏡臺。
時時勤拂拭，莫使有塵埃。

　　菩提偈（惠能）
菩提本無樹，明鏡亦非臺。
本來無一物，何處惹塵埃。

六、隱逸詩

(一) 關於隱逸詩的研究情況

　　學界大多從廣義的角度來界定隱逸詩，是指與隱逸主題有關的，包括描述隱逸生活的、企慕隱逸生活的、吟詠隱士的、討論隱逸價值的作品。隱逸詩體現的是謙遜禮讓、功成身退、知足不辱等中華民族的傳統美德，主張崇尚平靜、祥和和天人合一。隱逸詩歌有其鮮明的特徵：複雜紛紜的隱逸詩類型，與

自然山水親近的題材，旁徵博引的隱逸內容，怡然自適的詩人心境，超乎塵外的藝術想像等，更多的是一種真實自然的狀態。隱逸詩表現出來的人生哲理、抒發的情感、營造的生活空間、展現的精神風貌，應該成為喧囂的現代人的最佳教材，值得花大力氣去研究。

1949—1980 年，可見的有關隱逸詩的研究論文基本上以研究陶淵明的隱逸詩為主。20 世紀最後 20 年，中國學界對隱逸文化的研究逐漸增多，六朝隱逸詩的研究也取得了一些成果，據統計，這 20 年發表的相關論文近 50 篇，研究的角度和方法都有新的拓展，有進行隱逸詩人比較研究的，有進行隱逸心理研究的。雖然這 20 年的研究仍然為陶淵明為主，但是像謝朓、庾信、潘岳等人的隱逸詩作也引起了研究者的注意。進入 21 世紀，隱逸文化研究的視角越來越新，範圍越來越廣，研究成果越來越多，從 20 世紀學術研究的零敲散打，變為系統性的研究，對隱逸文化有了整體性的透視。近 10 年來，有關隱逸的論文頗多，四川大學肖玉峰（2006）博士論文《先秦隱逸思想及先秦兩漢隱逸文學研究》把隱逸思想與隱逸文學結合起來，按儒道兩家剖析隱逸思想的實質，隱逸詩學在先秦部分主要有《詩經》，而漢代部分主要是賦和傳記文學，較少涉及詩歌。上海師範大學周銀鳳（2007）碩士論文《東晉隱逸詩研究》根據詩歌形態內容，將隱逸詩分為五類，按類別依次考查各個階段的隱逸詩創作。復旦大學許曉晴（2005）博士論文《中古隱逸詩研究》對中古隱逸詩的界定與溯源、思想淵源及時代背景做了清楚的闡述，並做了較細緻的中古隱逸詩的分期研究、專題研究和文本分析，重點是隱逸詩在中古的發展演變軌跡及文本特徵，特別分析了隱逸詩產生與消亡的原因以及集體創作隱逸詩的情況。首都師範大學於春媚（2008）博士論文《道家思想與魏晉文學——以隱逸、遊仙、玄言文學為中心》以文學主題為核心，認為隱逸思想是道家自然社會人生思想的全面表現，隱逸避世是道家自然道論的直接指向，從哲學的角度尋找隱逸詩歌的本源。上海師範大學高智（2013）博士論文《六朝隱逸詩研究》對六朝時期的隱逸詩做了系統研究。

綜上所述，大量學者已經對隱逸詩做了大量的研究，取得了可喜的成績。但學術界對隱逸詩的英譯研究不夠，尤其是對於隱逸詩中文化負載詞的英譯研究。每種語言都存在著大量富有民族文化內涵的詞彙。這些文化詞彙除了與一般詞彙一樣有指稱意義外，還有豐富的內涵意義。內涵意義因民族文化背景不同而不同，與各民族長期所處的生活環境、歷史背景和民族心理等有著緊密的聯繫。常敬宇在《漢語詞彙與文化》一書中稱：「文化詞彙是指特定文化範疇的詞彙，它是民族文化在語言詞彙中直接或間接的反應」。這些詞彙載有明確

的民族文化信息，與各民族的物質文化、制度文化和心理文化等不可分割。由於文化詞彙具有豐富的內涵意義，承載著各民族的文化信息，因此在跨文化交際中，文化詞彙的翻譯往往是譯者最棘手的問題。

隨著中國經濟社會的快速發展，中國在世界上不斷展示影響力與競爭力，中國文化也越來越引起世界人民的關注。加強中國文化建設已勢在必行，這樣不僅有利於增加中國的軟實力，而且有利於中國文化走向世界。作為重塑中國文化的一種重要手段，翻譯的作用不言而喻。詩歌濃縮著文化的精華，常常在外交中使用，因此詩歌翻譯具有一定的價值和意義。當前的研究主要停留在宏觀的闡釋方面，而對隱逸詩歌譯本中意象、文化詞彙、音韻等微觀層面的專項研究暫時空缺。

(二) 隱逸詩代表作

鹿柴（王維）
空山不見人，但聞人語響。
返景入深林，復照青苔上。

竹里館（王維）
獨坐幽篁里，彈琴復長嘯。
深林人不知，明月來相照。

辛夷塢（王維）
木末芙蓉花，山中發紅萼。
澗戶寂無人，紛紛開且落。

第二節　唐詩的詩歌風格

唐詩的形式和風格是豐富多彩、推陳出新的。它不僅繼承了漢魏民歌、樂府的傳統，並且大大發展了歌行體的樣式；唐詩不僅繼承了前代的五言、七言古詩，還發展為敘事言情的長篇巨制；唐詩不僅擴展了五言、七言形式的運用，還創造了風格特別優美整齊的近體詩。近體詩是當時的新體詩，它的創造和成熟是唐代詩歌發展史上的一件大事。它把中國古曲詩歌的音節和諧、文字精練的藝術特色推到前所未有的高度，為古代抒情詩找到一個最典型的形式，至今還特別為人民所喜聞樂見。

一、高適詩歌分類及風格

高適詩題材廣泛，內容豐富，現實性較強。其詩歌分類及風格概述如下：

(一) 詩歌分類

1. 邊塞詩成就最高

高適的邊塞詩代表作如《燕歌行》《薊門行五首》《塞上》《塞下曲》《薊中作》《九曲詞三首》等，歌頌了戰士奮勇報國、建功立業的豪情，也寫出了他們從軍生活的艱苦及向往和平的美好願望，同時揭露了邊關將領的驕奢淫逸、不恤士卒和朝廷的賞罰不明、安邊無策，流露出憂國愛民之情。

2. 反應民生疾苦的詩

這些詩比較深刻地揭露了統治者與廣大人民之間的矛盾，如《自淇涉黃河途中作十三首》之九、《東平路中遇大水》等，真實地描寫了廣大農民遭受賦稅、徭役和自然災害的重壓，對他們的困苦境遇表示同情。他還寫過一些贊美「良吏」的詩，從「仁政」思想出發，提倡輕徭薄賦，在當時也有一定的進步作用。

3. 諷時傷亂詩

高適的諷時傷亂詩大抵指斥弊政，對統治者的驕奢淫逸有所批判，如《古歌行》《行路難二首》等。還有一些詩作於安史之亂後，對政局流露出憂慮和憤慨之情，如《酬裴員外以詩代書》《登百丈峰二首》等。

4. 詠懷詩

高適的詠懷詩數量最多，思想內容比較複雜。例如，《別韋參軍》《淇上酬薛三據兼寄郭少府微》《效古贈崔二》《封丘作》等，抒寫了懷才不遇、壯志難酬的憂憤，對現實有所不滿。

(二) 詩歌風格

「雄渾悲壯」是高適邊塞詩的突出特點。其詩歌尚質主理，雄壯而渾厚古樸。高適少孤貧，有遊俠之氣，曾漫遊梁宋，躬耕自給，加之本人豪爽正直的個性，故詩作反應的層面較廣闊，題旨亦深刻。高適的心理結構比較粗放，性格率直，故其詩多直抒胸臆，或夾敘夾議，較少用比興手法。

高適詩歌的注意力在於人而不在於自然景觀，故很少單純寫景，常在抒情之時伴有寫景的部分，因此這景帶有詩人個人主觀的印記。《燕歌行》中用

「大漠窮秋塞草衰，孤城落日鬥兵稀」描繪淒涼場面，用大漠、枯草、孤城、落日進行排比，組成富有主觀情感的圖景，把戰士們戰鬥不止的英勇悲壯烘托得更為強烈。高適在語言風格上用詞簡淨，不加雕琢。

高適以古之大將軍自詡，可見胸中豪氣。他縱酒馳獵，狂狷之處不亞李白，其所賦名篇《別董大》足以見其風采：

千里黃雲白日曛，北風吹雁雪紛紛。

莫愁前路無知己，天下誰人不識君。

高適第一次趕赴的邊塞乃河北節度使張守珪鎮御的東北邊防地段。該地北鄰突厥，東北鄰契丹與奚。唐築居庸隘以阻突厥，建營州以鎮馭奚與契丹。他的邊塞生活留下了不少優秀詩篇，如《營州歌》：

營州少年愛原野，狐裘蒙茸獵城下。

虜酒千鐘不醉人，胡兒十歲能騎馬。

詩人還憑藉想像，展現了邊防戰士奮勇殺敵的壯烈畫面，如《薊門行》：

黯黯長城外，日沒更煙塵。

胡騎雖憑陵，漢兵不顧身。

古樹滿空塞，黃雲愁殺人。

高適的名篇《同李員外賀哥舒大夫破九曲之作》就是為慶祝前方勝利而寫作的：

遙傳副丞相，昨日破西蕃。

作氣群山動，揚軍大旆翻。

奇兵邀轉戰，連弩絕歸奔。

泉噴諸戎血，風驅死虜魂。

頭飛攢萬戟，面縛聚轅門。

鬼哭黃埃暮，天愁白日昏。

石城與巖險，鐵騎若雲屯。

長策一言決，高蹤百代存。

威稜慴沙漠，忠義感乾坤。

老將黯無色，儒生安敢論。

解圍憑廟算，止殺報君恩。

唯有關河渺，蒼茫空樹墩。

高適第二次赴塞外，所詠不限於河西戰場，對於更為遼遠的西部邊塞——安西大都護府治下的西域局勢也很關切。高適本人固然未嘗親履西域，但同他相過往的朋友中卻不乏其人。在其所賦贈別詩中反應了他的關切之情，

如《送李侍御赴安西》：
>行子對飛蓬，金鞭指鐵驄。
>功名萬里外，心事一杯中。
>虜障燕支北，秦城太白東。
>離魂莫惆悵，看取寶刀雄。

另一首題為《送裴別將之安西》的五律，風格也與此類似：
>絕域眇難躋，悠然信馬蹄。
>風塵經跋涉，搖落怨暌攜。
>地出流沙外，天長甲子西。
>少年無不可，行矣莫淒淒。

二、王維詩歌風格

王維的詩風雖然是發展的、變化的、多樣的，但是他的詩風以衝淡著名；他之所以成為唐代詩壇的大家，就是由於他的衝淡是無與倫比的。他雖然也偶有豪放之作（如《從軍行》《燕支行》《老將行》），但在總體上遠不及李白；他雖然也偶有沉鬱（如《隴頭吟》《嘆白髮》《寄荊州張丞相》《凝碧詩》），但遠遠趕不上杜甫。然而，他卻以衝淡獨樹一幟，無人匹敵。因而，王維不能為李白之豪放、杜甫之沉鬱，李、杜也不能為王維之衝淡。

所謂衝淡，就是衝和、淡泊。衝淡含有閒逸、靜默、淡泊、深遠等特點。如果用四個字來概括，就是閒、靜、淡、遠。王維的山水田園詩就是如此，王維是衝淡派的大師。且看以下作品：

>鳥鳴澗
>人閒桂花落，夜靜春山空。
>月出驚山鳥，時鳴春澗中。

>辛夷塢
>木末芙蓉花，山中發紅萼。
>澗戶寂無人，紛紛開且落。

>鹿柴
>空山不見人，但聞人語響。
>返景入深林，復照青苔上。

木蘭柴
秋山斂餘照，飛鳥逐前侶。
彩翠時分明，夕嵐無處所。

　　欹湖
吹簫凌極浦，日暮送夫君。
湖上一回首，山青卷白雲。

　　這些詩，不僅出現了閒、靜、寂、無、空等衝淡的字眼，而且出現了衝淡的意境。這裡，沒有城市的喧囂，沒有人間的紛爭，沒有外界的紛擾，只有大自然的寧靜、山水花鳥的生機。詩人盡情地消受著、欣賞著、陶醉著，簡直是投入大自然的懷抱之中，變成了大自然的有機體了。詩人筆下的大自然，無處不跳動著詩人的脈搏，回旋著詩人的聲音，震盪著詩人的靈魂。因此，大自然已被人格化了。王維筆下的大自然，就是王維自己。它反應了王維衝淡的心情。王維已衝淡到忘我的程度。他把自己消融在大自然中了。這種消融，意味著衝淡。

　　然而，詩人難道真能百分之百地達到忘我、無我的極境嗎？當然不是。詩人所希冀的只是忘掉官場的挫折、命運的坎坷、人世的煩惱，也就是把人生道路上所遭遇的險惡風雲忘得一干二淨；他所向往的是悠然自得、安謐恬淡的生活。

　　心境衝和、氣質舒緩、和藹可親、平易近人乃是衝淡的一個特點。可細細品味以下詩作：

　　臨湖亭
輕舸迎上客，悠悠湖上來。
當軒對尊酒，四面芙蓉開。

　　白石灘
清淺白石灘，綠蒲向堪把。
家住水東西，浣紗明月下。

　　雜詩三首·其二
君自故鄉來，應知故鄉事。
來日綺窗前，寒梅著花未？

田園樂七首·其四
萋萋春草秋綠，落落長鬆夏寒。
牛羊自歸村巷，童稚不識衣冠。

詩人信筆所寫，著手成春，隨手拈來，絕不故意用力，故行文沒有波瀾，而是平靜如水，其節奏不是大起大落的，而始終是緩慢舒展的。這種出神入化的功力，可與陶淵明的詩相比。

飲酒
結廬在人境，而無車馬喧。
問君何能爾？心遠地自偏。
採菊東籬下，悠然見南山。
山氣日夕佳，飛鳥相與還。
此中有真意，欲辨已忘言。

淡泊寧靜，潔身自處，意境清幽，淡而有味，均是衝淡的特點。王維的衝淡，是衝衝和之、淡淡出之。它淡而深，淡而遠，淡而幽，淡而雅，淡而古，淡而淳，淡而清，淡而閒，淡而有致，淡而有味，味在淡中，亦味在淡外。這種淡，只可意會，難以言傳。在色彩上，它不用濃墨，不愛華豔，而追求蕭疏清淡。在運筆上，既非精雕細刻，又非粗線勾勒，而是點點染染，意到筆隨。在情趣上，王維不作驚人語，不崇尚誇飾，不出大言，不吞吐日月，不豪情滿懷，也不執著於現實，不留意生活的紛爭，不關心人事的糾葛，不激動，不悲痛，不狂歡，不愁苦，而是潔身自好，孤身靜處，獨善其身，寄情山水，吟誦風月，始終保持這內心的和平與淡泊。如以下詩作：

青溪／過青溪水作
言入黃花川，每逐清溪水。
隨山將萬轉，趣途無百里。
聲喧亂石中，色靜深鬆裡。
漾漾泛菱荇，澄澄映葭葦。
我心素已閒，清川澹如此。
請留盤石上，垂釣將已矣。

孟浩然的詩，衝淡得就像一杯白開水。白開水，雖不稀奇，卻是人人需要的。它沒有一點斧鑿的痕跡。孟浩然詩的衝淡是當之無愧的。如以下詩作：

宿建德江
移舟泊煙渚，日暮客愁新。
野曠天低樹，江清月近人。

這裡的境況一曠一清。詩人極目遠眺，蒼茫遼闊，連天也顯得低了，樹也顯得小了，這不是曠嗎？俯視江水，明澄淨澈，月影浮現，嫵媚皎潔，這不是清嗎？這一遠一近、一暗一明的對照手法，把清曠的景象就鮮明地描繪出來了。這種清曠正是孟浩然衝淡詩風的一個特點。王維、孟浩然雖同樣具有衝淡中「清」的特點，但王維偏重一個「秀」字，孟浩然偏重一個「曠」字。如以下詩作：

　　秋登蘭山寄張五
　北山白雲里，隱者自怡悅。
　相望試登高，心隨雁飛滅。
　愁因薄暮起，興是清秋發。
　時見歸村人，沙行渡頭歇。
　天邊樹若薺，江畔洲如月。
　何當載酒來，共醉重陽節。

詩人登高遠眺，不禁心曠神怡。遠處飛雁上下，時出時沒，把詩人開闊的胸懷開拓得更遼闊了。平沙渡頭歇著歸村人，給這遼闊的平原增添了活氣，詩人再把視野伸向遠處，江畔之舟小如月，更為遙遠寬闊的是詩人通達曠遠的心境。它與清曠之景相疊合，就顯得格外情景交融、魅力誘人了。如果說這首詩在清曠之中偏重於「曠」的話，那麼，《夏日南亭懷辛大》則偏重於「清」。

　　夏日南亭懷辛大
　山光忽西落，池月漸東上。
　散髮乘夕涼，開軒臥閒敞。
　荷風送香氣，竹露滴清響。
　欲取鳴琴彈，恨無知音賞。
　感此懷故人，中宵勞夢想。

這裡，不僅出現了「清」「閒」的字樣，而且從氛圍、環境、心境上烘托出清閒的情思與雅興。在池月光輝的撫摸下，詩人自由自在地散開頭髮，打開窗戶，閒散地躺著納涼，這是多麼清爽舒服啊！加之荷風飄香，竹露滴響，既美嗅覺，又美聽覺，就更增添了一種清興雅趣。詩人不禁情思萌動，對他的同鄉人還思念不已。這就把他的清興提到了藝術的高尚境界，顯示出詩人對於知音的企求。從以上分析可以看出，孟浩然的清曠，就是清靜、閒逸、豁達、曠遠。這正是孟浩然詩的一個重要特色。

此外，孟浩然詩的衝淡，樸素自然，脫口而出，如話家常，親切感人，富於泥土味。如以下詩作：

過故人莊
　故人具雞黍，邀我至田家。
　綠樹村邊合，青山郭外斜。
　開軒面場圃，把酒話桑麻。
　待到重陽日，還來就菊花。

　　此詩寫作者與田家老友促膝談心之事，情感真摯，平易近人，可謂衝而不稀，淡而不薄。如以下詩作：

　　　春曉
　春眠不覺曉，處處聞啼鳥。
　夜來風雨聲，花落知多少。

　　春眠本是處於靜謐狀態的，然而春曉鳥鳴，生機蓬勃，打破了酣睡狀態，可謂由靜入動。此時，風停雨歇，本屬靜態，但詩人巧妙地把筆鋒倒轉，在時間上回到夜裡，又回思起風雨聲而聯想到花的飄零，這就又把動的景象寫活了。從全詩看，詩人似漫不經心，但出口成詩。詩人的心情也是悠閒恬適的。

　　我們如果把王、孟的衝淡做個比較，就可體味出他們之間的區別：王維的衝淡，高雅清秀，空靈閒寂；孟浩然的衝淡，淳樸清曠，平靜悠遠。

　　王維在詩歌上的成就是多方面的，無論邊塞詩、山水詩、律詩還是絕句等都有流傳的佳篇。

　　王維詩歌風格關鍵詞：繪影繪形，有寫意傳神、形神兼備之妙。王維以清新淡遠、自然脫俗的風格，創造出一種「詩中有畫，畫中有詩」「詩中有禪」的意境，在詩壇樹起了一面不倒的旗幟。王維詩歌文學特色表現如下：

　　第一，詩如畫卷，美不勝收。蘇軾曾說：「味摩詰之詩，詩中有畫，觀摩詰之畫，畫中有詩」(《東坡志林》)。王維多才多藝，他把繪畫的精髓帶進詩歌的天地，以靈性的語言，生花的妙筆為我們描繪出一幅幅浪漫、空靈、淡遠的傳神之作。他的山水詩勝於著色取勢，如「漠漠水田飛白鷺，陰陰夏木囀黃鸝」(《積雨輞川莊作》)、「雨中草色綠堪染，水上桃花紅欲燃」(《輞川別業》)、「白水明田外，碧峰出山後」(《新晴野望》)。

　　王維的山水詩勝於結構畫面，其層次豐富，遠近相宜，乃至動靜相兼，聲色俱佳，更多一層動感和音樂美，如「鬆含風裡聲，花對池中影」(《林園即事寄舍弟》)、「萬壑樹參天，千山響杜鵑。山中一夜雨，樹杪百重泉」(《送梓州李使君》、「郡邑浮前浦，波瀾動遠空」(《漢江臨眺》)、「草間蛩響臨秋急，山裡蟬聲薄暮悲」(《早秋山中作》)，又如《山居秋暝》：空山新雨後，天氣晚來秋。明月鬆間照，清泉石上流。竹喧歸浣女，蓮動下漁舟。隨意春芳

歇，王孫自可留。該詩有遠景近景，仰視俯視，冷色暖色，人聲水聲，把繪畫美、音樂美與詩歌美充分地結合起來。王詩的畫境，具有清淡靜謐的人性特徵。如《竹里館》：獨坐幽篁裡，彈琴復長嘯，深林人不知，明月來相照。幽靜的竹林，皎潔的月光，讓詩人不禁豪氣大發，仰天長嘯，一吐胸中鬱悶。而千思萬緒，竟只有明月相知。

神韻的淡遠，是王維詩中畫境的靈魂。《鹿柴》雲：「空山不見人，但聞人語響，返景入深林，復照青苔上。」詩中著意描寫了作者獨處於空山深林，看到一束夕陽的斜暉，斜暉透過密林的空隙，灑在林中的青苔上，在博大紛繁的自然景物中，詩人捕捉到最引人入勝的一瞬間，用簡淡的筆墨，細緻入微地描繪出一幅寂靜幽清的畫卷，意趣悠遠，令人神往。

第二，情景交融、渾然天成。王維山水詩寫景如畫，在寫景的同時，不少詩作也飽含濃情。王維的很多山水詩充滿了濃厚的鄉土氣息和生活情趣，表現自己的閒適生活和恬靜心情。如《田園樂七首》其六曰：「桃紅復含宿雨，柳綠更帶朝烟。花落家童未掃，鶯啼山客猶眠。」《輞川閒居贈裴秀才迪》曰：「寒山轉蒼翠，秋水日潺湲。倚杖柴門外，臨風聽暮蟬。渡頭餘落日，墟里上孤煙。復值接輿醉，狂歌五柳前。」王維在優美的景色和濃厚的田園氣氛中抒發自己衝淡閒散的心情。再如《渭川田家》：「斜光照墟落，窮巷牛羊歸。野老念牧童，倚杖候荊扉。雉雊麥苗秀，蠶眠桑葉稀。田夫荷鋤立，相見語依依。即此羨閒逸，悵然吟《式微》。」王維從細微處入筆，捕捉典型情節，抒發無限深情。

王維寫情還多言及相思別離之情和朋友間的關懷、慰勉之情。王維在《淇上別趙仙舟》一詩中寫道：「相逢方一笑，相送還成泣。祖帳已傷離，荒城復愁入。天寒遠山淨，日暮長河急。解纜君已遙，望君猶佇立。」濃鬱深情，扑面而至。

王維詩歌中借景寓情、以景襯情的手法，使他描寫的景物饒有餘味，抒情含蓄不露。如《臨高臺送黎拾遺》：「相送臨高臺，川原杳何極。日暮飛鳥還，行人去不息。」寫離情卻無一語言情而只摹景物。《送楊長史赴果州》：「鳥道一千里，猿啼十二時。」既是景語，也是情名，將道路的荒涼之景與行者的淒楚之情融為一體，自然、含蓄而又回味深長。

在王維的詩歌中，有不少採用了直抒胸臆的表達方式，而且往往顯得自然流暢，蘊藉含蓄。比如《送元二使安西》：「渭城朝雨浥輕塵，客舍青青柳色新。勸君更盡一杯酒，西出陽關無故人。」詩人關懷體貼之情溢於言表。

王維寫情之妙還在於對現實情景平易通俗的描寫中，蘊含深沉婉約的綿綿

情思。其《相思》一篇，托小小紅豆，咏相思情愫，堪稱陶醉千古相思的經典之作。

王維寫情，又多隱喻比興。如《雜詩二首》：「家住孟津河，門對孟津口。常有江南船，寄書家中否。君自故鄉來，應知故鄉事。來日綺窗前，寒梅著花未。已見寒梅發，復聞啼鳥聲。心心視春草，畏向階前生。」全篇不著「相思」二字，看似信手拈來，實則句句意深。詩人藉「寒梅」「春草」喻義，相思之情躍然紙上。

第三，詩滲禪意，流動空靈。與上述相反，王維又有很多詩清冷幽邃，遠離塵世，無一點人間菸氣，充滿禪意，山水意境已超出一般平淡自然的美學，含義進入一種宗教的境界，這正是王維佛學修養的必然體現。王維生活的時代，佛教繁興。士大夫學佛之風很盛。政治上的不如意，王維一生幾度隱居，一心學佛，以求看空名利，擺脫煩惱。

王維有些詩尚有蹤跡可求，如《過香積寺》雲：「不知香積寺，數里入雲峰。古木無人徑，深山何處鐘。泉水咽危石，日色冷青鬆。薄暮空潭曲，安禪制毒龍。有些詩顯得更空靈，不用禪語，時得禪理，如羚羊掛角，無跡可求，代表詩句如下：行到水窮處，坐看雲起時。偶然值林叟，談笑無還期（《終南別業》）；鬆風吹解帶，山月照彈琴。君問窮通理，漁歌入浦深（《酬張少府》）；空山不見人，但聞人語響。返景入深林，復照青苔上（《鹿柴》）；木末芙蓉花，山中發紅萼，澗戶寂無人，紛紛開且落（《辛夷塢》）；人間桂花落，夜靜春山空。月出驚山鳥，時鳴春澗中（《鳥鳴澗》）。一切都是寂靜無為的，虛幻無常，沒有目的，沒有意識，沒有生的喜悅，沒有死的悲哀，但一切又都是不朽的，永恆的，還像胡應麟《詩藪》和姚周星《唐詩快》所評：「讀之身世兩忘，萬念皆寂，不謂聲律之中，有此妙詮。」

三、李白詩歌風格

第一，情感激盪，格調昂揚。

情感激盪，格調昂揚，是李白豪放詩風的根本特點，如《司馬將軍歌》：

狂風吹古月，竊弄章華臺。北落明星動光彩，南徵猛將如雲雷。手中電擊倚天劍，直斬長鯨海水開。我見樓船壯心目，頗似龍驤下三蜀。揚兵習戰張虎旗，江中白浪如銀屋。身居玉帳臨河魁，紫髯若戟冠崔嵬。細柳開營揖天子，始知灞上為嬰孩。羌笛橫吹阿亸回，何月樓中吹落梅。將軍自起舞長劍，壯士呼聲動九垓。功成獻凱見明主，丹青畫像麒麟臺。

其氣概何其威嚴！其氣勢何其雄壯！其場面何其壯闊！

再如《結客少年場行》：

紫燕黃金瞳，啾啾搖綠騣。
平明相馳逐，結客洛門東。
少年學劍術，凌轢白猿公。
珠袍曳錦帶，匕首插吳鴻。
由來萬夫勇，挾此生雄風。
托交從劇孟，買醉入新豐。
笑盡一杯酒，殺人都市中。
羞道易水寒，從令日貫虹。
燕丹事不立，虛沒秦帝宮。
舞陽死灰人，安可與成功。

這首詩生動地描繪了少年任俠、輕生重義的英雄氣概，真是激昂慷慨，氣貫長虹！

再看看《蜀道難》：

噫吁嚱，危乎高哉！蜀道之難，難於上青天！蠶叢及魚鳧，開國何茫然！爾來四萬八千歲，不與秦塞通人煙。西當太白有鳥道，可以橫絕峨眉巔。地崩山摧壯士死，然後天梯石棧相鈎連。上有六龍回日之高標，下有衝波逆折之回川。黃鶴之飛尚不得過，猿猱欲度愁攀援。青泥何盤盤，百步九折縈岩巒。捫參歷井仰脅息，以手撫膺坐長嘆。

問君西遊何時還？畏途巉岩不可攀。但見悲鳥號古木，雄飛雌從繞林間。又聞子規啼夜月，愁空山。蜀道之難，難於上青天，使人聽此凋朱顏！連峰去天不盈尺，枯松倒掛倚絕壁。飛湍瀑流爭喧豗，砯崖轉石萬壑雷。其險也如此，嗟爾遠道之人胡為乎來哉！

劍閣崢嶸而崔嵬，一夫當關，萬夫莫開。所守或匪親，化為狼與豺。朝避猛虎，夕避長蛇；磨牙吮血，殺人如麻。錦城雖雲樂，不如早還家。蜀道之難，難於上青天，側身西望長咨嗟！

此詩起句就氣勢非凡，令人有昂首天外之感。詩人的一聲驚呼，就緊緊抓住你的心弦。接著，就把你隨手拋入天際，忽聽鏘然一聲，便飄落在高聳入雲、崎嶇險峻的巴山之巔。

由於豪放的情緒是激越的、格調是昂揚的，因而決定了它所馳騁的空間必然是浩渺無垠的；它的情感必然是外溢的，而不是內向的；它的節奏必然是疾速的，而不是徐緩的；它的氣勢必然是衝擊型的，而不是迂迴型的；它的風度

必然是倜儻不羈的，而不是謹言方正的；它的胸襟必然是曠達的，而不是狹窄的；它的格局必然是宏偉的，而不是玲瓏的。如《古風五十九首》其三十九：

登高望四海，天地何漫漫。
霜被群物秋，風飄大荒寒。
榮華東流水，萬事皆波瀾。
白日掩徂輝，浮雲無定端。
梧桐巢燕雀，枳棘棲鴛鸞。
且復歸去來，劍歌行路難。
登高望四海，天地何漫漫。
霜被群物秋，風飄大荒寒。
殺氣落喬木，浮雲蔽層巒。
孤鳳鳴天倪，遺聲何辛酸。
遊人悲舊國，撫心亦盤桓。
倚劍歌所思，曲終涕泗瀾。

第二，想像奇特，誇張出格。

豪放不僅需要想像，而且需要誇張。豪放所要求的誇張，往往是出格的。它可誇大如李白所說的「燕山雪花大如席」（《北風行》）、「白髮三千丈」（《秋浦歌》），又可縮小為李白所說的「黃河如絲天際來」（《西岳雲臺歌送丹邱子》）、「興在一杯中」（《江夏別宋之悌》）。

誇張必須合情合理。誰見過「白髮三千丈」呢？但李白接著寫道「緣愁似個長」（《秋浦歌》）。這就一語道破了它的秘密。它和「橫江欲渡風波惡，一水牽愁萬里長」（《橫江詞》）有異曲同工之妙。當你聯想到在漫漫黑夜裡，無數仁人志士追求美好理想而不能實現時，當你仿佛看到他們一生窮愁潦倒的情景時，你就會相信那白髮真有三千丈，非三千丈不可。這是荒誕的，確實逼真的，唯其荒誕才更逼真。

李白的豪放詩風，以情感激盪、格調昂揚、想像奇特、誇張出格著稱於世。但李白絕不濫用自己的感情、亂彈高亢的音調，從不胡思亂想、愛說大話，李白的豪放，雖屬水到渠成、自然而為，但卻基於詩人遠大的目的，出於詩人宏偉的抱負。

第三，氣吞宇宙，力拔山河。

正由於詩人志向高遠，襟懷曠達，所以詩人之詩描繪了廣闊的天地，容量極大，力量極大，從而表現在豪放的詩風上就形成了另一個特點：氣吞宇宙，力拔山河。

欲令豪放風格氣吞宇宙、力拔山河，必須出言不遜，既要氣魄大，又要口氣大。如《上李邕》：

大鵬一日同風起，扶搖直上九萬里。
假令風歇時下來，猶能簸卻滄溟水。
世人見我恒殊調，聞餘大言皆冷笑。
宣父猶能畏後生，丈夫未可輕年少。

首句顯然受《莊子·逍遙遊》的啓發，緊接著詩人別出心裁，想像風歇時大鵬猶可簸卻海水，足見其威力之大。詩人描寫至此，並不諱言是他口出「大言」的結果。再看如下詩句：「雲龍風虎盡交回，太白入月敵可摧」（《胡無人》）。「墨池飛出北溟魚，筆鋒殺盡山中兔」（《草書歌行》）。「旌旗繽紛兩河道，戰鼓驚山欲傾倒」（《猛虎行》）。「百年三萬六千日，一日須傾三百杯。遙看漢水鴨頭綠，恰似葡萄初醱醅」（《襄陽歌》）。「興酣落筆搖五岳，詩成笑傲凌滄洲」（《江上吟》）。「身騎飛龍耳生風，橫河跨海與天通」（《元丹邱歌》）。這些詩句生動地表現了李白詩風的氣概與魄力。

第四，傲骨嶙峋，倜儻不羈。

正由於李白之詩氣吞宇宙，力拔山河，故能揮斥萬物。對於達官權貴，李白往往採取不屑一顧的態度。這樣，就形成了他豪放詩風的另一個特點：傲骨嶙峋，倜儻不羈。

李白的豪放詩風推崇一個「傲」字，突出一個「狂」字，如「安能摧眉折腰事權貴，使我不得開心顏」（《夢遊天姥吟留別》）。李白的傲骨，正表現了中國古代文人不阿諛奉承、不低三下四、正直無私、不懼邪惡的高尚品格。

正由於傲，所以也顯得狂。所謂狂，就是狂蕩不羈，倜儻不群，自由自在，無拘無束，而絕不是瘋狂、癲狂。他狂而有責，蕩而不浮，而不是放浪形骸，爛醉如泥，如「我本楚狂人，鳳歌笑孔丘」（《廬山謠寄盧侍御虛舟》）。詩人擺出一副挑戰傳統禮教、儒學的姿態。李白詩風之狂，正是詩人自由自在的表現。李白，就是一個口出狂言的人，一個個性狂蕩的人，一個舉止狂放的人，一個喜交狂士的人，一個狂歌縱飲的人。

四、杜甫詩歌風格

豪放仿佛火山爆發，沉鬱好似海底潛流。當詩人飄逸飛動、奔放不羈時，就形成豪放；當詩人沉思默處、憂憤填膺時，就變得沉鬱。李白和杜甫，在唐代詩壇上，一個豪放，一個沉鬱，是後代詩人不可企及的典範。

李白豪放，其體輕，其氣輕，故裊裊上升，飛入雲霄，若野鶴閒雲，隨處飄逸。杜甫沉鬱，其體重，其氣濁，故沉沉下墜，潛入心海，感慨激盪，迴旋迂折。

豪放和沉鬱是兩種截然不同的風格。它形象地表明，李白和杜甫，儘管所處的時代大致相同，儘管都有很高的詩名，儘管是相互尊重的朋友，但豪放飄逸，卻是李白卓絕；沉鬱頓挫，則為杜甫獨劍。二人各有特色，不可代替。李白飄飄欲仙，有凌雲之志，有「詩仙」之稱；杜甫博大精深，有「詩聖」之譽。

首先，杜甫之詩，博大精深，浩瀚汪洋，變幻莫測，為沉鬱之極致。沉鬱的根本特點是深厚，但沉鬱所要求的深厚，卻具有自己的特色。首先，它是忠厚的、誠實的，而無半點虛偽和矯飾，所謂「忠厚之至，亦沉鬱之至」，所謂「沉鬱頓挫，忠厚纏綿」，無不把忠厚與深厚連接在一起。杜甫之詩，就是極忠厚，極誠實的，故也極深厚。

其次，沉鬱所要求的深厚，扎根於生活的最底層，具有濃鬱的泥土味。所謂「沉厚之根底深也」。唯其根深，故必然含蓄，但含蓄不見得都沉鬱。二者雖然都有言已殫而意未盡的特點，但含蓄卻是泛指，而沉鬱則更進一步，它所要求的含蓄是特指。它深邃幽絕，妙不可測。如《送鄭十八虔貶臺州司戶傷其臨老陷賊之故闕為面別情見於詩》：

鄭公樗散鬢成絲，酒後常稱老畫師。
萬里傷心嚴譴日，百年垂死中興時。
蒼惶已就長途往，邂逅無端出錢遲。
便與先生應永訣，九重泉路盡交期。

可以清楚地看出，杜甫是極其忠厚、誠實的，絕不願在送別時講些違心的話。同時，我們也可體察到杜詩情感的深沉、濃鬱、悲痛、淒絕。它不是酒席上為人祝福的套話，而是在心靈深處迴盪著的情感波瀾。

最後，沉鬱所要求的深厚和憂憤結下了不解之緣。它喜歡與悲慨、憤疾結伴，而不願同滑稽為鄰。杜甫之詩，或悲或愁，或哀或憤，或涕或嘆，堪稱沉鬱之絕唱。杜甫的很多詩，從題目上，就可窺見沉鬱的氛圍，如《悲陳陶》《悲青坂》《哀江頭》《恨別》《愁》《逃難》等。

五、白居易、元稹詩歌風格

白居易有意識地追求通俗。蘇軾贊之為「白俗」，王安石譽之為「白俚」。

在唐代詩人中，從理論上到創作實踐上都提倡通俗的，是白居易和元稹。他倆既是詩友，又是摯友，世稱元白。通俗的根本特點就是質樸、率真、切實。這裡，通俗已不僅是個形式問題，而且也是個內容問題。內容是求實的，形式是純樸的，才符合通俗的要求。白居易在《寄唐生》詩中言道：「篇篇無空文，句句必盡規……非求宮律高，不務文字奇。唯歌生民病，願得天子知。」可見，他之所以不尚華彩，只求通俗，乃是為了歌咏蒼黎的痛苦，希望皇帝能夠知道，這就顯示出白詩「白俗」的人民性和現實主義精神，說明詩人之所以追求通俗，並不單是為了博取百姓的青睞，而是為了反應人民的疾苦，因此，詩人追求通俗的目的是高尚的，而不是為通俗而通俗。作為新樂府運動的倡導者，白居易所提倡的通俗，開一代詩風，成為中唐詩歌發展史上的巨大潮流。

白居易不僅在理論上提倡通俗，而且在創作上也實踐通俗。他的《秦中吟》《新樂府》就是推行通俗詩風的力作。在《輕肥》中，詩人揭露了統治階級內臣、大夫、將軍山珍海味的奢侈生活，最後以「是歲江南旱，衢州人食人」作結。這種強烈的對比，與杜甫寫的「朱門酒肉臭，路有凍死骨」有異曲同工之妙，如《杜陵叟》：

杜陵叟，杜陵居，歲種薄田一頃餘。
三月無雨旱風起，麥苗不秀多黃死。
九月降霜秋早寒，禾穗未熟皆青乾。
長吏明知不申破，急斂暴徵求考課。
典桑賣地納官租，明年衣食將何如？
剝我身上帛，奪我口中粟。
虐人害物即豺狼，何必鈎爪鋸牙食人肉？
不知何人奏皇帝，帝心惻隱知人弊。
白麻紙上書德音，京畿盡放今年稅。
昨日里胥方到門，手持敕牒榜鄉村。
十家租稅九家畢，虛受吾君蠲免恩。

該詩對封建官吏的揭露，可謂字字見血，淋灘盡致！仿佛連珠炮似的打在統治者身上。

通俗既追求藝術表達的淺顯，又追求思想內容的深刻。因此，它淺而深，而不是淺而薄。它淺中藏深，寓深於淺。淺，顯示它的通脫、俗拙；深，表明它的深刻、充實。通俗富有強烈的泥土味，它濃鬱芬芳，撲鼻誘人，耐人尋味，如《觀刈麥》：

田家少閒月，五月人倍忙。

夜來南風起，小麥覆隴黃。
婦姑荷簞食，童稚攜壺漿，
相隨餉田去，丁壯在南岡。
足蒸暑土氣，背灼炎天光，
力盡不知熱，但惜夏日長。
復有貧婦人，抱子在其旁，
右手秉遺穗，左臂懸敝筐。
聽其相顧言，聞者為悲傷。
家田輸稅盡，拾此充饑腸。
今我何功德，曾不事農桑。
吏祿三百石，歲晏有餘糧。
念此私自愧，盡日不能忘。

「田家少閒月，五月人倍忙。夜來南風起，小麥覆隴黃。」這類詩句，脫口而出，像從地裡順手揀來一樣。接著，詩人描寫了拾麥穗的貧婦的悲嘆：「家田輸稅盡，拾此充饑腸。」這裡形象地反應了農民生活之苦和官府租稅之重，流露出詩人對人民的深切同情。

白居易、元稹的詩之所以能不脛而走，風靡天下，雄視百代，同詩人錘煉字句有關。因此，白居易、元稹之通俗，絕非粗製濫造，而是千錘百煉的。在錘煉過程中，詩人盡量採用民間語言，以口語入詩，並對口語進行加工改造，唯求詞能達意，明白曉暢。詩人盡量少用成語典故，凡晦澀難懂的詞語，經詩人筆底，均一掃而空。如此成詩，人們語言中生動活潑、富於生命力的成分便跳躍於詩人筆底，因而也給詩人的通俗灌注了生氣。可見，通俗詩風是汲取了人民的乳汁營養而形成的。

六、李商隱詩歌風格

李商隱通常被視作唐代後期最傑出的詩人，他流傳下來的詩歌共594首，在唐朝的優秀詩人中，他的重要性僅次於杜甫、李白、王維等人。就詩歌風格的獨特性而言，他與其他任何詩人相比都不遜色。李商隱的詩具有鮮明而獨特的藝術風格，文辭清麗、意韻深微，有些詩可含義豐富，好用典，有些詩較晦澀。李商隱的無題詩堪稱一絕；李商隱擅作七律和五言排律，七絕也有不少傑出的作品。清朝詩人葉燮在《原詩》中評李商隱的七絕道：「寄託深而措辭婉，實可空百代無其匹也。」

他的格律詩繼承了杜甫的詩歌技巧，也有部分作品風格與杜甫相似。李商隱的詩經常用典，而且比杜甫用得更深更難懂。他在用典上有所獨創，喜用各種象徵、比興手法，有時讀了整首詩也不清楚目的為何。而典故本身的意義，常常不是李商隱在詩中所要表達的意義。例如，有人直觀認為《常娥》（嫦娥）是詠嫦娥之作，紀昀認為是悼亡之作，有人認為是描寫女道士之作，甚至認為是詩人自述之作，眾說紛紜。

　　也正是他好用典故的風格，形成了他作詩的獨特風格。據宋代黃鑒的筆記《楊文公談苑》記載，李商隱每作詩，一定要查閱很多書籍，屋子裡到處亂攤，被人比作「獺祭魚」。明王士楨也以玩笑的口吻說：「獺祭曾驚博奧彈，一篇錦瑟解人難」《戲仿元遺山論詩絕句》。也有人認為他有時用典太過，犯了晦澀的毛病，使人無法瞭解他的詩意。魯迅曾說：「玉溪生清詞麗句，何敢比肩，而用典太多，則為我所不滿。」（1934 年 12 月魯迅致楊霽雲的信）

　　此外，李商隱的詩詞藻華麗，並且善於描寫和表現細微的感情。李商隱以無題詩著名。根據《李商隱詩歌集解》裡所收詩歌的統計，基本可以確定詩人寫作時以《無題》命名的詩共有 15 首：《無題》（八歲初照鏡）、《無題》（照梁初有情）、《無題二首》（昨夜星辰；聞道閶門）、《無題四首》（來是空言；颯颯東南；含情春晼晚；何處哀箏）、《無題》（相見時難）、《無題》（紫府仙人）、《無題二首》（鳳尾香羅；重帷深下）、《無題》（近知名阿侯）、《無題》（白道縈回）、《無題》（萬里風波），另有 5 首在目前通行的詩集中經常被標為「無題」：「幽人不倦賞」「長眉畫了」「壽陽公主」「待得郎來」「戶外重陰」。經馮浩、紀昀等人考訂，他們認為多半是版本問題產生了原題丟失情況，並非為真正的無題詩。

　　李商隱的詩的社會意義雖然不及李白、杜甫、白居易，但是李商隱是對後世最有影響力的詩人，因為愛好李商隱詩的人比愛好李、杜、白詩的人更多。在清代孫洙編選的《唐詩三百首》中，收入李商隱的詩作 22 首，數量僅次於杜甫（38 首）、王維（29 首）、李白（27 首），居第四位。這個唐詩選本在中國家喻戶曉，由此也可以看出李商隱在普通民眾中的巨大影響。

　　第一，情致深蘊。情致深蘊是李商隱詩歌的根本特徵。李商隱無論感時、抒懷、吊古、咏物或言情，詩詞中莫不滲透著詩人的真情實感，具有一唱三嘆的韻味。例如，「身無彩鳳雙飛翼，心有靈犀一點通」（《無題二首》），寥寥 14 個字，把那種受阻隔的痛苦和心有默契的喜悅以及愈受阻隔愈感到默契可貴和愈有默契愈覺得阻隔難堪的矛盾心理，揭示得極其深刻動人。再如「春心莫共花爭發，一寸相思一寸灰」（《無題四首》），表面上寫絕望的悲哀，骨

子裡卻又透露了絕望掩蓋下相思如春花萌發、不可抑止的熾熱情懷，顯得分外沉痛且富有感染力。劉熙載所謂「深情綿邈」（《藝概・詩概》），張採田所謂「哀感沉綿」（《李義山詩辨正》），都是指他詩歌的這個特點。李商隱詩歌的抒情，較少採用直抒胸臆的方式，而特別致力於婉曲見意。詩人喜歡把自己的藝術構思錘煉得千迴百轉，一波三折。他常避免正面抒情，而借助於環境景物的描繪來渲染氣氛，烘托情思，如《日射》《宿駱氏亭寄懷崔雍崔袞》。他善於驅遣想像，將實事實情轉化為虛擬的情境畫面，如《夜雨寄北》《嫦娥》。他愛好綉織麗字，鑲嵌典故，細針密線，造成光怪陸離而又朦朧隱約的詩歌意象，如《錦瑟》《碧城三首》。他又大量運用比興寄託的手法，或借古諷今，或託物喻人，或言情感慨，往往寄興深微，寓意空靈，索解無端，而又餘味無窮。前人說他「總因不肯吐一平直之語，幽咽迷離，或彼或此，忽斷忽續，所謂善於埋沒意緒者」（馮浩《玉溪生詩集箋註》），分析是很中肯的。當然，刻意求深求曲，也會帶來晦澀費解的弊病。詩人的一部分作品迷離恍惚，旨意難明，有的甚至成為千古揭不破的「詩謎」，導致妄為比附、影射的索隱風氣，他也難辭其咎。婉曲見意的表現形式，同「深情綿邈」的內涵相結合，做到「寄託深而措辭婉」（葉燮《原詩》），這就是李商隱詩歌的基本風格。在晚唐採縟藻繁的詩風影響下，李商隱的詩歌也自有富麗精工的一面。但他不局限於華豔，而能夠在絢麗之中時帶沉鬱，流美之中不失厚重，這與他情深詞婉的作風分不開。約略而辭採相近的作家中，如果說李賀的特點是瑰奇，杜牧是俊爽，溫庭筠是綺密，那麼李商隱恰恰就是深婉。

第二，含蓄隱秀，奧僻幽邃。

高棅在《唐詩品匯總序》中用「隱僻」來概括晚唐詩人李商隱的詩歌風格，稱為「李商隱之隱僻」。所謂「隱僻」，就是含蓄隱秀，奧僻幽邃。所謂隱，就是言外之旨；所謂秀，就是篇中之萃。李商隱的詩風就以隱秀為特色。如《初食筍呈座中》：

嫩籜香苞初出林，於陵論價重如金。
皇都陸海應無數，忍剪凌雲一寸心。

此詩中，詩人以初出土的嫩筍自況，言其價重如金。皇廷海內應有無數嫩筍之才，須珍惜呵護，始可物盡其用，人盡其才。詩人以筍寄情，寓情於景，充分表現出含隱蓄秀的風格美。

第三，言雖殫而意無窮。

李商隱詠史詩顯著的藝術特色是言雖殫而意無窮。李商隱的詠史詩七律、七絕較多，但在壓縮的形式中都包含著十分豐富的內容。重大的歷史事件、豪

華的宮廷生活、熱鬧的歌舞場面、富麗的宮殿建築、嚴重的歷史教訓、深沉的思想情調都隱藏在凝練的語言中,可謂由博返約,以少總多,含一蓄十,寓無限於有限。它表面上似乎一平如水,骨子裡卻滾動著起伏的波瀾。它有時言內無一字觸及當時的政治,但在言外卻無不戳及當時皇帝的痛處,如《夜雨寄北》:

君問歸期未有期,
巴山夜雨漲秋池。
何當共剪西窗燭,
卻話巴山夜雨時。

再如《宿駱氏亭寄懷崔雍崔袞》:
竹塢無塵水檻清,相思迢遞隔重城。
秋陰不散霜飛晚,留得枯荷聽雨聲。
以上兩首詩均含隱蓄秀,韻味深長。

第二章　唐詩英譯理論研究

　　唐代文化昌盛，詩人輩出，唐詩成了中國文化的瑰寶。唐詩以它深邃的意境，精巧的思想概括、雋永的藝術魅力，使難以觸摸的情緒化而為可見可聞、有聲有色的形象，對後世的文學發展有著極其深遠的影響。「熟讀唐詩三百首，不會吟詩也會吟」。可見，讀唐詩對提高詩學修養有著不可忽略的作用。因此，古今中外許多翻譯大家都在為唐詩走向世界做著不懈的努力。唐詩是中國文學寶庫中的精華，在世界文學史上的地位也是非常高的。十九世紀末期，英國劍橋大學教授翟理思（Herbert A. Giles）曾將李白、王維、李商隱等詩人的名篇譯成韻文，譯文能夠吸引讀者，有獨特的風格，得到評論界的贊賞。英國文學家萊頓斯特（Lytten Strachey）就說過，翟理思譯的唐詩是那個時代最好的詩，他譯的唐詩集在世界文學史上佔有獨一無二的地位。二十世紀英國漢學家阿瑟‧韋利（Arthur Waley）也認為翟理思善於將詞義和韻律巧妙地結合起來。

　　不但是在中國，就是在全世界，正如諾貝爾文學獎評獎委員會主席埃斯普馬克說的：「世界上哪些作品能與中國的唐詩和《紅樓夢》相比呢?」早在19世紀末，英國漢學家翟理斯（Giles）曾把唐詩譯成韻文，得到評論家的好評，如英國作家斯特萊徹（Strachey）說：翟譯唐詩是那個時代最好的詩，在世界文學史上佔有獨一無二的地位。但20世紀初期英國漢學家韋利（Waley）認為譯詩用韻不可能不因聲損義，因此他把唐詩譯成自由詩或散體。中國學者翁顯良先生也是散體的身體力行者之一。一方面，他主張古典漢詩英譯要保有中國的情味，「完全西化，本色盡喪」。另一方面，他又認為「但求形似，勢必變相；舍形取神，才能保持本色」。在他看來，對英漢兩種語言、兩種文化傳統、兩種民族心理，要見其同，尤其要見其異；要見其外表的差異，尤其要見其深刻的內在差異。

　　翻譯主體的首次提出引導人們認識主體對翻譯的重要性，突出了人的主體的自覺性以及主體對於翻譯所形成的先決條件。人們不再像以往那樣，一味突

出單一主體的作用，而不顧及翻譯的對話性質及其牽涉到的各個主體所具有的複雜性以及眾多主體的創發作用。

第一節　翻譯的主體和客體

主體和客體是一對哲學範疇。西方哲學中主體與客體的概念起源很早，但作為二元對立的範疇始於十七世紀，那時是從人的角度界定主體和客體的。笛卡兒、康德、費希特、黑格爾和費爾巴哈都將人的理性和感性視為主體，與主體對立的就是客體，客體是主體實踐的對象。翻譯主體和客體研究是向哲學的借鑑。翻譯理論界已經有很多學者對翻譯主體和客體進行過探討，但何為翻譯主體？何為翻譯客體？翻譯界尚無定論。不少學者對這個問題都給出了自己的答案，但是觀點不一，存在著很大的分歧。許鈞教授歸納出以下4種答案：譯者是翻譯主體；原作者和譯者是翻譯主體；譯者與讀者是翻譯主體；原作者、譯者、讀者都是翻譯主體[1]。確定翻譯主體和客體是翻譯本體研究的基石，具有重要意義：一方面為了更好地發揮主體的主導性，譯者具備充分的「酌情善斷」的權力；另一方面強調和提升客體的職能可以抑制主體的凌駕性，使主體的活動處在客體可容性的制約之下，主體不能無視和破壞客體的格局。筆者將在本文中就翻譯主、客體進行界定，並對翻譯的主體和客體的關係進行探討。

一、翻譯主體和翻譯客體

哲學中的主體和客體有狹義和廣義之分。「廣義的主體和客體指的是在普遍存在的事物相互作用中能動的、主動的一方與受動、被動的一方，因而廣義的主、客體關係，也就是事物互相作用過程中能動與受動、主動與被動的關係。狹義的主體和客體不是以事物之間的作用，而是以人的活動的發出和指向為尺度來區分的。在這個意義上的主體是活動著的人，客體則是人的活動所指向的對象」[2]。人們提到的主、客體關係常常指狹義的主、客體關係。

主體具有兩大屬性：一是自然屬性，表現為人對自然的依附存在，即沒有

---

[1] 許鈞.「創造性的叛逆」和譯者主體性的確立 [J]. 中國翻譯, 2003, 24 (1): 10.
[2] 郭湛. 主體性哲學：人的存在及其意義 [M]. 昆明：雲南人民出版社, 2002: 12.

自然界就沒有人以及人對自身生理機能的依附存在；二是人的社會屬性，表現為人對他所在的社會的依附，人通過自己的社會實踐實現自己的目的和價值。人的精神和意志通過社會實踐才能體現。笛卡兒所說的「我思故我在」就是近代哲學史上人對主體性的最初宣言。主體的這兩大屬性又衍生出三大主體特徵。一是主導性，它是人這個主體的內在規定性，即主體總是以自己的意識、意向、目的為前提或主導而行事。其二是主體的主觀性，即主體在行事的過程中具有強烈的自我傾向，有意或無意地在行事過程中表現出自己的影響力。在行事過程中，主體能發揮自己的潛力，認識客體，把握客體，總是以自己的目的和意向對客體進行認識和改造。主體能動性是主體價值的體現。其三是主體的能動性，它是主體的價值之源。

客體是一個相對主體而言的實體概念。客體也具有兩大特徵：第一，客體具有客觀自身規定性，它永遠排斥主體對它的隨意描寫或認定，拒絕主體對它實施凌駕性；第二，客體具有一種外在實在性，存在於不依主體為轉移的外在空間；第三，客體具有對象性，客體是主體行事所指向的對象。「客體既可以被本體本質力量所及但又不能被主體本質力量所完全覆蓋。它永遠大於或超出主體本質力量在一定的時空條件下的『活動域』。它本身常常是一個系統，一個網絡或者是一個多維的複合體」①。

在翻譯活動中，翻譯主要涉及以下幾個對象：譯者、譯文、作者、原文讀者和譯文讀者。到底誰是翻譯主體呢？有些學者認為，他們都是翻譯主體。「翻譯是兩種語言文化之間的對話、交流與協商的過程。在這種對話、交流與協商的過程中，原文、原文作者、譯者、（原）譯文、讀者，有時還有翻譯發起人、出版商或贊助人等，都會參與到翻譯活動中來……原文作者、（原）譯者、復譯者、讀者、原文、（原）譯文、復譯文本都是文學作品復譯中的主體」②。是不是翻譯過程中所涉及的所有因素包括原文作者、（原）譯者、復譯者、讀者、原文、（原）譯文、復譯文本等都是翻譯主體呢？對於李明的觀點，筆者不敢苟同。首先，根據哲學對主、客體的界定可知主體是參與實踐活動的人。哲學中提到的主體和翻譯主體是普遍與特殊的關係，翻譯主體也不例外，應該是人，不能是物，因此文本包括原文文本和譯文文本等都不是翻譯主體。其次，主體是人，但並不是說人就是主體，二者不等同。只有當人參與了某一活動，才能成為這一活動的主體。原文作者、讀者他們雖然是人，但並沒

---

① 劉宓慶. 翻譯與語言哲學 [M]. 北京：中國對外出版社，2001：53.
② 李明. 從主體間性理論看文學作品的復譯 [J]. 外國語. 2006, 166 (4)：68

有參與翻譯活動，他們只是譯者翻譯時考慮的對象，因此也不是翻譯主體。

根據上面提到的主體特徵可以得知翻譯主體是指從事翻譯實踐的人，只有譯者才有資格勝任這個稱呼。因為翻譯是譯者實現主體價值的實踐活動，筆者認為譯者的翻譯主體地位不能模糊，不能忽略，不能讓讀者、原文作者佔據中心，從而使譯者成為一個邊緣人。原文作者和讀者雖然可以成為主體，但不是翻譯主體。作者創作了原文，是原文的創作主體，但他沒有參與翻譯這一實踐活動，因而不是翻譯的主體；讀者是閱讀活動的主體，也不是翻譯主體。「因此，我們可以說，翻譯活動過程中的主體，無論在理論上還是在實踐中，應該是譯者，因為他是翻譯活動過程中的行為者和實踐者，其目的是為了使客體——譯作在最大程度上滿足不同主體（包括個人主體、群體主體、社會主體等）的需要」①。

翻譯客體是指在翻譯過程中，翻譯主體指向、認識、改造的對象。在翻譯的過程中，作者和讀者成為譯者研究和利用的對象，成為譯者翻譯實踐活動的所指，已經由原來的主體衍化成客體。原文文本是譯者直接改造的對象，因而是翻譯客體。總的來說，對原文文本的改造，對讀者反應的認識，對原作者的創作意圖的瞭解等都是翻譯實踐活動的一部分，都是譯者在翻譯過程中的所指，都是翻譯客體。因此，翻譯的客體是一個多維的複合體，它包括了原文作者、讀者和原文文本。

二、翻譯主體和翻譯客體的關係

翻譯主、客體關係是改造與被改造、認識與被認識的關係。翻譯客體是譯者（翻譯主體）所指向的對象，是譯者行事的依據。它具有客觀的自身規定性，反對譯者對其任意描寫，凌駕其上。而翻譯主體即譯者具有強烈的自我傾向，具有主導性，具有主觀能動性，有權對翻譯客體進行改造，但如果譯者一味地將自己的目的、意願凌駕於翻譯客體之上，試圖臣服翻譯客體，超越翻譯客體所能接受的極限，那譯者就越出了其權界，成為翻譯客體所不能接受的不稱職的翻譯主體。「因此，我們在理解主體性內涵時要避免兩種極端：一是無視客體的制約性，過分誇大主體能動性；二是過分強調客體的制約性，完全排除主體的能動性」②。在翻譯的過程中，翻譯主體既受制於翻譯客體即原文、

---

① 胡牧. 主體性、主體間性抑或總體性——對現階段翻譯主體性研究的思考 [J]. 外國語，2006, 166 (6): 69.
② 陳大亮. 誰是翻譯的主體 [J]. 中國翻譯，2004, 25 (2): 4.

原文作者、譯文、讀者等，也可以利用翻譯客體所授予的權力發揮其主觀能動性。這種能動性必須以翻譯客體為依據，不能以徵服者的姿態將原作者擠出文本。翻譯畢竟不同於創造，譯者不能毫無限制地發揮主觀創造性。

　　翻譯客體是多維的，譯者對待這些不同的客體應該有所區別。原文文本是譯者直接改造的對象，當然是譯者把握的重中之重，離開了原文文本，譯者的主體地位也就不復存在。因此，對原文文本的認知是翻譯的前提。傅雷在《給羅新璋的信》（1963 年 1 月）中曾這樣寫道：「事先熟讀原著，不厭其詳，尤為要著。任何作品，不精讀四五遍決不動筆，是為譯事基本法門。第一要求將原作（連同思想、感情、氣氛、情調等等）化為我有，方能談到譯。平時除鑽研外文外，中文亦不可忽視，舊小說不可不多讀，充實辭匯，熟讀吾國固有句法及行文習慣。」① 可見，大譯家都注重對原文本的理解。黑格爾曾經說過：「原文文本猶如從樹上摘下的果實，已經脫離了它已有的價值觀，倫理道德等生存土壤，已經沒有它們具體存在的真實生命，給予我們的只是對這種現實性的朦朧的回憶。」解構主義者也認為：「原文文本在不斷重寫，每一次閱讀、翻譯都是對原文文本的重構。」② 不同的時代，由於價值取向不同，譯者對文本有不同的理解，文本的意義在時空的流變中得到豐富。因此譯者應該充分發揮主觀能動性，有必要通過原文作者對原文文本進行解讀，熟讀原文文本，從而達到更好的認識原文文本的目的，為良好的翻譯邁好第一步。

　　原文作者雖然不是譯者所改造的對象，但對原文作者的瞭解可以使譯者更好地把握原文文本的內容。譯文讀者作為譯者成果的品評者，無時無刻不影響著譯者在操作過程中的思維取向、價值取向等。一部譯作如果不能被同代讀者認可，那麼譯者就應該好好地反思其翻譯活動。好的譯作往往易於被讀者廣泛接受，譯者一般傾向於用適合讀者品味的方式進行翻譯。當然，不能否認，時代在變，讀者的品位也在改變。某一時代被認可的優秀的譯作隨著時間的改變可能得不到後來讀者的認可，這另當別論，如中國著名翻譯家林紓的翻譯就如此。質量低劣的譯作得不到讀者的認可，對譯者是一個督促。因此，譯者不得不考慮讀者因素。譯者首先以讀者的身分認識原文文本。對於譯者來說，在翻譯過程中及時瞭解其他讀者的反應是非常必要的。但是，只將讀者反應作為譯作的衡量標準是不可取的，這樣做是翻譯客體一元論的表現，其實質是忽略了不同的人對同一文本的反應具有差異性，不同民族對同一文本的反應具有個

---

① 周儀，羅平. 翻譯與批評 [M]. 武漢：湖北教育出版社，1999：198-200.
② Edwin Gentzler. Contemporary Translation Theories [M]. Shanghai：Shanghai Foreign Language Education Press, 2004：149.

性。總之，在翻譯過程中，過分地誇大譯者的主體性，使譯者凌駕於原文文本之上是應該避免的誤區。同時，過分地誇大翻譯客體的功能，使譯者充當讀者和文本的僕人，反客為主也是不對的。

三、對翻譯主、客體關係認識的歷時演變

學界對主、客體地位的認識大約經歷了三個階段：首先是從客體入手，強調客體的重要性，而主體的地位沒有受到應有的重視。其次是從主體入手，提升主體的地位。相比之下，客體地位被忽視。最後才從主、客體統一觀入手，注重主、客體的協調發展。在原始社會、奴隸社會和封建社會，人作為改造客觀世界的主體被客體所主宰，對客觀世界頂禮膜拜。在資本主義社會，人逐漸擺脫了客觀世界的束縛，感覺已成為世界的主宰，開始根據自己的意願對客觀世界任意地加以改造，將其意志凌駕於客體之上，結果遭到了客觀世界的報復。現代社會開始辯證地對待客體，開始注重人與自然的和諧發展。主客體的關係的變化總體上體現了這樣的特徵。在譯學領域，翻譯主體和翻譯客體地位的變化也具有相似的特徵：先重視翻譯客體，後重視翻譯主體，最後注重翻譯主、客體的和諧發展。

在中國早期的佛經翻譯過程當中，有文質之爭。文派要求譯者有更多的自由空間，文本不應該束縛譯者，而質派則強調譯者應該忠於文本，不得修飾譯本，改變原文本的意思。在佛經翻譯《法句經序》中，維祇難曰：「佛言，依其義不用飾，取其法不以嚴。其傳經者，當令易曉，勿失厥義是則為善。」[1]維祇難的這番話體現了中國早期質派的譯學觀點，即要求翻譯主體忠實於翻譯客體，翻譯客體的地位受到了極度的重視。即使是好文的支謙在《法句經序》中也提出「因循本旨，不加文飾」的譯學觀點[2]。在這場爭辯中，質派最終取勝，這實際上暗示著翻譯客體重要於翻譯主體。唐代的玄奘提出了求真喻俗的翻譯標準。在他的譯文中，翻譯主體和翻譯客體的地位都受到同樣的重視，既重視發揮譯者的能動性，也重視尊重原文文本的客觀實在性。翻譯主體和客體的關係達到了和諧的統一。到了近代，嚴復提出了信達雅的翻譯標準，指出譯文應該達雅，為譯者主體的發揮留下了空間，但忠於原文文本還是第一要的。現代翻譯家魯迅先生提出了寧信勿順的翻譯標準，把對原文的忠實又一次當作

---

[1] 陳福康. 中國譯學理論史稿 [M]. 上海：上海外語出版社，2000：6.
[2] 陳福康. 中國譯學理論史稿 [M]. 上海：上海外語出版社，2000：8.

翻譯的首要條件，對客體的忠實又一次蓋過了主體能動性的發揮。但是，就在對忠實標準高唱贊歌的時候，傅雷提出了「重神似不重形似」的翻譯觀，而翻譯大師錢鐘書把化境作為翻譯的至高標準，他說：「譯作就像原作的『投胎轉世』，軀體換了一個，而精魂依然故我。」① 中國當代翻譯家許淵衝則提倡發揮譯者的主觀能動性同原作競賽。王東風等學者則在《中國翻譯》上撰文，指出忠實是一個神話，要解構忠實。譯者的地位又一次得到重視。中國譯界對翻譯標準的探討過程總體上反應了中國翻譯研究開始重視翻譯客體，繼而重視翻譯主體的過程，而中國當代翻譯研究更注重翻譯主、客體辯證統一，提出了翻譯間性的觀點，提出翻譯過程中涉及的不同主體應該平等對話，強調既要堅持發揮翻譯主體的主觀創造性，又要尊重翻譯客體的客觀實在性。

西方的翻譯研究雖然有別於中國的翻譯研究，但基本上也體現了這樣的發展規律。古希臘時期，七十二子的聖經翻譯本著絕對忠實的翻譯標準逐字翻譯。譯者的主體性受到了苛刻的壓縮，被喻為帶著鐐銬跳舞。古羅馬時期，在羅馬勢力剛剛興起之時，「希臘文化依然高出一籌，或者說羅馬文化才開始進入模仿希臘文的階段，希臘的作品被羅馬譯者奉為至寶，因而在翻譯中譯者亦步亦趨，緊隨原文，唯一目的在於傳遞原文內容，照搬原文風格」② 此時翻譯客體的地位顯然高過翻譯主體。後來羅馬勢力逐漸勃興，古羅馬人為了體現他們在文化上優於古希臘文化，把古希臘的文學作品也當成戰利品，在翻譯古希臘文學作品的時候，任意刪改原作，充分發揮譯者的主觀能動性，同原作一較高下。其中的突出代表是西塞羅，他在《論最優秀的演說家》第五卷第十四章中說：「我不是作為解釋員，而是作為演說家來翻譯的……在這一過程中，我認為沒有必要字當句對，而是保留語言總的風格和力量。因為我認為不應當像數錢幣一樣把原文詞語一個個數給讀者，而是應該把原文重量稱給讀者。」③ 他的這一觀點突出了譯者的主體性地位，影響了後來許多翻譯家，如賀拉斯、昆體良、哲羅姆、泰特勒等。昆體良甚至認為：「我所說的翻譯，並不僅僅指意譯，而且還指表達同一意思上與原作者搏鬥競賽。」④ 現付、當代西方翻譯理論體現了多樣性的特徵，其中既不乏尊重翻譯客體、堅持對等翻譯的聲音，也不缺強調發揮主觀能動性、堅持活譯、創譯的聲音。釋意派、解構

---

① 陳福康. 中國譯學理論史稿 [M]. 上海：上海外語出版社，2000：418.
② 譚載喜. 西方翻譯簡史 [M]. 北京：商務印書館，2004：187.
③ Robison, Douglas. The Translation's Turn [M]. Baltimore：The John's Hopkins University Press, 1991：7.
④ 譚載喜. 西方翻譯簡史 [M]. 北京：商務印書館，2004：22.

派認為意義是遊離不定的，在不同的時間域延異，因此忠實的翻譯是不存在的。多元系統派等文藝學派更強調發揮譯者的主觀能動性，強調翻譯文學在不同時期的語言文學的建構中發揮著不同的作用，扮演著不同的角色。而語篇語言學派、翻譯科學派等語言學派等以原文文本分析為基礎，更強調譯者應忠實翻譯客體。當然其中也不乏翻譯主、客體應該協調統一的聲音，如德國近代翻譯理論家施萊馬赫指出譯者通過翻譯客體來再現自身，翻譯客體在制約譯者的同時，正好為譯者提供了一個發揮能動性的契機。

縱觀整個東西方譯論史不難發現：在整個翻譯過程中，每個階段都體現了一定的特徵：早期的翻譯研究更重視對翻譯客體的重視，中後期則更強調發揮翻譯主體的能動性，而現當代翻譯理論者對翻譯主、客體關係的認識趨向多樣化。隨著翻譯主體間性論的提出，當代翻譯更重視翻譯過程中所涉及的不同主體之間的平等對話，包括譯者與讀者、譯者與作者等。總之，發揮翻譯主體的主觀能動性與尊重翻譯客體的客觀實在性這兩種觀點通過互相對立而推動翻譯理論的發展。筆者相信翻譯客體中心論和翻譯主體中心論中的兩個中心將會消解，取而代之的是翻譯主客體之間的平等對話。

本書利用哲學的觀點，借鑑地探討了翻譯主客體的本質特徵及其關係。在翻譯的過程中，譯者需要從翻譯主客體關係入手，精確地界定翻譯主體的權限，準確地瞭解原文文本所表達的內容。作為翻譯主體的譯者必須明確文本所賦予他的權力，應該以文本為基礎，利用自身的可變性，努力適應翻譯客體所允許的變化範圍，而不應該脫離文本，濫用其權力，借翻譯之名，陳述自己的觀點。那樣的翻譯，嚴格來講，不能稱之為翻譯，應該是創作。譯者必須注重翻譯客體的客觀自身規定性，不能把自己的主觀意志強加在翻譯客體之上，但也不必過分強調翻譯客體的地位，為翻譯客體所制約，做客體的奴隸，從而影響譯者主觀能動性的發揮。翻譯客體的多維性使翻譯主客體關係複雜化。原文文本是譯者實踐的對象，是譯者關注的焦點，譯者進行翻譯活動時應該以文本為中心。當然，因為任何語言中的語言現象及其內涵和外延都具有不確定性和模糊性，且原文作者在運用語言的過程中難以避免其所思和其所說之間存在的矛盾，所以正確地解讀文本離不開對文本作者的解讀。對文本作者清晰的認識可幫助譯者更清楚地解讀原文文本。此外，對原文文本的理解會隨著時間的變化而變化。因此，譯者對原文文本的理解也受制於讀者。譯者在翻譯的時候也必須瞭解讀者的反應，在其可變性範圍內發揮能動性的同時，對原文文本保持一種與讀者一致的審美反應，積極地利用讀者反饋的信息及時地對譯文做出修改，既發揮譯者主觀能動性，又尊重翻譯客體的客觀實在性。因此，譯者應該

準確地把握翻譯客體的多維特徵，充分發揮主體的主觀能動性，使翻譯主、客體達到完美的結合。

第二節 直譯與意譯

翻譯是指在準確通順的基礎上，把一種語言信息轉變成另一種語言信息的活動。美國翻譯理論家奈達認為，譯文讀者對譯文的反應如能與原文讀者對原文的反應基本一致，翻譯就可以說是成功的，奈達還主張翻譯所傳達的信息不僅包括思想內容，還應包括語言形式。譯者不能隨意增加原作沒有的思想，更不能隨意地刪減原作的思想。英語和漢語是兩種不同的語言。前者注重結構形式，而且往往利用緊湊的結構來體現思維的邏輯性；而後者強調的是觀點，並且用合理地調整語序來整體地反應思維的邏輯性。因此，當我們進行翻譯時，必須掌握原作的思想和風格，同時也必須把原作的思想和風格當作譯語的思想和風格。此外，原作的理論、事實和邏輯也應當作譯語的理論、事實和邏輯。我們不能用個人的思想、風格、事實、理論與邏輯代替原作的這些特徵。

一、直譯與意譯的定義

在中國乃至世界翻譯史上，長期以來一直存在著關於不同翻譯方法的論爭，其中最有代表性也是論爭最為激烈的就是直譯與意譯。之所以出現這些論爭，原因十分複雜，其中既有技術層面上的優劣之辯，也有文化意義上的短長之較，甚至還有形而上的對翻譯使命的不同思考。此外，論爭還有一個根源，也是我們不能忽視的，那就是不同的人對翻譯方法的概念往往有不同的認識，因而導致討論的前提就不一致，其結論也就自然難以令人信服了。因此，對翻譯方法的討論，首先必須界定不同的概念，對其內涵有清楚的、科學的說明。

直譯（Literal Translation），是在譯入語語法能力所允許的範圍內，盡可能貼近原文內容與形式的翻譯方法。魯迅就是倡導直譯的方法的，在他看來，「翻譯必須兼顧兩面，一則當然求其易懂，一則保持著原作的風姿，但這樣，卻又常常和易懂相矛盾：看不慣了。不過它原是洋鬼子，當然誰也看不慣，為順眼起見，只能改換他的衣裳，卻不該削低他的鼻子，剜掉他的眼睛」[1]。

---

① 羅新璋編.翻譯論集［M］.北京：商務印書館，1984：301.

魯迅這段話，十分形象地道出了直譯的精神，也就是說，直譯首先需要尊重原文，要「保持著原作的風姿」，但直譯又不能完全拘泥於原文的字法句法，而是還要「求其易懂」，要尊重本民族語言的約定俗成，否則即是死譯。因此所謂直譯者，是要在傳達原文的精神和形式之間求一個平衡。

在翻譯過程中，譯語不要求等同於原語的數量和表現形式，但在內容方面要保持與原語一致。我們不能隨便增減原作的文字和意義，增減文字或意思要取決於表達方式和語言的特徵。這些原則都是直譯與意譯應該遵從的，也就是說，所有這些都是他們的共同點。因此，二者是相互聯繫、相互協調的。直譯出現於五四運動時期，它強調必須忠實於原文，這樣，翻譯才能實現「達」和「雅」。直譯並不是機械地逐字翻譯。由於英文和中文有著不同的結構，所以不可能都進行逐字翻譯。直譯就是既要全面準確地闡明原作的含義，又無任何失真或隨意增加或刪除原作的思想，同時還要保持原有的風格。有時甚至連原來的情緒或情感，比如憤怒或窘迫，挖苦或諷刺，喜悅或幸福都不應忽視。傅斯年、鄭振鐸都主張直譯。在近現代中國翻譯史上，直譯是壓倒一切的準則。魯迅和其弟周作人的作品《域外小說集》被視為直譯的代表。意譯則從意義出發，只要求將原文大意表達出來，不需過分注重細節，但要求譯文自然流暢。在翻譯時，如果不能直接採用原作的結構和表達形式，我們必須根據表達形式和特點改變句子結構和表達方式來傳達原作的內涵。由於原語和譯語在語序、語法、變化形式和修辭之間存在著許多差異，我們只能用適當的方式來傳達原作的意思和再現原作的效果。在翻譯過程中，要使語言清晰、有說服力，並且符合語言習慣，譯者必須盡量遵照所使用的語言習俗和正確的用法，而不是堅持原作的表達模式。趙景深先生曾經說過，「一個通順流暢的版本比只注重於忠實於原作的版本更好」。顯而易見，趙景深先生贊成意譯，嚴復先生也喜歡意譯。嚴復的許多經典作品都採用了意譯，如《天演論》就是意譯典型的例子。在直譯中，忠實於原作的內容應放在第一位，其次是忠實於原作的形式，再次是翻譯語言的流暢性和通俗性；而在意譯中，忠實於原作的內容應放在第一位，翻譯語言的流暢性和通俗性位居第二，但意譯並不局限於原作的形式。可見，直譯與意譯都注重忠實於原作的內容。當原文結構與譯語結構不一致時，仍字字對譯，不能稱為直譯，是「硬譯或死譯」，即形式主義。憑主觀臆想來理解原文，不分析原文結構，只看字面意義，編造句子也不能稱為意譯，是「胡譯或亂譯」，即自由主義。由此可見，直譯和意譯各有所長，可以直譯就直譯，不可以直譯就採用意譯，甚至雙管齊下，兩者兼施，才能兼顧到譯文的表層結構和原文的深層意思。從上述分析我們可以得出：直譯與意譯

不是孤立的，而是相互聯繫、相輔相成、互為補充、不可分割的。

二、直譯與意譯應遵守的原則

在翻譯過程中，譯者應避免兩種極端。在運用直譯和意譯時，我們必須首先要透澈瞭解作者的思想和原文所要表達的情感，然後根據一些基本的翻譯準則和方法把原語翻譯成符合語言習慣的譯語。只有這樣，我們才能說既是對作者負責又是對讀者負責。所有這些都是他們的共同點。另外，在直譯時，我們應該竭力擺脫僵硬的模式並且嚴格堅持翻譯準則，設法靈活運用；在意譯實踐中，我們應該謹慎，避免主觀性、無根據的斷言或任意的組合。他們的最終目標就是：譯文必須忠於原作並且譯語通順流暢。不論在何種情況下，如果有必要，我們可以交替使用這兩種方法或者把二者相結合，當讀者讀譯品時，能夠收到和讀原作一樣的效果。從上述分析，我們可以斷定，直譯與意譯是相互協調、互相滲透的，他們互為補充、不可分割。我們不能否認其中任何一方。它們之間也沒有任何排斥的關係。在翻譯過程中，如果譯者不能把直譯與意譯完美地結合，那麼將不會有完美的譯品產生。總之，在翻譯過程中，直譯和意譯是相互依存、密切聯繫的，二者有其各自的功能，二者之間的差異和共同點是它們存在的依據和理由。我們反對任何否定或忽視直譯與意譯並存價值的觀點。我們也反對強調其一而忽視另一方的觀點。錢歌川先生說：「翻譯沒有固定的規則和方法。」我們只能在實踐中累積經驗，尋找出一些規律，把直譯和意譯自由地運用到翻譯實踐中。此外，譯者還要深深體會直譯和意譯之間的關係。

三、直譯、意譯與唐詩英譯

直譯中國古典詩詞，除了遵守翻譯的基本原則之外，譯者還必須把握一定的技巧，並附加簡要貼切的註釋，以便闡釋原詩的典故和難懂詞語。

中國古典詩詞的藝術結構，多數以意象的鋪列與組合而形成，多數情況下甚至不用或少用連接詞語，以便營造出充滿詩意的藝術氛圍和境界，令人產生無窮的遐思。作者以為，對「雞聲茅店月，人跡板橋霜」（溫庭筠）、「千里鶯啼綠映紅，水村山郭酒旗風」（杜牧）等名句，宜盡可能採用對等直譯的手段，將意象組合按一定方法排列，以便讓讀者直接去體味和感受原詩的意境。但是，中國詩詞意象用語，相對於西方文字來說，又過於複雜。在同義詞的詞與

詞之間還存在著詞義上微妙的差別，形成令讀者體味和感受大不相同的意境。如月亮的同義詞就有明月、皓月、冰輪、玉壺、玉兔、嬋娟、蟾宮、蟾蜍、廣寒宮等，如果在英譯中，一概用 The moon、The lunar Artemis、Phoebe 來對等表示，其詩意便會大打折扣，有礙於傳遞中國文化形態和神韻。因此，在翻譯詩中之月時，譯者可以用 bright moon、bright white moon、ice wheel、jade kettle、jade rabbit、Guang-Han palace 等對於英語來說具有異國情調的詞彙來直接表示，然後再加以註釋。實際上，就是對於大多數中國讀者來說，許多時候在詠讀古詩時，也是需要查看註釋才能讀明白的。

　　直譯中國古典詩詞，除了必要的翻譯理論和一些基本原則之外，譯者還必須把握一定的方法，掌握一定的技巧，如附加簡要註釋的方法和技巧，以便明白地闡釋原詩的典故和難懂詞語。例如，「但使龍城飛將在」（王昌齡）、「六龍回日之高標」（李白）、「三顧頻煩天下計」（杜甫）、「宛轉蛾眉馬前死」（白居易）、「報君黃金臺上意」（李賀）、「隔江猶唱《後庭花》」（杜牧）、「嫦娥應悔偷靈藥」（李商隱）、「六朝如夢鳥空啼」（韋莊）等，其詩中一些語詞的背後，都隱藏著一段跌宕的史實，一個曲折的故事，一個神奇感人的傳說。譯者應先分別直譯為：The fly Gen. of Dragon city, six dragons tow the sun, three times call on, the moth eyebrow died in front of horses, golden-Tai stage, thieve divine medicine, six dynasties as a dream 等，而後加以註釋。這種有註釋的譯文，才便於讀者接受與解讀。關於典故的英譯，在已故語言學家呂叔湘《中詩英譯比錄》中也有所提及：「熟語之極致為『典故』，此則不僅不得其解者無從下手，即得其真解亦不易達其意蘊。如小杜金谷園結句『落花猶似墜樓人』，Giles 譯作 Petals, like nymphs from balconies, come tumbling to the ground, 誠為不當，即 Bynner 譯為 Petals are falling like a girl's robe long ago, 若非加註亦不明也……仍不得不乞靈於附註。」由此可知，呂老亦主張詩詞中典故的翻譯採用直譯並再加以註釋，才能完整真實地傳遞出中國古典詩詞完整真實的信息。此外還能使外國讀者，逐漸熟悉和理解中國文化的亙古淵源。

　　中國古典詩詞中用了很多人名、地名、度量衡、朝代、紀年、天文、官銜、署銜等專有名詞、如蠶叢、魚鳧、劍外、薊北等，舉不勝舉。對此，原則上都應音譯或、直譯，即譯為 Can-Cong, Yu-Fu, Tai-Bai, outside of Jian-Ge, northward of Ji, 並加以註釋。此外，中國古代的度量衡均採用市制，如寸、丈、門、錢、時辰等。關於這些度量衡單位名稱的翻譯，絕對不能像科技翻譯，甚至像在有的譯詩中那樣，將其換算為現代的公制或英制單位。市制單位在英語的對等詞中，有「兩」為 liang, 「尺」為 chi, 「畝」為 mu, 顯然這些都

是英語的音譯外來詞。因此，對於其他市制單位，亦可如法炮製地譯為：cun, zhang, dou, qian, jin, shi-chen 等，然後，在註釋中將其分別換算成公制或英制單位，加以闡明，使外國讀者也能逐漸熟悉中國古代的環境和習俗民風。

中國古典詩詞的詩句中，有許多特殊語法現象。例如，雙關語情況：東邊日出西邊雨，道是無晴卻有晴（劉禹錫），其中的「晴」就是與「情」字（feeling or affection）的雙關。這種情況，仍可用註釋做個案處理。前者可將原文譯為：The east is sunny but west is rain, Saying as Fine or not Fine. 其中雙關詞按大寫字母開頭，然後註明：In Chinese,「Fine」and「feeling」were both pronounced「情 Qing」。另外，中國唐詩的詩句中，還有許多疊字、疊句，如瑟瑟、嘈嘈切切、蕭蕭、滾滾、歷歷、萋萋等字、詞的疊加，可以強烈地提高意象的表達力，激發讀者情感和思緒的共鳴。而在英文詩中也有疊詞、疊句的修辭手法，關於這點，可從蘇格蘭偉大的農民詩人羅伯特・彭斯（Robert Burns, 1759—1796 年）的「A red, red rose」（被譯作《一朵紅紅的玫瑰》）的詩中「red, red」「O, my love is like…O, my love is like…」的疊詞、疊句中得到印證。筆者主張譯詩中應保留疊字、疊句的風格，在轉譯時應盡量採取作者的這種能加強語氣和意象表達的修辭手法。除上述之外，漢詩中還有許多回文詩。這是由漢語方塊字及以字組詞的特點才能達到的巧妙結構。這種詩詞幾乎是無法翻譯的，只能寄希望於有能力的外國讀者在中國古典詩詞原文中欣賞了。

中國唐詩中，大都存在著畫龍點睛之筆，即一些關鍵的動詞。如「秋風吹渭水，落葉滿長安」（賈島憶：江上吳處士），其中的「吹」與「滿」；賈島著名的詩句「鳥宿池邊樹，僧敲月下門」中，用「推」好抑或「敲」好？都是幾經詩人推敲所得的「詩眼」。譯文中不可忽視，宜盡可能找到相應妙詞，如也能獲取點睛之筆，則原詩的神韻便自在其中了。

中國格律詩詞具有嚴格的字數、對仗、平仄和音韻的規範。譯者要將這種格律形式移植到屬於不同文化圈語言的譯文中，幾乎是不可能的。只好退而求其次，首先考慮譯文按目的語的押韻，而後盡量照顧目的語詩歌的格律。漢詩翻譯應著重於在尾韻（End rhyme），但要按英詩音韻翻譯，弄不好還會以韻害意，更談不上詩的神韻了。因此，關於譯文的押韻，寧肯放寬一些，有時反而更好。關於韻律（Metre），建議基本按照漢詩的「言」數來安排，即五言詩句，大體按五音步（Pentameter）；七言詩句，大體按七音步（Heptameter），如此等等，只要大概統一即可，不可過於勉強。

將漢詩譯為英詩，使之語言通順，已屬不易，更別說達到諸「美」的高標準了，如果大動干戈，添加一些原詩中沒有的成分，則違背了要求直譯，即達

到譯文異化的初衷。因此，許多學者認為，對於詩歌的翻譯，在詞語和語法上，不能提出過於苛刻的標準。否則，可能畫虎不成而適得其反。錢鐘書在《談藝錄》中寫道：詩歌語言必有「突出處」，不惜乖違習用「標準語言」之文法、詞律，刻意破常示異……詩歌語言每「不通不順」，實則詩歌乃反常之語言……在常語為「文理欠通」或「不妥不適」者，在詩文中則為「奇妙」而「通順」和「妥適」之至也！詩歌既然受到音韻和格律的限制，那麼，文法上必然應該放寬。因此，古今詩人都享有對語言「破格和創造詩家語的特權」。因此，詩人為在自己的詩歌作品中選用最恰當、最具有表達力、在特定的語域中能產生某種表達效果，常常有意違背語言運用的常規，產生語言運用中的變異，是十分常見的現象。

在譯文中，除註釋之外，譯者還應以附註形式，簡明扼要地介紹該篇唐詩寫作的時代背景、環境、作者生平、內容分析等。作為對中國詩詞欣賞的導讀或輔導材料，特別是在向外國讀者介紹中國古典詩歌時，是非常必要的。

直譯加註釋翻譯，能夠忠實於原詩作者表達的意象和想要營造的意境、意蘊，又可幫助外國讀者理解中國古代詩詞中典故及背景知識。譯者在宏揚中國的傳統文化的同時，也使得唐詩與西方文化和諧共處，盡可能達到跨文化相互交流溝通和積極對話的目的。

第三節　歸化與異化

翻譯既是兩種不同語言的轉換過程，又是兩種不同文化之間的移植和傳遞過程，因此譯者在翻譯過程中必然產生了一個語言與文化之間關係的問題。「語言與文化是不可分割的。沒有語言，文化就不可能存在；語言也只有能反應文化才有意義」[1]。不同文化的語言在相互轉換的過程中，文化差異是影響其翻譯過程的最大因素，尤其是源語文化與目的語文化差異較大的文本。那麼，如何處理文本中的文化因素呢？翻譯界產生了分歧，即產生了所謂「異化」（Alienation）與「歸化」（Adaptation），兩種處理文化翻譯的基本策略。

---

[1] 郭建中. 翻譯中的文化因素：異化與歸化 [M] //郭建中. 文化與翻譯. 北京：中國對外翻譯出版公司，2000：285.

一、歸化與異化的概念與歷史沿革

異化與歸化的說法起源於 19 世紀初，由西方翻譯理論家提出的。1813 年，德國古典語言學家、翻譯理論家施萊爾‧馬赫（Schlerer Machre）在《論翻譯的方法》中提出，「翻譯的途徑只有兩種：一種是盡可能讓作者安居不動而引導讀者去接近作者，另一種可能是讓讀者安居不動而引導作者去接近讀者」。施萊爾馬赫只是描述了他所說的兩種翻譯方法，但並未授之以名稱。

翻譯中的「歸化」（Demestication）和「異化」（Foreignization）是翻譯研究領域的熱門話題。這兩個概念最初是由美國翻譯理論家勞倫斯‧韋努蒂（Lawrence Venuti）於 1995 年在《譯者的隱身》（*The Translator's Invisibility: A History of Translation*）一書中提出來的，將上述兩種方法稱為「異化法」（Foreigning Method or Alienation），將第二種方法稱作「歸化法」（Domesticating Method or Adaptation）。根據他的看法，歸化翻譯是「採用透明的、流暢的風格為譯文把陌生感降到最小的翻譯策略」[①]，而異化翻譯則是「通過保留原文的某些成分有意地打破目的文化的規範」[②]。

歸化（Demestication）和異化（Foreignization）是兩種翻譯策略。「歸化」，通常是指譯者在翻譯時採用透明而流暢的譯文，從而使得原語文本對於讀者的陌生感（Strangeness）降至最低；所謂「異化」，則是指譯者在翻譯時故意保留原語文本當中的某些異質性（Foreignness），以此打破譯入語的種種規範。之所以說這兩種翻譯策略截然相反，是因為二者的傾向性明顯不同，前者傾向於原語文化和原文作者（SL Culture or Author Oriented），後者則傾向於譯入語文化和譯文讀者（TL Culture or Reader Oriented）。在《譯者的隱身》一書中，韋努蒂明確表示自己傾向於「異化」策略。韋努蒂的異化理論一經提出，便在譯界產生了廣泛的影響，不少翻譯學者從異化論的角度出發，對翻譯理論中的一些基本概念，如直譯、意譯、對等、忠實等，進行了重新審視。

歸化的翻譯以原語與譯入語文化之間的有效交際與溝通為目標，充分考慮到譯入語讀者的接受心理和審美感受，用地道的本族語表達方式來傳遞原語文本的信息，避免給讀者的閱讀造成障礙。一般來說，由於歸化的翻譯採用了具有譯入語文化色彩的詞語，表達上更加符合譯入語的言語規範，譯文讀起來地

[①] Shuttleworth, Mark, Moira Cowie. Dictionary of Translation Studies [M]. Shanghai: Shanghai Foreign Language Education Press, 2004: 43.

[②] 陳福康. 中國譯學理論史稿 [M]. 上海：上海外語出版社，2000: 59.

道自然，因而易於為讀者所喜愛和接受，這是歸化的優勢所在。

與歸化翻譯相比，異化的翻譯則更注重體現原語文本在語言和文化上的差異性，盡可能多地保留原語文化的特色和作者的獨特表達方式，使得讀者能夠領會到原作的風貌，有身臨其境的感受。美國意象派詩人埃茲拉・龐德翻譯的中國古詩可謂是「異化法」的典範，翻譯如下：

抽刀斷水水更流，舉杯銷愁愁更愁。
Drawing sword, cut into water, water again flows.
Raise up, quench sorrow, sorrow again sorrow.

翻譯中的「歸化」和「異化」不僅是不矛盾的，而且是互為補充的，文化移植本來就需要不同的方法和模式。根據不同的情況和需要，譯者既可採用「歸化」的原則和方法，也可以採用「異化」的原則和方法；至於在譯文中必須保留哪些原語文化，怎樣保留，哪些原語文化的因素必須做出調整以適應譯入語文化，都可以根據實際情況來加以選擇。對譯者來說，重要的是在翻譯過程中要有深刻的文化意識，即意識到兩種文化的異同①。

需要補充說明的是，譯者在具體的翻譯實踐中對於歸化和異化策略的選擇，事實上受到很多因素的影響，如作者意圖、文本類型、譯者水準、翻譯目的、讀者對象、大的翻譯環境等。

實際上，歸化異化可以看作是直譯和意譯的延伸，但兩者之間也存在差異。韋努蒂曾說歸化策略就是「把原作者帶入譯入語文化」②即譯者向目的語讀者靠攏；而異化策略則是「接受外語文本的語言及文化差異，把讀者帶入外國情境」③，即讓讀者向作者靠攏。由此可知，直譯和意譯側重語言層面，而歸化和異化偏向文化層面。

二、主要觀點

1. 國外研究

韋努蒂的觀點是施萊爾馬赫的繼承與發展，他認為「異化法要求譯者向讀者靠攏，採取相應於作者所使用的源語表達方式來傳達原文內容，而歸化法則要求譯者向目的語靠攏，採取目的語讀者所習慣的目的語表達方式來傳達原文

---

① 郭建中. 翻譯中的文化因素：異化與歸化 [M] //郭建中. 文化與翻譯. 北京：中國對外翻譯出版公司, 2000：287.
② Lawrence Venuti. The Translator's Invisibility [M]. London：Routledge Press, 1995：20.
③ 陳福康. 中國譯學理論史稿 [M]. 上海：上海外語出版社, 2000：20.

內容」。這正是翻譯界的兩種對立觀點，也可以說是直譯和意譯之爭的延伸。而韋努蒂可以說是異化的代表人物。韋努蒂對歸化翻譯並不贊同，這可以從他對歸化翻譯下的定義看出：遵守目標語言文化的主流價值觀，公然對原文採用保守的同化手段，使其迎合本土的典律、出版潮流和政治需求。看來英美文化體系中歸化策略的選擇不僅僅是為了方便譯文讀者的需要，更重要的是強勢文化企圖將自己的價值觀和文化觀強加給弱勢文化以實現對後者的殖民統治。「而異化策略所要做的就是忠實於原文，尊重源語文化，保留異域情趣，再現原文特有的文化思想和藝術特色，使源語文化中有價值的信息完整地融入並豐富目的語的語言及文化，從而促進不同國家之間語言和文化的相互交流和滲透」。

歸化翻譯的代表人物是美國著名的翻譯家理論家尤金奈達（Eugene A Nida）。奈達提倡歸化，他「強調最近似的自然對等物」，即譯語文本應在交際功能上與源語文本實現對等，可以不考慮源語語言表達形式等因素，盡可能保證目標語讀者產生與原語讀者基本相同的反應。

2. 中國歸化異化代表人物及其對應的翻譯理論觀

中國較早提出「歸化」這一說法的是魯迅。但是，他提出的與歸化對應的詞不是異化，而是「保留洋氣」和「歐化」。中國第一篇含有「異化」字樣的翻譯研究論文是郭建中於 1998 年在《外國語》第二期上發表的「翻譯中的文化因素：歸化與異化」。

中國現當代學者也很重視翻譯中的異化問題。魯迅主張「寧信而不順」，實際上是提倡異化。錢鐘書強調要化境，提醒譯者不要因為中外語文習慣的差異而露出生硬牽強的痕跡，這是針對異化而採取的對策。許淵衝對中外語言與文化的差異提出「優勢競賽論」，也涉及翻譯的異化問題。

而提到翻譯的異化與歸化，就不得不提起直譯與意譯。「直譯」和「意譯」是屬於翻譯技巧範疇的兩種具體的翻譯方法。直譯是指譯者在譯文中採用原作的表現法；意譯是指譯者在譯文中另外尋找新的表現法，來表達原文的邏輯內容和形象內容[①]。

歸化與異化之爭可以說是歷史上直譯與意譯之爭的延伸，但並不完全等於直譯與意譯。直譯、意譯是具體的翻譯方法，而異化歸化是指導翻譯方法運用的策略。直譯和意譯只是語言層面上的討論，關注的核心是形式和內容的關係。而歸化異化則是在後殖民的大背景下提出來的，強勢文化為其理論預設背

---

① 張今，張寧. 文學翻譯原理 [M]. 北京：清華大學出版社，2005：232-233.

景，並將語言層面的討論延續升至文化、詩學和政治層面。

三、歸化、異化與唐詩英譯

唐詩，一個內涵豐富的中華文化瑰寶，譯者翻譯時不僅要注意英漢語言的差異和轉換，更要考慮不同的文化背景和社會習俗之間的差異。以下我們選取了許淵衝和弗萊徹的《長恨歌》英譯本，以此來深入分析在歸化與異化的翻譯策略指導下古詩英譯在文化傳播中的作用。

1. 歸化策略的應用

漢語古詩的一個特色就是主語的省略。通常，中國讀者能猜出詩歌的主語，而對於國外讀者來說就比較困難了。「漢語語法重意合而輕形合，最典型的就是主語的省略。在漢詩英譯時，絕大部分譯者都採用補出主語這一技巧，即增益法，屬結構增益」①。在古詩英譯中，大部分譯者都會選擇歸化的方法即補出主語來達到英語語法的要求，從而更好地進行文化傳播。例如，對「回眸一笑百媚生」的翻譯，許淵衝的譯文是「Turning her head, she smiled so sweet and full of grace」②。弗萊徹的譯文是「If she but turned her smiling, a hundred loved were born」③。在這一句詩裡，詩人只是說「回眸一笑」，並沒有說是誰，但在漢語中，正是因為主語的省略使這句詩具有別樣的魅力，且成為千古名句。翻譯為英語時，兩位譯者不約而同都選擇了增益的方法填補了主語。中國古典詩歌內涵豐富，用詞凝練，對具有豐富文化氣息的古詩翻譯而言，使用歸化的方法主動增補能讓譯語讀者更加瞭解中國的文化，彌補歷史文化背景的缺陷，從而有效地進行文化傳播。

「簡化是讓譯文更簡潔更易懂的過程」④。在歸化的翻譯策略中也有簡化翻譯技巧的運用。詩的後文「梨園弟子白髮新，椒房阿監青娥老」，許淵衝譯為「Actors although still young, began to have hair gray; Eunuchs and waiting maids looked old in palace deep」⑤。弗萊徹的版本則是「Tresses of her comrades. Were

---

① 李正栓，賈曉英. 歸化也能高效地傳遞文化——以樂府詩為例 [J]. 中國翻譯，2011 (4): 51-53.
② 許淵衝. 文學與翻譯 [M]. 北京：北京大學出版社，2003: 329.
③ 陳福康. 中國譯學理論史稿 [M]. 上海：上海外語出版社，2000: 318.
④ 李正栓，賈曉英. 歸化也能高效地傳遞文化——以樂府詩為例 [J]. 中國翻譯，2011 (4): 53.
⑤ 許淵衝. 文學與翻譯 [M]. 北京：北京大學出版社，2003: 331.

newly streaked with grey. The eunuchs of her palace. And women pined away」①。許淵衝把「梨園弟子」直接譯為「actor」，因為對譯語讀者來說他們或許不知道「梨園」在中國是戲院的意思，「梨園弟子」就是戲曲演員。在不影響詩歌原意的前提下，簡化翻譯為「actor」，對他們來說更容易理解且不會造成閱讀受阻。而弗萊徹則譯為「comrades」，雖然也運用了簡化的方法，但傳達的原意並不充分。

2. 異化策略的應用

在中國的文化語境下，「芙蓉」「荷花」和「蓮花」通常指代一種花，它們寓意著高貴、典雅和富貴。在《長恨歌》中有一句「芙蓉帳暖度春宵」，下面比較一下許淵衝和弗萊徹的譯文：

「How warm in her pure curtains to pass a night of spring!」②（弗萊徹）

「In lotus-flower curtain she spent the night blessed.」③（許淵衝）

首先來看「芙蓉帳」的翻譯。弗萊徹把它譯為「pure curtain」，而許淵衝則直譯為「lotus-flower」。實際上，在其他國家的文化背景下，「芙蓉」或許並沒有「典雅、富貴」之說，按照許譯，則會讓譯語讀者瞭解到楊玉環生活的富足以及「芙蓉」在中國的寓意，這裡的異化策略就有效地傳遞了中國文化。而在「春宵」的翻譯中，弗萊徹直譯的「night of spring」與許淵衝的「night blessed」相比更容易使譯語讀者產生共鳴。「spring」比「blessed」更能讓譯語讀者在直觀上體會到漢語特有的「春宵」的含義。此時弗萊徹的異化策略就更勝一籌。

在《長恨歌》中還有另外一個非常出名的典故「金屋藏嬌」，如詩句「金屋妝成嬌侍夜」。「金屋藏嬌」的典故起源於漢武帝。漢武帝年幼時，他的姑姑想把自己的女兒阿嬌許配給他，童稚的皇帝當場回答說「若得阿嬌作婦，當作金屋貯之也」，「金屋」即被後世指稱為華麗的房屋。許淵衝把此句譯為「Her beauty served the night when dressed in Golden Bower」④，弗萊徹則譯為「When dressed, in secret chamber, her beauty served the night」⑤。在這裡，弗萊徹間接地採用了異化的策略，因為人們有時也會使用「金屋藏嬌」來形容男子的家中有一位美麗的女子。但此處的異化譯法可能會使譯語讀者感到困惑，

---

① 陳福康. 中國譯學理論史稿［M］. 上海：上海外語出版社，2000：325.
② 陳福康. 中國譯學理論史稿［M］. 上海：上海外語出版社，2000：319.
③ 陳福康. 中國譯學理論史稿［M］. 上海：上海外語出版社，2000：330.
④ 許淵衝. 文學與翻譯［M］. 北京：北京大學出版社，2003：330.
⑤ 陳福康. 中國譯學理論史稿［M］. 上海：上海外語出版社，2000：320.

為什麼會把一位美麗的女子藏起來。許淵衝則直接採用了異化策略中經常使用的「直譯」的技巧，僅用一個「Golden」就完美地向譯語讀者闡釋了「華麗」的意思。

歸化和異化作為兩種翻譯策略是相輔相成的，綜觀《長恨歌》的這些譯文，我們可以看出，每種譯文都是歸化和異化策略使用的結合，譯者只選取一種策略而完全排除另一種策略的譯文是不存在的，也是不現實的。歸化策略和異化策略的選擇取決於具體的翻譯目的，若想要再現原文的風格，傳播濃厚的異國情調就可以採用異化策略；若想要保證譯文的可讀性，減少文化摩擦，可以採用歸化策略。但通過對不同版本的《長恨歌》譯本的分析我們可以得知，在特定情況下，為了交流的需要以及緩解文化衝突，古詩英譯的譯者也經常會使用歸化策略，從而有效地傳播中國文化。在古詩英譯的過程中，譯者要根據具體情況選擇適當的翻譯策略，達到翻譯目的，以期更忠實地傳播中國文化。

第四節　目的論

「目的論」是德國功能派學者費米爾和諾德等提出來的，它形成了功能翻譯理論的主流。翻譯目的論者認為，翻譯是一種交際行為，翻譯行為所要達到的目的決定整個翻譯行為的過程，即「目的決定手段」，翻譯策略必須由翻譯目的來確定。在這一原則的指導下，原文文本在翻譯中只起到「提供信息」的作用，為適應新的交際環境和疑問讀者的需求，更加有效地實現譯文的功能，譯者在整個翻譯過程中的參照系不應是「對等理論」中所注重的原文及其功能，而應是譯文在譯語環境中所期望達到的一種或幾種交際功能。因此譯者在翻譯過程中可以根據譯文預期的交際功能，結合譯文讀者的「社會文化背景知識」，對譯文的「期待」以及「交際需要」等，來決定處於特定譯語環境中文本的具體翻譯策略和方法。

一、目的論的定義

目的論從人類行為理論的視角來審視和研究翻譯活動，認為翻譯具有明確的目的性和意圖性，是一種在譯者的作用下以原文文本為基礎的跨文化人類交際活動。翻譯的意圖在於幫助那些由於語言障礙而無法實現交際的人們實現交際活動。目的論的核心概念是：翻譯方法和翻譯策略必須由譯文預期目的或功

能決定。德國翻譯功能學派學者費米爾根據行為理論提出翻譯（包括口譯、筆譯）是人類的一種行為活動，並且具有人類行為活動的一般共性——這是一種受特定背景影響的有目的的活動。同時，他提出「翻譯是一種人類行為」，而「任何行為都具有目的」「翻譯是一種目的性行為」。因此，翻譯是「在目的語情景中為某種目的及目的受眾而生產的語篇」。另外，費米爾強調，「目的論所指的意圖性並不是說一種活動本身具有意圖，而是指活動的參與者認為或解釋為有意圖；翻譯活動的意圖主要與譯者或翻譯活動的發起者有關」①。

目的論將翻譯視為一種人際間的互動活動，涉及譯文發起者、譯者、原文作者、譯文讀者和譯文文本的使用者等。翻譯活動的發起者確定翻譯目的並規定翻譯要求，其中包括：文本功能、譯語文本的接受者、接受文本的時代及地點、傳播文本的媒介、生產或接受文本的動機等。費米爾認為譯文接受者對於翻譯過程起著重要作用，因此任何有關譯文接受者的信息對於譯者來說都很重要。

目的論認為，「諸如特定歷史時期的政治、經濟、社會歷史文化、意識形態、居主導地位的文學體裁和文學規範等譯語文化語境會對翻譯活動產生重大的影響，因而制約著翻譯材料的選擇、翻譯目的的選擇、翻譯目的的確定、譯者對翻譯策略的選擇、譯文文本的生成以及譯語文本在譯語文化中的地位和作用。因此，作為翻譯活動中重要的參與者，譯者首先需要研究分析翻譯要求在法律經濟及意識形態方面的可行性和確定翻譯的必要性，然後再根據翻譯要求將原文文本翻譯成符合譯語功能的譯語文本」②。

二、目的論的發展

凱瑟琳娜·萊斯首次把功能範疇引入翻譯批評，將語言功能、語篇類型和翻譯策略相聯繫，發展了以原文與譯文功能關係為基礎的翻譯批評模式，從而提出了功能派理論思想的雛形。萊斯認為理想的翻譯應該是綜合性交際翻譯，即在概念性內容、語言形式和交際功能方面都與原文對等，但在實踐中應該優先考慮的是譯本的功能特徵。

漢斯·弗米爾（Vermeer）提出了目的論，將翻譯研究從原文中心論的束

---

① 程盡能，呂和發. 旅遊翻譯理論與實務 [M]. 北京：清華大學出版社，2008：19.
② 遲明彩. 功能派翻譯理論概述 [J]. 黑龍江教育學院學報，2010（3）：2.

縛中擺脫出來。該理論認為翻譯是以原文為基礎的有目的和有結果的行為，這一行為必須經過協商來完成；翻譯必須遵循一系列法則，其中目的法則居於首位。也就是說，譯文取決於翻譯的目的。此外，翻譯還須遵循「語內連貫法則」和「語際連貫法則」。前者指譯文必須內部連貫，在譯文接受者看來是可理解的，後者指譯文與原文之間也應該有連貫性。這三條原則提出後，評判翻譯的標準不再是「對等」，而是譯本實現預期目標的充分性。弗米爾還提出了翻譯委任的概念，即應該由譯者來決定是否、何時、怎樣完成翻譯任務。也就是說，譯者應該根據不同的翻譯目的採用相應的翻譯策略，而且有權根據翻譯目的決定原文的哪些內容可以保留，哪些需要調整或修改。

費米爾認為，「翻譯中的最高法則應該是『目的法則』。」也就是說，翻譯的目的不同，翻譯時所採取的策略、方法也不同。換言之，翻譯的目的決定了翻譯的策略和方法。對於中西翻譯史上的歸化、異化之爭，乃至近二三十年譯界廣泛討論的形式對等與動態對等，「目的論」都做出了很好的解釋。翻譯中到底是採取歸化還是異化，都取決於翻譯的目的。由於功能翻譯理論就是以「目的原則」為最高準則，而任何翻譯活動都是有目的的行為，如片名翻譯的最終目標和主要功能是幫助人們瞭解影片的主要內容，並激發觀眾的觀看慾望；菜名翻譯的最終目的就是讓人們清楚明白地瞭解這道菜的主料及烹飪方法。

賈斯塔・霍茨・曼塔里借鑑交際和行為理論，提出翻譯行為理論，進一步發展了功能派翻譯理論。該理論將翻譯視作受目的驅使的，以翻譯結果為導向的人與人之間的相互作用。該理論和目的論有頗多共同之處，費米爾後來也將二者融合。

克里斯汀娜・諾德全面總結和完善功能派理論。克里斯汀娜・諾德首次用英語系統闡述了翻譯中的文本分析所需考慮的內外因素以及如何在原文功能的基礎上制定切合翻譯目的的翻譯策略。克里斯汀娜・諾德對功能派各學說進行了梳理，並且提出譯者應該遵循「功能加忠誠」的指導原則，從而完善了該理論。

三、目的論的三項基本規則

目的規則：目的規則指翻譯應能在譯語情境和文化中，按譯語接受者期待的方式發生作用。決定翻譯過程的根本原則是整個翻譯活動的目的，即「結果決定方法」。這種目的有三種解釋：譯者的基本目的；譯文的交際目的；特

定翻譯策略或手段要達到的目的。但通常「目的」是指譯文的交際目的。即翻譯過程的發起者決定譯文的交際目的，發起者出於某一特殊需要，在理想狀況下，他會給出譯文的原因、譯文接受者使用譯文的環境、譯文應具有的功能以及與原因有關的細節等。這些構成了「翻譯要求」。翻譯要求向譯者指明了需要何種類型的譯文，而譯者並非被動地接受一切。他可以參與決定譯文的目的，特別是當發起者因為專業知識不足或某些原因對譯文的目的不甚明了的時候，譯者可以與發起者協商，從特殊的翻譯情況中得出譯文的目的。然而目的一詞常指譯文文本所要達到的目的即交際目的。除使用目的，費米爾還使用了幾個相關的概念即目標（aim）、目的（purpose）、意圖（intention）和功能（function），目標（aim）即行為要達到的最終結果，目的（purpose）指達到目標過程中的階段和結果，功能指接受者心目中文本意在傳達的意義，意圖指有目標的行為計劃，包括傳送者有目標地以某種適當的方式生產文本和接受者有目標地理解文本。區分傳送者和接受者的目標意圖很重要，因為傳送者和接受者從定義來看處於不同的文化背景和情境，這五個概念中目的（skopos）是類指概念，其餘四個是所屬概念。目的由翻譯發起者決定。

　　連貫規則：連貫規則指的是翻譯必須符合語內連貫的標準。語內連貫是指譯文必須能讓讀者理解，並在譯語文化以及使用譯文的交際環境中有意義。任何文本都只是信息提供者，譯者根據翻譯的目的法則只選取其中讓他感興趣的信息，再通過語言加工，譯入目的語使之成為新的信息提供者。在這種信息轉換過程中，譯者首先就應遵循語內連貫的原則。

　　忠實規則：既然翻譯是通過信息加工提供給譯語讀者信息的，譯文就應該是忠實於原文的。這就是譯者需要遵循的忠實性原則。忠實原則指原文和譯文應該在語際上連貫一致，即忠實於原文，忠實的程度和形式取決於譯文的目的和譯者對譯文的理解。

　　三條規則的關係：忠實規則服從於連貫規則，而這二者服從於目的規則，如果翻譯的目的要求改變原文功能，譯文的標準就不再是與原文文本的語際間的連貫而是符合翻譯目的，如果翻譯目的要求語際不連貫，則語際連貫規則不再有效。忠實的程度和形式宏觀上取決於翻譯目的的要求，忠實規則要服從於目的規則。如果翻譯目的要求譯文文本再現原文文本的特點、風貌，那麼忠實規則與目的規則相符合。譯者會盡最大努力再現原文的風格、內容及特點。如果翻譯目的要求譯文和原文有某種程度的差異時，譯者有可能背離原文，出現所謂的「激進」（Radical）功能主義翻譯。為此，諾德對功能主義觀的翻譯目的論進行修正，提出了「功能結合忠誠」（Loyalty）的原則，功能即譯文文本

在譯語情境中按讀者期待的方式發生作用，這和弗米爾的觀點一致。忠誠是指譯者在翻譯互動行為中對參與各方所應負的責任，忠誠屬於人與人之間的社會關係的範疇。對於原作者、發起人、譯語讀者，譯者有協調他們關係的責任，應該以忠誠贏得各方的信任，在這幾者之間取得平衡，協調譯入語文化和譯出語文化對翻譯的制約作用。作為對目的論的補充，功能加忠誠原則，要求譯者在翻譯行為中對翻譯過程中的各方參與者負責，竭力協調好各方關係。

「目的論」包含三點法則：「目的法則」「連貫法則」及「忠實法則」。其中「目的法則」是由費米爾提出的，然而，「目的法則」有不足之處。第一，不同讀者層對譯文期望不同，翻譯目的不可能同時滿足所有的譯語讀者；第二，翻譯目的有可能違背原文的寫作目的，有鑒於此，諾德在費米爾的「目的法則」基礎上提出了「忠誠原則」。「目的法則」認為翻譯行為所要達到的目的決定整個翻譯行為的過程。一切翻譯活動都由它的目的決定；而「忠誠原則」認為譯者在翻譯過程中要尊重原作者，也要對譯文讀者負責，翻譯原則要求譯文與原文作者意圖一致，不能與原作者意圖相差太遠，協調譯文目的和作文意圖，力求原文作者、翻譯活動發起者和譯文讀者之間的關係在譯文中達到一致。所謂「忠誠」是指譯語的目的必須與原作者的意圖相一致。也就是說，譯者既要對讀者負責，又必須尊重原文作者，協調譯文目的和作者意圖。此外，還有「連貫法則」，即譯文必須符合語內連貫的標準，也就是譯文必須能讓接受者理解，具有可讀性，並在的語文化及其譯文的交際環境中有意義。「忠誠原則」指出，在翻譯過程中，如果目的法則要求原文與譯文功能不同，那麼忠誠法則便不再適用；如果目的法則需要譯文不通順，既不符合語內連貫，連貫法則就不適用。「忠誠原則」從屬於「連貫法則」，但二者都必須服從「目的法則」。因此，所有的翻譯首要的原則就是「目的法則」，即目的決定手段。

四、目的論與唐詩英譯

威密爾如此解釋「目的法則」：每一文本是由一個既定目的產生的，應當為該目的服務。翻譯時，譯者應根據客戶或委託人的要求，結合翻譯的目的和譯文讀者的特殊情況，從原作所提供的原信息中進行選擇性的翻譯。譯者應該優先考慮譯文的功能。這一規則解決了直譯還是意譯、歸化還是異化、動態對等還是形式對等這些翻譯研究中的兩難問題，意味著譯者為達到某一特定的翻譯任務的目的可能直譯或意譯或在兩個極端之間，意味著接受方或者說讀者是

目標文本目的的主要決定因素。

　　不同的譯本因譯者的翻譯目的不同，其側重不同，分別反應了唐詩之美的某一個側面。迄今為止尚未出現唐詩的全譯本，因此各個譯者選取的唐詩各有不同，這也使得讀者可以通過閱讀不同的唐詩譯本，更廣泛地閱讀更多首唐詩。為了方便讀者欣賞譯者的成就，觀察到因翻譯目的之不同引起的翻譯策略、方法和最終譯品的差異，作者在本書僅以一首李白的《月下獨酌》為例，分析四位譯者不同的英譯本（具體譯文可參見第四章）。

　　從四首譯詩的形式上看，所有的譯詩都是用自由詩體的形式。但是，賓納以原作者感情變化為線索，將譯詩分成了兩個部分，以此從形式上凸現譯詩的情感張力。宇文所安的譯詩中每兩行分為一個詩節（Stanza），每個詩節中兩行詩的音節基本相同，這樣的處理方式在自由詩中最大限度保全了原詩的形式美。從譯詩的韻律方面看，賓納的譯詩在原詩相同位置押韻。這樣的處理方式符合目的論的觀點，即譯者的翻譯目的決定翻譯策略和方式。賓納是詩人，宇文所安是學者，故賓納在翻譯時更期望傳遞詩歌之美，而宇文氏則更需要盡可能地為其嚴謹的讀者傳達原詩的形美。

　　在李白的原詩中，頭兩行詩運用了中國古詩中常見的無人稱、無時態句，以突破空間和時間的局限，讓讀者有身臨其境之感，能夠換位到詩人的角度去體會詩人創作時的情感體驗。原詩的第一個字「花」是中國傳統文化中常見的意象，具幸福愉悅之情和欣欣向榮之態，此處用來和下文「獨酌無相親」形成強烈對比。四首譯詩中除了韋利，其他均用了 among 和 alone 這一對押頭韻的詞來複製這樣的對比。從語法和句法來看，四首譯詩的第一行前半句都採用了無動詞句來再現原作的語言形式和語法功能。這種違背英語語法規則的創造性叛逆在此處的恰當運用也使譯文保持了原詩的張力。而對於原詩第一行的無人稱問題的處理，所有譯文都運用了歸化策略，添加了主語「I」，使譯詩符合英語語法規範。在時態處理的問題上，韋利、羅鬱正和宇文所安的譯詩均選擇了一般現在時態，然而賓納在其譯詩中採用了一般過去時態。使用一般過去時態翻譯的缺陷在於：詩人情感被限定在具體的一段時間內，但是與譯詩的最後一句中的 I watch 使用的一般現在時形成了對比，更凸顯了詩人無盡的孤寂。另外，第一行後半句的邏輯關係表達上，只有韋利用了 for 將原詩模糊的因果關係清晰限定出來。這種超額翻譯的做法也是出於滿足普通大眾的目標讀者的需要。羅鬱正在譯文中使用了押頭韻的 kith and kin，以此來增加譯文的詩味（Rosa）和文學性。這跟羅氏以嚴謹的讀者為目標讀者也不無關係。

　　原詩「舉杯邀明月，對影成三人」使用移情手法，賦予了月亮和影子以人

的感情。在「邀」這個字的處理上，目標讀者的差異引起的翻譯目的的不同得到了體現：韋利用一個形象的 beckon 讓普通讀者看到一個用手召喚月亮靠近的詩人形象，而宇文所安使用的 beg 則向有良好文學素養的英美世界學者凸現了中國古代文人的真誠和謙卑。

在對「月既不解飲」的翻譯中，三首譯詩儘管措辭不同，但表達的意思是一致的：月亮不會喝酒。在羅譯文本中用了 unconcerned about，意思是月亮會喝酒，只是當下對喝酒沒有興致。這種理解更符合月亮在中國傳統文化中的形象：月亮是一個清冷之地，寧靜無欲。這樣涵義深刻的譯文固然要歸功於羅鬱正良好的中國文化功底，但其譯詩所欲達到的傳播中國傳統文化的目的應該是更大的原動力。

對於原詩中「我歌月徘徊」一句，譯者的理解則各有不同，羅鬱正和韋利的譯詩中月亮是隨著詩人歌聲的節拍，翩然起舞；賓納在譯詩中使用的 encourage 一詞，意思是月亮跳舞以鼓勵詩人繼續歌唱。而宇文所安採用 lingers on 一詞，表達了陶醉在詩人歌聲之中，不知不覺翩然而舞的月亮。另外，韋利譯文中「凌亂」被翻譯為 tangles and breaks，tangle 的發音與探戈（Tango）這個詞近似，tango 是一種具有強烈節奏感的舞蹈，給讀者以強烈節奏感。韋利的譯文正是通過使用同音異義字 tangle 和 tango，產生了濃烈的文學性。

在接下來的兩句詩的翻譯處理上，韋利和羅鬱正的譯詩與原詩同樣採用了對句的表達形式，保障原詩的形式美最大限度得以重現。

對於原詩的最後兩句的處理方法上，四首譯詩迥然各異。韋利的譯詩 May we long share our odd, intimate feast，字面上缺乏對應關係，語義上與原詩也有些出入，但卻恰如其分地傳達了原詩的意境。賓納的譯詩用了語義含混的 Shall goodwill ever be secure，應當說原詩的本意包含其中，然而這句話的含義更為豐富。羅和宇文氏的譯詩表達的意思是在原詩讀者中最廣為接受的含義。

再從整體上看，在原詩的進程中，首先浮現出「我」，隨後重新融入大千世界，人稱主語「我」用在詩的中間，而在開頭和結尾的詩句中都沒有出現。但是翻譯為英詩時，譯詩為了符合譯語的語法和句法規則，是無法保持與原詩那樣，讓活動主體自由出現或隱沒的。譯文受語言的限制，使得主體「I」預先就放置在詩中，而不能讓主體通過他者（影子等）認識到自身，只能通過主體認識到他者。四首譯詩中「我」均是周圍景物的描述者，周圍的景物均通過「我」的觀照表現出來。從整體的語言來看，韋利和賓納出於翻譯目的的考慮，均採用了簡單樸實的詞，方便譯詩為普通大眾所接受；羅鬱正和宇文所安譯詩的目的在於向英語世界傳播中國的傳統詩歌，因此用詞更接近原詩的意義

和中國古代文人的特點。

通過上文中的分析，我們不難看出，不同的譯者由於其目標讀者群的差異引起的翻譯目的的差異，還有因為大的社會文化背景導致的譯文文本在譯語文化系統中的需要承擔的功能的差異，在源文文本的選擇、翻譯策略和翻譯方法的選擇上都會有所不同。這種種不同必然會產生不同的譯品，即譯文文本。本書中筆者無意去評價這些不同譯本的優劣，因為正是由於這些不同譯者的譯文，唐詩之美才能夠更豐富更完善地展現給受眾。由於譯者翻譯目的的差別、中文詞彙的復義現象以及相對英文而言更加靈活多變的語法，加之譯者本身的能力不同，譯者有意無意對原詩進行了操縱，即將原詩特點通過譯文呈現給譯語讀者時進行了二次創作，凸現了他們最想表達的原詩特點。基於譯者不同的翻譯目的，譯者在翻譯過程中選擇不同的翻譯策略，創造性叛逆導致了同一首唐詩存在差異的英譯版本。不同譯者對唐詩作品的偏好差異，決定著翻譯選材的多樣性，而不同翻譯目的產生同一首唐詩的不同英譯文本，提供給以英語為語境文化的不同背景的讀者多樣性的選擇，更有助於以唐詩為代表的中國傳統詩歌在英美的傳播和接受。

第五節　三美論

談到中國古典詩歌英譯，就不能不提許淵衝先生。他不僅將歷代詩、詞、曲譯成英文，還能押韻自然，功力過人。更為可貴的是，他把將本國文化推向世界，成為全球文化的一部分，使世界文化更加燦爛輝煌作為己任，在翻譯實踐的同時，更是提出了富有創新的譯詩理論，即「美化之藝術，創優似競賽」。他的著名的「三美論」和「發揮譯語優勢論」在經受了實踐的考驗後，正在被越來越多的學者所接受。

許淵衝教授在《漢英對照唐詩三百首》（2000）的序言中提出，翻譯詩歌的標準是「意美、音美、形美」。這從理論上高度地概括了詩歌翻譯的要求和最終目標。意美、音美、形美是一個有機的整體，不可偏廢任何一個方面，其含義為：譯詩在意義、音韻、形式結構幾個層次上，都應該用與目的語相應、恰當的語言手段傳達出來，從而與原詩盡可能地吻合，使得讀者在心靈感受、聽覺和視覺上得到美的藝術享受。達意是譯詩的基本要求，原詩涉及哪些信息，或隱藏了哪些信息，是譯者必須把握的，一篇譯詩沒有傳達出原詩的基本含義，其翻譯必然是失誤的。但是讀者當然不能因為譯者在個別地方出現意義

傳遞的偏差就完全否定整首譯作。相對於達意，求得譯詩在音韻和形式上與原詩對等似乎更難。一般來講，不同語言創作的詩歌都有它們自己獨立的音韻和形式的表現方式，譯者所要做的就是在原詩和目的語之間架起一座橋樑，用目的語系統中恰當的詩歌音韻形式忠實地、對等地傳達原詩的音和形特徵。因為音韻和形式對於詩歌的整體風格和意境的表達是不可或缺的，一首好的詩歌必然十分注重音韻和形式。

如果譯者在譯詩的過程中做到了意美、音美和形美，實現了三種美的統一，就達到了詩歌翻譯的最高境界——傳神。傳神是衡量一首譯詩成功與否的終極標準。所謂「神」，其實是指詩歌的整體風格，即詩人通過具體的詩歌語言所表達出來的一種意境和這種意境對讀者的影響。

「三美論」即意美、音美、形美，是許淵衝先生在多年翻譯實踐經驗的基礎上，總結出來的一則實用且意蘊深刻的翻譯理論。許先生認為，譯文要像原文一樣能感化讀者的心，這是意美；要像原文一樣有悅耳的韻律，這是音美；還要盡可能地保持原文的形式，這是形美。其中，音美最重要，其次是音美，最後是行美。

許淵衝說的「意美」，不說「意似」，因為他覺得「意美」指的是深層結構，「意似」指的卻是表層結構。

一、三美論

「意美、音美、形美」，所謂「三美」並非許淵衝原創，而是魯迅在其《漢文學史綱要》中第一篇《自文字至文章》中提出來的：「誦習一字，當識形音義三：口誦耳聞其音，目察其形，心通其義，三識並用，一字之功乃全。其在文章……遂具三美：意美以感心，一也；音美以感耳，二也；形美以感目，三也。」[①] 魯迅的「三美」雖是針對文學創作而言，但在許淵衝看來，中國古詩（尤其是唐詩）講究格律、押韻有致、含蓄雋永、極富意境、美感十足，故此「三美」亦可用於譯詩。「譯詩要和原詩一樣能感動讀者的心，這是意美；要和原詩一樣有悅耳的韻律，這是音美；還要盡可能保持原詩的形式（如長短、對仗等），這是形美」[②]。這就是許淵衝的譯詩「三美」論。

具體地講，「意美」強調「詩歌的意境之美，譯者要盡力傳達原詩的思

[①] 魯迅. 漢文學史綱要 [M]. 北京：人民文學出版社，1976：3.
[②] 許淵衝. 文學與翻譯 [M]. 北京：北京大學出版社，2005：85.

想、情調與感情」①，讓人留有回味；「音美」除了選擇和原文相似的韻腳外，還要求譯者顧及原詩重複（如疊詞）和節奏等方面的問題；「形美」除了要求譯詩要和原詩長短相近、對仗工整之外，還要使其行數、詩行的排列與錯落和原詩一致。而同為詩歌翻譯的標準，「三美」的地位卻各有不同。其中，「意美」最重要，「音美」次之，最後才是「形美」。許淵衝認為，譯詩只有「三美」齊備才稱得上是好的譯詩。實際上，「三美」論作為詩歌翻譯的最高標準，譯者要完全傳達原詩的意美、音美、形美並不容易，能做的只是和原詩盡量接近而已。作為中國著名的翻譯理論家和實踐家，許淵衝先生有「書銷中外六十本，詩譯英法惟一人」之稱。由其英譯的中國古典詩詞（如《唐詩三百首》）在國內外享有盛譽，這和他「譯詩必『三美』」的原則是分不開的。

二、三美論與唐詩英譯

唐詩作為中國古詩藝術成就的傑出代表，其藝術魅力不言而喻。對譯者來說，在翻譯唐詩之前必須對原作的歷史背景、語言風格、情感態度等因素做一番徹底的瞭解，然後發揮想像力和創造力，再用最地道的譯文將原作的「三美」傳遞到目的語中，如此方能使譯詩取得和原詩同樣的審美效果，譯語讀者才能最大限度體會原詩的藝術美感。

許淵衝在唐詩翻譯領域可謂獨樹一幟，在長期的翻譯實踐和理論研究基礎上提出了自己的獨創性理論，其詩歌翻譯的「三美論」在譯界產生了深遠影響。三美即意美、音美、形美。許淵衝曾指出：「譯詩要和原詩一樣能感動讀者的心，這是意美；要和原詩一樣有悅耳的韻律，這是音美；還要盡可能保持原詩的形式（如長短、對仗等），這是形美。」翻譯時最重要的是意美，其次音美，再次形美。在傳遞意美的前提下，三美的和諧統一、三美齊備是詩歌翻譯的最高境界。

（一）意美

「三美論」的核心是意美，古詩的意美就在於它能夠以簡單的形式、精煉的文字構成一幅有動感、有神韻的詩畫。意境美是詩歌美的最高境界，音美和形美都要以意美為歸宿。許淵衝認為，在譯詩過程中，「傳達了原詩意美，而沒有傳達音美和形美的翻譯，雖然不是譯得好的詩，還不失為譯得好的散文；

---

① 馬紅軍. 從文學翻譯到翻譯文學 [M]. 上海：上海譯文出版社，2006：126.

如果譯詩只有音美和形美而沒有意美，那就根本算不上是好的翻譯」①。由此可見「意美」的重要性。唐詩語言優美，情感真摯，內容含蓄雋永，語義雙關，總能讓讀者感受到其中的深邃意境。譯者在翻譯過程中必須把傳達原詩的深層結構，也就是「意美」，作為首要目標，如此才能讓譯語讀者感受到原詩的藝術魅力。許教授的這種以意美為核心的翻譯觀在其翻譯的唐詩《西宮秋怨》中就很好地體現了出來：

芙蓉不及美人妝，水殿風來珠翠香。
誰分含啼掩秋扇，空懸明月待君王。
The lotus bloom feels shy beside the lady fair,
The breeze across the lake takes fragrance from her hair.
An autumn fan cannot conceal her hidden love,
In vain she waits for her lord with the moon above.

這是王昌齡的一首宮怨詩，反應了封建社會失寵宮女深居幽宮，虛度光陰，浪費青春的精神痛苦。同時也暗含了作者自己懷才不遇，遭受壓迫，對封建社會制度的不滿之情。對於第一句的翻譯，「不及」意為「比不上，比……差」，許淵衝教授在翻譯時不是平鋪直敘翻譯，而是獨具匠心地採用了擬人的修辭手法，用「lotus bloom feels shy」來反襯宮女容貌，雖然沒有直接說宮女好看，但用芙蓉害羞更加強烈地襯托出了宮女容貌的靚麗。本來是沒有生氣的花在譯者筆下一下子有了生命力，活了起來，可以說英譯比原詩更勝一籌，更富意境美。對於最後一句的翻譯，更是體現了許教授對意境美的重視。「空懸明月」中「空」代表徒勞，沒有結果，宮女靜靜地坐在後宮等待帝王的臨幸，但這種等待是徒勞的，擁有後宮佳麗三千的帝王早已將其拋之腦後另尋新歡了，陪伴她的只有頭頂的明月。靜靜的明月襯托出宮女內心的寂寞哀苦。英譯詩中「in vain」和「空」是對等的，「in vain she waits for her lord with the moon above」準確地傳遞了原詩的意思，並且也留給了讀者想像空間。「with the moon above」看似寥寥數語，卻和原詩一樣能讓讀者透過頭頂靜靜的月亮品味出宮女內心的痛苦，和原詩富有同樣的意境美。

(二) 音美

唐詩的藝術魅力經久不衰，除本身具有的深邃意境外，還與其平仄、押韻以及善用疊詞等特點所表現的音韻美息息相關。唐詩或五言或七言，或絕句或

---

① 張智中. 許淵衝與翻譯藝術 [M]. 武漢：湖北教育出版社，2006：58.

律詩，其最顯著的押韻方式莫過於尾韻，主要包括兩行轉韻（aabb）、隔行押韻（abcb）、隔行交互（abab）和交錯押韻（abba）四種押韻方式。許淵衝認為：「唐詩的『音美』，首先是押韻。因此，翻譯唐詩即使百分之百傳達了原詩的『意美』，如果沒有押韻，也不可能保存原詩的風格和情趣」[1]。由此可見，對於唐詩的英譯者來說，再現原詩的「音美」是十分必要的。

中國唐代詩歌追求音韻美，有著嚴格的平仄和韻律，因此讀起來朗朗上口，這也是唐詩的魅力之一。唐詩英譯時如果也追求音韻美，會極大地增加翻譯的難度，甚至有時是無法實現的，因為漢語和英語不是完全對等的。因此翻譯界有人認為詩歌翻譯不必追求音韻美，只要傳遞意境美就行了。持相反意見的人認為譯文如果放棄了這種押韻，其美感就會喪失很多，主張要盡可能再現原詩的音韻美。許淵衝教授就是主張以詩體譯詩的代表人物，他說：「以詩體譯詩好比把蘭陵美酒換成了白蘭地，雖然酒味不同，但多少還是酒；以散體譯詩就好像把酒換成了白開水……」他力求譯文具有嚴格的韻律、音步和句數，使譯文和原詩一樣和諧統一富於美感。以唐代詩人柳宗元的《江雪》為例：

千山鳥飛絕，萬徑人蹤滅。
孤舟蓑笠翁，獨釣寒江雪。
From hill to hill no bird in flight,
From path to path no man in sight.
A lonely fisherman afloat,
Is fishing snow in a lonely boat.

該詩描繪了一幅幽靜寒冷的江鄉雪景圖，山山是雪，路路皆白，飛鳥絕跡，人蹤湮滅，而一位身披蓑衣的老漁翁卻獨自在江心垂釣。全詩韻腳採用仄韻，即「絕、滅、雪」。許淵衝教授的翻譯也保留了原詩的韻腳，即「flight 和 sight」「afloa 和 boat」，因此讀起來朗朗上口，體現了詩歌的韻律美。相比之下，另一個譯本的翻譯如下，由於缺乏了韻律，從音韻美學角度來講就遜色很多：

Myriad mountains-not a bird flying,
Endless roads-not a trace of men.
Only an old fisherman in a lonely boat,
Angling silently in the river covered with snow.

---

[1] 顧延齡. 唐詩英譯的「三美」標準——兼評漢英對照唐詩一百五十首 [J]. 中國翻譯, 1987（6）.

（三）形美

對於一篇形如聖誕樹的詩來說，若其譯文看起來不像聖誕樹抑或相去甚遠，那麼無論其如何忠實於原文，意境如何優美，讀來如何朗朗上口，終究亦為敗筆。同樣，若一篇對仗工整的唐詩被譯成了散文，則無論其意境如何優美，原詩的「形美」亦會消失殆盡。「形美」雖位列「三美」之末，但其重要性亦不容忽視。唐詩以格律著稱，對仗工整，前後長短相同，錯落有致，譯者在翻譯時要盡可能讓譯語讀者讀到相同效果的譯文。

形美主要是指譯詩和原詩的行數是否一致，分節是否相當。如果譯詩和原詩行數一致，分節相當，在句子長短方面和對仗工整方面做到了形似，就基本體現了原詩的形美。以許譯李白的《夜下徵虜亭》為例：

船下廣陵去，月明徵虜亭。
山花如繡頰，江火似流螢。

My boat sails down toRiver Tower,
The tower's bright in the moonlight.
The flowers blow like cheeks aglow,
And lanterns beam as fireflies gleam.

從行數和分節來看，原詩是五言絕句，譯文行數與原詩一致，除第一句有九個音節外，其餘每句八個音節，較好地傳達了原詩的形美。從對仗來看，原詩是工整的對仗，「山花」對「江火」，「繡頰」對「流螢」，許譯也力求傳達這種形式之美，可以看到譯文後兩句也是對仗工整，令人嘆服的。

從以上三方面來看，許淵衝教授的「三美論」對古詩的英譯是有極大的啓發和幫助的。他的意美、音美、形美的翻譯理念能使讀者最大限度體會到原詩的意境、神韻和風姿。拜讀許先生的譯作，我們會為其高超的譯技折服，他的翻譯和翻譯理論把古詩翻譯推上了一個新的高度。總而言之，無論是許教授的精益求精，追求盡善盡美的工作態度，還是他令人拍案叫絕的翻譯作品，還是他獨樹一幟的翻譯理論都值得我們去好好學習，認真借鑑。

在「三美論」的指導下，許淵衝先生英譯的唐詩意美、音美、形美兼備，實可謂譯中精品。唐詩作為中國古典詩歌的傑出代表，字裡行間以含蓄為美，意境為上，譯者在翻譯過程中切不可拘於原詩形式，而應挖掘原詩的深層結構，以意美、音美、形美為標準，在借助譯語優勢的基礎上發揮主觀能動性，以使譯詩和原詩在意境、音律、對仗等方面具備同樣的感染力，最終傳達原詩的神韻。總之，譯者只有以「三美」為標準，才能使以唐詩為代表的中國古

典詩歌的藝術魅力在譯文中真正得以彰顯，中國文化也能在世界範圍內大放光彩。

譯者翻譯唐詩要盡可能傳達原詩的「意美」「音美」和「形美」。但是，「三美」的重要性並不是鼎足三分的。在許先生看來，最重要的是「意美」，其次是「音美」，最後是「形美」。換句話說，押韻的「音美」和整齊的「形美」是必須條件，而「意美」既是必需條件，又是充分條件。因此，在翻譯唐詩的時候，許先生要求在傳達原詩這種「音美」和這種「形美」的範圍之內，用「深化」「等化」「淺化」的譯法，盡可能傳達原詩的「意美」。

第六節　生態翻譯學

生態翻譯學（Eco-translatology）可以理解為一種生態學途徑的翻譯研究（An Ecological Approach to Translation Studies），抑或生態學視角的翻譯研究（Translation Studies from An Ecological Perspective）。肇始於中國的生態翻譯學自 2001 年提出以來，受到了國內外的廣泛關注。作為一個全新的翻譯理論，生態翻譯學擁有獨特的研究焦點和理論視角，是「運用生態理性、從生態視角對翻譯進行綜觀審視的整體性研究」，是一個「翻譯即適應與選擇」的生態範式和研究領域。經過十幾年的發展，針對生態翻譯學的理論研究和應用研究日漸增多，因此我們有必要對其研究發展狀況進行總結和回顧，以便為其他學者提供借鑒，更好地對其進行深度研究。

一、生態翻譯學定義

該理論提出的歷史不久，「起步於 2001 年，全面開展於 2009 年」。[1] 胡庚申教授將其定義為：「以生態整體主義為理念，以東方生態智慧為依歸，以『適應/選擇』理論為基石，是一項系統探討翻譯生態、文本生態和『翻譯群落』生態以及其相互作用、相互關係的跨學科研究，致力於對翻譯生態整體和翻譯理論本體做出符合生態理性的縱觀和描述。」[2] 翻譯適應選擇論引入了「翻譯生態環境」這一概念。翻譯生態環境指原文、源語和譯語所呈現出來的

---

[1] 胡庚申. 生態翻譯學：產生的背景與發展的基礎 [J]. 外語研究，2010（4）：62.
[2] 胡庚申. 生態翻譯學：建構與詮釋 [M]. 北京：商務印書館，2013.

世界,即語言、文化、社會以及作者、讀者、委託者等互聯互動的整體。

　　作為生態翻譯學的提出者,胡庚申教授對生態翻譯學的研究和發展做出了巨大貢獻。2001年10月22日,胡庚申教授在香港浸會大學翻譯學研究中心做了題為「從達爾文的適應與選擇原理到翻譯學研究」的講座,闡述了將達爾文的「自然選擇學說」應用於翻譯研究的可行性,進而提出了建立「翻譯適應選擇論」的初步構想。這一構想引起了與會研究者的廣泛關注和熱烈討論。緊接著,同年12月6日,胡庚申教授在國際譯聯第三屆亞洲翻譯家論壇上宣讀了題為《翻譯適應選擇論初探》的論文。該論文在適應與選擇角度對翻譯的定義、過程、原則和方法等方面都進行了重新闡釋和描述,初步形成了翻譯適應選擇論的基本框架(該文後來以《譯論的繁榮與困惑——探索適應與選擇視角的譯論研究》為題發表於《翻譯季刊》)。2001年就此標志著生態翻譯學研究的開端。

　　2002年,專題英文論文《Translation as Adaptation and Selection》在國際期刊上發表,文中,胡庚申教授將該項系統的理論研究定義為「一種生態學的翻譯研究途徑」。2004年,胡教授出版了《翻譯適應選擇論》一書,更為全面系統地總結了翻譯適應選擇論的產生背景、理論基礎和基本理論。2006年8月,胡庚申教授在「翻譯全球文化:走向跨學科的理論構建」國際會議上宣讀了《生態翻譯學詮釋》一文,生態翻譯學首次在國際場合提出。

　　生態翻譯學發展的十幾年間,作為生態翻譯學理論的奠基人,胡庚申教授對生態翻譯學理論框架進行了不斷的探索和完善。《翻譯適應選擇論的哲學理據》《適應與選擇:翻譯過程新解》《生態翻譯學解讀》《生態翻譯學:譯學研究的「跨科際整合」》以及《態翻譯學:產生的背景和發展的基礎》等文章從宏觀角度又對生態翻譯學這一全新理論進行了理論上的解釋和闡述,分析了生態翻譯學產生的背景、起源和發展。此外,胡教授發表的《從術語看譯論——翻譯適應選擇論概觀》《生態翻譯學的研究焦點與理論視角》《從「譯者中心」到「譯者責任」》等論文更為詳細地闡述和解釋了生態翻譯學的核心理念和視角。面對其他學者的質疑和不解,胡庚申教授也做出了回應,如《關於「譯者中心」問題的回應》。

　　胡庚申教授對生態翻譯學的研究不僅停留在理論層面,同時也有一些實證研究,將生態翻譯學應用於實際的翻譯中,以此來證實翻譯適應選擇論的可操作性和解釋力,如《譯論研究的一種嘗試——翻譯適應選擇論的實證調查》《例示「適應選擇論」的翻譯原則和解釋方法》和《從譯文看譯論——翻譯適應選擇論應用例析》等。此外,胡庚申教授還從生態翻譯學視角對傅雷的翻

譯思想進行了研究和全新詮釋。

　　生態翻譯學運用生態學的相關知識對翻譯現象和活動進行綜合性、整體性的研究，是一種翻譯即適應與選擇的生態範式和研究①。目前已有很多學者對生態翻譯學做了理論上的論述和闡發，如胡庚申先生（2004，2011，2014）對生態翻譯學的研究方法和理論體系做了深入的探討，王宏先生（2011）對生態翻譯學的核心理念做了論述。也有學者運用生態翻譯學分析相關翻譯活動和現象，如劉愛華（2011）從生態翻譯學的視角對徐遲的翻譯活動做了研究，認為徐遲的翻譯活動是一次次力圖適應多方面、多層次的翻譯生態環境，不斷做出選擇以獲得最高整合適應選擇度的探索歷程②。張麗麗（2014）從生態翻譯學的視角對歇後語的翻譯做了探討，認為譯者在翻譯歇後語時應該選擇恰當的翻譯策略以適應生態翻譯環境③。生態翻譯學將翻譯系統視為一個生態系統。在這個系統中，譯者、原作者、讀者、原作、譯作、翻譯贊助人、原語文化生態、譯語文化生態各自起著不同的作用，維持著某種動態平衡。物競天擇，適者生存，不適者淘汰，這是生態系統的主要特點，對翻譯現象同樣具有較強的解釋力。譯者唯有做出恰當的選擇，處理好各因素的關係，適應翻譯生態，才能在這個系統中謀得一席之地。他的譯作才可能適應讀者的品位，滿足贊助人提出的翻譯要求，在譯入語文化體系中煥發出新的生命，流傳下去。因此，選擇和適應是生態翻譯學的核心觀點。譯者在語言、文化、交際層面做出適當的選擇，使譯文符合譯入語文化生態，才能實現翻譯之目的。

二、生態翻譯學的「三維」轉換

　　生態翻譯學對翻譯的本質、過程進行了全新的描述和解釋，從而也給譯者提供了全新的翻譯方法、翻譯原則以及譯文評判標準。生態翻譯學主張用生態學的範式和視角來研究翻譯現象，興起於 21 世紀初，經過十幾年的發展現在已成為譯學研究的熱點之一。生態翻譯學認為譯者進行翻譯時，需要從「三維」（語言維、交際維、文化維）著手，使譯文能夠達到多維轉化的程度。翻譯原則也被定義為「多維度的選擇性適應與適應性選擇」④。生態翻譯學的相

---

① 胡庚申．翻譯適應選擇論［M］．武漢：湖北教育出版社，2004．
② 劉愛華．徐遲：絕頂靈芝、空谷幽蘭──生態翻譯學視角下的翻譯家研究［J］．中國外語，2011（4）．
③ 張麗麗．生態翻譯學視域中的歇後語翻譯［J］．外語學刊，2014（3）：102-105．
④ 胡庚申．生態翻譯學解讀［J］．中國翻譯，2008（6）．

關觀點已從不同角度不斷地得到闡釋和完善，被廣泛地用於翻譯實踐的探討，如文學翻譯、公示語翻譯、外宣資料翻譯、新聞翻譯、電影字幕以及民俗翻譯等。

從 2001 年最早提出生態翻譯學這一概念至今已有十幾年，生態翻譯學已經成為譯學界的研究熱點之一，這一理論從不同角度不斷地得到闡釋和完善，並被大量地運用到翻譯研究領域，如文本翻譯、公示語翻譯、翻譯思想的重新闡釋、外宣資料翻譯、新聞翻譯、電影字幕以及片名翻譯等，在民俗翻譯中也得到了應用，如廣西、廣東、福建、陝西等地民俗的翻譯研究。

生態翻譯學的翻譯方法可謂之「多維」轉換，主要落實在「三維」的轉換上，即在「多維度適應與適應性選擇」的原則下，相對集中於語言維、文化維和交際維的適應性選擇轉換。在生態翻譯學的視角下，「三維」轉換是翻譯的主要方法。在具體的翻譯過程中，譯者關注的不僅僅是語言維，文化維和交際維也不容忽視，三者相互交織，互聯互動。

(一) 語言維的適應性選擇轉換

語言維的適應性選擇轉換（Adaptive Transformation from the Linguistic Dimension）即譯者在翻譯過程中對語言形式的適應性選擇轉換。語言維的適應性選擇轉換，是指譯者要準確把握原文本的語言風格並將其體現在譯文中，這就要求譯者最大限度地對原文忠誠。語言維的轉換是在不同方面、不同層次上進行的，主要指的是譯者在翻譯過程中為適應譯文生態翻譯環境的需要，對語言形式進行的適應性選擇轉換。

(二) 文化維的適應性選擇轉換

文化維的適應性選擇（Adaptive Transformation from the Cultural Dimension）即譯者在翻譯過程中關注雙語文化內涵的傳遞與闡釋。文化維的適應性選擇轉換指的是譯者要重視雙語文化內涵和文字背後的文化意義，不僅要關注目標語與源語的轉換，更要從整個文化生態系統去深刻把握和審視。文化維的適應性選擇轉換要求譯者關注源語文化和譯語文化在性質和內容上存在的差異，避免從譯語文化出發去理解原文。中國文化典籍翻譯對於文化維的關注不容小覷。中國文化典籍蘊含著中國 5,000 多年的歷史和文化底蘊，具有鮮明的中國特色。在翻譯時，譯者一定要從文化系統整體上把握好中英兩種語言間的文化轉換。

（三）交際維的適應性選擇轉換

交際維的適應性選擇轉換（Adaptive Transformation from the Communicative Dimension）即譯者在翻譯過程中關注雙語交際意圖的適應性選擇轉換。交際維的適應性選擇轉換是指譯者除了進行語言信息和文化內涵的轉換之外，在翻譯過程中也要關注原文中暗含的交際意圖是否在譯文中得到體現。在翻譯過程中，譯者不僅要傳達原作品本身想表達的思想和意義，同時也要考慮譯者本身的需求及其交際目的。由於源語和目標語的語言形式和文化的差異以及譯者不一樣的生活經驗和認識，誤譯是必然存在的。一般來說，誤譯分為有意誤譯和無意誤譯兩種。當常規翻譯方法不能很好地體現原作的交際目的時，為了達到原作的交際目的，有時譯者不得不改變源語的形式，在源語的基礎上進行一定程度的刪除或添加，這被稱為有意誤譯。

三、生態翻譯學與唐詩英譯

肇始於中國、具有跨學科性質的生態翻譯學，走過了紮實又初見成效的十年，極有發展潛力和研究活力，它將翻譯過程類比生態環境，探究其相互關係，分析和闡釋翻譯中的各種現象，豐富了翻譯理論與實踐，相關研究方興未艾。以下將探析生態翻譯學角度下李白詩作《贈汪倫》的四種翻譯版本。

1. 原詩分析

《贈汪倫》是唐朝詩人李白於涇縣（今安徽皖南地區）遊歷桃花潭時寫給當地好友汪倫的一首留別詩，全詩簡短明了，語言清新自然，想像豐富奇特，四句僅 28 個字，朗朗上口，是李白詩中流傳最廣的七言絕句之一。

贈汪倫

李白乘舟將欲行，忽聞岸上踏歌聲。
桃花潭水深千尺，不及汪倫送我情。

此詩前兩句交代了事情的背景，起句先寫離去者，「將欲」表達出汪倫的送行出乎意料。次句繼寫送行者，用了曲筆，有人邊走邊唱前來送行。這出乎李白的意料，所以用「忽聞」而不用「遙聞」。只聞其聲，不見其人，但人已呼之欲出。人未到而聲先聞，表現出李白和汪倫這兩位朋友同是不拘俗禮之人；後兩句抒情，先用「深千尺」贊美桃花潭水的深度，緊接「不及」兩個字筆鋒一轉，用襯托的手法，把無形的情誼化為有形的千尺潭水，把情感的虛無縹緲轉變為現實的池水，生動形象地表達了汪倫對李白的那份真摯深厚的友

情。第三句遙接起句，「深千尺」既描繪了潭的特點，又為結句預伏一筆。結句迸出「不及汪倫送我情」，以比物手法形象性地表達了真摯純潔的深情。潭水已「深千尺」，那麼汪倫送李白的情誼必定更深，此句耐人尋味。「不及」二字不用比喻而採用比物手法，使得無形的情誼生動形象，空靈而有餘味，自然而又情真。後兩句詩極力贊美汪倫對詩人的敬佩和喜愛之情，也表達了李白對汪倫的深厚情誼。

2. 從「三維」適應性轉換角度比較《贈汪倫》譯本

《贈汪倫》有多個譯本，筆者首先根據翻譯的基本標準，對各種版本進行了初步的篩選，刪去了一些在「語法」和「意思」方面還存在明顯錯誤的版本，然後選出了以下四種流傳度較高的英譯本——許淵衝譯本、Tony Barnstone 與 Willis Barnstone 合作的譯本、Burton Watson 譯本以及 Obata 譯本。學界有較多研究是從事義學或者功能語篇的角度對譯本進行分析，下面筆者從生態翻譯學出發，從語言維、文化維、交際維的「三維」轉換視角，分析《贈汪倫》四個英譯本在各個方面的得失，從而得出「整合適應選擇度」相對較高的一個譯本。

譯文 1（許淵衝譯）：

I, Li Bai sit aboard a ship about to go, when suddenly on shore your farewell songs o'erflow. However deep the Lake of Peach Blossoms may be, it is not so deep, O Wang Lun, as your love for me.

譯文 2（Barnstone 譯）：

On board and about to set sail, I suddenly hear you stamping and singing on the shore. Peach Blossom Spring is a thousand fathoms deep, but your love for me is deeper as I leave.

譯文 3（Burton 譯）：

Li Bai on board, ready to push off, suddenly heard the tramping and singing on the bank. Peach Flower Pool a thousand feet deep, is shallower than the love of Wang Lun who sees me off.

譯文 4（Obata 譯）：

I was about to sail away in a junk, when suddenly I heard the sound of stamping and singing on the bank. The Peach Flower Lake is a thousand fathoms deep, but it cannot compare, O Wang Lun, with the depth of your love for me.

（1）語言維

由於漢英思維方式不同，漢語和英語在語言表達層面上存在很大的差異，

譯者在翻譯時應充分考慮翻譯的整體生態環境，對詩句的工整、音韻和句長進行處理。四種譯本在語言維上的選擇轉換如下：

首先，從形式上看，四種譯文都譯成了四行，既符合原文，也符合了譯入語英語詩歌的形式；其次，從韻律上看，原詩採取 aaba 韻，譯文 1、譯文 4 韻律整齊，為 aabb 韻，雖沒有與原詩完全一致，但以韻律對韻律，也體現了原詩的韻律美；而譯文 2、譯文 3 在韻律方面的把握不如譯文 1、譯文 4；再次，從時態角度看，譯文 1、譯文 2 全詩均採用現在時，而譯文 3、譯文 4 有明顯的時態變化，筆者認為本詩應是有感而發，有奮筆疾書之感，原文中沒有表現出明顯的過去時，因此建議用現在時。最後，從用詞來看，譯文 1 中「about to go」和「suddenly」體現出汪倫送行的意料之外，緊貼原文；「however deep」和「not so deep」相互呼應，符合英語的表達習慣。同時，許譯中開篇用同位語進行解釋，如「I, Li Bai」交待了送別的主客體，讓讀者理解更加順暢。在譯文 2 中，譯者忽略了送別的主客體；同時，在譯文 2 和譯文 4 中，「千尺」都屬直譯，譯文 3 中直接譯為「feet」，但通過對原文的分析會發現，這兩句話更多的是用來抒情，因此可以意譯。

從語言維層面上，許老先生的譯本實屬佳作。但值得注意的是，四位大家對「桃花潭」的翻譯有所不同，筆者認為，樹上開的花應使用 blossom，長在地上的花應使用 flower，因此桃花潭譯為 peach blossom lake 更為合適。

(2) 文化維

生態翻譯學主張譯者在文化維上突出文化內涵來宣傳——國的文化。而語言是文化的載體，通過對原詩進行分析，我們會發現「踏歌」是極具中國文化特色的一個詞語，是民間的一種唱歌形式，一邊唱歌，一邊用腳踏地打拍子，可以邊走邊唱，譯文 2、譯文 3、譯文 4 都對「踏歌」一詞進行了直譯，但是「踏歌」所唱的一定是送別的相關內容。因此，譯文 1 根據內容詩歌進行了意譯，但是並沒有對「踏歌」進行描述或者解釋。整體而言，譯文 1 的整合度相對較好。但在譯文 1 中，筆者認為英文中的 ship 和中國古代的「舟」有一定的區別，用 boat 應會更貼切。

(3) 交際維

生態翻譯學主張譯者在交際維上調整信息量來適應讀者的文化習慣，幫助讀者理解譯文，再現原文的交際意圖。中國古詩較少在詩中直呼姓名，而《贈汪倫》以詩人直呼自己姓名開始，以稱呼對方的名字作結，顯得直率和灑脫，也體現出兩人之間的深厚感情，而從英語方面，稱呼名字也代表著尊重和親切，從這一這方面看，譯文 2 和譯文 4 略有欠缺。

就全詩而言，許淵衝教授的譯本用詞簡潔、語言簡單樸素，卻貼近原文意境，在語言維、文化維和交際維方面都相對的成功，屬於整合適應度較高的一種譯作，值得學習研究。從生態翻譯學視角下對《贈汪倫》四種譯本進行探析，不難發現，四個譯本都各有千秋，但在交際維和文化維上與原文還存在一定的差距，整合適應度相對較高的是許淵衝先生的譯作。中國古典詩歌的翻譯仍然任重道遠，但同時，我們也發現生態翻譯學對翻譯工作有著較好的指導意義，極具活力。

第三章　唐詩文化詞彙及典故英譯研究

文化詞彙也稱文化負載詞。這類詞通過長時間的互文運用具有豐富的聯想意義、高度的互文性和民族性，承載著一個民族的文化基因。閱讀這類詞能給人們帶來獨特的審美體驗。一般說來，文化詞彙除了本身的所指意義外，還具有獨特的引申意義。詞義的疊加給文化詞彙的翻譯帶來了很大的難度。

第一節　中西思維方式對比

思維方式是溝通文化與語言的橋樑。思維方式的差異本質上是文化差異的表現。長久生活在不同區域的人，具有不同的文化特徵，因而也形成不同的思維方式。從地理和文化的角度看，全世界可以分為東方和西方兩大區域，東方以中國為代表，西方古代以希臘、羅馬為代表，近代以西歐和北美為代表。東方和西方具有不同的地理環境、生活方式、生產方式、行為方式、交往方式、歷史背景、政治制度、經濟制度、風俗習慣、宗教信仰、語言文字以及不同的哲學觀、倫理觀、價值觀、審美觀、時空觀、心理特徵、表達方式等，東方和西方的思維方式從總體上看具有不同的特徵，東方人偏重人文，注重倫理、道德，西方人偏重自然，注重科學、技術；東方人重悟性、直覺、意向，西方人重理性、邏輯、實證；東方人好靜、內向、守舊，西方人好動、外向、開放；東方人求同、求穩、重和諧，西方人求異、求變、重競爭；等等。

思維方式是一個複雜的系統，根據不同的角度、標準、特點，思維方式可以分為各式各樣的類型。下面將從四個方面對比東西方人民思維方式及語言結構特點。

1. 綜合與分析

綜合思維是指思想上將對象的各個部分聯合為整體，將它的各種屬性、方面、聯繫等結合起來。分析思維是指在思想上將一個完整的對象分解為各個組成部分，或者將它的各種屬性、方面、聯繫等區分開來。中國人偏好綜合，導致思維上整體優先，而西方人偏好分析，產生思維上部分優先的特點。

中國人習慣於整體思維的特點在漢語的形式上得到了充分的反應。中國人在表明時間、地理位置、人物身分等時，常常先整體後局部，以從大到小順序排列。而具有解析式思維的西方人的思維程序是從小到大，從局部到整體。例如，在時間順序的表達上，中國人是年→月→日→時→分→秒；而西方人特別是英國人恰恰相反，是秒→分→時→日→月→年。地址順序的表達上，西方人是門牌號碼→路或街→區→市→州→郵政編碼→國家；中國人正好相反，為國家→省→市→區→路或街→門牌號碼。在社會關係的屬性上，中國人的順序是姓→名，如果有職務，順序是姓→名→職務，而且，在交際中，為了提高對方的地位，如果職務是副職的話，還習慣上把「副」字省去；而西方人是名→姓，如果有職務，應該明確是正職還是副職，不可模糊，順序是職務→名→姓。

2. 直覺與邏輯

中國傳統思維注重實踐經驗，注重整體思考，因而借助直覺體悟，即通過靜觀、體忍、靈感、頓悟的知覺，從總體上模糊而直接地把握認識對象的內在本質和規律。西方傳統思維注重科學、理性、分析、實證，因而必然借助邏輯，在論證、推演中認識事物的本質和規律。舉例如下：

The isolation of the rural world because of distance and the lack of transport facilities is compounded by the paucity of information media.

因為距離遙遠，交通工具缺乏，農村與外界隔絕。這種隔絕又由於通信工具的不足而變得更加嚴重。

比較這兩句，英文句中只有一個主語和一個謂語動詞，其他都用名詞和介詞的形式將句子連成一體；而漢語句採用了數個動詞按照事理推移的順序，把一件件事情交代清楚。可見，英漢兩種語言在句式結構上的最大區別在於英語重形合而漢語重意合。英語句子以主謂結構為主幹，控制句內各成分之間的關係，其他動詞只能採用非限定形式，表示其與謂語動詞的區別。英語句子雖然看起來繁瑣累贅，實際上則是通過嚴整的結構表達出一種中心明確、層次清楚的邏輯意念。而漢語句子主要是連動句和流水句，不是以說明主語的謂語動詞為中心，而是按時間先後順序表達客觀事理。

3. 具象與抽象

從思維的結構分析，整體思維似乎偏愛具象的思維模式，即人們可能以經驗為基礎，通過由此及彼的類別聯繫，人與人、人與物、人與社會進行溝通，達到協同效應。而抽象思維是運用概念進行判斷、推理。從總體上看，傳統中國文化思維具有較強的具象性，而西方文化具有較強的抽象性。

體現在語言上，漢語用詞傾向以實的形式表達虛的概念，以具體的形象表達抽象的內容。示例如下：

In line with latest trends in fashion, a few dress designers have been sacrificing elegance to audacity.

譯文：有些服裝設計師為了趕時髦，捨棄了優雅別致的式樣，而一味追求袒胸露體的奇裝異服。

抽象名詞 elegance 和 audacity，對於習慣抽象思維的英美讀者來說，詞義明確，措辭簡練；但對於習慣於具體思維的中國讀者來說，譯者必須將這些抽象名詞所表達的抽象概念具體化，才符合漢語讀者的思維習慣和漢語遣詞造句的行文習慣。而英語用詞傾向於虛，大量使用抽象名詞和介詞。尤其在現代英語中，出現了介詞代替動詞、形容詞甚至一些語法結構現象，如要表達「這本書太難，我看不懂」，「The book is above/beyond me」比「The book is too difficult for me to read」顯得更簡練、生動。

4. 歸納與演繹

中國人受「天人合一」及「關係」取向的影響，說話寫文章往往表現出把思想發出去還要收攏回來，落到原來的起點上，這就使話語或語篇結構呈圓形，或呈聚集式。在談論某個問題時，中國人不是採取直線式或直接切題的作法，呈現一個由次要到主要、由背景到任務、從相關信息到話題的發展過程，往往把諸如對別人的要求和意見以及自己的看法等主要內容或關鍵問題保留到最後或含而不露，這是一種逐步達到高潮式。而演繹法不僅成為西方學者構建理論體系的一種手段，而且成了西方人比較習慣的一種思維方法。他們談話寫文章習慣開門見山，把話題放在最前面，以引起聽話人或讀者的重視。美國人看中國人的信是越看越糊塗，到信的末尾才有幾句是對方真正要談的問題，前面都是寒暄，美國人讀中國人的信往往先看後面。正如徐念詞先生所描述的，這是一種逆潮式，其特點是「起筆多突兀，結筆多瀟脫」。而中方語篇是「起筆多平鋪，結筆多圓滿」。西文語篇是「果」在前，「因」在後，與中文語篇的「因」在前，「果」在後形成鮮明對比。

第二節　孫大雨唐詩譯作中民俗文化詞彙的英譯

孫大雨是新月派詩人，與朱湘、饒孟侃、楊世恩等人被譽為新詩壇「清華四子」①。他幼年時期接受過良好的國學教育，青年時期負笈美國，接受西方文化的薰陶，學貫中西。孫大雨具有紮實的中西文化根底，再加上鐘情於詩歌，他在英詩中譯和中詩英譯兩方面都取得了不錯的成績。近年來，學術界對新月派代表性詩人的譯詩研究愈發深入，取得了豐碩的研究成果，如徐志摩、聞一多、朱湘等人譯詩的研究都要專著問世，而對孫大雨等其他一批詩人的研究愈顯邊緣化。然而，不論是在譯詩與作詩的實踐上，還是在理論上，這些邊緣化的詩人都有其獨特的貢獻。對他們進行研究既有利於挖掘出他們在實踐與理論上的成就，也有利於從縱深推動那些代表性詩人的研究。本書對孫大雨唐詩譯作中民俗文化詞彙的英譯進行研究，以期喚起學界同仁對他的關注。

一、孫大雨的翻譯成就

孫大雨的翻譯成就主要包括莎士比亞戲劇中譯、英詩中譯以及中國古詩詞英譯，共出版譯作十二部。其中，他譯有莎士比亞戲劇八部，包括《黎琊王》（即《李爾王》），《罕秣萊德》（即《哈姆萊特》）《奧賽羅》《麥克白斯》（即《麥克白》）（以上四種收入《莎士比亞四大悲劇》）以及《威尼斯商人》《冬日故事》《暴風雨》《蘿密歐與琚麗曄》（即《羅密歐與朱麗葉》）。此外，他譯有《英詩選譯集》一部以及三部中譯英詩集《屈原詩選英譯》《古詩文英譯集》《英譯唐詩選》。他的《英詩選譯集》主要選譯了喬叟（Geoffrey Chaucer）、約翰遜（Ben John）、彌爾頓（John Milton）、華茲華斯（Wordsworth）、拜倫（Byron）等十二位名家的作品。他的《古詩文英譯集》選譯了中國歷代三十八位名家的名作，時間跨度從戰國時期至宋代，譯文後的註釋多達一百五十多頁，足可以看出譯者對這部作品所付出的心血以及翻譯時所持的嚴謹的學術態度。

孫大雨先生是「音組」理論早期的提倡者和踐行者。他在《我與詩人朱

---

① 陳子善. 碩果僅存的「新月」詩人孫大雨 [M] //孫近仁, 孫大雨詩文集. 石家莊：河北教育出版社，1996：144.

湘》一文中提到音組，1925 年夏天，他「在浙江海上普陀山佛寺圓通庵客舍中」，「尋找出了一種新詩的格律形式」，那就是「以兩個或三個漢字為常數而有各種不同變化的『音組』結構來實現」①。因此，孫大雨先生稱自己是「音組」理論的首創者②。但目前學界對此有不同的看法，孫大雨先生於 1925 年提出了「音組」理論，但是是葉公超（1937）最早形諸於文字，所以也有學者把首創的光環歸功於葉公超先生③。不管怎麼說，說孫大雨先生是「音組」早期的提倡者和踐行者是不為過的。據孫大雨自述，1926 年 4 月，他在《晨報副刊·詩鐫》上發表的十四行體詩《愛》就是「用音組有意識地撰寫格律體新詩的首次實踐」，並稱「以後我用這個方法創作和翻譯了三萬行左右的詩行」④。由於孫大雨先生用音組翻譯莎劇和英詩，用詩體譯詩，因此他的譯文在音韻上能夠取得與原文大致相當的審美效果，在翻譯質量和數量上都取得了不錯的成績。

二、孫大雨唐詩英譯中民俗文化詞彙的翻譯特點

（一）詩歌中民俗文化詞彙的特點

民俗文化的形成與一個民族的居住環境、生活習慣分不開。人們在生活中形成的觀念、信仰有一部分會慢慢地沉澱下來，成為一種文化現象，一個民族的服飾穿著、審美心理、宗教信仰、圖騰崇拜、飲食習慣、神話傳說、歷史語境等都是民俗文化的一部分。這些民俗文化現象往往為這個民族所獨有，與其他民族的民俗文化相比，具有很大的差異性。語言是記載文化現象的工具，其中包含著大量的民俗文化詞彙。這些民俗文化詞彙或表現一個民族獨特的地理環境，或記錄一個民族特有的人文現象，具有豐富的聯想意義、高度的互文性，這是翻譯中的難點。

詩歌中的民俗文化詞彙具有更高的互文性、更深的情感意義以及更強的審美意義。這一點不難理解，因為詩歌在空間上具有限制性，即詩歌在詩行上有

---

① 孫大雨. 我與詩人朱湘 [M] //孫近仁. 孫大雨詩文集. 石家莊：河北教育出版社，1996：324.

② 陳福康. 中國譯學理論史稿 [M]. 上海：上海外語出版社，2000：318.

③ 龍清濤. 簡論孫大雨的「音組」——對新詩格律史上一個重要概念的辨析 [J]. 中國現代文學研究叢刊，2009（1）：156.

④ 孫大雨. 我與詩人朱湘 [M] //孫近仁. 孫大雨詩文集. 石家莊：河北教育出版社，1996：324.

一定的歸約性。因此，只有當詩歌中的語言具有高度的濃縮性時才能在短短的詩行中表達強烈的情感，營造理想的意境，創造鮮明的意象，產生強烈的審美效果。這樣，在詩歌創作中，詩人傾向於選擇精簡且意義豐富的詞語。這也是民俗文化詞彙很容易走進詩篇的原因。因此，與一般詞彙相比，詩歌中的民俗文化詞彙濃縮性更強，意義更為豐富。

（二）孫大雨唐詩英譯中民俗文化詞彙的翻譯方法

孫大雨主要採用了音譯、直譯、音譯加註、直譯加註、意譯等方法翻譯唐詩中的民俗文化詞彙。他靈活運用這些方法，因詞而異。即使在同一首詩中，如果遇到的詞語不同，他採用的翻譯方法也有所改變。這種變通的手法充分彰顯了這位翻譯老手的高超技藝，提升了譯文的質量。下面通過四篇名詩譯文來探討孫大雨先生如何使用這些譯法翻譯原詩中的民俗文化詞彙。

1.《涼州詞》中民俗文化詞彙的翻譯

《涼州詞》是唐代著名詩人王之渙的名篇。詩題「涼州詞」是唐代廣為流傳的一種曲調名，不是詩題名，而是涼州歌的唱詞。在這首詩中，詩人描繪了守邊士卒偏遠單調的生存境況，格調悲愴哀怨，聲律遼闊沉鬱，給人的印象非常深刻。原文及孫大雨先生的譯文如下：

涼州詞[①]
黃河遠上白雲間，
一片孤城萬仞山。
羌笛何須怨楊柳，
春風不度玉門關。

　　　　　Liang County Song
The Luteous River glares heavenwards to the white clouds,
And a lorn pile lies by a mount a hundred furlongs high.
Why need the Qiang flute plain in a song of Plucking Willows?
Spring breezes would not be wafted out of the Jade Gate Pass.

在這首詩中，詩人主要運用「黃河」「羌笛」「楊柳」「玉門關」等民俗文化詞彙創造意象，營造意境。「黃河」因流經黃土高原，河水泛黃而得名。「黃河」流域是中原文化的發源地，因此「黃河」成為中華民族文化的圖騰，被國人稱之為「母親河」。孫大雨先生將之譯為「Luteous River」，「luteous」

---

① 孫大雨. 古詩文英譯集[M]. 上海：上海外語教育出版社，1997：130-131.

是「黃金色的，黃中帶綠的」的意思，顯然採用了直譯的方法。羌指中國的一個民族，而「羌笛」是羌族的一種樂器。孫大雨先生將之譯為「the Qiang flute」，採用了音譯加意譯的方法。詩中「楊柳」是指當時歌曲《折楊柳》。因「柳」與「留」諧音，贈柳可以表示留念，故唐代有折柳贈別的風俗，而《折楊柳》是唐代廣泛流傳的送別歌曲，孫大雨先生將之譯為「a song of Plucking Willows」，採用了直譯的翻譯方法。「玉門關」是唐代出塞必經的關口，孫大雨先生將之譯為「Jade Gate Pass」，採用了直譯的方法。

觀察這首譯詩可以發現，孫大雨先生在翻譯民俗文化詞彙的時候採用的方法是靈活多變的。但是，儘管他採用的方法靈活多變，從中可以發現一個特點，他盡量保留原詩中民俗文化詞彙的特色，力圖原汁原味地介紹給英文讀者。在不影響民俗文化詞彙意象傳播的情況下，譯者能意譯則意譯，不能意譯則直譯，不能直譯則音譯。

2. 《送元二使安西》中民俗文化詞彙的翻譯

《送元二使安西》是盛唐著名詩人王維的送別詩，譜曲後廣為傳唱，別稱「陽關三疊」「渭城曲」。詩人王維因崇信佛教，詩中有禪，故稱為「詩佛」。蘇東坡贊他「詩中有畫」「畫中有詩」。這首詩就具有這中特徵，描寫了初春時節，一場細雨後，渭城邊客舍中詩人惜別朋友的畫面。該詩原文及孫大雨先生的譯文如下：

　　　送元二使安西①
渭城朝雨浥輕塵，客舍青青柳色新。
勸君更盡一杯酒，西出陽關無故人。
Bidding Adieu to Yuan Junior in His Mission to Anxi
The fall of morning drops in this Town of Wei
Its dust light doth moisten,
Tenderly green are the new willow sprouts
Of this spring-adorned tavern.
I pray thee to quench once more full to the brim
This farewell cup of wine,
For after thy departure from this western-most pass,
Thou will have no old friend of thine.

在這首詩中，詩人王維主要採用「安西」「渭城」「陽關」三個文化詞彙

---

① 孫大雨. 古詩文英譯集 [M]. 上海：上海外語教育出版社，1997：154-155.

營造詩境。

安西指唐代為統轄西域地區而設的安西都護府的簡稱，在今新疆維吾爾自治區庫車縣附近。孫大雨先生採用音譯將之譯為「Anxi」。渭城指秦時咸陽城，漢代改稱渭城（《漢書·地理志》），位於渭水北岸，唐時屬京兆府咸陽縣轄區。渭城實際上是指渭城縣的縣城。孫大雨先生採用意譯與音譯結合的方法將其譯為「Town of Wei」。由於「Town」在英語中比「Village」（村）大，比「City」（城）小，譯成漢語是「鎮」「城鎮」。因此，「Town of Wei」回譯成漢語就是「渭鎮」，與原詩中的「渭城」有別，縮小了行政級別，這是翻譯中的不足之處。但這小小瑕疵不掩譯文的光澤。陽關是漢朝設置的邊關名，古代與玉門關同是出塞必經的關口。據《元和郡縣志》載，關口因在玉門之南，故稱陽關，在今甘肅省敦煌縣西南。為了諧韻，孫大雨先生採用意譯將之譯為「the western-most pass」。但是，「the western-most pass」譯為漢語為「最西邊的關塞」，不僅與「陽關」所處的地理位置不太相符，而且也喪失了「陽關」在漢語文化圈所具有的文化內涵，是為不足之處。

在這首詩中，孫大雨先生主要採用音譯、意譯、音譯與意譯結合等譯法翻譯古詩中民俗文化詞彙，雖然存在一些小瑕疵，但總體上還是成功的。

3. 《清平調》中民俗文化詞彙的翻譯

《清平調》是唐代著名詩人李白的名篇，共三首，流傳非常廣，知名度非常高。這三首詩創作於開元年間，當時唐玄宗與楊貴妃、樂師李龜年一起在宮中沉香亭畔遊賞牡丹。面對美人與名花，再加上有大樂師相伴，唐玄宗興致高漲，便邀李白進宮寫出新詞，以供歌舞之用。李白很快以《清平調》為題，寫下了三首詩。下面以前兩首為例分析孫大雨先生如何翻譯詩中的民俗文化詞彙。

清平調（一）①

雲想衣裳花想容，春風拂檻露華濃。
若非群玉山頭見，會向瑤臺月下逢。

For Qing-ping Tunes

Tinged cloudlets are likened unto her raiment.
And the flowers unto her mien.
Spring zephyrs along the balustrade
Gently brush the crystal dew's sheen.

---

① 孫大雨. 古詩文英譯集［M］. 上海：上海外語教育出版社，1997：184-185.

If not seen on the wondrous Mount of Gems

At some enchanted strand,

She could be met with on the Magic Tower

In the moonlit fairyland.

在詩的第一、二行，李白通過把「雲」與「花」兩個意象與楊玉環衣貌進行比擬從而突出楊玉環的傾城之美，雖似寫花寫雲，實則運用比興手法贊美楊玉環的容貌。在詩的第一行，「想」與「像」諧音，給這行詩的闡釋提供了多維視角，彰顯該詩的魅力，起筆之格調就與眾不同，既可以理解為「看到美麗的白雲就讓人想到楊玉環漂亮的衣裳，看到華麗的牡丹花就讓人想到楊玉環迷人的容顏」，也可以理解為「燦爛的白雲就像楊玉環的衣裳，華麗的牡丹花就像楊玉環豔麗的容顏」，如此種種，從而可以看出李白作詩的天才之處。第三、四行承接第一、二而來，運用「群玉山」「瑤臺」兩個民俗文化詞的神話意象進一步突出楊玉環綽約若仙子、超凡脫俗的美。「群玉山」是傳說中西王母所住之地，孫大雨先生將之意譯為「Mount of Gems」，處理得比較成功。「瑤臺」在這裡是指神仙、仙女居住的地方，孫大雨先生採用意譯將之譯為「Magic Tower」。這樣譯雖然取得了相似的詩境，但還是不太準確。因為「Magic Tower」回譯成漢語是「魔力城」或「魔法塔」，與原詩中的「瑤臺」不太對等。

在這首詩中，孫大雨先生主要採用意譯的方式翻譯原詩中的民俗文化詞彙。意譯的名詞雖然有利於西方讀者接受和理解，但其不足之處也十分明顯。一方面，由於民俗文化詞彙為一個民族所獨有，往往很難在異族文化中找到完全對等的詞彙；另一方面，由於民俗文化詞彙的內涵非常豐富，在意譯的時候往往會顧此失彼，只能翻譯其中的一些義項，甚至可能導致誤譯。從上面這首詩的譯文來看，總體而言說孫大雨先生是處理得比較成功的，但是存在一些不足之處，翻譯得不夠精到。下面再來看看《清平調》第二首詩中民俗文化詞彙的翻譯。

清平調（二）①

一枝紅豔露凝香，雲雨巫山枉斷腸。

借問漢宮誰得似，可憐飛燕倚新妝。

For Qing-ping Tunes

A spray of fresh pink beauty sparkleth

---

① 孫大雨. 古詩文英譯集［M］. 上海：上海外語教育出版社，1997：184-185.

With dews full of scents sweet;

The clouds and showers of Mount Wu's Belle

Remain today a mere legend.

If it be asked who in the Han palace

Could ever be named as her like,

The answer is「The Flitting Swallow」

In her newly sewn skirt of gauze.

　　這首詩的第一句把楊玉環比喻成凝香帶露的牡丹花，第二句通過楊玉環與巫山神女的對比贊美唐玄宗對楊玉環的寵愛遠勝過楚懷王與巫山神女這個只會讓多情人斷腸的虛假傳說。第三、四句詩則通過楊玉環與漢代美女趙飛燕的對比突出楊玉環美壓群芳。即使漢代美女趙飛燕著上新妝也顯得遜色幾分。在這首詩中，李白通過使用「雲雨巫山」「漢宮」「飛燕」等民俗文化詞彙營造詩境，突出楊玉環的得寵與美豔。「雲雨巫山」出自宋玉的《高唐賦》：「妾在巫山之陽，高丘之阻。旦為朝雲，暮為行雨，朝朝暮暮，陽臺之下。」大意是楚懷王在高唐地區遊覽時，在睡夢中遇見一位美麗女子。女子稱自己是巫山之女，願獻枕席給楚王使用。楚王喜出望外，立即寵幸巫山美女。巫山神女告訴楚王，如果再想找她，就請楚王記住她住在巫山的南面，早上是「朝雲」，晚上是「行雨」。孫大雨先生將「雲雨巫山」直譯為「the clouds and showers of Mount Wu's Belle」。「Belle」有兩個意思，其一是 Annabella、Arabella、Isabella 等的昵稱，其二是美人、美女。這裡取第二個意思。這個詞語回譯成漢語就是「巫山美女的雲朵和雨點」，與原詩意義相當，比較忠實地再現了原詩的內容。孫大雨先生採用譯音與譯意結合的方法將「漢宮」譯成「Han palace」，也忠實於原詩內容。本詩中第四行中的民俗文化詞彙「飛燕」是指西漢漢成帝的皇後趙宜主。因其體態輕盈瘦美，故稱飛燕。孫大雨先生將之意譯為「the Flitting Swallow」，不用加註直接保留了原詩中人物形象的特徵，便於西方讀者接受和理解，應該說是比較成功的。

　　從這首詩中民俗文化詞彙的譯文來看，孫大雨先生處理得很成功，比前面兩首更為出色。通過這四首詩中民俗文化詞彙的譯文，我們可以發現孫大雨先生主要採用了音譯、直譯、意譯等方法翻譯詩中的民俗文化詞彙。在翻譯中，孫大雨先生以音譯為主，直譯、意譯為輔，盡量保留原文的文化意象，從中可以看出孫大雨先生所持的文化立場，即希望通過翻譯向西方讀者原汁原味地介紹中國文化，有利於中國文化與世界文化的對話與交流。

　　孫大雨先生是新月派詩人中重要的一員。在英詩中譯和中詩英譯兩個方面

都取得了很大的成就。他是「音組」理論早期的提倡者和踐行者，主張以詩譯詩。因此，他的譯文質量較高。在《涼州詞》《送元二使安西》《清平調》等詩歌的翻譯中，他主要採用音譯、直譯、意譯等方法翻譯詩歌中的民俗文化詞彙，以保留原詩的文化意象為宗旨，在不破壞原詩意象的情況下，能意譯的則意譯，不能意譯的則直譯，不能直譯的則音譯，比較成功地保留了原詩的詩境。當然，有時為了諧韻，孫大雨先生在保留原詩意象與追求譯詩音韻美之間進行過一些艱難的抉擇，有些抉擇難免存在一些瑕疵，導致原詩文化意象的變形。儘管如此，瑕不掩瑜，總體來說，孫大雨先生的譯詩是成功的，原詩中民俗文化詞彙所包含的文化意象在譯詩中比較完美地保留下來。孫大雨先生嚴謹的翻譯態度值得學習，其翻譯成果為中西文化交流做出了巨大貢獻。

第三節　《長干行》中文化詞彙的英譯

李白（791—762年）是盛唐最傑出的詩人之一，素有「詩仙」之稱。他的詩，想像力「欲上青天攬明月」，氣勢如「黃河之水天上來」。他的詩蘊含著豐富的中國傳統文化，題材廣泛，在中國詩歌的發展史上有著重要的地位和深遠的影響，不僅是中國文學的瑰寶，也是世界文學寶庫中的珍品。多年來不少中外譯者努力從事著李白詩歌英譯這項艱鉅任務，如楊憲益夫婦、許淵衝、翁顯良等。在國外，戴維斯（John Davis）、莊延齡（Edward Parke）、翟爾斯（Herbert Giles）和弗萊徹（William Fletcher）、龐德（Ezra Pound）等人也對李白的詩歌做過翻譯。

雖然有很多名家譯過李白的詩歌，但李白詩歌翻譯的研究還比較薄弱。到目前為止，對李白詩歌英譯研究的成果主要集中在兩個方面：其一，採用美學視角闡述李白詩歌譯本的相關成果，如《李白詩歌英譯美學探索》《從許淵衝三美原則角度論李白詩歌英譯的美感再現》等；其二，借助西方的研究視角闡釋李白詩歌譯本的成果，如《關聯理論視角下李白詩歌英譯的比較研究》《從巴斯奈特的文化翻譯觀研究李白詩歌的英譯》等。總體說來，當前的研究主要停留在宏觀的闡釋，而對李白詩歌譯本中意象、文化詞彙等微觀層面的專項研究暫時空缺。本書正是在當前這種研究背景下對李白詩歌英譯中文化詞彙這一微觀語言現象進行探討。

一、文化詞彙的特點及其翻譯

文化詞彙也稱文化負載詞。這類詞通過長時間的互文運用而具有豐富的聯想意義，文化詞彙具有高度的互文性和民族性，承載著一個民族的文化基因。閱讀這類詞能給人們帶來獨特的審美體驗。一般說來，文化詞彙除了本身的所指意義外，還具有獨特的引申意義。這兩類詞義的疊加給文化詞彙的翻譯帶來了很大的難度。

根據不同國家文化詞彙的對應程度，可以將文化詞彙的對應關係分為對應空缺、所指意義對應、引申意義對應、完全對應四種。對應空缺是指某一個國家的文化詞在另一國家的語言中找不到對應詞，如英語中大量的神話、典故等文化詞彙在漢語中找不到對應的詞彙，反之亦然。所指意義對應是指不同國家文化詞彙所指的事物一致，但引申意義不同，如英語的「chrysanthemum」和漢語中「菊花」所指的事物一致，但漢語中的「菊花」比英語中的「chrysanthemum」內涵豐富得多。引申意義對應是指不同國家文化詞彙所指的事物有所區別，但引申意義大體一致，如英語的「heaven」與漢語中「天堂」所指不同，一個是指基督教教徒向往的聖地，另一個是指佛教徒渴望的理想淨土，但引申意義差別不大，都是指聖潔的地方。完全對應是指不同國家文化詞彙的所指意義和引申意義都對應。一般來說，不同語系的語言很少有完全對應的文化詞彙。這種情況多見於同一語系下語言之間的互相借用，如中日兩種語言之間文化詞彙的互相借用，英法兩種語言之間文化詞彙的互相借用等。弄清這四種對應關係對理清文化詞彙的翻譯策略有一定的指導意義，如對應空缺的文化詞彙一般宜採用音譯和刪譯，完全對應的則宜直譯，所指意義對應的文化詞彙一般宜採用直譯或意譯，而引申意義對應的詞彙一般採用替代、刪譯等翻譯手段。

文化詞彙是指具有一定文化負荷的詞語。這些詞語「受文化制約（Culture-bound），從它們身上可映射出不同國家之間的文化差異」[1]。文化詞彙是語言詞彙體系中的精華，是一個民族的物質文化和精神文化的真實載體，是瞭解該民族文化的鏡子。每種語言中都存在著大量富有民族文化內涵的詞彙。「文化詞彙是指特定文化範疇的詞彙，它是民族文化在語言詞彙中直接或

---

[1] Larry A Samovar, Richard E Porter, Lisa A. Stefani Communication between Cultures [M]. Belmont: Wadsworth Publishing Company, 1998: 132.

間接的反應。文化詞彙與其他一般詞彙的界定有以下兩點：一是文化詞彙本身載有明確的民族文化信息，並且隱含著深層的民族文化的含義。文化詞彙的另一特點，是它與民族文化，包括……物質文化、制度文化和心理文化有各種關係，有的是該文化的直接反應，如『龍、鳳、華表』等；有的則是間接反應，如漢語中的紅、黃、白、黑等顏色詞及鬆、竹、梅等象徵詞語；有的和各種文化存在淵源關係，如來自文化典籍的詞語及來自宗教的詞語等。」①這些文化詞彙除了與一般詞彙一樣有指稱意義外，還有豐富的內涵意義。內涵意義因民族文化背景不同而不同，與各民族長期所處的生活環境、歷史背景和民族心理等有著緊密的聯繫。因此，文化詞彙的翻譯往往是譯者最棘手的問題。同樣，由於中國的哲學思想或價值觀念與西方人不同，中國傳統文化中很多文化詞彙也是難以傳達的，如陰陽八卦、天干地支等，在英語裡都沒有合適的對應詞。

對於文化詞彙的翻譯，「目前比較現實的做法是用漢語拼音拼寫、加註或是增譯、音譯和譯借」②以便保留詞語的民族文化內涵。下面將以李白詩歌《長干行》英譯為例，探討譯者對此詩中文化詞彙所採取的翻譯方法。

二、《長干行》英譯中文化詞彙的翻譯方法

「長干行」屬樂府《雜曲歌辭》調名。這首詩是商婦的自白，用纏綿婉轉的筆調，抒寫了她對在外經商丈夫的思念。從兩人天真爛漫的童年到丈夫遠離後深深的思念，將初嫁時的羞澀、新婚的喜悅和堅貞不渝的心願寫得十分細膩生動。全詩感情細膩，纏綿婉轉；語言坦白，音節和諧；格調清新雋永，是詩歌中的上品。

長干行

妾髮初覆額，折花門前劇。郎騎竹馬來，繞床弄青梅。
同居長干里，兩小無嫌猜。十四為君婦，羞顏未嘗開。
低頭向暗壁，千喚不一回。十五始展眉，願同塵與灰。
常存抱柱信，豈上望夫臺。十六君遠行，瞿塘灩澦堆。
五月不可觸，猿聲天上哀。門前遲行跡，一一生綠苔。
苔深不能掃，落葉秋風早。八月蝴蝶黃，雙飛西園草。
感此傷妾心，坐愁紅顏老。早晚下三巴，預將書報家。

---

① 常敬宇. 漢語詞彙與文化 [M]. 北京：北京大學出版社，1995：2.
② 金惠康. 跨文化交際續編 [M]. 北京：中國對外翻譯出版公司，2004：231.

相迎不道遠，直至長風沙。

這首詩先後被一些外國學者譯成英文。他們的譯作各有特色，但有些地方值得商榷。「唐人絕句是中國文學裡的珍寶，英文譯作如林，可不見得篇篇都好。」①下面我們選取《長干行》五種（Fletcher, Lowell, Ezra Pound, 羅志野、許淵衝）英譯文本，挑出原詩中有文化詞彙詩句的英譯，加以對比與分析。

1. 竹馬

譯者	郎騎竹馬來
Fletcher：	You riding came onhobby-horse astride,
Lowell：	Then you, my Lover, came riding a bamboo horse,
Pound：	You came by onbamboo stilts, playing horse.
羅志野：	you came to me with a bamboo as a horse
許淵衝：	Ona hobby horse you came upon the scene,

在中國，竹子與梅、蘭、菊被並稱為花中「四君子」，竹子以其中空、有節、挺拔的特性歷來為中國人所稱道，成為中國人所推崇的謙虛、有氣節、剛直不阿等美德的生動寫照。而在英語當中，竹子不會有此文化意象。Lowell 將「竹馬」譯為「a bamboo horse」（用竹子做的馬），這種譯法沒有準確傳達出原詩的文化內涵。Pound 譯成「bamboo stilts」（竹高蹺）也沒有完全傳達出原詩的文化內涵。原詩中沒有「踩竹高蹺」（bamboo stilts）之意，而是「騎著一根竹竿當馬」。Fletcher 和許淵衝譯成「hobby-horse」，雖然用瞭解釋詞語 hobby，在意思上比較接近詩歌中的「竹馬」，但還是沒有翻譯出「竹」這個意象，也沒有傳達出中國文化中「竹馬」的內涵意義。羅志野把「竹馬」譯成「a bamboo as a horse」，比較好地傳達出了原詩中的中國文化原有的意象。

2. 抱柱信②

譯者	常存抱柱信
Fletcher：	My troth to thee till death I keep for aye.
Lowell：	I often thought that you were the faithful man who clung to the bridgepost.

---

① 呂叔湘. 英譯唐人絕句百首 [M]. 長沙：湖南教育出版社，1980：1.
② 註釋：Fletcher, Ezra Pound, Lowell 的譯文均選自呂叔湘《中詩英譯比錄》，羅志野的譯文選自吳鈞陶編《唐詩三百首》，許淵衝的譯文選自許譯《唐詩三百首》。

Pound	Forever and forever and forever.
羅志野：	I desired to live with you forever.
許淵衝：	Rather than break faith, you declared you'd die.

「抱柱信」典出《莊子·盜跖》：「尾生與女子期於梁下，女子不來，水至不去，抱柱而死。」大意是說一位名叫尾生的男子，與他的愛人約定在橋下見面；尾生先到，忽然河水暴漲，他不肯失信，便緊抱橋柱，結果被大水淹死。這句的意思是說丈夫象尾生那樣堅貞不渝地愛著她。Fletcher 採用了意譯；Lowell 採用了直譯加釋義；Pound 採用意譯，他一連用了三個「forever」來譯「抱柱信」一句；羅志野把「抱柱信」一句的主語理解成「妾」，此譯文對原詩理解有誤，應該是對方（君）常存「抱柱信」，而不是敘述者商婦自己（妾）常存「抱柱信」。許淵衝也是採用了意譯。

3. 望夫臺

譯者	豈上望夫臺
Fletcher	My eyes still gaze adoring on my lord.
Lowell	That I should never be obliged to ascend to the Looking-for-Husband Ledge.
Pound：	Why should I climb the look-out?
羅志野：	And I, Did never think we would part some day
許淵衝：	Who knew I'd live alone in a tower high.

傳說古代有個女子，因丈夫久出不歸，她天天上山去盼望，結果變成了一塊石頭，狀如人形。後來人們稱此為望夫臺，山為望夫山。這些故事都是表達妻子如何望眼欲穿地盼著常年在外的丈夫的歸來。「豈上望夫臺」這句的意思是說她肯定不會登上望夫臺，去嘗受離別之苦。Fletcher 採用了意譯；Lowell 採用了直譯加釋義；Pound 採用直譯「望夫臺」直譯為「the look-out（望臺）」。妻子日夜思念丈夫，盼丈夫歸來的意象剎那變成了「瞭望」「放哨」。「龐德不懂漢語，誤解了不奇怪。」① 羅志野和許淵衝都是採用了意譯，試圖通過釋義方式來體現原詩中典故的涵義。

進行對《長干行》五種英譯文本中文化詞彙「竹馬」「抱柱信」和「望

---

① 翁顯良. 本色與變相——漢詩英譯瑣議之三 [J]. 外國語, 1982 (1): 23.

夫臺」英譯進行比較與分析，五個譯者在翻譯過程中，幾乎都是採用了直譯或是意譯。Fletcher、Pound 和 Lowell 等外國學者在翻譯這些文化詞彙時，譯文未能準確傳達出這些文化詞彙的文化內涵。原因為：一是不精通或不懂漢語；二是不瞭解中國文化或對中國文化瞭解不深入。畢竟他們各自的歷史和文化背景與我們中國文化大不相同。國內學者在翻譯這些文化詞彙的時候，他們也不能完全駕馭好文化詞彙的翻譯，充分傳達出各個文化詞彙的內涵意義。因為漢語和英語屬於不同語系，漢語重意合而英語重形合；英語中的時態和體態主要以動詞的曲折變化加以表示，而漢語的時態和體態較為鬆散和模糊，是通過詞彙手段來表示，從而就增加了國內學者英譯古詩的難度。

在詩歌的翻譯過程中，文化詞彙翻譯尤其困翻，因為文化詞彙本身承載著一國深厚的文化和歷史知識。中國古詩講求「神韻」「意境」「空靈」，力圖超越詩中的實境，去創造一種亦實亦虛、虛實相生的境界。如果不加註釋，再簡練的英語也不可能將中國文化中特有的文化詞彙用兩句話解釋清楚。在翻譯中國古詩時，譯者應首先理解原文，吃透原文的含義，把握原文的風格。表達時，譯者要「忠實」於原文。這就要求譯者一要具備熟練地運用兩種語言的能力，二要深刻理解兩種文化的異同。中外學者應該攜手合作，取人之長，補己之短。這樣譯出的作品才有生命力，能體現原詩的「風味」，引起英美讀者「心靈的共鳴」，才能讓他們更精確地瞭解中國的燦爛文化。

第四節　《清平調》中的典故英譯研究

典故包含了豐富的文化信息，含有大量的帶有民族印記的文化特徵和文化背景，是一個民族文化遺產不可或缺的組成部分。典故在《辭海》中釋義為：詩文中引用的古代故事和有來歷出處的詞語。其主要來源有：歷史故事或歷史事件，神話傳說，民間傳說，文學作品，寓言故事，民間習俗、諺語，等等[1]。因此在翻譯過程中，譯者如何恰當地翻譯中國文化中的典故是值得思考的問題。李白所作的《清平調》用了許多典故，諸如群玉山、瑤池、雲雨巫山、漢宮、飛燕、傾國傾城等。這些典故即使是對於中國讀者來說，恐怕也是較難理解。在翻譯時，兩國歷史、習俗、民情不同的情況，往往會使譯者陷入困境，有時即使翻譯出來了，也很難理解。本書從韋努蒂的文化翻譯策略視

---

[1]　包惠南. 文化語境與語言翻譯 [M]. 北京：中國對外翻譯出版公司，2001：243.

角，對比分析不同譯者運用翻譯策略的傾向性及其借鑑意義。

一、《清平調》的創作背景及其解讀

《清平調》三首詩是李白在長安供奉翰林時所作。唐玄宗和楊貴妃在宮中沉香亭觀賞牡丹花，伶人們正準備表演歌舞以助興。唐玄宗卻說：「賞名花，對妃子，豈可用舊日樂詞。」因急召翰林學士李白進宮寫新樂章。李白奉詔進宮，即在金花箋上作了這三首詩。

(一)
雲想衣裳花想容，春風拂檻露華濃。
若非群玉山頭見，會向瑤臺月下逢。
(二)
一枝紅豔露凝香，雲雨巫山枉斷腸。
借問漢宮誰得似，可憐飛燕倚新妝。
(三)
名花傾國兩相歡，長得君王帶笑看。
解釋春風無限恨，沉香亭北倚檻杆。

第一首寫楊貴妃的美豔。見到雲就使人想到她的衣裳，見到花使人想到她的容貌，春風吹拂著欄杆，在露水滋潤下的花朵更為豔濃。如此美人若不是在神仙居住的群玉山見到，也只能在瑤池的月光下才能遇到了。

第二首寫楊貴妃備受寵幸。您（貴妃）真像一支沾滿雨露、芳香濃鬱的盛開的牡丹花啊！傳說中楚王與神女在巫山的歡會那只是傳說而已，哪能比得上您受到君王的真正的恩寵呢？就算可愛無比的趙飛燕，還得穿上華麗的衣裳化好妝才能比得上。

第三首總承一、二兩首，把牡丹和楊貴妃與君王糅合，融為一體。牡丹與貴妃都如此美麗動人，惹得君王直笑看，此時即使心中有再大的恨意，只要和貴妃一起來到這沉香亭畔的牡丹園，也會消散得無影無蹤了。

全詩構思精巧，辭藻豔麗，將花與人渾融在一起寫，令人覺得人花交映，迷離恍惚，顯示了詩人高超的藝術功力。

二、異化、歸化翻譯策略

1995 年，美國翻譯理論家勞倫斯・韋努蒂（Lawrence Venuti）在《譯者的

隱身》(*The Translator's Invisibility: A History of Translation*) 一書中提出了歸化（Demestication）和異化（Foreignization）兩種翻譯策略。「歸化」，通常是指譯者在翻譯時採用流暢的譯文，從而使得原語文本對於讀者的陌生感（Strangeness）降至最低；歸化的翻譯充分考慮到譯入語讀者的接受心理和審美感受，用地道的本族語表達方式來傳遞原語文本的信息，避免給讀者的閱讀造成障礙，但會造成原文文化信息的損失，從而使原語文化處於失語狀態，不利於不同文化之間的平等交流與對話。「異化」，則是指譯者在翻譯時故意保留原語文本當中的某些異質性（Foreignness），盡可能地保留原語文化的特色和作者的獨特表達方式，使讀者能夠領會到原作的風貌，有身臨其境的感覺，異化可以最大限度地保留原語文化。韋努蒂認為這種翻譯策略有利於不同文化之間的平等交流與對話。歸化傾向於原語文化和原文作者（SL culture or author oriented），異化翻譯策略傾向於譯入語文化和譯文讀者（TL culture or reader oriented）①。韋努蒂的異化理論一經提出，便在譯界產生了廣泛的影響，學者們對歸化和異化提出了不同的闡釋。「異化原則強調的是最大限度地保留和介紹原文語言、文化的異質特徵，主張以原語的文化為取向，這包括原文語言文化的表現形式和內容」②。異化譯法就是在譯文中保留原文裡的文化意向，或按字面直譯③，目的是使譯文保持原文的語言風格，向譯文讀者介紹源語文化，並豐富譯入語及其文化。在翻譯實踐中，韋努蒂認為未來不同文化之間的平等交流中，譯者應該以異化翻譯為主，這也有利於彰顯譯者的主體性。下面將不同譯者對《清平調》中的典故的不同翻譯策略進行探討，分析並歸納他們的翻譯策略取向。

三、《清平調》中典故的不同英譯策略

本書所討論的六個譯本分別為 Bynner、趙彥春、孫大雨、唐一鶴、謝卓杰和許淵衝的譯本。下面逐一分析在不同的譯本中，這些譯者採用何種翻譯策略英譯漢詩中的典故。

1. 若非群玉山頭見，會向瑤臺月下逢。

關於群玉的記載方面。《山海經》中道：「山名。仙姑西王母所居之地，因山中多玉石，故名群玉山。」西王母，是中國神話中的至高女神，她是玉皇

---

① 姜倩，何剛強. 翻譯概論［M］. 上海：上海外語教育出版社，2008.
② 冒國安. 實用英漢對比教程［M］. 重慶：重慶大學出版社，2005：70.
③ 張春柏. 英漢漢英翻譯教程［M］. 北京：高等教育出版社，2003：213.

大帝的妻子。關於瑤臺的記載方面《太平御覽》中道：「西王母所住的宮殿。瑤臺又名瑤池。」《詞源》中道：「瑤池，神仙所居。《集仙傳》中道：西王母所居宮殿，在龜山昆侖之圃，閬風之苑，左帶瑤池，右環翠水。」

Bynner：
Is either the tip of earth's Jade Mountain
Or a moon-edged roof of Paradise.

趙彥春：
If not a fairy queen from Heav'n on high,
She's Goddess of Moon that makes flowers shy.

孫大雨：
If not seen on the wondrous Mount of Gems
At some enchanted strand,
She could be met with on theMagic Tower
In the moonlit fairyland①.

唐一鶴：
If such an extraordinary beauty doesn't appear
On the jade-group hills in sight,
She'd be met with on the Jasper Terrace
Under the moon light.②

謝卓杰、肖乙華：
Like Goddess witnessed on the crown ofJade Mountain,
Or met with in the moon by Fairyland Fountain③.

許淵衝：
If not a fairy queen from Jade-Green Mountains proud
She's Goddess of the Moon in Crystal Hall one sees④.

Bynner 採用異化策略，將「群玉山」直譯為「Jade Mountain」，符合典故中群玉山的形象。趙譯用「heaven」代替了「群玉山」，對西方讀者而言，在可接受性方面有一定優勢，但未能較好傳遞中國文化形象。孫大雨採用異化策略將「群玉山」直譯為「Mount of Gems」。「Gem」英語解釋是「precious stone or jewel, esp when cut and polished」，由「玉」變成了「寶石山」，與中國傳統文化形象有所改變。「Mount of Gems」採用復數形式表達了「群玉山」的形象，這一點難能可貴。唐一鶴採用異化策略，將其譯為「jade-group hills」，譯得過於直接。譯王母娘娘住所，hills 沒有 mountain 合適，hills 顯得有點美中不

---

① 孫大雨. 古詩文英譯集 [M]. 上海：上海外語教育出版社，1997：184-185.
② 唐一鶴. 英譯唐詩三百首 [M]. 天津：天津人民出版社出版，2005：130-131.
③ 陳福康. 中國譯學理論史稿 [M]. 上海：上海外語出版社，2000：105.
④ 許淵衝，等. 唐詩三百首新譯 [M]. 北京：中國對外翻譯出版公司，1997：105.

足。謝卓杰譯與 Bynner 一致，都採用異化策略，將「群玉山」譯為「Jade Mountain」，較符合地名形象。許淵衝把「群玉山」譯為「Jade‐Green Mountains」，也是採用異化策略，眼光獨到。

  Bynner 採用歸化策略將「瑤臺」譯為「a moon‐edged roof of Paradise」，體現出了宮殿的形象。趙譯採用歸化策略省譯了「瑤臺」。孫大雨採用歸化策略，將「瑤臺」譯為「Magic Tower（仙境中的魔幻城堡）」，利於西方讀者理解，但不利於傳播中國文化。唐一鶴採用異化策略，將「瑤臺」直譯為「the Jasper Terrace（碧玉平臺）」，而瑤臺是宮殿，與中國傳統形象有一定出入。謝譯採用歸化策略，將「瑤臺」意譯為「Fairyland Fountain（仙境中的噴泉）」，與原典故內涵有一定差異。許將「瑤臺」譯為「Crystal Hall（水晶宮）」，體現了典故內涵。在可接受性方面有優勢，用「Crystal Hall」譯瑤臺加上了自己的主觀創造性。

  2.「雲雨巫山枉斷腸」與「可憐飛燕倚新妝」

  關於雲雨巫山方面記載。宋玉《高唐賦》中道：「昔者先王嘗遊高唐，怠而晝寢，夢見一婦人，曰：『妾，巫山之女也。為高堂之客，原薦枕息。』王因幸之，去而辭曰：『妾在巫山之陽，高丘之姐，旦為行雲，暮為行雨，朝朝暮暮，陽臺之下。』」舊稱男女歡合為「雲雨」。宋玉在《神女賦》中對神女極力鋪陳：「茂矣美矣，諸好備矣。盛矣麗矣，難測究矣。上古既無，世所未見，瑰姿偉態，不可勝贊。」她如此美艷，集天下女性美於一身，使得楚襄王「回腸傷氣，顛倒失據，黯然而瞑，忽不知處」。這樣的絕色神女，也不及眼前楊貴妃的美貌。趙飛燕，西漢漢成帝的皇後，生得腰肢纖軟，善歌舞，人稱「飛燕身輕，掌上可舞」。然而，就連她也只能依仗新妝，哪裡比得上楊貴妃。

Bynner：	And a mist, through the heart, from the magical Hill of Wu; Not even Flying Swallow with all her glittering garments.
趙彥春：	Such nymphs, on earth or Heav'n, are really few; Lady Zhao, to shine, new clothes had to wear.
孫大雨：	The clouds and showers of Mount Wu's Belle, Remain today a mere legend; The answer is「The Flitting Swallow」, In her newly sewn skirt of gauze①.

---

① 孫大雨. 古詩文英譯集 [M]. 上海：上海外語教育出版社，1997：184‐185.

唐一鶴:	And compared to the Fairy Maiden On the cloudy and rainy Wu Mountain, Yearned for and dreamt of by Emperor Xiang Of the Kingdom of Chu; It was a pity only by wearing new fancy dress could Beauty Zhao Feiyan win the emperor's favor in the Kingdom of Han①.
謝卓杰、肖乙華:	Pains of lost love on Magic Hill all here adieu. Beauty, Flying Swallow's array cannot assume②.
許淵衝	Far fairer than the Goddess bringing showers in dreams. Not e'en the newly-dressed「Flying Swallow」, it seems. Note：The legend said that the king of a southern kingdom dreamed of the Goddess of Mount Witch with whom her made love and who would come out in the morning in the form of a cloud and in the evening in the form of a shower③.

　　Bynner 採用歸化策略，將「雲雨巫山」創造性地譯為「a mist（薄霧），through the heart, from the magical Hill of Wu」。「雲雨巫山」是指巫山女神與楊貴妃相比，自嘆不如，而 Bynner 譯成了薄霧，與原文典故內涵相去甚遠。譯者將「飛燕」意譯為「Flying Swallow」，譯文容易被西方讀者理解，但與典故內涵有一定的偏差。

　　趙譯採用異化策略使用增譯法，將巫山神女譯為「the oread（女神）Duke Xiang craved（渴望）」，用了後置定語，較好地保留了中華文化，但是對於西方讀者來說，較難理解 Duke Xiang 所指是誰，有過度翻譯之嫌。譯者將「飛燕」譯為「Lady Zhao」，西方讀者是很難理解的。

　　孫大雨採用異化策略，將「雲雨巫山」譯為「The clouds and showers of Mount Wu's Belle」，保留了中華文化，但西方讀者較難理解該譯文。孫大雨採用歸化策略將「飛燕」意譯為「The Flitting Swallow」，西方讀者容易理解。唐一鶴採用異化策略將「雲雨巫山」譯為「the Fairy Maiden On the cloudy and rainy Wu Mountain, Yearned for and dreamt of by Emperor Xiang Of the Kingdom of

---

① 唐一鶴. 英譯唐詩三百首 [M]. 天津：天津人民出版社出版，2005：130-131.
② 陳福康. 中國譯學理論史稿 [M]. 上海：上海外語出版社，2000：105.
③ 許淵衝，等. 唐詩三百首新譯 [M]. 北京：中國對外翻譯出版社，1997：105.

Chu」，也用了後置定語，較好地保留了中國文化；將「飛燕」譯為「Beauty Zhao Feiyan」，西方讀者較難理解其所指。謝卓杰採用歸化策略，將「雲雨巫山」譯為了「Magic Hill」，西方讀者較為容易理解，但與原典故內涵差異較大；將「飛燕」譯為「Beauty, Flying Swallow」，容易被西方讀者接受。許淵衝將「雲雨巫山」譯為「the Goddess bringing showers in dreams」並對典故做了較詳細的註釋，較好地保留了中國文化；與 Bynner 一樣，許淵衝將「飛燕」譯為「Flying Swallow」，容易為西方讀者接受。

　　分析以上 6 位譯者對兩個典故的翻譯，絕大多數譯者採用異化策略，積極向西方推廣了中國文化。但譯者面臨兩難處境，要在可接受性和傳播中國傳統文化之間進行選擇，有些譯者採用歸化變通的手法，雖然有利於西方讀者接受，但在傳達中國傳統文化方面有待進一步改進。

　　翻譯是一種創造性的工作，翻譯有法無定法。在翻譯過程中，譯者要注意民族語言的獨特性，語言可以相互借鑑、相互滲透、相互補充。「對譯者來說，重要的是在翻譯過程中要有深刻的文化意識，即意識到兩種文化的異同」①。通過六個譯本的對比發現，大部分譯者在英譯漢詩典故時以異化為主，在譯語中較好地保留了中國文化的特質，他們的翻譯策略取向為今後的漢詩典故英譯提供了可資借鑑的方法和策略。因此，將中國文化裡的典故譯成英語應該以異化翻譯為主，並且在翻譯過程中注重傳播原語文化，保留原語文化的異質性特徵，最佳地傳遞典故的文化內涵，使西方讀者能更好地瞭解中國文化。

第五節　《錦瑟》中的典故英譯研究

　　李商隱（公元813—858年），晚唐時期著名的詩人，其詩構思新奇，情感細膩。尤其以愛情詩為代表，其詩用典出神入化，優美動人，廣為傳誦。其詩風深受杜甫和韓愈的影響，用典頗多，歷來為詩評家所關注，故體現出晦澀難懂的特點。李商隱詩中典故的英譯難度較大。在李詩典故英譯中，不同譯者採用了不同的策略方法，可謂「見仁見智」。故本書以《錦瑟》為例，列舉出不同譯者對其詩中典故的英譯作品，從而為後來譯者提供可資借鑑的方法。

---

① 郭建忠. 文化與翻譯 [M]. 北京：中國對外翻譯出版公司，2000：287.

一、典故的英譯

「典故原指舊制、舊例，也是漢代掌管禮樂制度等史實者的官名。後來一種常見的意義是指關於歷史人物、典章制度等的故事或傳說。」《漢語大辭典》將典故定義為：「詩文中引用的古代故事和有來歷出處詞語。」[①]典故體現了中華五千年的文化內涵，是弘揚中國文明和傳統的一個載體。典故能把我們引入中華民族的歷史，體驗不同時期發生的歷史事件，瞭解各個不同時期的社會文化和生活狀態。當今世界經濟和文化交流日益頻繁，為了增進各民族之間的理解和交流，向世界其他國家傳播中國的傳統文化和向中國人民介紹西方的文化，典故的翻譯勢必將受到越來越多的關注。

國內有不少學者探討了典故的翻譯。武恩義博士（2005）對英漢典故的不同文化淵源、來源和類型、形成的理據以及語義上的對應與非對應關係進行了對比研究，論述了英漢典故的共性和差異性及其互譯。王軍（2005）對《紅樓夢》中的典故英譯進行比較分析，指出異化是極其合理必要的，而處理形式上最宜採取直譯加註。黃瓊英（2006）運用關聯翻譯理論標準，從認知語用學的角度對《自題小像》中典故的五種譯文進行比較分析。張英萍（2007）從異化與歸化原則探討了中文人名典故英譯；指出譯成英語時要遵循異化與歸化原則，根據具體的情況採取音譯、音意結合、意譯、約定俗成和對應意翻譯的方法與技巧，準確地將中文人名典故翻譯成英語。李箭（2008）以社會符號學為理論依據探討典故的語用意義，深入認識語境對典故翻譯的制約作用，結合功能目的論來討論典故的翻譯策略，以便達到翻譯的文化交流目的。陳靜博士（2010）對唐宋詩詞中典故英譯研究做了系統研究，涉及典故的分類及英譯方法；陳靜對各家的譯文進行比較，簡單分析各家譯文的長處和短處，並試圖找到一種合適的解決方法，從而避免出現文化丟失現象。本書將以《錦瑟》為例子，探討不同譯者對此詩中典故所採取的不同翻譯方法。

二、《錦瑟》中典故的翻譯

錦瑟

錦瑟無端五十弦，一弦一柱思華年。

---

① 陳靜. 唐宋詩詞中典故英譯研究 [D]. 杭州：浙江工業大學，2010：3.

莊生曉夢迷蝴蝶，望帝春心托杜鵑。
滄海月明珠有淚，藍田日暖玉生煙。
此情可待成追憶，只是當時已惘然。

李商隱的《錦瑟》是中國詩歌史上（除作為經書的《詩三百》）解人最多、爭論最大、聚訟最繁的一首詩。有人說是詩人寫給令狐楚家一個叫「錦瑟」的侍女的愛情詩；有人說是詩人睹物思人，寫給故去的妻子王氏的悼亡詩；也有人認為中間四句詩可與瑟的適、怨、清、和四種聲情相合，從而推斷為描寫音樂的詠物詩；此外還有影射政治、自敘詩歌創作等許多種說法。千百年來眾說紛紜，莫衷一是，大體而言，以「悼亡」和「自傷」說者為多。這首詩先後被一些國內外學者譯成英文，他們的譯作各有特色。「唐人絕句是中國文學裡的瑰寶，英文譯作如林，可不見得篇篇都好」①。筆者試圖選取幾種不同英文譯本，對比分析其中典故的英譯。

1. 莊生曉夢迷蝴蝶

此典故出自《莊子·齊物論》：「莊周夢為蝴蝶，栩栩然蝴蝶也；自喻適志與！不知周也。俄然覺，則蘧蘧然周也。不知周之夢為蝴蝶與？蝴蝶之夢為周與。」詩人李商隱在此引用莊周夢蝶的故事，以言人生如夢，往事如菸之意。佳人錦瑟，一曲繁弦，驚醒了詩人的夢境，不復成寐。這個典故反應了莊子哲學思想的一個方面。

譯者翻譯此典故時要注重「莊周」的譯法及對「迷」字的理解。「莊周」是具有中華文化特色的詞，翻譯時，譯者需要把莊子的哲學思想最大程度地表達出來，從而把中國文化傳譯出去。「迷」是「迷惑」，莊周面對蝴蝶分不清自己是蝴蝶還是二者合二為一。從這兩點來看，許譯把「迷」譯為「dream to be」，與原文有一定差異，譯文不夠忠實。戴乃迭、楊憲益把「迷」譯為「puzzled」，劉若愚譯為「confused」，均抓住了迷的主要意思，忠實於原文。John A. Turner 和 Bynner 將迷譯為 day-dreaming（白日夢），譯為胡思亂想，與原文有一定差異，不夠忠實。Graham 將迷譯為 lost its way（迷路），屬於誤譯，對典故理解欠妥。

許譯省譯了莊周，沒有傳達出原文的文化意蘊。戴乃迭、楊憲益將莊周譯為 Master Zhuang，劉若愚譯為 Master Chuang，Bynner 將莊周譯為 The sage Chuang-tzu，Graham 將其譯為 Chuang-tzu，均用音譯譯出了典故文化意向，從而這些譯本能更好地傳播中國文化。其中戴乃迭、楊憲益仔細介紹了該典故的

---

① 呂叔湘. 英譯唐人絕句百首 [M]. 長沙：湖南人民出版社，1980：1.

由來和基本意義，一定程度上彌補了譯文中無法表達出來的深層哲學思想，還是容易被讀者接受的。John A. Turner 泛化處理將其譯為 sage。

譯者	莊生曉夢迷蝴蝶
許淵衝：	Dim morning dream to be a butterfly.
戴乃迭、楊憲益：	Master Zhuang woke from a dream puzzled by a butterfly.
劉若愚：	Master Chuang, dreaming at dawn, was confused with butterfly.
John A. Turner：	The sage of his loved butterflies day-dreaming.
Bynner：	The sage Chuang-tzu is day-dreaming, bewildered by butterflies.
Graham.	Chuang-tzu dreams at sunrise that a butterfly lost its way.

註釋：According to a fable story, Zhuang Zi, a famous philosopher of the Warring States Period, dreaming of being a butterfly and when he woke up, he was so confused that he could not tell whether it was him that had dreamt of being a butterfly or it was a butterfly that was then dreaming of becoming him.（戴乃迭、楊憲益譯）。

2. 望帝春心托杜鵑

《華陽國志・蜀志》言：「杜宇稱帝，號曰望帝。……其相開明，決玉壘山以除水害，帝遂委以政事，法堯舜禪授之義，遂禪位於開明。帝升西山隱焉。時適二月，子鵑鳥鳴，故蜀人悲子鵑鳥鳴也。」子鵑即杜鵑，又名子規。蔡夢弼《杜工部草堂詩箋》一九《杜鵑》詩註引《成都記》：「望帝死，其魂化為鳥，名曰杜鵑，亦曰子規。」傳說蜀國的杜宇帝因水災讓位於自己的臣子，而自己則隱歸山林，死後化為杜鵑日夜悲鳴直至啼出血來。

譯者	望帝春心托杜鵑
許淵衝：	Amorous heart poured out in cuckoops cry.
戴乃迭、楊憲益：	Emperor Wang reposed his amorous heart to the cuckoo.
劉若愚：	Emperor Wang consigned his amorous heart in spring to the cuckoo.
John A. Turner：	The king that sighed his soul into a bird.
Bynner：	The spring heart of Emperor Wang is crying in a cuckoo.

Graham： Wang-ti bequeathed his spring passion to the nightjar.

　　從這典故中可以讀到詩句中的春心典故原指望帝在春天化為杜鵑，日夜悲鳴，表達其心聲。本詩此處引申為情人之間的愛戀。「托」是「托付」之意。對「春心」和「托」的翻譯是此句翻譯的難點之一，也是最能見譯者的匠心之處。許譯「春心」為 Amorous heart「托」為 poured out（傾盆而出），與原詩有一定差異不夠忠實，並對望帝進行了省譯處理，可見譯者把原詩的典故譯得較為模糊，對原詩進行了模糊化處理。戴乃迭、楊憲益從原詩意境出發，將「春心」譯為 amorous heart，省略了「春」；保留了文化意向「望帝」，將「托」譯為 reposed … to，與原詩意思比較接近。劉若愚將「托春心」譯為 consigned his amorous heart in spring to，最貼近典故的意義，在這六個譯本中最忠實。John A. Turner 採用了意譯，難能可貴的是保留了原典故的意境，尤其是 sighed his soul into a bird，頗有詩意。Bynner 保留了原典故的文化意向，將春心譯為 The spring heart，譯得較直，是一個比較不錯的譯法。Graham 整體譯本不錯，只是在個別詞的處理上值得斟酌，如「春心」spring passion「杜鵑」the nightjar（夜鶯）。

3. 藍田日暖玉生煙

　　《元和郡縣志》載「關內道京兆府藍田縣：藍田山，一名玉山，在縣東二十八里。」陸機《文賦》載：「石韞玉而山輝，水懷珠而川媚。」大意是山因其石含玉而熠熠生輝，河流因其中含有珠寶而顯得更加嫵媚。此詩李商隱借用日和玉的關係隱射他和他情人的關係，暗喻情人因他的存在而光彩照人。因此，在譯此詩時，譯者必須把握本典故的內涵，把握不準容易導致誤譯，從而譯文難以理解。在英譯時，譯者應該抓住日與玉的暗喻關係，玉因日而放彩，日與玉相得益彰。

譯者	藍田日暖玉生煙
許淵衝：	From sunburnt emeraldwatch vapor rise!
戴乃迭，楊憲益：	The sun is swarm at Lantian, The jade emits mist.
劉若愚：	At indigo field, the sun warms jade that engenders smoke.
John A. Turner：	Jade mists the sun distils from Sapphire Sward.
Bynner：	Blue fields are breathing their jade to the sun.
Graham：	On BlueMountain the sunwarms, a smoke issues from the jade.

許譯用「sunburnt」來譯日暖,「sunburn」是指「reddening and blistering of the skin caused by being in the sun too much（曬傷的皮膚、曬斑）」,不能較好地體現出日與玉的關係;「菸」應該是指玉放出的光彩因日的照耀玉則熠熠放彩,可以理解為光彩,vapor 指水汽（vapor: moisture or other substance spread about or hanging in the air）,用「vapor」譯「玉」不太確切。戴乃迭、楊憲益則把握了日與玉的關係,將「菸」意譯為「mist」。劉若愚將藍田譯為「indigo field（靛藍色的田）」,未能較好地保留原詩的文化,但很好地把握了日與玉的關係,指出了太陽使玉生輝,將「菸」直譯成「smoke」。John A. Turner 的理解出現了偏差,未能把握好日與玉的關係,誤譯為太陽因玉而放彩。Bynner 是創造性翻譯,譯文中沒有體現出日與玉的關係,而是強調藍田。Graham 雖是直譯,但很好地把握住了日與玉的關係,將「菸」譯為「smoke」,與劉若愚的譯文有異曲同工之妙。

通過幾組典故英譯的比較發現,在典故的翻譯方式上,不同譯者有著自己不同的翻譯方式。有的譯者從字面進行直譯,有的譯者習慣於用直譯再加註釋的方式翻譯,有的譯者則忽略了典故的翻譯,有的譯者則強調對典故的理解再進行翻譯。由於各國的文化差異,各民族人民的宗教信仰、歷史背景、生活習慣和思維方式不盡相同,不同的譯者會採取不同的翻譯方法和策略。但是忠實譯文需要譯者對原文的準確理解,好的理解是佳譯的前提。

翻譯是一種語言和文化的轉換。詩歌翻譯過程中,典故尤其難譯,因為典故承載了一個國家深厚的文化和歷史知識。譯者在翻譯時應該體現出中國特有的民族風格和語言風格,實現文化之間的交流。在翻譯中國詩詞時,譯者首先一定得吃透原文的含義,準確地理解原文。另外,譯者需深刻理解兩種文化的異同。這樣產出的譯文才能引起英美讀者的共鳴,才能更好地把中國文化傳遞出去。

附：不同譯本

The Inlaid Harp（Witter Bynner 譯）

I wonder why my inlaid harp has fifty strings,

Each with its flower-like fret an interval of youth.

The sage Chuangzi is day-dreaming, bewitched by butterflies,

The spring-heart of Emperor Wang is crying in a cuckoo,

Mermen weep their pearly tears down a moon-green sea,

Blue fields are breathing their jade to the sun.

And a moment that ought to have lasted for ever

Has come and gone before I knew.

Jewelled Zither (John Turner 譯)

Vain are the jewelled zither's fifty strings;
Each string, each stop, bears thought of vanished things.
The sage of his loved butterflies day-dreaming;
The king that sighed his soul into a bird;
Tears that are pearls, in ocean moonlight streaming;
Jade mists the sun distils from Sapphire Sward;
What need their memory to recall today?
A day was theirs, which is now passed away.

The Sad Zither (Xu Yuanzhong 譯)

Why should the zither sad have fifty strings?
Each string, each strain evoke but vanished springs.
At dawn the dream to be a butterfly;
At dusk the heart poured out in cuckoo's cry.
In moonlit pearls see tears of mermaid's eyes;
From sun burnt jade in Blue Field let smoke rise!
Such feeling cannot be recalled again,
It seemed long-lost e'en when it was felt then.

第四章　唐詩不同英譯本賞析

　　21世紀是全球化的世紀。新世紀的新人不但應該瞭解全球的文化，而且應該使本國文化走向世界，成為全球文化的一部分，使世界文化更加燦爛輝煌。如果說20世紀是美國世紀的話，那麼，19世紀可以說是英國世紀，18世紀則是法國世紀。再推上去，自7世紀至13世紀，則可以說是中國世紀或唐宋世紀，因為中國在唐代六百年間，政治制度先進，經濟繁榮，文化發達，是全世界其他國家難以企及的。唐代文化昌盛，詩人輩出，唐詩成了中國文化的瑰寶。唐詩包括了深邃的意境、精巧的思想概括、雋永的藝術魅力，使難以接觸的情緒化而為可見可聞，具有有聲有色的形象，對後世的文學發展有著極其深遠的影響。「熟讀唐詩三百首，不會吟詩也會吟」。可見，讀唐詩對提高詩學修養有著不可忽略的作用。因此，古今中外許多翻譯大家都在為唐詩走向世界做著不懈的努力。不但是在中國，就是在全世界，正如諾貝爾文學獎評獎委員會主席埃斯普馬克說的：「世界上哪些作品能與中國的唐詩和《紅樓夢》相比呢？」（《諾貝爾文學獎內幕》306頁）早在19世紀末，英國漢學家翟理斯（Giles）曾把唐詩譯成韻文，得到評論家的好評。英國作家斯特萊徹（Strachey）說：翟譯唐詩是那個時代最好的詩，在世界文學史上佔有獨一無二的地位。但20世紀初期英國漢學家韋利（Waley）認為譯詩用韻會因聲損義，因此他把唐詩譯成自由詩或散體，這就開始了唐詩翻譯史上的詩體與散體之爭。一般說來，散體譯文重真，詩體譯文重美，因此散體與詩體之爭也可以昇華為的真與美的矛盾。唐詩英譯的真與美之爭一直延續到了今天。

　　翻譯難，翻譯唐詩更難。其難就在於它不是一般的創作。創作只需忠於生活，而翻譯除了忠於生活外，還要忠於原文，再現原文風采。在這個意義上說，翻譯也是模仿。臨摹名畫，即使做到以假亂真，也難免在高明的藝術鑒賞家面前露出破綻，何況用一種語言再現作品中另一種語言的意蘊、風格、語調、色彩、形象、意境和韻味。

　　「把中國古詩翻譯成英文是漢譯英中難度最大的一件工作」（徐振忠，

2003)。不過,「詩雖難譯,但還是可譯」,隨著時代的進步、語言的發展和一些新的語言手段的出現,越來越多的優秀的外語人才加入到譯者的行列,詩歌翻譯呈現出一片欣欣向榮的繁榮景象。但是不同的譯者有不同的文化背景、不同的人生閱歷,對原詩意境有不同的理解。這些成功的譯作,也是異彩紛呈,各有千秋,都值得後來者研究、學習。

第一節　李白詩歌英譯賞析

一、《靜夜思》

　　　靜夜思（李白）
床前明月光,疑是地上霜。
舉頭望明月,低頭思故鄉。

譯文一

Nostalgia（翁顯良 譯）

A splash of white on my bedroom floor. Hoarfrost?
I raise my eyes to the moon, the same moon.
As scenes long past come to mind, my eyes fall again on the splash of white,
and my heart aches for home.

譯文二

Quiet Night Thoughts（趙甄陶 譯）

Moonlight before my bed,
Could it be frost instead?
Head up, I watch the moon;
Head down, I think of home.

譯文三

Thoughts in the Silent Night（楊憲益、戴乃迭 譯）

Beside my bed a pool of light,
Is it hoarfrost on the ground?

I lift my eyes and see the moon,
I bend my head and think of home.

譯文四

In the still of the night（徐忠杰 譯）

I descry bright moonlight in front of bed.
I suspect it to be hoary frost on the floor.
I watch the bright moon, as I tilt back my head.
I yearn, while stooping, for my homeland more.

譯文五

Thoughts on a Tranquil Night（許淵衝 譯）

Before my bed a pool of light,
O can it be hoar-frost on the ground?
Looking up, I find the moon bright;
Bowing, in homesickness I'm drowned.
Notes: Seeing a pool of moonlight, the poet is drowned in the pond of homesickness.

譯文六

Homesickness in a Silent Night（屠笛、屠岸 譯）

Before my bed the silver moonbeams spread,
I wonder if it is the frost upon the ground.
I see the moon so bright when raising my head,
Withdrawing my eyes my nostalgia comes around.

譯文七

Still Night Thoughts（Burton Watson 譯）

Moonlight in front of my bed,
I took it for frost on the ground!
I lift my eyes to watch the mountain moon,
Lower them and dream of home.

譯文八

In the Quiet Night (Witter Bynner 譯)

So bright a gleam on the foot of my bed,

Could there have been a frost already?

Lifting myself to look, I found that it was moonlight.

Sinking back again, I thought suddenly of home.

譯文九

Night Thoughts (John Turner 譯)

As by my bed the moon did beam,

It seemed as if with frost the earth were spread.

But soft I raise my head to gaze at the fair moon.

And now, With head bent low,

Of home I dream.

譯文十

Night Thoughts (Herbert A. Giles 譯)

I wake, and moonbeams play around my bed,

Glittering like hoar-frost to my wandering eyes;

Up towards the glorious moon I raise my head,

Then lay me down and thoughts of home arise.

譯文十一

On a Quiet Night (S. Obata 譯)

I saw the moonlight before my couch,

And wondered if it were not the frost on the ground.

I raised my head and looked out on the mountain moon,

I bowed my head and thought of my far-off home.

譯文十二

The Moon Shines Everywhere (W. J. B. Fletcher 譯)

Seeing the Moon before my couch so bright,

I thought hoar frost had fallen from the night.

On her clear face I gaze with lifted eyes:
Then hide them full of Youth's sweet memories.

譯文十三

Night Thoughts（Innes Herdan 譯）

The bright moon shone before my bed,
I wondered was it frost upon the ground?
I raised my head to gaze at the clear moon,
Bowed my head remembering my old home.

譯文十四

Thoughts in a Tranquil Night（L. Cranmer-Byng 譯）

Athwart the bed I watch the moonbeams cast a trail,
So bright, so cold, so frail,
That for a space it gleams,
Like hoar-frost on the margin of my dreams.
I raise my head,
The splendid moon I see:
Then droop my head,
And sink to dreams of thee,
My fatherland, of thee!

譯文十五

Night Thoughts（Amy Lowell 譯）

In front of my bed the moonlight is very bright.
I wonder if that can be frost on the floor?
I lift up my head and look at the full moon, the dazzling moon.
I drop my head, and think of the home of old days.

譯文十六

Calm Night Thought（Ezra Pound 譯）

The moon light is on the floor luminous,
I thought it was frost, it was so white.

Holding up head I look at mountain moon, That makes me lower head,
Lowering head think of old home.

譯文十七

Meditation in a Quiet Night（唐一鶴 譯）

The moon shines brightly in front of my bed.

It was frost on the ground,

I thought and said.

I gaze at the bright moon,

Raising my head.

I miss my native place,

When I bend my head.

譯文十八

Homesickness in a Quiet, Moonlit Night（王大濂 譯）

What bright beams are beside my bed in room!

Could on the ground there be the frost so soon?

Lifting my head I see a big full moon,

Only to bend to think of my sweet home.

譯文十九

In the Quiet of the Night（卓振英、劉筱華 譯）

The ground before my bed presents a stretch of light,

Which seems to be a tract of frost that's pure and bright.

I raise my head: a lonely moon is what I see;

I stoop, and homesickness is crying loud in me!

譯文二十

Thoughts in Night Quiet（David Hinton 譯）

Seeing moonlight here at my bed,

and thinking it's frost on the ground,

I look up, gaze at the mountain moon,

then back, dreaming of my old home.

譯文二十一

Moonlit Night（Rewi Alley 譯）

Over my bed the moonlight streams,

Making it look like frost-covered ground;

Lifting my head I see the brightness,

Then dropping it, and I filled with thoughts of home.

譯文二十二

Meditation on a Quiet Night（Robert Payne 譯）

I see the moonlight shining on my couch.

Can it be that frost has fallen?

I lift my head and watch the mountain moon,

Then my head droops in meditation of earth.

譯文二十三

Quiet Night Thoughts（Sam Hamill 譯）

A pool of moonlight on my bed this late hour,

Like a blanket of frost on the world.

I lift my eyes to a bright mountain moon.

Resigned, remembering my home, I bow.

譯文二十四

Thoughts in a Still Night（孫大雨 譯）

The luminous moonshine before my bed,

Is thought to be the frost fallen on the ground.

I lift my head to gaze at the cliff moon,

And then bow down to muse on my distant home.

譯文二十五

Night Thoughts（Arthur Cooper 譯）

Before my bed there is bright moonlight,

So that it seems like frost on the ground.

Lifting my head I watch the bright moon,
Lowering my head I dream that I'm home.

譯文二十六
Night Meditation（林建民 譯）

In front of my bed flooded with moonbeam,
I mistook for frost appears on the floor;
Lifting my head trying to watch the moon,
I drooped again for missing our hometown.

譯文二十七
Homesick at a Still Night（劉軍平 譯）

A silver moon hangs by the balustrade,
I fancy moonlight as frost on the ground.
Gazing up of the bright moon I'm looking,
Lowering my head of my native land I'm missing.

譯文二十八
Thinking Quietly at Night（朱曼華 譯）

Over my bed is the bright moonlight;
Is the frost painting ground in white?
I raise my head to see the moon bright,
Lower it to picture my home in mind.

譯文二十九
Night Thoughts（Peter Harris 譯）

There were bright moonbeams in front of my bed,
And I mistook them for frost on the ground.
I lifted my head and gazed at the bright moon;
I dropped my head again and thought of home.

譯文三十
Night Thoughts（Soame Jenyns 譯）

In front of my bed there is bright moonlight,

I think there must be hoar frost on the ground;
I raise my head and gaze at the bright moon,
Lowering it I think of the old country.

二、《長干行》

《長干行》（李白）
妾髮初覆額，折花門前劇。
郎騎竹馬來，繞床弄青梅。
同居長干里，兩小無嫌猜。
十四為君婦，羞顏未嘗開。
低頭向暗壁，千喚不一回。
十五始展眉，願同塵與灰。
常存抱柱信，豈上望夫臺！
十六君遠行，瞿塘灩澦堆。
五月不可觸，猿鳴天上哀。
門前遲行跡，一一生綠苔。
苔深不能掃，落葉秋風早。
八月蝴蝶來，雙飛西園草。
感此傷妾心，坐愁紅顏老。
早晚下三巴，預將書報家。
相迎不道遠，直至長風沙。

譯文一

The River-Merchant's Wife （艾茲拉·龐德 譯）

While my hair was still cut straight across my forehead.
I played about the front gate, pulling flowers.
You came by on bamboo stilts, playing horse,
You walked about my seat, playing with blue plums.
And we went on living in the village of Chokan:
Two small people, without dislike or suspicion.
At fourteen I married My Lord you.
I never laughed, being bashful.

Lowering my head, I looked at the wall.

Called to, a thousand times, I never looked back.

At fifteen I stopped scowling,

I desired my dust to be mingled with yours

Forever and forever and forever.

Why should I climb the look out?

At sixteen you departed,

You went into far Ku-to-en, by the river of swirling eddies,

And you have been gone five months.

The monkeys make sorrowful noise overhead.

You dragged your feet when you went out.

By the gate now, the moss is grown, the different mosses,

Too deep to clear them away!

The leaves fall early this autumn, in wind.

The paired butterflies are already yellow with August.

Over the grass in the West garden;

They hurt me. I grow older.

If you are coming down through the narrows of the river Kiang,

Please let me know beforehand,

And I will come out to meet you

As far as Cho-fu-Sa.

譯文二

Ballad of a Merchant's Wife (許淵衝 譯)

My forehead covered by my hair cut straight,

I played with flowers pluck'd before the gate.

On a hobby-horse you came on the scene,

Around the well we played with mums still green.

We lived, close neighbors on Riverside lane.

Carefree and innocent, we children twain.

I was fourteen when I became your young bride,

I'd often turn my bashful face aside,

Hanging my head, I'd look towards the wall,

A thousand times I'd not answer your call.

I was fifteen when I composed my brows,

To fix my dust with yours were my dear vows.

Rather than break faith, you declared you'd die.

Who knew I'd live alone in a tower high?

I was sixteen when you went far away,

Passing Three Canyons studded with rocks gray,

Where ships were wrecked when spring blood ran high,

Where gibbon's wails seemed coming from the sky.

Green moss now overgrows before our door,

Your footprints, hidden, can be seen no more.

Moss can't be swept away: so thick it grows,

And leaves fall early when the west wind blows.

The yellow butterflies in autumn pass,

Two by two o'er our western-garden grass.

The sight would break my heart, and I'm afraid,

Sitting alone, my rosy cheeks would fade.

Sooner or later, you'll leave the western land.

Do not forget to let me know beforehand.

I'll walk to meet you and not call it far,

To go to Long Wind Sands or where you are.

譯文三

Song of Wife in Chang Gang（江紹倫 譯）

While my hair was cut covering my forehead straight,

I played with flowers plucked from my front gate.

Riding on bamboo stilts you entered the scene,

Like a pair of green plums we played together so keen.

As neighbours at Chang Gann Lane,

We shared one another's joy with no guessing.

I was fourteen when I became your loving bride,

Bashful I often cast off any feelings of delight.

Lying sideways I turned to face the wall on my side,

Daring not to respond to your loving calls a thousand times.
At fifteen I opened my brows to find myself,
And decided to be with you in sickness or in health.
You declared to die rather than to betray our ties,
Who would know then I need to look for you all my life.
At sixteen you left to roam afar,
O'er river canyons studded with boulders large.
Where spring tides wreck boats sailing near,
As frightened gibbons wail asking heaven to interfere.
I count your every step outside our door,
Mosses now grow covering them all.
They penetrate so deep no sweeping will clear them away,
Early autumn winds are hurrying leaves to frail.
Butterflies arrive waiting not for August to appear,
They pair to fly all over our garden spheres.
Watching all these hurts my body and soul,
As I sit in solitude waiting to grow old.
One day you may decide to leave the gorges for home,
Do remember to send me a message to let me know.
To meet you I will walk to earth's end,
Stopping not even where winds and sands assault the land.

譯文四

Song of a Merchant's Wife (曾衝明 譯)

When my hair grew just so long as to hide my forehead,
And I begin to play with flowers about the front gate,
Also young, you came to me, riding on a bamboo horse,
And run around a merchant's store with greenish plums.
You and I lived in neighborhood at so-called Long Street;
We both were too young to love or to hate each other then.
I married you, knowing not happiness or sham at fourteen,
But lowering my head all day, I looked at your dim walls.
I never dare reply even if you call me a thousand times.

I made up my mind to be your wife for ever at fifteen,
I swear my dust should be mingled with yours till death.
I would be loyal to you and wish to live with you together.
But at sixteen you left home for business toSichuan Province,
Which is so far and you must passQutang Canyon in danger.
By the river of swirling eddies, especially in May with reefs,
You should bear the sorrowful noise out of monkeys overhead.
It's late fall now and the moss is grown on the door steps,
The thick moss covered your heavy footprints as you lingered.
The leaves fall early in wind to be so thick to clear out.
Come back home, early or late, I'm waiting for you, my dear!
If you are determined to come down through Three Canyons,
Please let me know beforehand and I will come out to meet you,
If I had to walk along the desert for thousands of miles.

譯文五

That Parting at Ch'ang-kan (W. J. B. Fletcher 譯)

When first o'er maiden brows my hair I tied,
In sport I plucked the blooms before the door.
You riding came on hobbyhorse astride,
And wreathed my bed with greengage branches o'er.
At Ch'ang-kan village long together dwelt,
We children twain, and knew no petty strife.
At fourteen years, lo! I became thy wife.
Yet ah! the modest shyness that I felt!
My shamefaced head I in a corner hung;
Nor to long calling answered word of mine.
At fifteen years my heart's gate open sprung,
And I were glad to mix my dustwith thine.
My troth to thee till death I keep for aye:
My eyes still gaze adoring on my lord.
When I was but sixteen you went away.
Heaven pity the voyager dear!

Where we bade each the other farewell at the gate,

The footprints are green with moss now,

Deep moss that clings fast to the unswept steps.

How early the wind strips the bough!

In the eighth moon the butterflies pale their bright hues,

But in pairs they flit through the west glade,

With a pang I remember it, sitting alone,

Old in heart though my cheek does not fade.

But surely, returning, he's made the Big Bend,

And the glad news my ears will soon greet.

If to welcome him alone I went seventy leagues,

I should count the road short, the toil sweet.

譯文六

Ch'ang Kan（Amy Lowell 譯）

When the hair of your Unworthy One first began to cover her forehead,

She picked flowers and played in front of the door.

Then you, my Lover, came riding a bamboo horse.

We ran round and round the bed,

And tossed about the sweetmeats of green plums.

We both lived in thevillage of Ch'ang Kan.

We were both very young, and knew neither jealousy nor suspicion.

At fourteen, I became the wife of my Lord.

I could not yet lay aside my face of shame;

I hung my head, facing the dark wall;

You might call me a thousand times, not once would I turn round.

At fifteen, I stopped frowning.

I wanted to be with you, as dust with its ashes.

I often thought that you were the faithful man who clung to the bridge-post,

That I should never be obliged to ascend to the Looking-for-Husband Ledge.

When I was sixteen, my Lord went far away,

To the Chū Tang Chasm and the Whirling Water Rock of the Yü River.

Which, during the Fifth Month, must not be collided with;

Where the wailing of the gibbons seems to come from the sky.
Your departing footprints are still before the door where I bade you good-bye,
In each has sprung up green moss.
The moss is thick, it cannot be swept away.
The leaves are falling, it is early for the Autumn wind to blow.
It is the Eighth Month, the butterflies are yellow,
Two are flying among the plants in the West garden;
Seeing them, my heart is bitter with grief,
They wound the heart of the Unworthy One.
The bloom of my face has faded, sitting with my sorrow.
From early morning until late in the evening, you descend the Three Serpent River.
Prepare me first with a letter, bringing me the news of when you will reach home.
I will not go far on the road to meet you,
I will go straight until I reach the Long Wind Sands.

譯文七

A Letter From Chang-Kan (S. Obata 譯)

(A river-merchant's wife writes)
I would play, plucking flowers by the gate;
My hair scarcely covered my forehead, then.
You would come, riding on your bamboo horse,
And loiter about the bench with green plums for toys.
So we both dwelt in Chang-kan town,
We were two children, suspecting nothing.
At fourteen I became your wife,
And so bashful that I could never bare my face,
But hung my head, and turned to the dark wall;
You would call me a thousand times,
But I could not look back even once.
At fifteen I was able to compose my eyebrows,
And beg you to love me till we were dust and ashes.
You always kept the faith of Wei-sheng,
Who waited under the bridge, unafraid of death,

I never knew I was to climb the Hill of Wang-fu,

And watch for you these many days.

I was sixteen when you went on a long journey,

Traveling beyond the Keu-Tang Gorge,

Where the giant rocks heap up the swift river,

And the rapids are not passable in May.

Did you hear the monkeys wailing Up on the skyey height of the crags?

Do you know your foot-marks by our gate are old,

And each and every one is filled up with green moss?

The mosses are too deep for me to sweep away;

And already in the autumn wind the leaves are falling.

The yellow butterflies of October Flutter in pairs over the grass of the west garden.

My heart aches at seeing them,

I sit sorrowing alone, and alas!

The vermilion of my face is fading.

Some day when you return down the river,

If you will write me a letter beforehand,

I will come to meet you--the way is not long,

I will come as far as theLong Wind Beach instantly.

譯文八

A Song Of Ch'ang-Kan（Witter Bynner 譯）

My hair had hardly covered my forehead.

I was picking flowers, playing by my door,

When you, my lover, on a bamboo horse,

Came trotting in circles and throwing green plums.

We lived near together on a lane in Ch'ang-kan,

Both of us young and happy-hearted.

At fourteen I became your wife,

So bashful that I dared not smile,

And I lowered my head toward a dark corner

And would not turn to your thousand calls;

But at fifteen I straightened my brows and laughed,

Learning that no dust could ever seal our love.
That even unto death I would await you by my post,
And would never lose heart in the tower of silent watching.
Then when I was sixteen, you left on a long journey,
Through the Gorges of Chü-t'ang, of rock and whirling water.
And then came the Fifth-month, more than I could bear,
And I tried to hear the monkeys in your lofty far-off sky.
Your footprints by our door, where I had watched you go,
Were hidden, every one of them, under green moss,
Hidden under moss too deep to sweep away.
And the first autumn wind added fallen leaves.
And now, in the Eighth-month, yellowing butterflies,
Hover, two by two, in our west-garden grasses.
And, because of all this, my heart is breaking,
And I fear for my bright cheeks, lest they fade.
Oh, at last, when you return through the three Pa districts,
Send me a message home ahead!
And I will come and meet you and will never mind the distance,
All the way to Chang-feng Sha.

三、《月下獨酌》

月下獨酌（李白）
花間一壺酒，獨酌無相親。
舉杯邀明月，對影成三人。
月既不解飲，影徒隨我身。
暫伴月將影，行樂須及春。
我歌月徘徊，我舞影零亂。
醒時同交歡，醉後各分散。
永結無情遊，相期邈雲漢。

譯本一

Last Words（Herbert A. Giles 譯）

An arbor of flowers and a kettle of wine:
Alas! In the bowers no companion is mine.
Then the moon sheds her rays on my goblet and me,
And my shadow betrays we're a party of three!
Thou' the moon cannot swallow her share of the grog,
And my shadow must follow wherever I jog,
Yet their friendship I'll borrow and gaily carouse,
And laugh away sorrow while spring-time allows.
See the moon-how she dances response to my song;
See my shadow-it dances so lightly along!
While sober I feel, you are both my good friends;
While drunken I reel, our companionship ends.
But we'll soon have a greeting without a goodbye,
At our next merry meeting away in the sky.

譯本二

Amongst the flowers is a pot of wine（Ezra Pound 譯）

Amongst the flowers is a pot of wine,
I pour alone but with no friend at hand.
So I lift the cup to invite the shining moon,
Along with my shadow we become party of three.
The moon although understands none of drinking,
And the shadow just follows my body vainly.
Still I make the moon and the shadow my company,
To enjoy the springtime before too late.
The moon lingers while I am singing,
The shadow scatters while I am dancing.
We cheer in delight when being awake,
We separate apart after getting drunk.
Forever will we keep this unfettered friendship,
Till we meet again far in the Milky Way.

譯本三

Drinking Alone by Moonlight（Arthur Waley 譯）

A cup of wine, under the flowering trees;
I drink alone, for no friend is near.
Raising my cup I beckon the bright moon,
For he, with my shadow, will make three men.
The moon, alas, is no drinker of wine;
Listless, my shadow creeps about at my side.
Yet with the moon as friend and the shadow as slave,
I must make merry before the Spring is spent.
To the songs I sing the moon flickers her beams;
In the dance I weave my shadow tangles and breaks.
While we were sober, three shared the fun;
Now we are drunk, each goes his way.
May we long share our odd, inanimate feast,
And meet at last on the Cloudy River of the sky.

譯本四

We Three（W. J. B. Fletcher 譯）

One pot of wine amid the Flowers,
Alone I pour, and none with me.
The cup I lift; the Moon invite;
Who with my shadow makes us three.
The moon then drinks without a pause.
The shadow does what I begin.
The shadow, Moon and I in fere,
Rejoice until the spring come in.
I sing: and wavers time the moon.
I dance: the shadow antics too.
Our joys we share while sober still.
When drunk, we part and bid adieu.
Of loveless outing this the pact,

Which we all swear to keep for aye.

The next time that we meet shall be

Beside yon distant milky way.

譯本五

On Drinking Alone by Moonlight（W. A. P. Martin 譯）

Here are flowers and here is wine,

But where's a friend with me to join.

Hand in hand and heart to heart,

In one full cup before we part?

Rather than to drink alone,

I'll make bold to ask the moon,

To condescend to lend her face,

The hour and the scene to grace.

Lo, she answers, And she brings my shadow on her silver wings;

That makes three, and we shall be.

I ween, a merry company,

The modest moon declines the cup,

But shadow promptly takes it up,

And when I dance my shadow fleet,

Keeps measure with my flying feet.

But though the moon declines to tipple,

She dances in yon shining ripple,

And when I sing, my festive song,

The echoes of the moon prolong.

Say, when shall we next meet together?

Surely not in cloudy weather,

For you my boon companions dear,

Come only when the sky is clear.

譯本六

Drinking Alone in the Moonlight（Florence Ayscough & Amy Lowell 譯）

A pot of wine among flowers.

I alone, drinking, without a companion.

I lift the cup and invite the bright moon.

My shadow opposite certainly makes us three.

But the moon cannot drink,

And my shadow follows the motions of my body in vain.

For the briefest time are the moon and my shadow my companions.

Oh, be joyful! One must make the most of Spring.

I sing, the moon walks forward rhythmically;

I dance, and my shadow shatters and becomes confused.

In my waking moments we are happily blended.

When I am drunk, we are divided from one another and scattered.

For a long time I shall be obligated to wander without intention.

But we will keep our appointment by the far-off Cloudy River.

譯本七

Three with the Moon and his Shadow（S. Obata 譯）

With a jar of wine I sit by the flowering trees.

I drink alone, and where are my friends?

Ah, the moon above looks down on me;

I call and lift my cup to his brightness.

And see, there goes my shadow before me.

Ho! We're a party of three, I say,

Though the poor moon can't drink,

And my shadow but dances around me,

We're all friends tonight,

The drinker, the moon and the shadow.

Let our revelry be suited to the spring!

I sing, the wild moon wanders the sky.

I dance, my shadow goes tumbling about.

While we're awake, let us join in carousal;

Only sweet drunkenness shall ever part us.

Let us pledge a friendship no mortals know,

And often hail each other at evening,

Far across the vast and vaporous space!

譯本八

Drinking Alone with the Moon（Witter Bynner 譯）

From a pot of wine among the flowers.

I drank alone, There was no one with me—

Till, raising my cup, I asked the bright moon,

To bring me my shadow and make us three.

Alas, the moon was unable to drink,

And my shadow tagged me vacantly;

But still for a while I had these friends,

To cheer me through the end of spring.

I sang. The moon encouraged me.

I danced. My shadow tumbled after.

As long as I knew, we were boon companions.

And then I was drunk, and we lost one another.

Shall goodwill ever be secure?

I watch the long road of the River of Stars.

譯本九

The Little Fete（J. C. Cooper 譯）

I take a bottle of wine and I go to drink it among the flowers.

We are always three,

Counting my shadow and my friend the shimmering moon.

Happily the moon knows nothing of drinking,

And my shadow is never thirsty.

When I sing, the moon listens to me in silence.

When I dance, my shadow dances too.

After all festivities the guests must depart;

This sadness I do not know.

When I go home,

the moon goes with me and my shadow follows me.

譯本十

Drinking Alone Under the Moon（Burton Watson 譯）

A jug of wine among flowers,

I drink alone, for there's no companion.

I raise the cup and invite the moon,

With my shadow we become three.

Of course the moon does not understand drinking;

The shadow purposelessly traces my body.

But I accompany the moon and the shadow anyway,

The pursuit of pleasures must continue until the spring.

The moon wanders as I sing;

The shadow rattles when I dance.

Still sober, we share our joys;

After drunk, each goes its way.

Permanently joined for feelingless journeys,

Perhaps to the remote Milky Way.

譯本十一

Drinking Alone by Moonlight（Stephen Owen 譯）

Here among flowers one flask of wine,

With no close friends, I pour it alone.

I lift cup to bright moon, beg its company,

then facing my shadow, we become three.

The moon has never known how to drink;

my shadow does nothing but follow me.

But with moon and shadow as companions a while,

this joy I find must catch spring while it's here.

I sing, and the moon just lingers on;

I dance, and my shadow flails wildly.

When still sober we share friendship and pleasure,

Then, utterly drunk, each goes his own way,

Let us join to roam beyond human cares,

And plan to meet far in the river of stars.

譯本十二

Drinking Alone under the Moon（許淵衝 譯）

Amid the flowers, from a pot of wine,
I drink alone beneath the bright moonshine.
I raise my cup to invite the Moon who blends,
Her light with my Shadow and we're three friends.
The Moon does not know how to drink her share;
In vain my Shadow follows me here and there.
Together with them for the time I stay
And make merry before spring's spent away.
I sing and the Moon lingers to hear my song;
My Shadow's a mess while I dance along.
Sober, we three remain cheerful and gay;
Drunken, we part and each may go his way.
Our friendship will outshine all earthly love,
Next time we'll meet beyond the stars above.

譯本十三

Drinking Alone under the Moon（孫大雨 譯）

With a jug of wine among the flowers,
I drink alone sans company.
To the moon aloft I raise my cup,
With my shadow to form a group of three.
As the moon doth not drinking ken,
And shadow mine followeth my body,
I keep company with them twain,
While spring is here to make myself merry.
The moon here lingereth while I sing,
I dance and my shadow spreadeth in rout.
When sober I am, we jolly remain,
When drunk I become, we scatter all about.
Let's knit our carefree tie of the good old day;

We may meet above sometime at the milky way.

譯本十四
Drinking Alone under the Moon（林語堂 譯）
A pot of wine amidst the flowers,
Alone I drink sans company.
The moon I invite as drinking friend,
And with my shadow we are three.
The moon, I see, she does not drink,
My shadow only follows me;
I'll keep them company a while,
For spring's time for gayety.
I sing: the moon she swings her head;
I dance: my shadow swells and sways.
We sport together while I awake,
While drunk, we all go our own ways.
An eternal, speechless trio then,
Till in the clouds we meet again!

四、《送友人》

送友人（李白）
青山橫北郭，白水繞東城。
此地一為別，孤蓬萬里征。
浮雲遊子意，落日故人情。
揮手自茲去，蕭蕭班馬鳴。

譯文一
Taking Leave of a Friend（Ezra Pound 譯）
Blue mountains to the north of the walls,
White river winding about them;
Here we must make separation,
And go out through a thousand miles of dead grass.

Mind like a floating wide cloud.

Sunset like the parting of old acquaintance.

Who bow over their clasped hands at a distance.

Our horses neigh to each other as we are departing.

譯文二

A Farewell（A. Giles 譯）

Where blue hills cross the northern sky,

Beyond the moat which girds the town,

Twas there we stopped to say Goodbye!

And one white sail alone dropped down,

Your heart was full of wondering thought;

For me, my sun had set indeed;

To wave a last adieu we thought,

Voiced for us by each whinnying steed!

譯文三

Adieu（W. J. B. Fletcher 譯）

Athwart the northern gate the green hills swell,

White water round the eastern city flows.

When once we here have bade a long farewell,

Your lone sail struggling up the current goes.

Those floating clouds are like the wanderer's heart,

Yon sinking sun recalls departed days.

Your hand waves us adieu; and lo! You start,

And dismally your horse retiring neighs.

譯文四

Taking Leave of a Friend（S. Obata 譯）

Blue mountains lie beyond the north wall;

Round the city's eastern side flows the white water.

Here we part, friend, once forever.

You go the thousand miles, drifting away

Like an unrooted water-grass.
Oh, the floating clouds and thoughts of wanderer!
Oh, the sunset and the longing of an old friend!
We ride away from each other, waving our hands,
While our horses neigh softly, softly.

譯文五

A Farewell to a Friend（Witter Bynner 譯）
With a blue line of mountains north of the wall,
And east of the city a white curve of water,
Here you must leave me and drift away,
Like a loosened water-plant hundreds of miles.
I shall think of you in a floating cloud;
So in the sunset think of me.
We wave our hands to say good-bye,
And my horse is neighing again and again.

譯文六

Farewell to a Friend（許淵衝 譯）
Green mountains bar the northern sky;
White water girds the eastern town.
Here is the place to say good-bye;
You'll drift like lonely thistledown.
Like floating cloud you'll float away;
With parting day I'll part from you.
We wave and you start on our way;
Your horse still neighs:「Adieu, adieu!」

五、《早發白帝城》

早發白帝城（李白）
朝辭白帝彩雲間，千里江陵一日還。
兩岸猿聲啼不住，輕舟已過萬重山。

譯文一

Leaving the White Emperor Town at Dawn (許淵衝 譯)

Leaving at dawn the White Emperor crowned with cloud.
I've sailed a thousand miles through canyons in a day.
With monkeys' sad adieus the river banks are loud:
My skiff has left ten thousand mountains far away.

譯文二

Set off from White Emperor Town at Morn (Peter Cooper 譯)

From White Emperor Town in rosy clouds I leave at morn,
Down for Jiang Ling thousand miles away I reach in a day.
Along the Yangzi River comes the continuous apes' moan;
Unawares, my wherry's flown o'er lofty mountains in brisk way.

Notes: a. White Emperor Town: A town located on the top of Mount White Emperor in Chongqing, China.

b. Jiang Ling: A county of Hu Bei Province.

譯文三

Homeward! (翁顯良 譯)

Good bye to the city high in the rosy clouds of dawn.
Homeward, out the gorges, out today!
Let the apes wail. Go on.
Out shoots my boat. The serried mountains are all behind.

譯文四

The River Journey from White King City (Obsta 譯)

At dawn I left the walled city of White King,
Towering among the many-coloured clouds;
And came down stream in a day,
One thousand li to Jiangling.
The screams of monkeys on either bank,
Had scarcely ceased echoing in my ear.

When my skiff had left behind it,
Ten thousand ranges of hills.

譯文五

Sailing from White King Town（王大濂 譯）

Having left White King Town at dawn, where red clouds play;
I'm back to Jiangling through sailing long miles one day.
With monkey's cried along both banks still ringing in my ears,
My skiff has passed by mountains, one and all, in cheers.

譯文六

Starting from White King Town at Down（曾衝明 譯）

My journey starts at dawn from this high town amid the clouds,
Through Three Gorges my boat arrives at Jiang Ling this night.
As I hear monkeys cry without stopping on the mountainous banks,
Through the thousands of hills the swift boat has already sailed.

譯文七

Quitting Poti at Dawn（W. J. B. Fletcher 譯）

Poti amid its rainbow clouds we quitted with the dawn,
A thousand li in one day's space to Kiang-ling are borne.
Ere yet the gibbon's howling along the banks was still,
All through the cragged Gorge our skiff had fleeted with the morn.

譯文八

Through the Yangzi Gorges（Witter Bynner 譯）

From the walls of Baidi high in the coloured dawn,
To Jiangling by night-fall is three hundred miles.
Yet monkeys are still calling on both banks behind me,
To my boat these ten thousand mountains away.

譯文九

Embarking fromBaidi Town at Early Morn（孫大雨 譯）

Leaving Baidi on high at down,

Among the clouds in blaze gay.
A thousand li to Jiangling City
I sped within a day.
Unceasingly the gibbons screeched,
On both banks of the River,
As my light skiff shot through the folds,
Of mounts ten thousand with a whirr.

六、《黃鶴樓送孟浩然之廣陵》

　黃鶴樓送孟浩然之廣陵（李白）
故人西辭黃鶴樓，煙花三月下揚州。
孤帆遠影碧空盡，唯見長江天際流。

譯文一

Seeing Meng Hao-Ran off at Yellow Crane Tower（許淵衝 譯）

My friend has left the west where the Yellow Crane towers;
For River Town green with willows and red with flowers.
His lessening sail is lost in the boundless blue sky;
Where I see but the endless River rolling by.

譯文二

Seeing Meng Haoran Off from Yellow Crane（楊憲益、戴乃迭 譯）

At Yellow Crane Tower in the west my old friend says farewell;
In the mist and flowers of spring he goes down to Yangzhou;
Lonely sail, distant shadow, vanish in blue emptiness;
All I see is the great river flowing into the far horizon.

譯本三

Seeing Meng Haoran Off to Guangling on the Yellow Crane Tower（孫大雨 譯）

Mine old friend leaveth the West,
From the Yellow Crane Tower.
In this flowery April clime,

For thickly peopled Yangzhou.
A solitary sail's distant speck,
Vanisheth in the clear blue:
What could be seen heavenward,
Flowing is but the Long River.

譯文四

A Farewell Song to Meng Haoran at Yellow Crane Tower（王大濂 譯）

From west Crane Tower my friend is on his way,
Down to Yangzhou in misty, flowery May.
A sail's faint figure dots the blue sky's end,
Where seen but River rolling till its bend.

譯本五

Saying Goodbye to Meng Haoran at the Yellow Crane Tower（Roger Mason 譯）

Goodbye, old friend, at the Yellow Crane Tower,
As eastward in April, Yangzhou bursts in flower.
Your sail fades in the distance against the blue sky,
And to the horizon, theGreat River flows by.

譯文六

At Yellow Crane Tower Taking Leave of Meng Hao-jun as He Sets Off for Kuang-ling（Burton Waston 譯）

My old friend takes leave of the west at Yellow Crane Tower,
In misty third-month blossoms goes downstream to Yang-chou.
The far-off shape of his lone sail disappears in the blue-green void,
And all I see is the long river flowing to the edge of the sky.

譯文七

Farewell on seeing Meng Haojan off fromBrown Crane Tower as he took his departure for Kuangling（John A. Turner 譯）

And so, dear friend, at Brown Crane Tower you,
Bidding the west adieu,

Mid April mists and blossoms go,
Till in the vast blue-green.
Your lonely sail's far shade no more is seen,
Only on the sky's verge the River's flow.

譯文八
A Farewell to Meng Haoran on His Way to Yangzhou（Witter Bynner 譯）
You have left me behind, old friend, at the Yellow Crane Terrace,
On your way to visit Yangzhou in the misty month of flowers;
Your sail, a single shadow, becomes one with the blue sky,
Till now I see only the river, on its way to heaven.

譯文九
Seeing Meng Haoran Off to Kuangling（Paul Kroll 譯）
My old friend, going west, bids farewell at Yellow Crane Terrace,
Among misty blossoms of the third month, goes down to Yang-chou.
His long sail's far shadow vanishes into the azure void,
Now, only the Long River flowing to the sky's end.

七、《清平調》

清平調·其一（李白）
雲想衣裳花想容，
春風扶檻露華濃。
若非群玉山頭見，
會向瑤臺月下逢。

清平調·其二（李白）
一枝紅豔露凝香，
雲雨巫山枉斷腸。
借問漢宮誰得似？
可憐飛燕倚新妝。

清平調·其三（李白）
名花傾國兩相歡，
長得君王帶笑看。
解釋春風無限恨，
沉香亭北倚闌干。

譯文一

Pure Peace Tune（趙彥春 譯）

Her clothes like plumage and her face a rose,
Breeze pets the rails and the belle in repose.
If not a fairy queen from Heav'n on high,
She's Goddess of Moon that makes flowers shy.

A rosebud red glistens with fragrant dew,
Such nymphs, on earth or Heav'n, are really few.
The oread Duke Xiang craved couldn't compare,
Lady Zhao, to shine, new clothes had to wear.

The rose and reigning belle smile each to each;
His Majesty's eyes make a happy reach.
Thus dissolves the melancholy of breeze.
Amidst the balm they lean on rail at ease.

譯文二

The Beautiful Lady Yang（秦大川 譯）

Cloud is likened to the dress, and flower the mien of thee,
The dewy flower gleams over the balcony in vernal breeze.
If not seen among the wondrous Jadite Mountains,
From the moonlit celestial palace you must be.

A spray of brilliant red soaked in dew is so sweet;
Vainly do the fabled lovers painfully weep.
Who can match you, even from the old Han Palace?

Flipping Swallow depended but on her new piece.

Th' flower and the crushing beauty in each other rejoice,
Alway winning the monach's gaze in smiling glee.
The endless woeful cares are blowing in the spring wind;
On the rails north of Aloe Arbour you lean at ease.

譯文三

Three Songs of the Beauty (曾衝明 譯)
Her dress is like a cloud and her pretty face a rose.
She shows beauty when vernal breeze kisses railings.
The beauty and the beautiful picture must be found,
Either at Fairy Terrace or Jade Mount in moonlight.

A red peony shows its fragrance and its beauty,
The Goddess is sorrowful in vain on Wu Mount.
Who in the palace of Xan Dynasty could do so?
It is only Zhao Feiyan known as Flying Swallow.

This flower and this beauty are both famous and delightful,
The latter was often favorited by the Emperor with smiles.
The vernal breeze might get rid of her boundless sorrows.
She'd lean on the raillings north of the Pavilion beautiful.

八、《怨情》

怨情（李白）
美人卷珠簾，
深坐顰蛾眉。
但見淚痕濕，
不知心恨誰。

譯文一

Waiting In Vain（許淵沖 譯）

A lady fair uprolls the screen,

With eyebrows knit she waits in vain.

Wet stains of tears can still be seen.

Who, heartless, has caused her the pain?

譯文二

Tears（Herbert A. Giles 譯）

A fair girl draws the blind aside,

And sadly sits with drooping head;

I see her burning tear-drops glide,

But know not why those tears are shed.

譯文三

Passionate Grief（Amy Lowell 譯）

Beautiful is this woman who rolls up the pearl-reed blind.

She sits in an inner chamber,

And her eyebrows, delicate as a moth's antennae,

Are drawn with grief.

One sees only the wet lines of tears.

For whom does she suffer this misery?

We do not know.

第二節　杜甫詩歌英譯賞析

一、《春望》

春望（杜甫）

國破山河在，城春草木深。

感時花濺淚，恨別鳥驚心。

烽火連三月，家書抵萬金。

白頭搔更短，渾欲不勝簪。

譯文一

Spring View（許淵衝 譯）

On war-torn land streams flow and mountains stand;
In vernal town grass and weeds are overgrown.
Grieved over the years, flowers make us shed tears;
Hating to part, hearing birds breaks our heart.
The beacon fire has gone higher and higher;
Words from household are worth their weight in gold.
I cannot bear to scratch my grizzled hair;
It grows too thin to hold a light hairpin.

譯文二

Spring Scene（Wai-Lim Yip 譯）

All ruins, the empire; mountains and rivers in view.
To the city, spring: grass and trees so thick.
The times strike. Before flowers, tears break loose.
Separation cuts. Birds startle our heart.
Beacon fires continued for three months on end.
A letter from home is worth thousands of gold pieces.
White hair, scratched, becomes thinner and thinner.
So thin it can hardly hold a pin.

譯文三

Spring View（Gary Snyder 譯）

The nation is ruined, but mountains and rivers remain.
This spring the city is deep in weeds and brush.
Touched by the times even flowers weep tears.
Fearing leaving the birds tangled hearts.
Watch-tower fires have been burning for three months.
To get a note from home would cost ten thousand gold.
Scratching my white hair thinner.

Seething hopes all in a trembling hairpin.

譯文四

Spring Prospect（Burton Watson 譯）

The nation shattered, hills and streams remain.

The city in spring, grass and trees deep:

Feeling the times, flowers draw tears;

Hating separation, birds alarm the heart.

Beacon fires three months running,

A letter from home worth ten thousand in gold.

White hairs, fewer for the scratching,

Soon too few to hold a hairpin up.

譯文五

Spring—Looking into the Distance（Florence Ayscough 譯）

The State is destroyed; hills, rivers remain;

Spring: within the city wall, grass, trees are thick.

Emotion, fitting to the season; flowers bring a rush of tears;

I hate being cut apart; the song of birds quickens my heart.

Beacon fires burn incessantly; their flames connect this Third Moon with that of last year;

A letter from home would be worth ten thousand ounces of gold.

I scratch my white head; the hair is shorter than ever;

It is matted; I should like to knot it, but cannot succeed in thrusting through the jade hair-pin.

二、《望岳》

望岳（杜甫）

岱宗夫如何，齊魯青未了。

造化鍾神秀，陰陽割昏曉。

蕩胸生層雲，決眦入歸鳥。

會當凌絕頂，一覽眾山小。

譯文一

Looking up at Mountain Tai (何功杰 譯)

What a majestic sight of holy Mountain Tai!

Vast greens stretch across Qi and Lu, the two lands high.

The Maker endowed all the mystic Nature grace here,

And a day at once into dawn and dusk comes by.

Colorful clouds lave my bosom free and easy,

And the birds fly back and forth before my strained eye.

Once climbing to the top of the peek, one would see.

The other mountains all appear dwarfs under the sky.

譯文二

Gazing at the Great Mount (John A. Turner 譯)

To what shall compare,

The sacred Mount that stands,

A balk of green that hath no end.

Betwixt two lands!

Nature did fuse and blend,

All mystic beauty there,

Where Dark and Light,

Do dusk and dawn unite.

Gazing, soul-cleansed, at Thee.

From clouds upsprung,

one may Mark with wide eyes the homing flight of birds.

Some day must I thy topmost height Mount,

At one glance to see Hills numberless Dwindle to nothingness.

譯文三

Gazing at Mount Tai (許淵衝 譯)

O Peck of Pecks, how high it stands!

Once boundless green o'erspreads two States.

A marvel done by Nature's hands,

O'er light and shade it dominates.
Clouds rise therefrom and lave my breast;
I strain my eyes and see birds fleet.
I must ascend the mountain's crest;
It dwarfs all peaks under my feet.

三、《登高》

登高（杜甫）
風急天高猿嘯哀，渚清沙白鳥飛回。
無邊落木蕭蕭下，不盡長江滾滾來。
萬里悲秋常作客，百年多病獨登臺。
艱難苦恨繁霜鬢，潦倒新停濁酒杯。

譯文一

On the Height（許淵衝 譯）

The wind so swift, the sky so wide, apes wail and cry;
Water so clear and beach so white, birds wheel and fly.
The boundless forest sheds its leaves shower by shower;
The endless river rolls its waves hour after hour.
A thousand miles from home, I'm grieved at autumn's plight;
Ill now and then for years, alone I'm on this height.
Living in times so hard, at frosted hair I pine;
Cast down by poverty, I have to give up wine.

譯文二

Climbing a Terrace（楊憲益、戴乃迭 譯）

Wind blusters high in the sky and monkeys wail;
Clear the islet with white sand where birds are wheeling;
Everywhere the leaves fall rustling from the trees,
While on for ever rolls the turbulent Yangtze.
All around is autumnal gloom and I, long from home,
A prey all my life to ill heath, climb the terrace alone;

Hating the hardships which have frosted my hair,

Sad that illness has made me give up the solace of wine.

譯文三

The Heights (W. J. B. Fletcher 譯)

The wind so fresh, the sky so high,

Awake the gibbons' wailing cry.

The islet clear-cut, the sand so white,

Arrest the wheeling sea-gulls' flight.

Through endless space with rustling sound,

The falling leaves are whirled around.

Beyond my ken a yeasty sea.

The Yangtze's waves are rolling free.

From far away, in autumn drear,

I find myself a stranger here.

With dragging years and illness wage.

Lone war upon this lofty stage.

With troubles vexed and trials sore

My locks are daily growing hoar:

Till Time, before whose steps I pine,

Set down this failing cup of wine!

譯文四

Written on an Autumn Holiday (Rewi Alley 譯)

These days of autumn, the clouds Are high; wind rises in strength;

Far away the cry of monkeys can Be heard, giving people a sorrowful

Feeling;

Skimming the white sands And the water, waterfowl fly;

Falling Leaves rustle as they come through

The air;

The Yangtse seems endless

With its waters rolling on incessantly;

So many autumns have I now spent Away from home, with sickness for

A companion;

Now do I climb high Above the river by myself,

Troubles and sorrow have turned my hair Grey;

Sick and poor, I now Even stop drinking wine!

譯文五

I Climb High (Florence 譯)

Wind is strong, sky is high, gibbons wail sadly;

Shoals are bright, sand gleam white, birds fly in circles.

Without bounds is the forest, leaves fall, swish, swish, they drop;

No ending has Great River, swirl, swirl, it comes.

Ten thousand li sad Autumn! Have been long a wanderer;

A hundred years, many illnesses! Alone I climb the tower.

Sorrows, hardships, bitterness, grief, thickly frosted hair on my brows,

Inert I sink to ground; all fellowship ended; I drink muddy wine in my cup.

譯文六

A Long Climb (Witter Bynner 譯)

In a sharp gale from the wide sky apes are whimpering,

Birds are flying homeward over the clear lake and white sand,

Leaves are dropping down like the spray of a waterfall,

While I watched the long river always rolling on.

I have come three miles away. Sad now with autumn.

And with my hundred years of woe, I climb this height alone.

Ill fortune has laid a bitter frost on my temples,

Heart-ache and weariness are a thick dust in my wine.

譯文七

Climbing on the Double Ninth Day (Wai-Lim Yip 譯)

Shrill winds, high sky, monkeys' heart-reading cry.

Clear river, white sand, birds soar and wheel.

Leaves, leaves of a rimless forest rustle down.

Waves upon waves, the endless Yangtze comes drumming in.

A million miles of grievous autumn, constantly a traveler.
Entire life in sickness; I alone climb up the terrace.
Hardships, bitter regrets propagates my frosty hair.
Wretched! That I have recently stopped going for the cup!

譯文八

Climbing the Heights（謝文通 譯）

Swift wind and a high ceiling mournful the monkeys sound,
From island to white beach the birds are wheeling round.
Everywhere falling leaves fall rustling to,
The waves of the Long River onrushing without bound.
Who grieves for Autumn a thousand miles from home.
Despite lifelong illness I climb the terrace alone.
Hardships and bitterness frosting many a hair,
I abjure the cup of wine that stopped my moan.

譯文九

On the Heights（李惟建 譯；翁顯良 校）

High wind blowing, high clouds floating, gibbons wailing,
Sandbars gleaming white, the waters rippling clear,
Birds coming home, leaves rustling down,
And the great river rolls on, ceaseless.
A stranger here, far, far, from home,
I can't help feeling sad in autumn.
Life is short, my health failing, here I stand alone.
Life is hard, my temples greying,
I'm filled with regret.
Down and out, can't even drink now,
Can't even drink now.

譯文十

Ascent（章學清 譯）

The wind so wild, the sky so high,

The moody monkeys sorely sigh.
The isle so drear, the sand so pale,
The lingering gulls in circles sail.
All over such a vast expanse,
The rustling leaves off branches dance.
The Yangtse River rises yon,
And passes raging on and on.
Apart from home so far and long,
With autumn, myriad sorrows throng.
With illness all my life to fight,
I now alone ascend this height.
Weighed down in troubled times with care,
I hate the growing hoary hair.
A broken heart, for cups I pine;
Oh, if my health permitted wine!

譯文十一

An Ascent（徐忠杰 譯）
A stiff breeze is up; the vault of heaven seems high.
Monkeys on the hills are making their plaintive cry.
The islets become clearer; the sandbanks, clean and white;
Water-birds are hovering over them in their flight.
For miles around, rustling leaves are falling without pause.
The Yang-tze-kiang is tumbling on in its onward course.
Far from home, autumn strikes me as adding to my grief.
An invalid, I mount the heights alone for relief.
Long suffering has left its cruel mark on my hair.
I've ceased anew to drink in utter despair.

譯文十二

Mounting（吳鈞陶 譯）
From heaven high the winds are whirling down with monkey's whine,
And over the white sanded hursts the birds are cleaving fine.

The boundless forests shed their yellow leaves with rustles;
The everflowing Yangtze on its way rolls and wrestles.
Autumn is chilling me-always a thousand-miles-roameer,
Alone mounting the mountain, and a life-long sufferer.

譯文十三

Ascending a Height (秦大川 譯)

The swift gusts, vaulted sky and wails of apes,
The clean shoal, white sand and birds on their way.
Boundless tree leaves fall drear and desolate;
The infinite Yangtse rolls forth wave on wave.
Oft a world rover, lamenting the fall days,
I scale the terrace by myself, ill and aged.
Hardship and pain have my hair whiter turned,
Down and out, I've quited coarse brew of late.

譯文十四

Reciting My Poem at a High Terrace (曾衝明 譯)

The winds blow strong in the sky,
The monkeys in mountains all cry;
The islet is brilliant with sand white,
Gulls fly all around over the riverside.
Leaves fall off endless woods rustling.
Waves roll in the Yangtse River roaming.
I've left home so far away as a stranger.
Climbing a high terrace alone in sad fall.
My temples grow white because of hardships,
And along with hatred as well as sorrows.
In such a condition I have to abandon,
Even a cup of muddy wine once again.

四、《春夜喜雨》

春夜喜雨（杜甫）
好雨知時節，當春乃發生。
隨風潛入夜，潤物細無聲。
野徑雲俱黑，江船火獨明。
曉看紅濕處，花重錦官城。

譯文一

Spring Night, Delighting in Rain（Burton Watson 譯）

The good rain knows when to fall,
Stirring new growth the moment spring arrives.
Wind-borne, it steals softly into the night,
Nourishing, enriching, delicate, and soundless.
Country paths black as the clouds above them;
On a river boat a lone torch flares.
Come dawn we'll see a landscape moist and pink,
Blossoms heavy over the City of Brocade.

譯文二

Rain On A Spring Night（David Young 譯）

Congratulations, rain,
You know when to fall coming at night.
Quiet walking in the wind,
Making sure things get good and wet.
The clouds hang dark over country roads,
There's one light from a boat coming down river in the morning。
Everything's dripping red flowers everywhere.

譯文三

A Spring Night-Rejoycing in Rain（William H. Nienhauser 譯）

A good rain knows its season,

Comes forth in spring.

Follows the wind, steals into the night;

Glossing nature, delicate without a sound.

Clouds on country road, all black,

Sparks of a lantern from a river boat, the only light.

Morning will see red steeped spots:

Flowers heavy on the City ofBrocade.

譯文四

Good Rain on a Spring Night（Rewi Alley 譯）

A good rain falling Just when it should,

In springtime riding

On the wind it falls,

A whole night, soaking.

The land with its goodness;

Clouds hang heavily over Country paths;

A lone light Shines from a passing boat;

Morning and I see a damp Redness on the branches,

Laden down with flowers.

譯文五

Spring Night, Happy Rain（Florence Ayscough 譯）

Happy rain knows time and season;

Should come in Spring, cause life to rise.

Borne on wind, secretly it enters night;

Soaks all growing things, is fine without sound.

On path in outskirts, clouds all black;

On boat in river, light shines lone.

At dawn see places where vermilion blooms are wet,

Flowers hang heavy in Embroidered Official City.

譯文六

The Kindly Rain（W. J. B. Fletcher 譯）

The kindly rain its proper season knows.
With gentle Spring aye born in fitting hour.
Along the Wind with cloaking Night it goes.
Enmoistening, fine, inaudible it flows.
The clouds the mountain paths in darkness hide.
And lonely bright the vessels' lanterns glower.
Dawn shows how damp the blushing buds divide,
And flowers droop head-heavy in each bower.

譯文七

The Little Rain（L. Cranmer-Byng 譯）

Oh, she is good, the little rain!
And well she knows our need.
Who cometh in the time of spring to aid the sun-drawn seed;
She wanders with a friendly wind through silent nights unseen,
The furrows feel her happy tears, and lo!
The land is green.
Last night cloud shadows gloomed the path that winds to my abode,
And the torches of the river-boats like angry meteors glowed.
Today fresh colors break the soil, and butterflies take wing.
Down broidered lawns all bright with pearls in the garden of the King.

譯文八

Rejoicing in Rain on a Spring Night（謝文通 譯）

The good rain knows its season when to fall,
As it does whenever Spring comes round.
Stealing into the night behind the wind,
To moisten all things fine without a sound.
On country paths the clouds are a dark pall,
The river boats pinpoint with light for a foil.
At dawn we see on the trail of sodden pink,

The flowers hang heavy from the city wall.

譯文九

Welcome Rain One Spring Night（楊憲益、戴乃迭 譯）

A good rain knows its season,

And comes when spring is here;

On the heels of the wind it slips secretly into the night,

Silent and soft, it moistens everything.

Now clouds hang black above the country roads,

A lone boat on the river sheds a glimmer of light;

At dawn we shall see splashes of rain-washed red,

Drenched, heavy blooms in the City of Brocade.

譯文十

Happy Rain（翁顯良 譯）

Happy rain comes not by happy chance; of spring's return it's well aware.

Soft as the breeze, quiet as the night, it soothes the thirsting multitudes.

Out there, the fields, the paths, by dark clouds blanketed; Here in my river boat, the only light, burning bright.

Morning reveals glistening spots of crimson: flowers, heavily beaded, smiling on the waking city.

譯文十一

Night a Spring Rain（徐忠杰 譯）

Good rain chooses the proper season to fall.

In spring, all trees and flowers, to life it recall.

With a mild breeze, it continues into the night.

In silence, it gives the needed moisture aright.

Darkness shuts off the field paths and the clouds from sight.

Only the lamps of river boats emit some light.

Morning sees tops of trees wet with a red stain.

Flowers in Chengdu are fresh and heavy with rain.

譯文十二

Rain in a Spring Night（吳鈞陶 譯）

The favorable rain its season knows,
It drizzles down when Spring her breaths blows.
Diving and melting into night with winds,
It mutely moistens Earth with wary minds.
The clouds and the wild path are very dark,
The only light is from the river bark.
At day-break in Chengdu where is red and wet,
There you'll see blooms now under heavy weight.

譯文十三

Happy Rain on a Spring Night（許淵衝 譯）

Good rain knows its time right;
It will fall when comes spring.
With wind it steals in night;
Mute, it moistens each thing.
O'er wild lanes dark cloud spreads;
In boat a lantern looms.
Dawn sees saturated reds;
The town's heavy with blooms.

譯文十四

Propitious Rain in a Spring Night（章學清 譯）

Propitious rain comes opportunely not past reason,
To its best knowledge, none but spring is its prime season.
With breeze, it slips into night, a silent, soft descent,
To gratify the thirst of life to heart's content.
The paths of yonder clad in clouds no more in sight,
The candled boat on river all the more shines bright.
Just fancy everywhere in radiant red at morn,
The City with pearl-laden flowers to adorn!

譯文十五

Good Rain on a Spring Night（曾衝明 譯）

The good rain knows when to fall,
It falls just the time spring comes.
Stealing into the night with the wind,
It nourishes everything without a sound.
Country paths are as black as the rainy clouds;
Flaring on the river, boats appear here and there.
We'll see tomorrow good landscape after rain at dawn,
When red flowers are heavy all around the Chengdu City.

五、《兵車行》

兵車行（杜甫）

車轔轔，馬蕭蕭，行人弓箭各在腰。
耶娘妻子走相送，塵埃不見咸陽橋。
牽衣頓足攔道哭，哭聲直上干雲霄。
道旁過者問行人，行人但雲點行頻。
或從十五北防河，便至四十西營田。
去時裡正與裹頭，歸來頭白還戍邊。
邊庭流血成海水，武皇開邊意未已。
君不聞漢家山東二百州，千村萬落生荊杞。
縱有健婦把鋤犁，禾生隴畝無東西。
況復秦兵耐苦戰，被驅不異犬與雞。
長者雖有問，役夫敢申恨。
且如今年冬，未休關西卒。
縣官急索租，租稅從何出。
信知生男惡，反是生女好。
生女猶是嫁比鄰，生男埋沒隨百草。
君不見，青海頭，古來白骨無人收。
新鬼煩冤舊鬼哭，天陰雨濕聲啾啾。

譯文一

A Song Of War-Chariots (Witter Bynner 譯)

The war-chariots rattle,

The war-horses whinny.

Each man of you has a bow and a quiver at his belt.

Father, mother, son, wife, stare at you going,

Till dust shall have buried the bridge beyond Ch'ang-an.

They run with you, crying, they tug at your sleeves,

And the sound of their sorrow goes up to the clouds;

And every time a bystander asks you a question,

You can only say to him that you have to go.

We remember others at fifteen sent north to guard the river,

And at forty sent west to cultivate the camp-farms.

The mayor wound their turbans for them when they started out.

With their turbaned hair white now, they are still at the border,

At the border where the blood of men spills like the sea,

And still the heart of Emperor Wu is beating for war.

Do you know that, east of China's mountains, in two hundred districts,

And in thousands of villages, nothing grows but weeds.

And though strong women have bent to the ploughing,

East and west the furrows all are broken down?

Men of China are able to face the stiffest battle,

But their officers drive them like chickens and dogs.

Whatever is asked of them,

Dare they complain?

For example, this winter,

Held west of the gate,

Challenged for taxes,

How could they pay?

We have learned that to have a son is bad luck,

It is very much better to have a daughter.

Who can marry and live in the house of a neighbour,

While under the sod we bury our boys.

Go to the Blue Sea, look along the shore,
At all the old white bones forsaken.
New ghosts are wailing there now with the old,
Loudest in the dark sky of a stormy day.

譯文二

Conscripts Leaving for the Frontier（Charles Budd 譯）
Chariots rumbling; horses neighing;
Soldiers shouting martial cries;
Drums are sounding; trumpets braying;
Seas of glittering spears arise.
On each warrior's back are hanging,
Deadly arrows, mighty bows;
Pipes are blowing, gongs are clanging,
On they march in serried rows.
Age-bowed parents, sons and daughters,
Crowd beside in motley bands;
Here one stumbles, there one falters,
Through the clouds of blinding sands.
Wives and mothers sometimes clinging,
To their loved ones in the ranks,
Or in grief their bodies flinging,
On the dusty crowded flanks.
Mothers', wives', and children's weeping,
Rises sad above the din,
Through the clouds to Heaven creeping.
Justice begging for their din.
「To what region are they going」
Asks a stranger passing by;
To the Yellow River, flowing,
Through the desert bare and dry!
Forced conscription daily snapping,
Ties which bind us to our clan;

Forced conscript, slowly sapping;
All the manhood of the Han.
And the old man went on speaking,
To the stranger from afar:
Tis the Emperor, glory seeking,
Drives them neath his baleful star.
Guarding river; guarding passes,
On the frontier, wild and drear;
Fighting foes in savage masses,
Scant of mercy, void of fear.
Proclamations, without pity,
Rain upon us day by day,
Till from village, town, and city.
All our men are called away.
Called away t swell the flowing,
Of the streams of human blood,
Where the bitter north wind blowing,
Petrifies the ghastly flood.
Guarding passes through the mountains,
Guarding rivers in the plain;
While in sleep, in youth's clear fountain,
Scenes of home come back again.
But, alas! The dream is leaded,
With the morn's recurring grief,
Only few return grey-headed,
To their homes, for days too brief.
For the Emperor, still unheeding,
Starving homes and lands untilled,
On his fatuous course proceeding,
Swears his camps shall be refilled.
Hence new levies are demanded,
And the war goes on apace,
Emperor and foemen banded,

In the slaughter of the race.
All the region is denuded,
Of its men and hardy boys,
Only women left, deluded,
Of life's promise and its joys.
Yet the prefects clamour loudly,
That the taxes must be paid,
Ride about and hector proudly!
How can gold from stones be made?
Levy after levy driven,
Treated more like dogs than men,
Over mountains, tempest river,
Through the salty desert fen.
There by Hun and Tartar harried,
Ever fighting, night and or day;
Wounded, left to die, or carried,
Far from kith and kin away.
Better bring forth daughters only,
Than male children doomed to death,
Slaughtered in the desert lonely,
Frozen by the north wind's breath.
Where their bodies, left unburied,
Strew the plain from west to east,
While above in legions serried,
Vultures hasten to the feast.
Brave men's bones on desert bleaching,
Far away from home and love,
Spirits of the dead beseeching,
Justice from the heaven above.

譯文三

The Chariots Go Forth to War（Henry H. Hart 譯）
The chariots go forth to war,

Rumbling, roaring as they go;
The horses neigh and whinny loud,
Tugging at the bit.
The dust swirls up in great dense clouds,
And hides the Han Yang bridge.

In serried ranks the archers march,
A bow and quiver at each waist;
Fathers, mothers, children, wives,
All crowd around to say farewell.
Pulling at clothes and stamping feet,
The force the soldiers' ranks apart,
And all the while their sobs and cries,
Reach to the skies above.

「Where go you to-day?」a passer-by,
Calls to the marching men.
A grizzled old veteran answers him,
Halting his swinging stride:
At fifteen I was sent to the north,
To guard the river against the Hun;
At forty I was sent to camp,
To farm in the west, far, far from home.
When I left, my hair was long and black;
When I came home, it was white and thin.
To day they send me again to the wars,
Back to the north frontier,
By whose gray towers our blood has flowed,
In a red tide, like the sea.
And will flow again, for Wu Huang Ti,
Is resolved to rule the world.

Have you not heard how in far Shantung,

Two hundred districts lie.

With a thousand towns and ten thousand homes,

Deserted, neglected, weed-grown?

Husbands fighting or dead, wives drag the plow,

And the grain grows wild in the fields.

The soldiers recruited in Shansi towns,

Still fight; but with spirit gone,

Like chickens and dogs they are driven about,

And have not the heart to complain.

I am greatly honored by your speech with me.

Dare I speak of my hatreds and grief?

All this long winter, conscription goes on,

Through the whole country, from the east to the west,

And taxes grow heavy. But how can we pay,

Who have nothing to give from our hand?

A son is a curse at a time like this,

And daughters more welcome far;

For, when daughters grow up, they can marry, at least,

And live on a neighbor's land.

But our sons? We bury then after the fight,

And they rot where the grass grows long.

Have you not seen at far Ching Hai,

By the waters of Kokonor,

How the heaped skulls and bones of slaughtered men,

Lie bleaching in the sun?

Their ancient ghosts hear our own ghosts weep,

And cry and lament in turn;

The heavens grow dark with great storm-clouds,

And the specters wail in the rain.

譯文四

Ballad of the Chariots (Tommy W. K. Tao 譯)

Chariots rumble,

Horses neigh,

Men marching, bow and arrows at the waist.

So much dust, you cannot see the bridge o'er River Wei.

Fathers, mothers, wives and children run along to bid farewell,

Clutching at clothes, stamping their feet, standing in the way, wailing.

Wailing so loud it pierces the clouds.

A passerby asks a soldier.

The soldier simply says:

Conscription again.

Going north to guard Huanghe, one is probably just fifteen;

Sent west to till the land, he would be then already forty.

Leaving, wearing a headscarf tied by the village elder;

Returning, hoary-headed, still to guard the border.

The border is a sea of blood.

Emperor Wu still intends to push ahead.

Have you not heard, in the two hundred districts of Guandong,

Thousands of villages o'ergrown with bramble and medlar?

Even with sturdy women to hoe and plow,

The rice paddies grow haphazardly, no east, no west.

The Guanxi forces, moreover, have endured a drawn out war,

And are driven about like dogs and chickens.

Though an elder may kindly ask,

Dare a soldier speak his heart?

This winter, for instance,

No rest for the Guanxi soldiers,

While district governors press hard for land taxes.

Taxes to come from where?

Now I know, to have a son is no blessing.

Indeed, It's better to have a daughter.

A daughter can be married to a neighbour.

A son is sure to die, in the wilderness to lie.

Have you not seen, at the shores of Lake Qinghai,

White bones have lain ungathered for ages?

When the sky is overcast, and the air is wet with rain,

You can hear a haunting howl:

New ghosts moan,

Old ghosts cry.

譯文五

The Chariots Go Forth to War (W. J. B. Fletcher 譯)

Chariots rumble and roll; horses whinny and neigh.

Footman at their girdle bows and arrows display.

Fathers, mothers, wives, and children by them go.

It's not the choking dust alone that strangles what they say!

Their clothes they clutch; their feet they stamp; their crust blocks up the way,

The sounds of weeping mount above the clouds that gloom the day.

The passers-by inquire of them, 「But whither do you go?

They only say: 「We're mustering—do not disturb us so.」

These, fifteen years and upwards, the Northern Pass defend;

And still at forty years of age their service does not end.

All young they left their villages—just registered were they—

The war they quitted sees again the same men worn and gray.

And all along the boundary their blood has made a sea.

But never till the World is his, will Wu Huang happy be!

Have you not heard—in Shantung there two hundred districts lie.

All overgrown with briar and weed and wasted utterly?

The stouter women swing the hoe and guide the stubborn plough,

The fields have lost their boundaries—the corn grows wildly now.

And routed bands with hunger grim come down in disarray.

To rob and rend and outrage them, and treat them as a prey.

Although the leaders question them, the soldiers' plaints resound.

And winter has not stopped the war upon the western bound.
And war needs funds; the Magistrates for taxes press each day.
The land tax and the duties—Ah! How shall these be found?
In times like this stout sons to bear is sorrow and dismay.
Far better girls—to marry to a home not far away.
But sons!—are buried in the grass!—you Tsaidam's waste survey!
The bones of those who fell before are bleaching on the plain.
Their spirits weep our ghosts to hear lamenting all their pain.
Beneath the gloomy sky there runs a wailing in the rain.

譯文六

War Chariots（Florence Ayscough 譯）

Lin! Lin! Chariots jangle; Hsiao! Hsiao! Horses snort;
Men move forward; at his hip each wears arrows and a bow.
Fathers, mothers, wives, children, all come out to say farewell;
Dust in clouds: they cannot see the near-by Hsien Yang Bridge.
They drag at the men's coats, fell beneath their feet, obstruct the road, weeping;
Sound of weeping rises straight; divides the soft white clouds.
On the road, passers-by question the marching men;
Marching men reply,「Dots against our names; we are hurried away.」
Followers who are ten years and five, go North to guard the river;
When they reach four tens, go West to dig encampment fields.
On leaving, Village Senior wraps a cloth about their heads;
On returning, their hair is white; they have continuously kept watch at frontiers.
At frontier territories blood flows like waters of the sea;
To open those frontiers is the unceasing desire of the Military Emperor.
Does my Lord not hear? the Han Clan have two hundred prefectures East of the Mountain;
In a thousand hamlets, a myriad abodes, brambles, alders grow.
Propriety is outraged; the stronger women grasp the hoe, the plough;
Grain springs on dykes, in fields; divisions East and West are wiped out.
Moreover, soldiers of Ch'in again endure hardships of battle;
They submit to being driven on, as though they did not differ from dogs or fowls.

Even if the elders ask questions,
How dare conscript soldiers express resentment?
Thus it is in the winter of this very year:
West of the Pass arming of soldiers does not cease.
The Official of the Central District urgently seeks taxes in kind;
Where shall they come from, rentals, taxes in kind?
We must admit, giving birth to sons is bad;
All is changed: giving birth to daughters is good.
A daughter is born: we still can give her in marriage, —keep her as a neighbour;
A son is born: he is buried without rites among the one hundred grasses.
Does my Lord not see? —at the head of the Green Lake,
White bones have lain since early ages, and none to gather them.
New ghosts are perplexed at wanton ill-usage; old ghosts cry;
Dark sky, wetting rain; sound of their cries—chiu! Chiu!

第三節　白居易詩歌英譯賞析

一、《賦得古原草送別》

賦得古原草送別（白居易）
離離原上草，一歲一枯榮。
野火燒不盡，春風吹又生。
遠芳侵古道，晴翠接荒城。
又送王孫去，萋萋滿別情。

譯文一

Grass（許淵衝 譯）

Wild grasses spreading over the plain,
With every season come and go.
Health fire can't burn them up, again,
They rise when the vernal winds blow.
Their fragrance over runs the pathway;

Their color invades the ruined town.

Seeing my friend going away,

My sorrow grows like grass over grown.

譯文二

The Grass on the Old Plain (Arthur Waley 譯)

Thick, thick the grass grows in the fields;

Every year it withers, and springs anew.

The prairie fires never burn it up;

The spring wind blows it into life again.

Its sweet smell carries to the old road;

Its green haze touches the crumbling wall.

Now that we are seeing our noble friend on his way.

Its close verdure fills our parting thoughts.

譯文三

Grass (Witter Bynner 譯)

Boundless grasses over the plain,

Come and go with every season;

Wildfire never quite consumes them,

They are tall once more in the spring wind.

Sweet they press on the old high-road,

And reach the crumbling city-gate.

O Prince of Friends, you are gone again,

I hear them sighing after you.

譯文四

Grass (M. C. Doo 譯)

How verdant the grasses on the plain!

Each year they flourish, then die away again.

Never burnt up by prairie fire,

In spring winds' breath they grow up higher.

Their drifting scents the ancient path pervade.

The verdure reaches to the walls decayed.
Here again as I bid my princely friend goodbye,
My parting sorrow grows as deep as the grass is high.

譯文五

The Grass upon the Ancient Plain: A Song of Parting (Zhang Tiangchen、Bruce M. Wilson 譯)

Green green the grass upon the plain,
That each year dies to flourish anew,
That's scorched by flames yet unsubdued,
Surging back when spring winds blow.
Its fresh fragrance over runs the ancient roads;
Its sun filled greenness meets the ruined city's wall.
When once again we meet to say adieu,
Deep green are these parting thoughts of you.

二、《長恨歌》

長恨歌（白居易）

漢皇重色思傾國，御宇多年求不得。楊家有女初長成，養在深閨人未識。
天生麗質難自棄，一朝選在君王側。回眸一笑百媚生，六宮粉黛無顏色。
春寒賜浴華清池，溫泉水滑洗凝脂。侍兒扶起嬌無力，始是新承恩澤時。
雲鬢花顏金步搖，芙蓉帳暖度春宵。春宵苦短日高起，從此君王不早朝。
承歡侍宴無閒暇，春從春遊夜專夜。後宮佳麗三千人，三千寵愛在一身。
金屋妝成嬌侍夜，玉樓宴罷醉和春。姊妹弟兄皆列土，可憐光彩生門戶。
遂令天下父母心，不重生男重生女。驪宮高處入青雲，仙樂風飄處處聞。緩歌慢舞凝絲竹，盡日君王看不足。
漁陽鼙鼓動地來，驚破霓裳羽衣曲。九重城闕煙塵生，千乘萬騎西南行。
翠華搖搖行復止，西出都門百餘里。六軍不發無奈何，宛轉蛾眉馬前死。
花鈿委地無人收，翠翹金雀玉搔頭。君王掩面救不得，回看血淚相和流。
黃埃散漫風蕭索，雲棧縈紆登劍閣。峨嵋山下少人行，旌旗無光日色薄。
蜀江水碧蜀山青，聖主朝朝暮暮情。行宮見月傷心色，夜雨聞鈴腸斷聲。
天旋日轉回龍馭，到此躊躇不能去。馬嵬坡下泥土中，不見玉顏空死處。

君臣相顧盡沾衣，東望都門信馬歸。歸來池苑皆依舊，太液芙蓉未央柳。
芙蓉如面柳如眉，對此如何不淚垂。春風桃李花開夜，秋雨梧桐葉落時。
西宮南內多秋草，落葉滿階紅不掃。梨園弟子白髮新，椒房阿監青娥老。
夕殿螢飛思悄然，孤燈挑盡未成眠。遲遲鐘鼓初長夜，耿耿星河欲曙天。
鴛鴦瓦冷霜華重，翡翠衾寒誰與共。悠悠生死別經年，魂魄不曾來入夢。
臨邛道士鴻都客，能以精誠致魂魄。為感君王輾轉思，遂教方士殷勤覓。
排空馭氣奔如電，升天入地求之遍。上窮碧落下黃泉，兩處茫茫皆不見。
忽聞海上有仙山，山在虛無縹緲間。樓閣玲瓏五雲起，其中綽約多仙子。
中有一人字太真，雪膚花貌參差是。金闕西廂叩玉扃，轉教小玉報雙成。
聞到漢家天子使，九華帳裡夢魂驚。攬衣推枕起徘徊，珠箔銀屏邐迤開。
雲鬢半偏新睡覺，花冠不整下堂來。風吹仙袂飄搖舉，猶似霓裳羽衣舞。
玉容寂寞淚闌干，梨花一枝春帶雨。
含情凝睇謝君王，一別音容兩渺茫。昭陽殿裡恩愛絕，蓬萊宮中日月長。
回頭下望人寰處，不見長安見塵霧。唯將舊物表深情，鈿合金釵寄將去。
釵留一股合一扇，釵擘黃金合分鈿。但教心似金鈿堅，天上人間會相見。
臨別殷勤重寄詞，詞中有誓兩心知。七月七日長生殿，夜半無人私語時。
在天願作比翼鳥，在地願為連理枝。天長地久有時盡，此恨綿綿無絕期。

譯文一

Song of Eternal Sorrow（楊憲益、戴乃迭 譯）

Appreciating feminine charms,

The Han emperor sought a great beauty.

Throughout his empire he searched,

For many years without success.

Then a daughter of the Yang family,

Matured to womanhood.

Since she was secluded in her chamber,

None outside had seen her.

Yet with such beauty bestowed by fate,

How could she remain unknown?

One day she was chosen,

To attend the emperor.

Glancing back and smiling,

第四章　唐詩不同英譯本賞析 | 169

She revealed a hundred charms.
All the powdered ladies of the six palaces,
At once seemed dull and colourless.
One cold spring day she was ordered,
To bathe in the Huaqing Palace baths.
The warm water slipped down,
Her glistening jade-like body.
When her maids helped her rise,
She looked so frail and lovely,
At once she won the emperor's favour.
Her hair like a cloud,
Her face like a flower,
A gold hair-pin adorning her tresses.
Behind the warm lotus-flower curtain,
They took their pleasure in the spring night.
Regretting only the spring nights were too short;
Rising only when the sun was high;
He stopped attending court sessions,
In the early morning.
Constantly she amused and feasted with him,
Accompanying him on his spring outings,
Spending all the nights with him.
Though many beauties were in the palace,
More than three thousand of them,
All his favours were centred on her.
Finishing her coiffure in the gilded chamber,
Charming, she accompanied him at night.
Feasting together in the marble pavilion,
Inebriated in the spring.
All her sisters and brothers,
Became nobles with fiefs.
How wonderful to have so much splendour,
Centred in one family!

All parents wished for daughters,
Instead of sons!
The Li Mountain lofty pleasure palace,
Reached to the blue sky.
The sounds of heavenly music were carried,
By the wind far and wide.
Gentle melodies and graceful dances,
Mingled with the strings and flutes;
The emperor never tired of these.
Then battle drums shook the earth,
The alarm sounding from Yuyang.
The Rainbow and Feather Garments Dance
Was stopped by sounds of war.
Dust filled the high-towered capital.
As thousands of carriages and horsemen,
Fled to the southwest.
The emperor's green-canopied carriage,
Was forced to halt,
Having left the west city gate,
More than a hundred li.
There was nothing the emperor could do,
At the army's refusal to proceed.
So she with the moth-like eyebrows,
Was killed before his horses.
Her floral-patterned gilded box,
Fell to the ground, abandoned and unwanted,
Like her jade hair-pin,
With the gold sparrow and green feathers.
Covering his face with his hands,
He could not save her.
Turning back to look at her,
His tears mingled with her blood.
Yellow dust filled the sky;

The wind was cold and shrill.
Ascending high winding mountain paths,
They reached the Sword Pass,
At the foot of the Emei Mountains.
Few came that way.
Their banners seemed less resplendent;
Even the sun seemed dim.
Though the rivers were deep blue,
And the Sichuan mountains green,
Night and day the emperor mourned.
In his refuge when he saw the moon,
Even it seemed sad and wan.
On rainy nights, the sound of bells,
Seemed broken-hearted.
Fortunes changed, the emperor was restored.
His dragon-carriage started back.
Reaching the place where she died,
He lingered, reluctant to leave.
In the earth and dust of Mawei Slope,
No lady with the jade-like face was found.
The spot was desolate.
Emperor and servants exchanged looks,
Their clothes stained with tears.
Turning eastwards towards the capital,
They led their horses slowly back.
The palace was unchanged on his return,
With lotus blooming in the Taiye Pool,
And willows in the Weiyang Palace.
The lotus flowers were like her face;
The willows like her eyebrows.
How could he refrain from tears,
At their sight?
The spring wind returned at night;

The peach and plum trees blossomed again.
Plane leaves fell in the autumn rains.
Weeds choked the emperor's west palace;
Piles of red leaves on the unswept steps.
The hair of the young musicians of the Pear Garden.
Turned to grey.
The green-clad maids of the spiced chambers,
Were growing old.
At night when glow-worms flitted in the pavilion,
He thought of her in silence.
The lonely lamp was nearly extinguished,
Yet still he could not sleep.
The slow sound of hells and drums,
Was heard in the long night.
The Milky Way glimmered bright.
It was almost dawn.
Cold and frosty the paired love-bird tiles;
Chilly the kingfisher-feathered quilt,
With none to share it.
Though she had died years before,
Even her spirit was absent from his dreams.
A priest from Linqiong came to Chang'an,
Said to summon spirits at his will.
Moved by the emperor's longing for her,
He sent a magician to make a careful search.
Swift as lightning, through the air he sped,
Up to the heavens, below the earth, everywhere.
Though they searched the sky and nether regions,
Of her there was no sign.
Till he heard of a fairy mountain,
In the ocean of a never-never land.
Ornate pavilions rose through coloured clouds,
Wherein dwelt lovely fairy folk.

One was named Taizhen,

With snowy skin and flowery beauty,

Suggesting that this might be she.

When he knocked at the jade door,

Of the gilded palace's west chamber,

A fairy maid, Xiaoyu, answered,

Reporting to another, Shuangcheng.

On hearing of the messenger,

From the Han emperor,

She was startled from her sleep,

Behind the gorgeous curtain.

Dressing, she drew it back,

Rising hesitantly.

The pearl curtains and silver screens,

Opened in succession.

Her cloudy tresses were awry,

Just summoned from her sleep.

Without arranging her flower headdress,

She entered the hall.

The wind blew her fairy skirt,

Lifting it, as if she still danced,

The Rainbow and Feather Garments Dance.

But her pale face was sad,

Tears filled her eyes,

Like a blossoming pear tree in spring,

With rain drops on its petals.

Controlling her feelings and looking away,

She thanked the emperor.

Since their parting she had not heard,

His voice nor seen his face.

While she had been his first lady,

Their love had been ruptured.

Many years had passed,

On Penglai fairy isle.

Turning her head,

She gazed down on the mortal world.

Chang'an could not be seen,

Only mist and dust.

She presented old mementos,

To express her deep feeling.

Asking the messenger to take,

The jewel box and the golden pin.

「I'll keep one half of the pin and box;

Breaking the golden pin,

And keeping the jewel lid.

As long as our love lasts,

Like jewels and gold,

We may meet again,

In heaven or on earth.」

Before they parted,

She again sent this message,

Containing a pledge,

Only she and the emperor knew.

In the Palace of Eternal Youth,

On the seventh of the seventh moon,

Alone they had whispered,

To each other at midnight:

「In heaven we shall he birds,

Flying side by side.

On earth flowering sprigs,

On the same branch!」

Heaven and earth may not last for ever,

But this sorrow was eternal.

譯文二

The Everlasting Regret (許淵衝 譯)

The beauty-loving monarch longed year after year,
To find a beautiful lady without peer.
A maiden of the Yangs[1] to womanhood just grown,
In inner chambers bred, to the world was unknown.
Endowed with natural beauty too hard to hide,
One day she stood selected for the monarch's side.
Turning her head, she smiled so sweet and full of grace,
That she outshone in six palaces the fairest face.
She bathed in glassy water of warm-fountain pool,
Which laved and smoothed her creamy skin when spring was cool.
Upborne by her attendants, she rose too faint to move,
And this was when she first received the monarch's love.
Flowerlike face and cloudlike hair, golden-headdressed,
In lotus-flower curtain she spent the night blessed.
She slept till sun rose high, for the blessed night was short,
From then on the monarch held no longer morning court.
In revels as in feasts she shared her lord's delight,
His companion on trips and his mistress at night.
In inner palace dwelt three thousand ladies fair;
On her alone was lavished royal love and care.
Her beauty served the night when dressed in Golden Bower,
Or drunk with wine and spring at banquet in Jade Tower.
All her sisters and brothers received rank and fief,
And honours showered on her household, to the grief.
Of the fathers and mothers who'd rather give birth,
To a fair maiden than any son on earth.
The lofty palace towered high into blue cloud,
With wind-borne music so divine the air was loud.
Seeing slow dance and hearing fluted or stringed song,
The emperor was never tired the whole day long.
But rebels[2] beat their war drums, making the earth quake,
And「Song of Rainbow Skirt and Coat of Feathers」break.

A cloud of dust was raised o'er city walls nine-fold;
Thousands of chariots and horsemen southwestward rolled.
Imperial flags moved slowly now and halted then,
And thirty miles from Western Gate they stopped again.
Six armies would not march, what could be done? with speed,
Until the Lady Yang was killed before the steed.
None would pick up her hairpin fallen to the ground,
Or golden bird and comb with which her head was crowned.
The monarch could not save her and hid his face in fear;
Turning his head, he saw her blood mix with his tear.
The yellow dust spread wide, the wind blew desolate;
A serpentine plank path led to cloud-capped Sword Gate.
Below the Eyebrow Mountains wayfarers were few;
In fading sunlight royal standards lost their hue.
On western waters blue and western mountains green,
The monarch's heart was daily gnawed by sorrow keen.
The moon viewed from his tent shed a soul-searing light,
The bells heard in night rain made a heart-rending sound.
Suddenly turned the tide. Returning from his flight,
The monarch could not tear himself away from the ground,
Where mid the clods beneath the slope he couldn't forget.
The fair-faced Lady Yang, who was unfairly slain.
He looked at ministers, with tears his robe was wet;
They rode east to the capital, but with loose rein.
Back, he found her pond and garden in the old place,
With lotus in the lake and willows by the hall.
Willow leaves like her brows and lotus like her face;
At the sight of all these, how could his tears not fall.
Or when in vernal breeze were peach and plum full-blown,
Or when in autumn rain parasol leaves were shed?
In western as in southern court was grass o'ergrown;
With fallen leaves unswept the marble steps turned red.
Actors, although still young, began to have hair grey;

Eunuchs and waiting maids looked old in palace deep.
Fireflies flitting the hall, mutely he pined away;
The lonely lampwick burned out; still he could not sleep.
Slowly beat drums and rang bells; night began to grow long;
Bright shone the Milky Way; daybreak seemed to come late.
The lovebird tiles grew chilly with hoar frost so strong,
And his kingfisher quilt was cold, not shared by a mate.
One long, long year the dead and the living were parted;
Her soul came not in dreams to see the brokenhearted.
A Taoist sorcerer came to the palace door,
Skilled to summon the spirit from the other shore.
Moved by the monarch's yearning for the departed fair,
He was ordered to seek for her everywhere.
Borne on the air, like flash of lightning he flew;
In heaven and on earth he searched through and through.
Up to the azure vault and down to deepest place,
Nor above nor below could he find her trace.
He learned that on the sea were fairy mountains proud,
That now appeared, now disappeared amid the cloud.
Of rainbow colours where rose magnificent bowers,
And dwelt so many fairies as graceful as flowers.
Among them was a queen whose name was Ever True;
Her snow-white skin and sweet face might afford a clue.
Knocking at western gate of palace hall, he bade,
The porter fair to inform the queen's waiting maid.
When she heard there came the monarch's embassy,
The queen was startled out of dreams in her canopy.
Pushing aside the pillow, she rose and got dressed,
Passing through silver screen and pearl shade to meet the guest.
Her cloudlike hair awry, not full awake at all,
Her flowery cap slanted, she came into the hall.
The wind blew up her fairy sleeves and made them float,
As if she danced the 「Rainbow Skirt and Feathered Coat.」

Her jade-white face crisscrossed with tears in lonely world
Like a spray of pear blossoms in spring rain impearled.
She bade him thank her lord, lovesick and brokenhearted;
They knew nothing of each other after they parted.
Love and happiness long ended within palace walls;
Days and months appeared long in the fairyland halls.
Turning her head and fixing on the earth her gaze,
She saw no capital mid clouds of dust and haze.
To show her love was deep, she took out keepsakes old,
For him to carry back, hairpin and case of gold.
Keeping one side of the case and one wing of the pin,
She sent to her dear lord the other half of the twin.
「If our two hearts as firm as the gold should remain.
In heaven or on earth we'll sometime meet again.」
At parting she confided to the messenger,
A secret vow known only to her lord and her.
On seventh day of seventh moon when none was near,
At midnight in Long Life Hall he whispered in her ear,
「On high, we'd be two lovebirds flying wing to wing;
On earth, two trees with branches twined from spring to spring.」
The boundless sky and endless earth may pass away,
But this vow unfulfilled will be regretted for aye.

[1] Yang Yu-huan (719-756) was the favourite mistress of Emperor Xuan Zong (reigned 725-768) of the Tang Dynasty.
[2] The revolt broke out in 755 and forced the emperor to flee from the capital.

三、《琵琶行》

琵琶行（白居易）

元和十年，予左遷九江郡司馬。明年秋，送客湓浦口，聞舟中夜彈琵琶者，聽其音，錚錚然有京都聲。問其人，本長安倡女，嘗學琵琶於穆、曹二善才，年長色衰，委身為賈人婦。遂命酒，使快彈數曲。曲罷憫然，自敘少小時

歡樂事，今漂淪憔悴，轉徙於江湖間。予出官二年，恬然自安，感斯人言，是夕始覺有遷謫意。因為長句，歌以贈之，凡六百一十六言，命曰《琵琶行》。

潯陽江頭夜送客，楓葉荻花秋瑟瑟。
主人下馬客在船，舉酒欲飲無管弦。
醉不成歡慘將別，別時茫茫江浸月。
忽聞水上琵琶聲，主人忘歸客不發。
尋聲暗問彈者誰？琵琶聲停欲語遲。
移船相近邀相見，添酒回燈重開宴。
千呼萬喚始出來，猶抱琵琶半遮面。
轉軸撥弦三兩聲，未成曲調先有情。
弦弦掩抑聲聲思，似訴平生不得志。
低眉信手續續彈，說盡心中無限事。
輕攏慢捻抹復挑，初為《霓裳》後《六幺》。
大弦嘈嘈如急雨，小弦切切如私語。
嘈嘈切切錯雜彈，大珠小珠落玉盤。
間關鶯語花底滑，幽咽泉流冰下難。
冰泉冷澀弦凝絕，凝絕不通聲暫歇。
別有幽愁暗恨生，此時無聲勝有聲。
銀瓶乍破水漿迸，鐵騎突出刀槍鳴。
曲終收撥當心畫，四弦一聲如裂帛。
東船西舫悄無言，唯見江心秋月白。
沉吟放撥插弦中，整頓衣裳起斂容。
自言本是京城女，家在蝦蟆陵下住。
十三學得琵琶成，名屬教坊第一部。
曲罷曾教善才服，妝成每被秋娘妒。
五陵年少爭纏頭，一曲紅綃不知數。
鈿頭銀篦擊節碎，血色羅裙翻酒污。
今年歡笑復明年，秋月春風等閒度。
弟走從軍阿姨死，暮去朝來顏色故。
門前冷落鞍馬稀，老大嫁作商人婦。
商人重利輕別離，前月浮梁買茶去。
去來江口守空船，繞船月明江水寒。
夜深忽夢少年事，夢啼妝淚紅闌干。

我聞琵琶已嘆息，又聞此語重唧唧。
同是天涯淪落人，相逢何必曾相識！
我從去年辭帝京，謫居臥病潯陽城。
潯陽地僻無音樂，終歲不聞絲竹聲。
住近湓江地低濕，黃蘆苦竹繞宅生。
其間旦暮聞何物？杜鵑啼血猿哀鳴。
春江花朝秋月夜，往往取酒還獨傾。
豈無山歌與村笛？嘔啞嘲哳難為聽。
今夜聞君琵琶語，如聽仙樂耳暫明。
莫辭更坐彈一曲，為君翻作《琵琶行》。
感我此言良久立，卻坐促弦弦轉急。
淒淒不似向前聲，滿座重聞皆掩泣。
座中泣下誰最多？江州司馬青衫濕。

譯文一

Pipa Germination of（David Wei 譯）

The Xunyang River pier night to send the guests,
A Maples and autumn winds and miscanthus flowers.
And master dismount-the passenger on ship their,
Where raised wine-cup you but no orchestral.
So not a happy drunk, the empty miserable farewell,
While the vast river the moonlight-dip.

Suddenly, where the water came music Piba,
The master forgot to return, the boat was not starting up.
To explore the acoustic Lute secretly asked Who?
The Lute muise stops, and like language to defer;
And move the boat close to each other, invite each other,
Then added wine back to the light to re-open the feast.
The long-awaited and call, who was out,
Still holding a Piba;
A one half face masked the where rotation the axis masked three twice,
That unsuccessfully melody first mood.

When string and chord of, hide control sounds minds,

Or Like her life unsuccessful hint.

O beautiful bows, accompanied by free hands plucked the heart,

To say the minds of infinite thing it.

One gently stroked slowly twist, wipe, then provoked OK!

The beginning of「Seduction」and「Of the Six Shake」,

Cao Cao as big chord rapid rain,

Gentle as a small string whisper;

Cao Cao-murmur mixed play;

When big and pearls and little Falling-into one jade plate.

And wooden wheels rhythms like orioles, over the flower mood,

The resentment spring sound like that in the ice.

When cold spring and bitter cold and strings solidified,

That bleak despair, the music pause.

In addition there are quiet melancholy to give birth secretly hate,

This time, silence was better than the sound.

And suddenly felling, like silver bottle burst suddenly sputtered,

And cavalry-storm appeared along with swords ringing;

At the end of the tune, plucked strings such as heart light painting,

That last four strings sound like tearing brocade.

O, east of the boat, west of the boats, silent-silent,

Only saw the river central pale fall moon was,

O pondered with the plectrum inserting strings the,

Rhythm, sorting clothes, stood up to clean up the appearance.

Then said to herself, her essentially is the capital of the woman,

Family lived in the Frog Mausoleum.

And thirteen study completed Pibas,

In the name belonged to the Royal Music School of First Division.

Then every the music ended, gave people understood music breaths,

And I was good makeup, always been a Fallmoon-beauty jealousy.

So the capital spoiled rich kid fight gifts,

A「red silk song」Then I do not know the numbers.

So gold headdress, silver grate, that break the chastity,

And bloody, silk satin skirts waved with wine and dirt.
That smile fairs this year to repeat next year; the spring winds,
And autumn moon, the scenery powerless to spend.
While brother in the army, gone; aunt died,
And twilight came and went, so color it.
Then doors to cold, pommels horse scarce,
And aging older, so married businessman wife the,
Businessman, materialistic-contempt in parting, yes,
And previous month, over the floating bridge to buy tea and.
So the river of, who go-come back often to keep the empty boat,
Follow the sun-moon changes boat entangled in the cold rivers.
Sometimes, late at night suddenly dreamed boy things,
The dream to cry, wet clothes makeup, tears drip dry until nights.

When I have heard sighing Lute,
Again the words of this woman, and more pity;
The same world people;
We meet why have known!
And left the capital last year I, now,
Demotion? Confined to bed in Xunyang city;
Xunyang secluded no joy Concert,
Throughout the year, do not listen to orchestral sound.
The residence near the river flowing in humidity,
Yellow reeds, low and long sections of bamboo growing around house.
You Living in the middle of the morning-evening news what things?
When Cuckoos blood, whether ape whine the,
Then river in spring, the bloom early sun and the autumn moonlight;
Wine also often taken trance alone dump is,
Is not the village folk flute?
Nor is it; is elegant enough and noisy mocking my minds.
Tonight I hear your Piba languages,
Such as listening to fairy music, the ears temporarily out.
And organization silently rhetoric, late at night play a song for you it,

For us to re-write an「Pipa Germination.」

I say these words to feel her beautiful long standing,
But sitten down the chord chord turn pro anxious.
Although still desolately, but do not like the forward of sounds,
And people here, hear the multiple meanings, all cover weep.
That among those who tears up?
Jiangzhou Sima-General greener gown wet downs-ups.
Preface:

Tang of Yuan dynasty years and I moved to Jiujiang-County Sima post. The fall of the second year, visitor out flowing of water PuKou, who heard the boat the night playing the Pipa, listen to which voice, clank and then-there capital sound. Asked the man, she replied originally Chang'an showgirl, once try learning the Luto in Mu Cao two teachers; after seniors and useless, committed a businessman's wife. Then ordered wine, playing a few songs so fast. End of the song-compassion naturally born. while the autobiography of joy when she was young thing, now drift perish haggard, was removed in between the rivers and the lakes. And I am out of the capital two years, a quiet calm and self-peaceful, thinking her speech perception, the night began to feel the exile meaning. So do long sentences, the songs to grant her; the usual text-totaling six hundred ten six words. Title *Pipa Germination.*

譯文二

Song of the Lute Player（楊憲益、戴乃迭 譯）

In the tenth year of the reign of Yuanhe, I was demoted to the assistant prefectship of Jiujiang. The next autumn, while seeing a friend off atPengpu, I heard someone strumming a lute in a boat at night, playing with the touch of a musician from the capital. I found upon inquiry that the lutist was a courtesan from Chang'an who had learned from the musicians Mu and Cao but growing old and losing her looks, she had married a merchant. Then I ordered drinks and asked her to play a few tunes. After playing, in deep distress, she told me of the pleasures of her youth and said now that her beauty had fades she was drifting from place to place by rivers and lakes. In my two years as an official away from the capital I had been resigned enough, my mind at peace, but moved by her tale that night I began to take my demotion and exile to heart. So I wrote a long poem and presented it to her. It has 612 words and I call it *the Song of the Lute Player.*

    By theXunyang River a guest is seen off one night;
    Chill the autumn, red the maple leaves and in flower the reeds;
    The host alights from his horse, the guest is aboard,
    They raise their cups to drink but have no music.
    Drunk without joy, in sadness they must part;
    At the time of parting the river seems steeped in moonlight;
    Suddenly out on the water a lute is heard;
    The host forgets to turn back, the guest delays going.
    Seeking the sound in the dark, we ask who is the player.
    The lute is silent, hesitant the reply.
    Rowing closer, we ask if we may meet the musician,
    Call for more wine, trim the lamp and resume our feast;
    Only after a thousand entreaties does she appear,
    Her face half-hidden behind the lute in her arms.
    She tunes up and plucks the strings a few times,
    Touching our hearts before even the tune is played;
    Each chord strikes a pensive note,
    As if voicing the disillusion of a lifetime;
    Her head is bent, her fingers stray over the strings,
    Pouring out the infinite sorrows of her heart.
    Lightly she pinches in the strings, slowly she strums and plucks them;
    First *The Rainbow Garments*, then *The Six Minor Notes.*
    The high notes wail like pelting rain,
    The low notes whisper like soft confidences;
    Wailing and whispering interweave,
    Like pearls large and small cascading on a plate of jade,
    Like a warbling oriole gliding below the blossom,
    Like a mountain brook purling down a bank,
    Till the brook turns to ice, the strings seem about snap,
    About to snap, and for one instant all is still,
    Only an undertone of quiet grief,

Is more poignant in the silence than any sound;
Then a silver bottle is smashed, out gushes the water,
Armoured riders charge, their swords and lances clang!
When the tune ends, she draws her pick full across,
And the four strings give a sound like the tearing of silk.
Right and left of the boat all is silence,
We see only the autumn moon, silver in midstream.
Pensively she puts the pick between the strings,
Straightens her clothes, rises and composes herself.
She is, she says, a girl from the capital,
Whose family once lived at the foot of Toad Hill.
At thirteen she learned to play the lute,
And ranked first among the musicians;
Her playing was admired by the old masters,
Her looks were the envy of other courtesans;
Youths from wealthy districts vied in their gifts to engage her,
A single song brought her countless rolls of red silk;
Men smashed jeweled and silver trinkets to mark the beat;
Silk skirts as red as blood were stained by spilt wine.
Pleasure and laughter from one year to the next.
While the autumn moon and spring breeze passed unheeded.
Then her brother joined the army, her aunt died,
The days and nights slipped by and her beauty fades,
No more carriages and horsemen thronged her gate,
And growing old she became a merchant's wife.
The merchant thought only of profit: to seek it he leaves her.
Two months ago he went to Fuliang to buy tea,
Leaving her alone in the boat at the mouth of the river;
All around the moonlight is bright, the river is cold,
And late at night, dreaming of her girlhood,
She cries in her sleep, staining her rouged cheeks with tears.
The music of her lute has made me sign,
And now she tells this plaintive tale of sorrow;

We are both ill-starred, drifting on the face of the earth;

No matter if we were strangers before this encounter.

Last year I bade the imperial city farewell;

A demoted official, I lay ill in Xunyang;

Xunyang is a paltry place without any music,

For one year I heard no wind instruments, no strings.

Now I live on the low, damp flat by the River Pen,

Round my house yellow reeds and bitter bamboos grow rife;

From dawn till dusk I hear no other sounds

But the wailing of night-jars and the moaning of apes.

On a day of spring blossoms by the river or moonlit night in autumn

I often call for wine and drink alone;

Of course, there are rustic songs and village pipes,

But their shrill discordant notes grate on my ears;

Tonight listening to your lute playing

Was like hearing fairy music; it gladdened my ears.

Don't refuse, but sit down and play another tune,

And I'll write a *Song of the Lute Player* for you.

Touched by my words, she stands there for some time,

Then goes back to her seat and played with quickened tempo

Music sadder far than the first melody,

And at the sound not a man of us has dry eyes.

The assistant prefect of Jiangzhou is so moved

That his blue coat is wet with tears.

譯文三

Song of the Pipa（張廷琛、魏博思 譯）

In 815, the tenth year of Yuan He, I was demoted and sent to Jiujiang to assume the duties of Assistant Prefect. The following autumn, seeing off a friend at Penpu, I heard someone skillfully playing the pipa aboard a boat. Inquiring, I learned that the player was a former courtesan from Chang-an who had studied the pipa with famous masters. Growing old and losing her looks, she had married a merchant. Then I ordered wine and asked her to play. After her performance, deeply distressed, she told me of her youth and of her present life of drifting from place to place. I thought that I had long become resigned to my own fall in life, but after hearing her story I began to take my exile more to heart. So I wrote this long poem of Six hundred and sixteen characters to present to her. I call it *the Song of the Pipa*.

> One night, while maples and flowering reeds,
> Were rustling in the wind,
> I saw a friend off by theXunyang River.
> Having dismounted our horses and boarded his boat,
> We raised our cups, in silence, having ordered no music,
> To find that drunkenness could not dispel our grief at parting.
> As the moon sank into the mist-covered river,
> Suddenly upon the waters came the music of the pipa,
> And I forgot my turning home, my friend his setting forth.
> Following the sound, in a low voice I asked who played.
> The music halted, but the player would not respond.
> We relit the lanterns, replenished food and wine,
> And moved the boat around to issue our invitation.
> Only after much cajoling did she then appear,
> Cradling the pipa, her face half hidden.
> Just her turning of the frets to tune the instrument,
> Sang the depth of her emotion.
> Every not and every chord,
> Gave utterance to a life of yearning,
> With lowered head, she played as if at random,
> Emptying her heart of endless passion.
> Pressing, sliding, stroking, plucking,
> First she played The Rainbow Skirts and then Six Minor Notes.
> Loud as drumming rain, soft as whispered secrets,
> Pearls of varied sizes cascaded on a tray of jade,
> An oriole warbled from within the flowery branches,
> A stream sobbed its way across its sandy shoals.
> The stream then turned to ice, the note to crystal,

To a perfect crystal silence that spoke more loudly than sound.
As water gushes forth from a shattered silver bottle,
And armored steeds charge into clashing sword and spear,
She swept her plectrum across the strings to make an end.
The four strings sounding together,
Like a single piece of splitting silk.
All round us the boats were silent,
We could only see the mid-stream whiteness of the autumn moon.

Pensively, she slipped the plectrum back beneath the strings,
And, straightening her clothes, she rose with great solemnity.
In the capital I was born,
In a household just below Xia Muoling.
Mastering the pipa at thirteen,
I was ranked among the most accomplished in the land.
Famed masters listened spellbound to my playing.
Made up, I was the envy of all the other courtesans.
Young dandies vied to give me silk.
In a single performance I don't know
How many bolts of silk they threw me,
How many precious things they broke while beating time,
How many blood red robes of silk they ruined spilling wine.
Year after year I spent in ceaseless gaiety,
Minding neither spring wind nor autumn moon.
My brother went to war, my aunt died;
As dawn yields to dusk my beauty faded,
And before my gate the carriages were few.
Too old, I married a merchant,
Who values profit and makes light of parting.
Last month he went to Fuliang to buy tea;
By the river's mouth I've waited on an empty boat,
Chill moonlit water my only company.
Deep in the night I'll dream suddenly of youth,

And dreaming, stain roughed cheeks with tears.

Already, the pipa's song had made me sign,
But there words made me utterly forlorn.
Both losers in this wider world,
By chance both here,
It mattered not that we had never met before.
Last year I left the capital.
Demoted, lying ill in Xunyang,
Throughout the year I've been deprived of music.
I live by the River Pen, in a low, damp place,
Surrounded by yellow reeds and bitter bamboo.
Morning to evening nothing can be heard.
But cuckoos' bloody cry, and the lonely wail of apes.
On flowery spring mornings or moonlit autumn nights,
I take my wine along the riverside and drink alone.
Of course there are the caws and grunts and whoops,
That they call music here,
But tonight it seemed that fairy music sharpened my senses once again.
Please don't refuse to sit and play another piece,
And for you I'll write the「Song of the Pipa.」
Moved by my words, she stood long in silence,
Then sat down to play with great intensity,
And with even greater sadness than before,
So that we hid our tears behind uplifted sleeves.
Among us, none wept more bitterly than I:
Drenched with tears are the robes of office,
Of the Assistant Prefect of Jiujiang.

譯文四

Song of a Pipa Player（許淵衝 譯）

One night by riverside I bade a friend goodbye;
In maple leaves and rushes autumn seemed to sigh.

My friend and I dismounted and came into the boat;
Without flute songs we drank our cups with heavy heart;
The moonbeams blended with water when we were to part.
Suddenly o'er the stream we heard a pipa sound;
I forgot to go home and the guest stood spell-bound.
We followed where the music led to find the player,
But heard the pipa stop and no music in the air.
We moved our boat towards the one whence came the strain,
Brought back the lamp, asked for more wine and drank again.
Repeatedly we called for the fair player still.
She came, her face half hidden behind a pipa still.
She turned the pegs and tested twice or thrice each string;
Before a tune was played we heard her feelings sing.
Each string she plucked, each note she struck with pathos strong,
All seemed to say she'd missed her dreams all her life long.
Head bent, she played with unpremeditated art,
On and on to pour out her overflowing heart.
She lightly plucked, slowly stroked and twanged loud,
The song of 「Green Waist」 after that of 「Rainbow Cloud」.
The thick strings loudly thrummed like the pattering rain;
The fine strings softly tinkled in a murmuring strain.
When mingling loud and sot notes were together played,
You heard orioles warble in a flowery land,
Then a sobbing stream run along a beach of sand.
But the stream seemed so cold as to tighten the string;
From tightened strings no more song could be heard to sing.
Still we heard hidden grief and vague regret concealed;
Then music expressed far less than silence revealed.
Suddenly we heard water burst a silver jar,
And the clash of spears and sabers come from afar.
She made a central sweep when the music was ending;
The four strings made one sound, as if silk one was rending.
Silence reigned left and right of the boat, east and west;

We saw but autumn moon white in the river's breast.
She slid the plectrum pensively between the strings,
Smoothed out her dress and rose with a composed mien.
「I spent,」she said,「in the capital my early springs,
Where at the foot of Mount of Toads my home had been.
At thirteen I learned on the pipa how to play,
And my name was among the primas of the day.
I won my master's admiration for my skill;
My beauty was envied by songstresses fair still.
The gallant young men vied to shower gifts on me;
One tune played, countless silk rolls were given with glee.
Beating time, I let silver comb and pin drop down,
And spilt-out wine oft stained my blood-red silken gown.
From year to year I laughed my joyous life away,
On moonlit autumn light as windy vernal day.
My younger brother left for war, and died my maid;
Days passed, nights came, and my beauty began to fade.
Fewer and fewer were cabs and steeds at my door;
I married a smug merchant when my prime was o'er.
The merchant cared for money much more than for me;
One month ago he went away to purchase tea,
Leaving his lonely wife alone in empty boat;
Shrouded in moonlight, on the cold river I float.
Deep in the night I dreams of happy bygone years,
And woke to find my rouged face crisscrossed with tears.
Listening to her story, I signed again and again.
Both of us in misfortune go from shore to shore.
Meeting now, need we have known each other before?
I was banished from the capital last year,
To live degraded and ill in this city here.
The city's too remote to know melodious song,
So I have never heard music all the year long.
I dwell by riverbank on a low and damp ground,

In a house with wild reeds and stunted bamboos around.

What is here to be heard from daybreak till nightfall,

But gibbon's cry and cuckoo's homeward-going call?

By blooming riverside and under autumn moon,

I've often taken wine up and drunk it alone.

Thought I have mountain songs and village pipes to hear,

Yet they are crude and strident and grate on the ear.

Listening to you playing on pipa tonight,

With your music divine e'en my hearing seems bright.

Will you sit down and play for us a tune once more?

I'll write for you an ode to the pipa I adore.

Touched by what I said, the player stood for long,

Then sat down, tore at strings and played another song.

So sad, so drear, so different, it moved us deep;

Those who heard it hid the face and began to weep.

Of all the company at table who wept most?

It was none other than the exiled blue-robed host.

第四節　王維詩歌英譯賞析

一、《相思》

相思（王維）
紅豆生南國，春來發幾枝，
願君多採擷，此物最相思。

譯本一

Love Beans（許景城 譯）

Red beans in South grow.

Spring comes, sprays aglow.

Pick more beans, may thou?

Of love they're best show!

譯本二

Love Seeds（W. J. B. Fletcher 譯）

The red bean grows in southern lands.

With spring its slender tendrils twine.

Gather for me some more, I pray.

Of fond remembrance It's the sign.

譯本三

One-Hearted（Witter Bynner 譯）

When those red berries come in springtime,

Flushing on your southland branches,

Take home an armful, for my sake,

As a symbol of our love.

譯本四

Love Seeds（許淵衝 譯）

The red beans grow in southern land.

How many load the autumn trees!

Gather them till full is your hand!

They would revive fond memories.

譯本五

Lovesickness（辜正坤 譯）

In the south red bean shrubs grow,

In spring abundant seeds they bear.

Gather them more, please, you know

They are the very symbol of love and care.

譯本六

Red Beans（吳鈞陶 譯）

Red Beans come from the Southern Land,

In spring, the trees grow some new wands.

Please pluck more of these seeds with your hands,
To show your love to friends it's grand.

譯本七

Red Beans（徐忠杰 譯）

Red Beans are grown in a southern clime,
A few branches burgeon in spring time.
On your lap, try to gather as many as you can,
The best reminder of love between woman and man.

譯本八

Red Love Beans（杜承南 譯）

The red beans are grown in the south,
Their flowers are blooming when spring comes.
Try to gather more to your heart's content,
They always remind you of the loving feelings.

譯本九

Lovesickness-Seeds（朱曼華 譯）

Lovesickness-seeds planted in the Southland,
Young twigs are growing up in the vernal wind.
I advise you to pick up much more seeds.
With best understanding lovesickness.

譯本十

Love sickness（王道餘 譯）

The berries red in the south land grow,
How many shoots in spring it brings?
May you gather as many as you can,
For my lovesickness these things best stand.

譯本十一

Love's Yearnings（龔景浩 譯）

The Red Beans grow in the South,

Each spring this tall shrub puts out some new twigs.

I hope you would pick a great deal,

They bring on the most exquisite love's yearnings one can feel.

譯本十二

The Love Peas（顧丹柯 譯）

In the southern land grow the love peas,

With spring the first sprouts begin to swell.

Gather more of them, please,

For my fond memories they can best tell.

二、《送元二使安西》

送元二使安西（王維）

渭城朝雨浥輕塵，客舍清清柳色新。

勸君更盡一杯酒，西出陽關無故人。

譯文一

Farewell to an Envoy on His Mission to Anxi（郭著章 譯）

What's got Weicheng's path dust wet is the morning rain,

The willows near the Hotel become green again.

I urge you to empty another cup of wine,

West of the Yangguan Pass you'll see no more of mine.

譯文二

A Farewell Song（許淵衝 譯）

No dust is raised on the road wet with morning rain,

The willows by the hotel look so fresh and green.

I invite you to drink a cup of wine again;

West of the Sunny Pass no more friends will be seen.

譯文三

Bidding Adieu to Yuan Junior in HisMission to Anxi Song of the Town of Wei
(孫大雨 譯)

The fall of morning drops in this Town of Wei.

Its dust light doth moisten,

Tenderly green are the new willow sprouts.

Of this spring adorned tavern.

I pay thee to quench once more full to the brim.

This farewell cup of wine,

For after thy departure from this western most pass,

Thou will have no old friend of mine.

譯文四

Seeing off Yuan Second on a Mission An-his (James J. Y. Liu 譯)

The light dust in the town of Wei is wet with morning rain;

Green, green, the willows by the guest house their yearly freshness regain.

Be sure to finish yet another cup of wine, my friend,

West of the Yang Gate no old acquaintance will you meet again.

譯文五

A Song at Weicheng (Witter Bynner 譯)

A morning-rain has settled the dust in Weicheng;

Willows are green again in the tavern dooryard.

Wait till we empty one more cup,

West of Yang Gate there'll be no old friends.

三、《送別》

送別 (王維)

下馬飲君酒，問君何所之？

君言不得意，歸臥南山陲。

但去莫復問，白雲無盡時。

譯文一

Dismounting（許淵衝 譯）

I invite you to drink wine;

Where are you leaving for? Is there a place fine?

Unheeded by the world, home you'll your way.

To lie down atZhongnan Mountain's foot, you say,

No more questionsI'll put but bid you good-bye;

The endless clouds are waiting for you on high.

譯文二

Goodbye to Meng Hao-jan（Herbert A. Giles 譯）

Dismounted, o'er wine we had said our last say;

Then I whisper,「Dear friend, tell me whither away.」

「Alas!」he replied,「I am sick of life's ills.」

「And I long for repose on the slumbering hills.」

「But oh seek not to pierce where my footsteps may stray.」

「The white clouds will soothe me for ever and ay.」

譯文三

So Farewell. And If for Ever, Still for Even Fare Ye Well

（W. J. B. Fletcher 譯）

Quitting my horse, a cup with you I drank.

And drinking, asked you whither you were bound.

Your hopes unprospered, said you, turned you round.

You went. I asked no more. The white clouds pass,

And never yet have any limit found.

譯文四

At Parting（Witter Bynner 譯）

I dismount from my horse and I offer you wine.

And I ask you where you are going and why.

And you answer:「I am discontent,

And would rest at the foot of the southern mountain.
So give me leave and ask me no questions.
White clouds pass there without end.」

译文五
To See a Friend Off（Wai-Lim Yip 译）
Dismount and drink this wine.
Where to? I ask.
At odds with the world:
Return to rest by the South Hill.
Go. Go. Do not ask again.
Endless, the white clouds.

译文六
Seeing Someone Off（Burton Waston 译）
We dismount; I you wine,
And ask, where are you off to?
You answer, nothing goes right!
Back home to lie down by Southern Mountain.
Go then, I'll ask no more,
There's no end to white clouds there.

四、《鹿柴》

鹿柴（王维）
空山不见人，但闻人语响。
返景入深林，复照青苔上。

译文一
Deer-park Hermitage（Witter Bynner 译）
There seems to be on one on the empty mountain.
And yet I think I hear a voice.
Where sunlight, entering a grove,

Shines back to me from the green moss.

譯文二

Deer Enclosure (Jerome Ch'en and Michael Bullock 譯)

On the lonely mountain I met no one,

I hear only the echo of human voices.

At an angle the sun's rays enter the depths of the wood,

And shine upon the green moss.

譯文三

Deer Enclosure (Wai-Lim Yip 譯)

Empty mountain: no man.

But voices of men are heard.

Sun's reflection reaches into the woods.

And shines upon the green moss.

譯文四

Deer Enclosure (Victor H. Mair 譯)

On the empty mountain, seeing no one,

Only hearing the echoes of someone's voice;

Returning light enters the deep forest,

Again shining upon the green moss.

譯文五

Deep in the Mountain Wilderness (Kenneth Rexroth 譯)

Deep in the mountain wilderness,

Where nobody ever comes.

Only once in a great while,

Something like the sound of a far off voice.

The low rays of the sun,

Slip through the dark forest,

And gleam again on the shadowy moss.

第五節　孟浩然詩歌英譯賞析

一、《春曉》

春曉（孟浩然）
春眠不覺曉，處處聞啼鳥。
夜來風雨聲，花落知多少。

譯文一

Spring Morn（許景城 譯）
Spring sleep, coming morn, unaware.
Awake, hearing birds' song everywhere.
After last night's wind and rain,
how many flowers fallen fair?

譯文二

Spring Dawn（宇文所安 譯）
Sleeping in spring, unaware of the dawn,
Then everywhere I hear birds singing.
Last night, the sound of wind and the rain,
Flowers have fallen, I wonder how many.
選自：Stephen Owen. The Great Age of Chinese Poetry: The High T'ang [M]. Yale University Press, 1981: 86.

譯文三

A Spring Morning（許淵衝 譯）
This morning of spring in bed I'm lying.
Not woke up till I hear birds crying.
After a night of wind and showers,
How many are the fallen flowers?
選自：許淵衝. 唐詩三百首新譯 [M]. 北京：商務印書館，1988：28.

譯文四

A Spring Morning（Witter Bynner、江亢虎 譯）

I awake light-hearted this morning of spring,
Everywhere round me the singing of birds.
But now I remember the night, the storm,
And I wonder how many blossoms were broken.

譯文五

Dawn in Spring（John Turner 譯）

How suddenly the morning comes in Spring!
On every side you can hear the sweet birds sing.
Last night amidst the storm-Ah, who can tell?
With wind and rain, how many blossoms fell.

譯文六

Spring Dawn（孫大雨 譯）

Feeling not when cometh the peep of spring dawn,
Everywhere birds' songs I hear in my slumber.
Though the sounds of wind and rain all the night long,
Know I not how many the flowers fall in number.

譯文七

The Dawn of Spring（Rewi Alley 譯）

Spring dreams that went on well past dawn;
And I felt that all around me was the sound of birds singing;
But really night was full of the noise of rain and wind,
And now I wonder how many blossoms have fallen.

譯文八

At dawn in Spring（王守義、約翰·諾弗爾 譯）

Slept so well I didn't know it was dawn.
Birds singing in every courtyard woke me up.

The wind and rain troubled my dream last night.
I think of all those petals swept to the ground.

譯文九

Spring Morn（卓振英 譯）

Awakening from slumber to a morn of spring,
I hear the birds everywhere beautifully sing.
The winds shatter'd and the rains splatter'd yesternight;
How many flowers have dropp'd in a wretched plight?

譯文十

One Morning in Spring（翁顯良 譯）

Late! This spring morning as I awake I know.
All around me the birds are crying, crying.
The storm last night, I sensed its fury. How many,
I wonder, are fallen, poor dear flowers!

譯文十一

A Morn in Spring（王大濂 譯）

It's after dawn when I awoke this morn in spring;
Then everywhere around me I heard birds all sing.
I now recall the sound of big storm late atnight;
How many flowers would have been blown to ground insight?

譯文十二

Spring Dawn（文殊 譯）

Oversleeping in spring I missed the dawn,
Now everywhere the cries of birds are heard.
Tumult of wind and rain had filled the night.
How many blossoms fell during the storm,
Oh, what a flowery-falling sight.

譯文十三

Spring Mornings（徐忠杰 譯）

One slumbers late in the morning in spring,
Everywhere, one hears birds warble or sing.
As the night advances, rain spatters; winds moan.
How many flowers have dropped? Can that be known?

譯文十四

Spring Dawn（張廷琛、魏博思 譯）

Oversleeping in spring I missed the dawn;
Now everywhere the cries of birds are heard.
Tumult of wind and rain had filled the night
How many blossoms fell during the storm?

譯文十五

The Spring Dawn（吳均陶 譯）

Slumbering, I know not the spring dawn is peeping.
But everywhere the singing birds are cheeping.
Last night I heard the rain dripping and the wind weeping.
How many petals were now on the ground sleeping.

譯文十六

Spring Dawn（Adele 譯）

Asleep in the spring, I missed the dawn.
Until I heard the birds singing everywhere.
Wind and rain had clamored last night.
How many flowers fell during the storm?

譯文十七

Daybreak in Spring（唐一鶴 譯）

In spring the sleeper doesn't know,
It's daybreaking.
Everywhere birds are heard Chirping.

Last night there came sounds of,

Wind blowing and rain pattering.

A lot of petals must have fallen,

He's thinking.

譯文十八

Spring Dawn（趙甄陶 譯）

Unconscious of dawning in the spring,

I hear birds crying all around.

There was sound of wind and rain all night;

How many flowers have fallen aground?

二、《宿建德江》

宿建德江（孟浩然）

移舟泊煙渚，

日暮客愁新。

野曠天低樹，

江清月近人。

譯文一

Night on the Great River（Carlos Williams 譯）

Steering my little boat towards a misty islet,

I watch the sun descend while my sorrows grow.

In the vast night the sky hangs lower than the treetops,

But in the blue lake the moon is coming close.

譯文二

Night on the Great River（Kenneth Rexroth 譯）

We anchor the boat alongside a hazy island.

As the sun sets I am overwhelmed with nostalgia.

The plain stretches away without limit.

The sky is just above the tree tops.

The river flows quietly by.

The moon comes down amongst men.

譯文三

Mooring on Chien-te River（Gary Snyder 譯）

The boat rocks at anchor by the misty island,

Sunset, my loneliness comes again.

In these vast wilds the sky arches down to the trees.

In the clear river water, the moon draws near.

譯文四

Mooring on the River at Jiande（許淵衝 譯）

My boat is moored near an isle in mist gray,

I'm grieved anew to see the parting day.

On boundless plain trees seem to touch the sky,

In water clear the moon appears so nigh.

譯文五

At Anchor（Herbert A. Giles 譯）

I steer my boat to anchor by the mist-clad river,

And mourn the dying day that brings me nearer to my fate.

Across the woodland wild I see the sky lean on the trees,

While close to hand the mirror moon floats on the shining seas.

譯文六

Mooring on the River at Jiande（W. J. B. Fletcher 譯）

Our boat by the mist-covered islet we tied.

The sorrows of absence the sunset brings back.

Low breasting the foliage the sky loomed black.

The river is bright with the moon at our side.

譯文七

A Night-Mooring on the Jiande River（Witter Bynner 譯）

While my little boat moves on its mooring mist,
And daylight wanes, old memories begin.
How wide the world was, how close the trees to heaven!
And how clear in the water the nearness of the moon!

三、《夏日南亭懷辛大》

夏日南亭懷辛大（孟浩然）
山光忽西落，池月漸東上。
散髮乘夕涼，開軒臥閒敞。
荷風送香氣，竹露滴清響。
欲取鳴琴彈，恨無知音賞。
感此懷故人，中宵勞夢想。

譯文一

In Summer At The South Pavilion Thinking Of Xing（Witter Bynner 譯）

The mountain-light suddenly fails in the west,
In the east from the lake the slow moon rises.
I loosen my hair to enjoy the evening coolness,
And open my window and lie down in peace.
The wind brings me odours of lotuses,
And bamboo-leaves drip with a music of dew.
I would take up my lute and I would play,
But, alas, who here would understand?
And so I think of you, old friend,
O troubler of my midnight dreams!

譯文二

In Dreamland（Herbert A. Giles 譯）

The sun has set behind the western slope,
The eastern moon lies mirrored in the pool;

With streaming hair my balcony I ope,
And stretch my limbs out to enjoy the cool.
Loaded with lotus-scent the breeze sweeps by,
Clear dripping drops from tall bamboos I hear,
I gaze upon my idle lute and sigh.
Alas no sympathetic soul is near!
And so I doze, the while before mine eyes,
Dear friends of other days in dream-clad forms arise.

譯文三

A Reverie in a Summer-House（Charles Budd 譯）
The daylight fades behind theWestern Mountains,
And in the east is seen the rising moon,
Which faintly mirrored in the garden fountains,
Foretells that night and dreams are coming soon.

With window open-hair unloosed and flowing,
I lie in restful ease upon my bed.
The evening breeze across the lilies blowing,
With fragrant coolness falls upon my head.

And in the solemn stillness all prevailing,
The fall of dewdrops from the tall bamboos.
Which grow in graceful rows along the railing,
Sounds through the silence soft as dove's faint coos.

On such an eve as this I would be singing,
And playing plaintive tunes upon the lute,
And thus to mind old friends and pleasures bringing;
But none are here to join with harp and flute!

So in a pleasant stillness I lie dreaming,
Of bygone days and trusty friends of old,

Among whom Sin-tze's happy face is beaming;
I would my thoughts could now to him be told.

第六節　李商隱詩歌英譯賞析

一、《夜雨寄北》

夜雨寄北（李商隱）
君問歸期未有期，
巴山夜雨漲秋池。
何當共剪西窗燭，
卻話巴山夜雨時。

譯文一

Note On A Rainy Night To A Friend In The North（Witter Bynner 譯）
You ask me when I am coming. I do not know.
I dream of your mountains and autumn pools brimming all night with the rain.
Oh, when shall we be trimming wicks again, together in your western window?
When shall I be hearing your voice again, all night in the rain?

譯文二

Written on Rainy Night to My Wife in the North（許淵衝 譯）
You ask me whenI can come back but I don't know.
The pools in western hills with autumn rain o'er flow.
When by our window can we trim the wicks again.
And talk about this endless, dreary night of rain?

譯文三

Souvenirs（Herbert A. Giles 譯）
You ask when I'm coming: alas not just yet.
How the rain filled the pools on that night when we met!
Ah, when shall we ever snuff candles again,

And recall the glad hours of that evening of rain?

譯文四

Night Rains: A Letter to Go North（Wai-Lim Yip 譯）

You ask: when to return? Don't know when.

Pa Shan's night rain swell autumn pools.

When can we trim candles together at West Window,

And talk of Pa Shan, Pa Shan of night rains?

譯文五

Lines Sent to the North Written during Night Rains（孫大雨 譯）

Being asked for my home-coming date,

I tell thee I'm not sure when that'll be,

As night rains on the mounts of Ba fall,

And autumn pools are brimmed from the lea.

Then we shall by the west window sit,

Clipping the candle wick in some night,

And talk of the night rains on the Ba mounts,

When I think of thee with mute delight.

譯文六

Lines Sent North One Rainy Night（張廷琛，Bruce M. Wilson 譯）

You ask me for the date of my return: I have no date,

In the Ba mountains, rain fills the autumn pond.

When will we sit together in the western window,

Trimming the candle, and talking about this rainy night in Ba?

Ba: In Sichuan, where the poet has been posted.

二、《無題四首（二）》

　　無題四首（二）（李商隱）

相見時難別亦難，東風無力百花殘。

春蠶到死絲方盡，蠟炬成灰淚始干。

曉鏡但愁雲鬢改，夜吟應覺月光寒。
蓬山此去無多路，青鳥殷勤為探看。

譯文一
To One Unnamed（許淵沖 譯）
It's difficult for us to meet and hard to part;
The east wind is too weak to revive flowers dead.
Spring silkworm till its death spins silk from love-sick heart;
A candle but when burned out has no tears to shed.
At dawn I'm grieved to think your mirrored hair turns grey;
At night you would feel cold while I croon by moonlight.
To the three fairy hills it is not a long way.
Would the blue birds oft fly to see you on the height?
(The poet writes this poem for his unnamed lover compared to a fairy living in the three mountains on the sea where only the mythical blue birds could bring messages.)

譯文二
An Untitled Poem（林建民 譯）
It's excitedly unbearable to meet as well as to depart,
Easterly wind weakens while all kinds of flowers faded;
Spring silkworm died after it ended fibre productions,
A candle turns to ashes when shedding of tears dries up;
Looking at morning mirror I worry my temple is changed.
Humming verse at night moonlight appeared to be chilly;
As the legendary Mount Fenglai isn't far from my place,
I asked the blue bird to convey you my kindest regards.

譯文三
A Titleless Poem（卓振英 譯）
It's hard for us to meet, but separation's harder still.
When breezes languish, fall and wither all the flowers will.
The silkworm ceases not to spin her thread before she's dead;
Unless burnt to ashes endless tears a candle'll shed.

At dawn the mirror may betray your dread of aging hair;
Reciting poems at night I feel the moon's chill in the air.
As Mount Penglai is not very long a distance away,
The Blackbird may be kind enough to you frequent, I pray!

譯文四
Untitled（張廷琛、Bruce M. Wilson 譯）
Difficult it was for us to meet, and difficult to part.
Now the east wind has failed, and all the flowers wither.
The silkworm labors until death its fine thread severs;
The candle's tears are dried when it itself consumes.

Before the mirror, you will fret to find those cloudlike tresses changing.
Making rhymes at night, you'll find the moonlight has grown chill.
The fairy mountain Peng is not so far from here:
Might the Blue Bird become our go between?

Fairy mountain Peng: One of the fairy mountains believed to lie in the Eastern Sea.

Blue Bird: Messenger that heralded the arrival of the Queen Mother of the West to the court of the Han Emperor Wu: a go-between.

三、《錦瑟》

錦瑟（李商隱）
錦瑟無端五十弦，
一弦一柱思華年。
莊生曉夢迷蝴蝶，
望帝春心托杜鵑。
滄海月明珠有淚，
藍田日暖玉生煙。
此情可待成追憶，
只是當時已惘然。

譯文一

The Sad Zither (許淵衝 譯)

Why should the zither sad have fifty strings?
Each string, each strain evokes but vanished springs:
Dim morning dream to be a butterfly;
Amorous heart poured out in cuckoo's cry.
In moonlit pearls see tears in mermaid's eyes;
From sunburnt emerald let vapour rise.
Such feeling cannot be recalled again;
It seemed long lost e'en when it was felt then.

譯文二

The Gorgeous Zither (戴乃迭、楊憲益 譯)

For no reason the gorgeous zither has fifty strings,
Each string, each fret, recalls a youthful year.
Master Zhuang woke from a dream puzzled by a butterfly,
Emperor Wang reposed his amorous heart to the cuckoo.
The moon shines on the sea, pearls look like tears,
The sun is warm at Lantian, The jade emits mist.
This feeling might have become a memory to recall,
But, even then, it was already suggestive of sorrows.

According to a fable story, Zhuang Zi (369-286BC), a famous philosopher of the Warring States Period, dreamt of being a butterfly and when he woke up, he was so confused that he could not tell whether it was him that had dreamt of being a butterfly or it was a butterfly that was then dreaming of being him.

A legendary king who had an affair with his prime minister's wife and after his death his spirit change into the cuckoo.

A hill famous for its jade in present—day Lantian County, Shaanxi Province.

譯文三

Jewelled Zither (John A. Turner 譯)

Vain are the jeweled zither's fifty strings,

Each string, each stop, bears thought of vanished things.
The sage of his loved butterflies day-dreaming,
The King that sighed his soul into a bird.
Tears that are pearls, in ocean moonlight streaming,
Jade mists the sun distils from Sapphire Sword.
What need their memory to recall today?
A day was theirs, which is now passed away.

第七節　唐朝諸家詩選譯

一、《春江花月夜》

　　張若虛的《春江花月夜》共三十六句，每四句一換韻，以富有生活氣息的清麗之筆，創造性地再現了江南春夜的景色，如同月光照耀下的萬里長江畫卷，同時寄寓著遊子思歸的離別相思之苦。詩篇意境空明，纏綿悱惻，洗淨了六朝宮體的濃脂膩粉，詞清語麗，韻調優美，膾炙人口，乃千古絕唱，素有「以孤篇壓倒全唐」之譽，聞一多稱之為「詩中的詩，頂峰上的頂峰」。

　　　春江花月夜（張若虛）
春江潮水連海平，海上明月共潮生。
灩灩隨波千萬里，何處春江無月明！
江流宛轉繞芳甸，月照花林皆似霰。
空裡流霜不覺飛，汀上白沙看不見。
江天一色無纖塵，皎皎空中孤月輪。
江畔何人初見月？江月何年初照人？
人生代代無窮已，江月年年只相似。
不知江月待何人，但見長江送流水。
白雲一片去悠悠，青楓浦上不勝愁。
誰家今夜扁舟子？何處相思明月樓？
可憐樓上月徘徊，應照離人妝鏡臺。
玉戶簾中卷不去，搗衣砧上拂還來。
此時相望不相聞，願逐月華流照君。
鴻雁長飛光不度，魚龍潛躍水成文。

昨夜閒潭夢落花，可憐春半不還家。
江水流春去欲盡，江潭落月復西斜。
斜月沉沉藏海霧，碣石瀟湘無限路。
不知乘月幾人歸？落花搖情滿江樹。

譯文一

Moon Thoughts（W. J. B. Fletcher 譯）

Over a river by the ocean floating,
That flows not for the tide.
The moon uprises on the waters' motion,
With equal kingdom wide.
The Ocean's face is radiant with her glory.
Perfumed through flowery banks the river flows.
And serpents with a winding desultory,
By flowering woods that gleam as purest snows,
So white that ivory no outline shows,
Nor seen the white sand on the shore thereby.
The fleckless sky meets with the stainless sea,
And wheel-large floats in vast eternity,
The moon upon the flawless crystal sky.

Who by this river first beheld her face?
Whom by this river did the moon first see?
Ah, many generations of his race,
Have come, and past into infinity,
While she rode lightly in immensity.
I do not know for whom her beams always,
Shine—but the river waters flow away!
And one white fleck of cloud them follows too,
Tracing their windings with its pearly hue.
To-night who floats upon the tiny skiff?
From what high tower yearns out upon the night.
The dear beloved in the pale moonlight,

Alone, so lonely with the lonely moon?

In the deep chamber where her hair she braids,
And where the moon oft kissed our arms entwined.
Where, oh, we parted—lo, she rolls the blind.
And inward steps the moon with silent pace.
Or noiseless gazes on her thoughtful face,
When busied in the working of her maids.

To each unknown our thoughts go forth to meet.
How would I ride the moonbeams to thy feet!
The wild swans and the geese go sailing by,
But rob not any brightness from the sky,
And fishes ripples on the water pleat.

Last night, when dreaming, ah, I seemed to see,
That many flowers had fallen by this stream.
And low I moaned, 「Already spring will flee,
And I can barely see thee in a dream.」
The waters bear away the spring; and now,
But scattered stars remain upon the bough.
The moon is sinking to her western hall,
Darkened and drooping in the sea mists' pall.

From thee to me I cannot tell how far!
How many with the moon home wandered are.
I cannot tell—But as the shadowy trees,
Stir on the stream with sighings sad and lone,
So sighs my soul to thee, my own, my own!

譯文二

A Moonlit Nighton the Spring River (許淵衝 譯)

In spring the river rises as high as the sea,

And with the river's rise the moon uprises bright.
She follows the rolling waves for ten thousand li,
And where the river flows, there overflows her light.

The river winds around the fragrant islet where,
The blooming flowers in her light all look like snow.
You cannot tell her beams from hoar frost in the air,
Nor from white sand upon Farewell Beach below.

No dust has stained the water blending with the skies;
A lonely wheel like moon shines brilliant far and wide.
Who by the riverside first saw the moon arise?
When did the moon first see a man by riverside?

Ah, generations have come and pasted away;
From year to year the moons look alike, old and new.
We do not know tonight for whom she sheds her ray,
But hear the river say to its water adieu.

Away, away is sailing a single cloud white;
On Farewell Beach pine away maples green.
Where is the wanderer sailing his boat tonight?
Who, pining away, on the moonlit rails would learn?

Alas! The moon is lingering over the tower;
It should have seen the dressing table of the fair.
She rolls the curtain up and light comes in her bower;
She washes but can't wash away the moonbeams there.

She sees the moon, but her beloved is out of sight;
She'd follow it to shine on her beloved one's face.
But message-bearing swans can't fly out of moonlight,
Nor can letter-sending fish leap out of their place.

Last night he dreamed that falling flowers would not stay.
Alas! He can't go home. although half spring has gone.
The running water bearing spring will pass away;
The moon declining over the pool will sink anon.

The moon declining sinks into a heavy mist;
It's a long way between southern rivers and eastern seas.
How many can go home by moonlight who are missed?
The sinking moon sheds yearning o'er riverside trees.

譯文三

The River by Night in Spring (Charles Budd 譯)

In Spring the flooded river meets the tide,
Which from the ocean surges to the land;
The moon across the rolling water shines,
From wave to wave to reach the distant strand.

And when the heaving sea and river meet,
The latter turns and floods the fragrant fields;
While in the moon's pale light as shimmering sleet
Alike seem sandy shores and wooded wealds.

For sky and river in one colour blend,
Without a spot of dust to mar the scene;
While in the heavens above the full-orbed moon,
In white and lustrous beauty hangs serene.

And men and women, as the fleeting years,
Are born into this world and pass away;
And still the river flows, the moon shines fair,
And will their courses surely run for ay.

But who was he who first stood here and gazed,
Upon the river and the heavenly light?
And when did moon and river first behold,
The solitary watcher in the night?

The maples sigh upon the river's bank,
A white cloud drifts across the azure dome;
In yonder boat some traveler sails to-night,
Beneath the moon which links his thoughts with home.

Above the home it seems to hover long,
And peep through chinks within her chamber blind;
The moon-borne message she cannot escape,
Alas, the husband tarries far behind!

She looks across the gulf but hears no voice,
Until her heart with longing leaps apace,
And fain would she the silvery moonbeams follow,
Until they shine upon her loved one's face.

「Last night,」she murmured sadly to herself,
「I dreamt of falling flowers by shady ponds;
My spring, ah me! Half through its course has sped,
But you return not to your wedded honds.」

Forever onward flows the mighty stream;
The spring, half gone, is gliding to its rest;
While on the river and the silent pools,
The moonbeams fail obliquely from the west.

And now the moon descending to the verge,
Has disappeared beneath the sea-borne dew;
While stretch the waters of the 「Siao and Siang」,

And rocks and cliffs, in never-ending view.

譯文四
Spring, River, Flower, Moon, Night（趙彥春 譯）
The spring river swells, level withthe sea,
Wherein, the moon rises with tide, so fair.
Her light follows waves for ten thousand li,
And the spring river is bright everywhere.
The river winds across a fragrant mead;
The moon snows the blooms with her snowy light.
Of hoarfrost in the air one takes no heed,
And on the shoal you fail to see sand white.
No dust, of one hue are river and sky;
So lone, the moon above shines bright and bright.
Who riverside did the moon first espy?
To whom the moon riverside first shed light?
From older generations new ones grow,
And find the moon this year just like that last.
For whom the moon's waiting for I don't know,
And only see the river flowing past.
Away, away floats a wisp of cloud white;
On the Green Maple Shoal I feel so sad.
Who's rowing a canoe against the night?
Who's by a moonlit rail missing her lad?
Over her roof the moon lingers to stay,
And illumines her dresser through the door.
The screen rolled down, the light won't go away;
Brushed offthe block, it comes along once more.
They gaze far, each out of the other's sight,
She'd go with the moonbeams to fondle him.
But wild geese can never outfly the light.
Nor can fish leap overthe ocean's brim.
Last night some flowers fell he had a dream;

Though spring's half over, he can't go back yet.
Spring's fleeting off with the water downstream,
And the moon's westering again to set.
The slanting moon looms amid the sea brume;
From him to her stretches an endless way.
How many can by moonlight return home?
The moon moves the riverside trees to sway.

二、《登幽州臺歌》

登幽州臺歌（陳子昂）
前不見古人，後不見來者。
念天地之悠悠，獨愴然而涕下。

譯文一

Song On Climbing You-Chou Gate Tower（Burton Watson 譯）
Behind me I do not see the ancient men,
Before me I do not see the ones to come.
Thinking of the endlessness of heaven and earth,
Alone in despair, my tears fall down.

譯文二

Regrets（Herbert A. Giles 譯）
My eyes saw not the men of old,
And now their age away had rolled.
I weep to think I shall not see,
The heroes of posterity!

譯文三

Loneliness（Xu Yuanchong 譯）
Where are the great men of the past,
And where are those of future years?
The sky and earth forever last,

Here and now I alone shed tears.

譯文四

I See Them Not（Weng Xianliang 譯）

Men there have been, I see them not.
Men there will be, I see them not.
The world goes on, world without end.
But here and now, alone I stand in tears.

譯文五

Upon ascending the parapet at Youzhou

（Zhang Tingchen、Bruce W. Wilson 譯）

Before me, unseen are the ancients,
Behind me, unseen those to come.
Thinking of this infinite universe,
Alone, in my sorrow, I shed tears.

譯文六

On a Gate-tower at Yuzhou（Witter Bynner 譯）

Where, before me, are the ages that have gone?
And where, behind me, are the coming generations?
I think of heaven and earth, without limit, without end.
And I am all alone and my tears fall down.

譯文七

A Song on Ascending Youzhou Terrace（Zong-qi Cai 譯）

I do not see the ancients before me,
Behind, I do not see those yet to come.
I think of the mournful breadth of heaven and earth,
Alone, grieving-tears fall.

譯文八

Song on Ascending the Youzhou Terrace（Sun Dayu 譯）

Descrying nor the ancients of long yore,

Nor those that are to come in the future far,

I muse on the eternity of heaven and earth.

And, all alone, grieve mutely with tears for my lorn star.

三、《望月懷遠》

望月懷遠（張九齡）
海上生明月，天涯共此時。
情人怨遙夜，竟夕起相思。
滅燭憐光滿，披衣覺露滋。
不堪盈手贈，還寢夢佳期。

譯文一

By Moonlight（Herbert A. Giles 譯）
Over the sea the round moon rises bright,
And floods the horizon with its silver light.
In absence lovers grieve that nights should be,
But all the livelong night I think of thee.
I blow my lamp out to enjoy the rest,
And shake the gathering dewdrop from my vest.
Alas! I cannot share with thee these beams.
So lay me down to seek thee in my dreams.

譯文二

Moon Thoughts（W. J. B. Fletcher 譯）
The clear moon uprises, new-born from the sea.
This hour is the same through the bourne of the skies.
With night my love grieves to be so far from me.
As evening approaches, our longings arise.
When I put out the candle, I long for the light;
And outside I find, ah! How rich is this dew.
Unable in handfuls to give it to you,

In dream of sweet meetings I pass the long night.

譯文三

Looking at the Moon and Thinking of one Far Away（Witter Bynner 譯）

The moon, grown full now over the sea,
Brightening the whole of heaven.
Brings to separated hearts,
The long thoughtfulness of night.
It is no darker though I blow out my candle,
It is no warmer though I put on my coat.
So I leave my message with the moon,
And turn to my bed, hoping for dreams.

譯文四

Watching the Moon with Thoughts of Far Away（Burton Watson 譯）

Bright moon born of the sea,
At sky's farthest edges we share it now.
A man of heart, hating the long night,
Till the end of evening wakeful, remembering,
I put out the lamp, marvel at the moonlight's fullness,
Don a cloak, aware of the dampness of dew.
No way to send my gift, this handful of moonbeams,
I go back to bed, dreaming of good times.

四、《回鄉偶書》

回鄉偶書（賀之章）

少小離家老大回，鄉音無改鬢毛衰。
兒童相見不相識，笑問客從何處來。

譯文一

Coming Home（Xu Yuanchong 譯）

I left home young and not till old do I come back,

My accent is unchanged, my hair no longer black.

The children don't know me, whom I meet on the way,

「Where do you come from, reverend sir?」they smile and say.

譯文二

The Return（Herbert A. Giles 譯）

Bowed down with age I seek my native place,

Unchanged my speech, my hair is silvered now,

My very children do not know my face,

But smiling ask,「O stranger, whence art thou?」

譯文三

Coming Home（Witter Bynner 譯）

I left home young. I returned old;

Speaking as then, but with hair grown thin;

And my children, meeting me, do not know me.

They smile and say:「Stranger, where do you come from?」

譯文四

Written Impromptu upon Returning to My Hometown（Victor H. Mair 譯）

I left home as a youth and am returning an old man,

The sounds of my hometown have not changed,

Yet the hair on my temples is receding;

The children look at me but do not recognize me,

Laughing, they ask,「Guest, where have you come from?」

五、《白雪歌送武判官歸京》

白雪歌送武判官歸京（岑參）
北風卷地白草折，胡天八月即飛雪。
忽如一夜春風來，千樹萬樹梨花開。
散入珠簾濕羅幕，狐裘不暖錦衾薄。
將軍角弓不得控，都護鐵衣冷難著。

瀚海闌干百丈冰，愁雲慘淡萬里凝。
中軍置酒飲歸客，胡琴琵琶與羌笛。
紛紛暮雪下轅門，風掣紅旗凍不翻。
輪臺東門送君去，去時雪滿天山路。
山回路轉不見君，雪上空留馬行處。

譯文一

Parting Amid a Snowstorm（翁顯良 譯）

Sudden the blasts from the north in mid-autumn, flattening the pallid gross, driving snowflakes across barbaric skies. Behold!

The woods have taken on the look of a pear orchard in full blossom, as if capricious spring, returning in the night, had breathed itsmagic into this Tatar land.

Such a snowstorm makes the naught of drapery pearled or silken.

Nor fur of fox, nor broidered quilt, is proof against its bitter cold.

Even seasoned soldiers, hands benumbed, find it hard to draw the bow.

Even the old marshal, eying his coat of mail, feels the chill in its steely sheen.

Forbidding, indeed, the frozen vastness, the towering masses of chaotic ice, the pall of curdled clouds drab and drear.

At headquarter a farewell feast is spread, with music of flute and fiddle, zither and lute.

Towards evening, when its time to part, the snow thickens, coming down in swirls.

Not a flutter in our bright red standard, though. Stiff with rime, it stands like a sculpture atop the garrison gate.

The garrison gate—the city gate—would that I could go farther.

There lies the way home, eastward throughTian Shan, now smothered in snow.

Adieu, my friend! Adieu!

I watch him ride into the storm, round a bend in the road, and pass out of sight.

His tracks, too, will soon be obliterated by the drifting snow.

譯文二

A song of white snow in farewell to field-clerk Wu going home

（Witter Bynner 譯）

The north wind rolls the white grasses and breaks them;

And the Eighth-month snow across the Tartar sky.
Is like a spring gale, come up in the night,
Blowing open the petals of ten thousand pear-trees.
It enters the pearl blinds, it wets the silk curtains;
A fur coat feels cold, a cotton mat flimsy;
Bows become rigid, can hardly be drawn,
And the metal of armour congeals on the men;
The sand-sea deepens with fathomless ice,
And darkness masses its endless clouds;
But we drink to our guest bound home from camp,
And play him barbarian lutes, guitars, harps;
Till at dusk, when the drifts are crushing our tents,
And our frozen red flags cannot flutter in the wind.
We watch him through Wheel-Tower Gate going eastward.
Into the snow-mounds of Heaven-Peak Road.
And then he disappears at the turn of the pass,
Leaving behind him only hoof-prints.

譯文三

The White Snow Song; A Farewell to Wu P'an-kuan on His Return Home
（C. Gaunt 譯）
The north wind rolls the dust along, and snaps the grass sere.
Why do the snowflakes fill the sky in the eighth moon of this year?
It's just as on a night in spring sudden the wind doth wail,
Then from a myriad pear trees fly the blossoms scattered.
And through the pearly lattice dew the curtains of my bed.
The fox-fur coat, nor quilted vest, may mitigate the cold;
But no respite tends the bowmen who escort the chieftain bold,
Who despite the bitter frost are clad in coat of iron mail.
From mile on mile the ice-bound tracts hedge in the Gobi Plains,
And league on league the sad clouds lower, and frozen silence reigns.
Last night the bold lieutenant purchased wine to speed the guest,
And music rose from lute, guitar, and sweet flute of the west.

Outside the yamen gate the snow drifted confusedly,

And rigid in the biting wind the red flag stood on high.

Escorting you upon your way, to the Eastern Gate I rode,

And there I marked the mountain path was filled with drifting snow;

Full soon you disappeared as up the winding way you go,

And wistfully I lingered where the snow your horses trode.

六、《逢雪宿芙蓉山主人》

逢雪宿芙蓉山主人（劉長卿）
日暮蒼山遠，天寒白屋貧。
柴門聞犬吠，風雪夜歸人。

譯文一

A Winter Scene（W. J. B. Fletcher 譯）

The daylight far is dawning across the purple hill,

And white the houses of the poor with winter's breathing chill.

The house dog's sudden barking, which hears the wicket go,

Greets us at night returning through driving gale and snow.

譯文二

Encountering A Snowstorm, I Stay Withthe Recluse Of Mount Hibiscus
（Dell R. Hale, 譯）

Dark hills distant in the setting sun,

Thatched hut stark under wintry skies.

A dog barks at the brushwood gate,

As someone heads home this windy, snowy night.

譯文三

Putting Up At Thehibiscus Mountain On A Snowy Evening（劉軍平 譯）

The dark mountains lose themselves as dusk draws near,

In the coldness I see a thatched house for the poor.

Approaching the wooden gate I could hear a dog's bark,

It's me the traveler who arrives after the storm dark.

譯文四

Seeking Shelter In Lotus Hill On A Snowy Night（許淵沖 譯）

At sunset hillside village still seems far;
Cold and deserted the thatched cottages are.
At wicket gate a dog is heard to bark;
With wind and snowI come when night is dark.

譯文五

Snow-Retained Lodging in Mt. Hibiscus（Huang Long 譯）

The vesper bedims the remote grey hill,
Frigidity reigns over a shabby paintless domicile.
Outside the humble gate travels a barking sound,
From amidst the blizzard a soul's homebound.

七、《遊子吟》

遊子吟（孟郊）

慈母手中線，遊子身上衣。
臨行密密縫，意恐遲遲歸。
誰言寸草心，報得三春暉？

譯文一

The wandering Son's Song（Sun Dayu 譯）

The thread from my dear mother's hand,
Was sewn in the clothes of her wandering son.
For fear of my belated return,
Before my leave they were closely woven.
Who says mine heart like a blade of grass
Could repay her love's gentle beams of spring sun?

譯文二

A Traveller's Song (Witter Bynner 譯)

The thread in the hands of a fond-hearted mother,
Makes clothes for the body of her wayward boy;
Carefully she sews and thoroughly she mends,
Dreading the delays that will keep him late from home.
But how much love has the inch-long grass,
For three spring months of the light of the sun?

譯文三

The Song of the Wandering Son (W. J. B. Fletcher 譯)

In tender mother's hands the thread,
Made clothes to garb her paring son.
Before he left, how hard she spun,
How diligently wove; in dread.
Ere he return long years might run!
Such life-long mother's love how may
One simple little heart repay?

譯文四

Sung to the Air:「The Wanderer」(Amy Lowell 譯)

Thread from the hands of a doting mother,
Worked into the clothes of a far-off journeying son.
Before his departure, were the close, fine stitches set,
Lest haply his return be long delayed.
The heart, the inch-long grass,
Who will contend that either can repay,
The gentle brightness of the Third Month of Spring.

譯文五

Song of a Roamer (Xu Yuanchong 譯)

The threads in a kind mother's hand,
A gown for her son bound for far-off land.

Sewn stitch by stitch before he leaves,

For fear his return be delayed.

Such kindness as young grass receives,

From the warm sun can't be repaid.

八、《江雪》

江雪（柳宗元）
千山鳥飛絕，萬徑人蹤滅。
孤舟蓑笠翁，獨釣寒江雪。

譯文一

Snowing on the River (Sun Dayu 譯)

Not a bird over hundreds of peaks,

Not a man on the thousands of trails.

An old angler alone in a boat,

With his rod and line, in raining outfit,

Is fishing on the river midst the snowdrift.

譯文二

Fishing in Snow (Xu Yuanchong 譯)

From hill to hill no bird in flight,

From path to path no man in sight.

A straw-cloak'd man afloat, behold!

Is fishing snow on river cold.

譯文三

River Snow (Burton Watson 譯)

From a thousand hills, bird flights have vanished,

On ten thousand paths, human traces wiped out.

Lone boat, an old in straw cape and hat,

Fishing alone in the cold river snow.

譯文四

River Snow (Wai-Lim Yip 譯)

A thousand mountains—no bird's flight.
A million paths—no man's trace.
Single boat. Bamboo-leaved cape. An old man
Fishing by himself: ice-river Snow.

譯文五

River Snow (Gary Snyder 譯)

These thousand peaks cut off the flights of birds,
On all the trails, human tracks are gone.
A single boat—coat—hat—an old man!
Alone fishing chill river snow.

譯文六

River-snow (Witter Bynner 譯)

A hundred mountains and no bird,
A thousand paths without a footprint;
A little boat, a bamboo cloak,
An old man fishing in the cold river-snow.

譯文七

River Snow (Kenneth Rexroth 譯)

A thousand mountains without a bird.
Ten thousand miles with no trace of man.
A boat. An old man in a straw raincoat,
Alone in the snow, fishing in the freezing river.

參考文獻

英文參考文獻

[1] Ivan Morris. Madly Singing in the Mountains: An Appreciation and Anthology of Arthur Waley [M]. London: George Allen &Un Win Ltd, 1970.

[2] Bassnett S, Lefevere A CEDs. Translation, History and Culture: a Source Book [M]. London: Routledge, 1992: 26.

[3] Chan T, Fung E, Cody M, et al. Review: The Selected Poems of Du Fu [J]. Asian Studies Review. September 2004, 28 (3): 313-344.

[4] David Hawkes. Review: Cold Mountain: 100 Poems by the T'ang poet Han-shan by Burton Watson; Han-shan [J]. Journal of the American Oriental Society, 82 (4): 596-599.

[5] Edwin Gentzler. Contemporary Translation Theories [M]. Shanghai: Shanghai Foreign Language Education Press, 2004.

[6] Eugene A Nida, Charles R Taber. The Theory and Practice of Translation [M]. Shanghai: Shanghai Foreign Language Education Press, 2004.

[7] Jeremy Munday. Introducing Translation Studies [M]. Routledge: London and New York, 2001. 146.

[8] Gramham A C. Poems of the Late Tang [M]. Middlesex: Penguin Book, 1965.

[9] Nord, Christiane. Translation as a Purposeful Activity: Functional Approaches Explained [M]. Shanghai: Shanghai Foreign Language Education Press, 2001.

[10] Shuttleworth Mark, Moira Cowie. Dictionary of Translation Studies [M]. Shanghai: Shanghai Foreign Language Education Press, 2004: 43.

［11］Venuti, Lawrence. The Translator's Invisibility：A History of Translation［M］. London：Routledge, 2004.

［12］Vincent Y C Shih. Review：Cold Mountain［J］. The Journal of Asian Studies, 1963, 22（4）：475-476.

［13］Robison, Douglas. The Translation's Turn［M］. Baltimore：The John's Hopkins University Press, 1991.

［14］Watson, Burton. Cold Mountain：100 Poems by the T'ang Poet Han-shan［M］. New York：Columbia University Press, 1962.

［15］Watson, Burton. Po Chu-i：Selected Poems［M］. New York：Columbia University Press, 2000.

中文參考文獻

［1］阿成, 楊憲益, 戴乃迭. 唐詩［M］. 北京：外文出版社, 2003：275.

［2］包惠南. 文化語境與語言翻譯［M］. 北京：中國對外翻譯出版公司, 2001.

［3］曹陽. 關聯理論與王維禪詩英譯［D］. 石家莊：河北師範大學, 2006.

［4］常敬宇. 漢語詞彙與文化［M］. 北京：北京大學出版社, 1995.

［5］陳大亮. 誰是翻譯的主體［J］. 中國翻譯, 2004, 25（2）：3-4.

［6］陳福康. 中國譯學理論史稿［M］. 上海：上海外語出版社, 2000.

［7］陳靜. 唐宋詩詞中典故英譯研究［D］. 杭州：浙江工業大學, 2010.

［8］程盡能, 呂和發. 旅遊翻譯理論與實務［M］. 北京：清華大學出版社, 2008,（6）：19.

［9］陳聖白. 國內生態翻譯學十年發展的文獻計量分析研究［J］. 河北聯合大學學報, 2014（3）：140-143.

［10］陳子善. 碩果僅存的「新月」詩人孫大雨［M］//孫近仕. 孫大雨詩文集. 石家莊：河北教育出版社, 1996.

［11］遲明彩. 功能派翻譯理論概述［J］. 黑龍江教育學院學報, 2010,（3）：2.

［12］鄧炎昌, 劉潤清. 語言與文化——英漢語言文化對比［M］. 北京：外語教學與研究出版社, 1989：9-10.

［13］段政絲. 本雅明翻譯理論下的中國古典禪意詩英譯研究——以王維

禪意詩為例 [D]. 西安：西北大學, 2014.

[14] 方夢之. 翻譯新論與實踐 [M]. 青島：青島出版社, 2002：34.

[15] 付天爵. 以目的論為視角分析電影字幕的英譯漢策略 [J]. 長治學院學報, 2009 (6)：51.

[16] 傅曉玲, 尚媛媛. 英漢互譯高級教程 [M]. 廣州：中山大學出版社, 2005：34

[17] 高智. 六朝隱逸詩研究 [D]. 上海：上海師範大學, 2013.

[18] 顧延齡. 唐詩英譯的「三美」標準——兼評漢英對照唐詩一百五十首 [J]. 中國翻譯, 1987, (6).

[19] 顧正陽. 古詩詞曲英譯美學研究 [M]. 上海：上海大學出版社, 2006.

[20] 郭建中. 翻譯中的文化因素：歸化與異化 [J]. 外國語, 1998 (2).

[21] 郭建忠. 文化與翻譯 [M]. 北京：中國對外翻譯出版公司, 2000.

[22] 郭建中. 翻譯中的文化因素：異化與歸化 [M] //郭建中. 文化與翻譯. 北京：中國對外翻譯出版公司, 2000：285-296.

[23] 郭善芳. 典故的認知模式 [J]. 貴州大學學報, 2015 (3)：139.

[24] 郭湛. 主體性哲學：人的存在及其意義 [M]. 昆明：雲南人民出版社, 2002.

[25] 何宇茵. 基於美國當代英語語料庫的中國文化詞彙研究 [J]. 山東外語教學. 2010 (1)：7-11.

[26] 賀茉莉. 從關聯理論看電影字幕的翻譯 [J]. 中國校外教育, 2009 (10).

[27] 蘅塘退士. 唐詩三百首 [M]. 北京：中華書局, 1959：257.

[28] 胡安江. 美國學者伯頓·華生的寒山詩英譯本研究 [J]. 解放軍外國語學院學報, 2009 (6)：75-80.

[29] 胡庚申. 生態翻譯學：建構與詮釋 [M]. 北京：商務印書館, 2013.

[30] 胡庚坤. 生態翻譯學的「異」與「新」 [J]. 中國外語, 2014 (5).

[31] 胡庚申. 翻譯適應選擇論 [M]. 武漢：湖北教育出版社, 2004.

[32] 胡庚申. 生態翻譯學解讀 [J]. 中國翻譯, 2008 (6).

[33] 胡庚申. 生態翻譯學：生態理性特徵及其對翻譯研究的啟示 [J]. 中國外語, 2011 (6)：96-109.

[34] 胡庚申. 傅雷翻譯思想的生態翻譯學詮釋 [J]. 外國語, 2009 (2).

[35] 胡筱穎. 從目的論看唐詩英譯——以《月下獨酌》為例 [J]. 西南民族大學學報 (人文社會科學版), 2011 (11).

[36] 胡衛平. 高級翻譯 [M]. 上海：華東師範大學出版社, 2011.

[37] 華滿元, 華先發. 漢詩英譯名篇選讀 [M]. 武漢：武漢大學出版社, 2014.

[38] 華茲生. 杜甫詩選 [M]. 長沙：湖南人民出版社, 2009.

[39] 黃國文. 翻譯研究的語言學探索：古詩詞英譯本的語言學分析 [M]. 上海：上海外語教育出版社, 2006.

[40] 黃瓊英. 魯迅《自題小像》中典故英譯的關聯理論評析 [J]. 山東外語教學, 2006,（2）：7-11.

[41] 霍劍波. 隱逸詩研究 [D]. 西安：陝西師範大學, 2005.

[42] 賈文波. 應用翻譯功能論 [M]. 北京：中國對外出版公司, 2004.

[43] 江嵐. 唐詩西傳史論——以唐詩在英美的傳播為中心 [M]. 北京：學苑出版社, 2013.

[44] 姜倩, 何剛強. 翻譯概論 [M]. 上海：上海外語教育出版社, 2008.

[45] 蔣洪新, 尹飛舟. 伯頓華茲生的《韓非子》英譯本漫談 [J]. 外語與外語教學, 1998（6）：46-47.

[46] 蔣紹愚. 唐詩語言研究 [M]. 鄭州：中州古籍出版社, 1990.

[47] 蔣驍華, 宋志平. 生態翻譯學理論的新探討 [J]. 上海翻譯, 2011（4）.

[48] 蔣驍華, 宋志平, 孟凡君. 生態翻譯學理論的新探索——首屆國際生態翻譯學研討會綜述 [J]. 中國翻譯, 2011（1）：34-36.

[49] 金秀敏. 王維山水詩：禪文化解讀及其翻譯 [J]. 上海工程技術大學教育研究, 2006,（4）.

[50] 孔莎. 從中國英語音譯詞論漢語文化負載詞的英譯策略 [J]. 四川理工學院學報, 2012（3）：73-75.

[51] 李箭. 典故的文化翻譯策略 [J]. 鹽城師範學院學報（人文社會科學版）, 2008, 28（4）：93-97.

[52] 李淼. 唐詩三百首譯析 [M]. 長春：吉林文史出版社出版, 2005.

[53] 李明. 從主體間性理論看文學作品的復譯 [J]. 外國語. 2006, 166（4）：68.

[54] 李明. 翻譯批評與賞析 [M]. 武昌：武漢大學出版社, 2006.

[55] 廖七一. 當代西方翻譯理論探索 [M]. 南京：譯林出版社, 2002.

[56] 劉愛華. 徐遲：絕頂靈芝、空谷幽蘭——生態翻譯學視角下的翻譯家研究 [J]. 中國外語, 2011（4）.

[57] 劉宓慶. 文體與翻譯 [M]. 北京：中國對外翻譯出版公司, 1998.

[58] 劉宓慶. 文化的翻譯論綱 [M]. 北京：中國對外翻譯出版公司, 2006.

[59] 劉宓慶. 新編英漢對比與翻譯 [M]. 北京：中國對外翻譯出版公司, 2006.

[60] 劉季春. 實用翻譯教程 [M]. 廣州：中山大學出版社, 1996.

[61] 劉利艾. 從目的論析電影字幕的翻譯 [J]. 安徽文學, 2008 (12).

[62] 龍清濤. 簡論孫大雨的「音組」——對新詩格律史上一個重要概念的辨析 [J]. 中國現代文學研究叢刊, 2009 (1).

[63] 劉雲虹, 許鈞. 一部具有探索精神的譯學新著——《翻譯適應選擇論》評析 [J]. 中國翻譯, 2004 (6)：40-43.

[64] 魯迅. 漢文學史綱要 [M]. 北京：人民文學出版社, 1976：3.

[65] 羅新璋. 翻譯論集 [M]. 北京：商務印書館, 1984.

[66] 周儀, 羅平. 翻譯與批評 [M]. 武漢：湖北教育出版社, 1999.

[67] 呂瑞昌, 喻雲根, 張復星, 等. 漢英翻譯教程 [M]. 西安：陝西人民出版社, 2001：138-143.

[68] 呂叔湘. 英譯唐人絕句百首 [M]. 長沙：湖南人民出版社, 1980.

[69] 呂叔湘. 中詩英譯比錄 [M]. 北京：中華書局, 2002.

[70] 馬紅軍. 從文學翻譯到翻譯文學 [M]. 上海：上海譯文出版社, 2006：126.

[71] 馬會娟, 苗菊. 當代西方翻譯理論選讀 [M]. 北京：外語教學與研究出版社, 2009.

[72] 毛發奮. 漢語古詩英譯比讀與研究 [M]. 上海：上海社會科學出版社, 2007：81.

[73] 冒國安. 實用英漢對比教程 [M]. 重慶：重慶大學出版社, 2005.

[74] 聶廣橋. 論寒山子與白居易「禪詩」的差異 [J]. 山東社會科學, 2015, (1).

[75] 錢書華. 從《長干行》的英譯談中國古詩翻譯 [J]. 徐州師範大學學報, 1998 (4).

[76] 秦小紅. 模糊理論與翻譯的模糊對等：以王維《鳥鳴澗》三個譯本為例 [J]. 西安科技大學學報（社會科學版）, 2013, (2).

[77] 沈松勤, 胡可先, 陶然. 唐詩研究 [M]. 杭州：浙江大學出版社, 2006.

[78] 宋錦波. 從目的論視角看菜單翻譯 [D]. 金華：浙江師範大學，2009：11.

[79] 孫大雨. 我與詩人朱湘 [M]. 孫近仁. 孫大雨詩文集. 石家莊：河北教育出版社，1996.

[80] 孫大雨. 古詩文英譯集 [M]. 上海：上海外語教育出版社，1997.

[81] 孫欽善. 高適集校註 [M]. 北京：中華書局，1981.

[82] 譚載喜. 翻譯學 [M]. 武漢：湖北教育出版社，2005.

[83] 譚載喜. 西方翻譯簡史 [M]. 北京：商務印書館，2004.

[84] 唐一鶴. 英譯唐詩三百首 [M]. 天津：天津人民出版社出版，2005：130-131.

[85] 王宏. 生態翻譯學核心理念考辨 [J]. 上海翻譯，2011（4）：10-11.

[86] 王軍. 漢語典故英譯的異化處理 [J]. 廣州大學學報（社會科學版），2005，4（7）：42-44.

[87] 王明居. 唐詩風格論 [M]. 合肥：安徽大學出版社，2001.

[88] 王明樹.「主觀化對等」對原語文本理解和翻譯的制約 [D]. 重慶：西南大學，2010.

[89] 王寧. 全球化時代的文化研究和翻譯研究 [J]. 中國翻譯，2000，(1).

[90] 王寧. 文化翻譯與經典闡釋 [M]. 北京：中華書局，2006.

[91] 汪榕培. 英語詞彙學研究 [M]. 上海：上海外語教育出版社，2000.

[92] 魏家海. 譯畫入詩、譯禪入詩和譯典入詩：宇文所安的英譯王維詩的翻譯詩學 [J]. 中譯外研究，2014，(2).

[93] 翁顯良. 本色與變相：漢詩英譯瑣議之三 [M]. 北京：中國對外翻譯出版公司，1983.

[94] 翁顯良. 古詩選譯 [J]. 現代外語，1981.

[95] 翁顯良. 譯詩管見 [J]. China Academic Journal Electronic Publishing House，2016.

[96] 翁顯良. 意象與聲律：談詩歌翻譯 [J]. China Academic Journal Electronic Publishing House，2016.

[97] 翁顯良. 自由與不自由：試譯稼軒詞十首附言 [M]. 北京：中國對外翻譯出版公司，1983.

[98] 翁顯良. 本色與變相——漢詩英譯瑣議之三 [J]. 外國語，1982 (1).

[99] 武恩義. 英漢典故對比研究 [D]. 北京：中央民族大學，2005：75.

[100] 吳鈞陶. 唐詩三百首 [M]. 長沙：湖南出版社出版，1997.

[101] 夏芳莉. 從目的論角度談中式菜名的英譯 [D]. 青島：中國海洋大學，2008：23.

[102] 夏徵農，陳至立. 辭海 [M]. 上海：上海辭書出版社，2009.

[103] 謝卓杰，肖乙華. 談李白《清平調》三章詩的英譯 [J]. 湖南大學學報，1991（6）：98-105.

[104] 徐振忠. 林健民和他的中國古詩英譯藝術 [J]. 泉州：黎明職業大學學報，2003，(4).

[105] 徐守勤，徐守平. 浪漫中華古詩英譯賞析 [M]. 合肥：安徽科學技術出版社，2006.

[106] 徐宜華，廖志勤. 從王維《鹿柴》三個英譯文本看翻譯審美再現 [J]. 西南科技大學學報（哲學社會科學版），2014，(4).

[107] 許均. 文學翻譯的理論與實踐——翻譯對話錄 [M]. 南京：譯林出版社，2001.

[108] 許鈞. 當代英國翻譯理論 [M]. 武漢：湖北教育出版社，2004.

[109] 許鈞. 當代美國翻譯理論 [M]. 武漢：湖北教育出版社，2002.

[110] 許曉晴. 中古隱逸詩研究 [D]. 上海：復旦大學，2005.

[111] 許淵衝. 翻譯的藝術 [M]. 北京：中國對外翻譯出版公司，1984.

[112] 許淵衝，等. 唐詩三百首新譯 [M]. 北京：中國對外翻譯出版社，1997.

[113] 許淵衝. 唐詩三百首 [M]. 北京：高等教育出版社，2000.

[114] 許淵衝. 文學與翻譯 [M]. 北京：北京大學出版社，2005.

[115] 許淵衝. 唐詩三百首（中英文對照）[M]. 北京：中國對外翻譯出版公司，2007.

[116] 許淵衝. 譯筆生花 [M]. 鄭州：文心出版社，2005.

[117] 許淵衝. 翻譯的藝術 [M]. 北京：五洲傳播出版社，2006.

[118] 許淵衝. 中詩英韻探勝——從《詩經》到《西廂記》[M]. 北京：北京大學出版社，1992

[119] 許淵衝. 漢英對照唐詩一百五十首 [M]. 西安：陝西人民出版社，1984.

[120] 薛宗正. 歷代西陲邊塞詩研究 [M]. 蘭州：敦煌文藝出版社，1993：70.

[121] 楊德峰. 漢語與文化交際 [M]. 北京：北京大學出版社，1999：135.

[122] 晏小花，劉祥清. 漢英翻譯的文化空缺及其翻譯對策［J］. 中國科技翻譯，2002（1）.

[123] 徐國良，文炳. 關於異化翻譯的再思考［J］. 外語學刊，2009.

[124] 於春媚. 道家思想與魏晉文學［D］. 北京：首都師範大學，2008.

[125] 張傳彪. 詩筆·譯筆·鈍筆：英漢語翻譯與比較縱談［M］. 北京：國防工業出版社，2005：39-40.

[126] 張春柏. 英漢漢英翻譯教程［M］. 北京：高等教育出版社，2003.

[127] 張建民. 意境為上——從認知能力、價值取向分析一首漢詩的英譯［J］. 美中外語，2004（3）.

[128] 張今，張寧. 文學翻譯原理［M］北京：清華大學出版社，2005：232-233.

[129] 張麗麗. 生態翻譯學視域中的歇後語翻譯［J］. 外語學刊，2014（3）：102-105.

[130] 張梅. 唐詩直譯加註釋的策略分析［J］. 人文雜志，2012（7）.

[131] 張南峰，陳德鴻. 西方翻譯理論精選［M］. 香港：香港城市大學出版社，2000.

[132] 張廷琛，魏博思. 唐詩一百首：漢英對照［M］. 中國對外翻譯，2007.

[133] 張英萍. 談中文人名典故英譯的異化與歸化原則［J］. 咸寧學院學報，2007，27（1）：94-95.

[134] 張智中. 許淵衝與翻譯藝術［M］. 武漢：湖北教育出版社，2006.

[135] 趙彥春. 翻譯學歸結論［M］. 上海：上海外語教育出版社，2005：98.

[136] 鄭在瀛. 李商隱詩集今註［M］. 武漢：武漢大學出版社，2001.

[137] 周儀，羅平. 翻譯與批評［M］. 武漢：湖北教育出版社，1999.

[138] 周銀鳳. 東晉隱逸詩研究［D］. 上海：上海師範大學，2007.

[139] 朱徽. 唐詩在美國的翻譯與接受［J］. 四川大學學報，2004（4）.

[140] 朱徽. 中國詩歌在英語世界［M］. 上海：上海外語教育出版社，2009.

[141] 朱健平. 翻譯：跨文化解釋——哲學詮釋學與接受美學模式［M］. 長沙：湖南人民出版社，2007.

[142] 朱立元. 接受美學導論［M］. 合肥：安徽教育出版社，2004.

網絡參考連結

[1] https://www.douban.com/note/562206047/

[2] https://baike.baidu.com/item/高適/15618

[3] https://baike.baidu.com/item/李白/1043

[4] http://blog.sina.com.cn/s/blog_86235a600101cwbr.html

[5] https://wenku.baidu.com/view/a1fb293eaeaad1f346933ffd.html

[6] http://blog.sina.com.cn/s/blog_1534238f70102woqm.html

[7] https://www.wenjiwu.com/doc/eackni.html

[8] http://blog.sina.com.cn/s/blog_1534238f70102xtah.html

[9] http://blog.sciencenet.cn/blog-300826-559691.html

[10] http://blog.sina.com.cn/s/blog_1534238f70102wpe5.html

[11] http://blog.sina.com.cn/s/blog_1534238f70102xozy.html

[12] http://blog.sina.com.cn/s/blog_8f5f12730100xgfx.html

[13] http://www.putclub.com/html/ability/Chiliterature/20121226/63480.html

[14] http://blog.sina.com.cn/s/blog_4aa74b37010005fd.html

[15] http://www.zihua01.com/article/show-1904.aspx

[16] http://baike.baidu.com/link?url=C_6NBJcuBjC83Yq-1qA7vOFmX_WH85O2HaibcoN0xs4u_QwJO_cvMu9gOU4FWCcFgmKOR-mG0biTEuXQiR3qF_

[17] http://www.24en.com/column/zhaoyanchun/2012-06-14/144439.html

[18] http://baike.baidu.com/link?url=j74BhJ8Co2kMylLGR6eDzb4wuQ_Krpcq4utUD3UsDQQk3EeS38HD1_6ikuObkwgZ

[19] http://baike.soso.com/h5622859.htm?sp=l5622860

[20] http://www.douban.com/group/topic/3671960/

[21] http://blog.sina.com.cn/s/blog_721fbb990102w6pb.html

後記

　　自 2007 年碩士生畢業參加工作以來，筆者一直在從事大學英語教學與翻譯研究方面的工作。這 10 年來，筆者一直在思考如何提高大學生的翻譯水準，大學英語教師應該如何激發學生學習本課程的興趣，從而改變學生學習熱情不高的情況。在工作之餘，筆者將自己的點滴經驗和思考寫成論文，試著去解決大學英語教學中面臨的問題，為同行提供相關參考和借鑑。因此，這 10 年來，筆者斷斷續續地在一些學術期刊上發表了一些論文，累積了一些研究成果，但回想起來，總感覺到有些意猶未盡，研究成果的條理性和系統性還需提高。因此，筆者決定寫作一部專著，將自己前期取得的成果以及最近的一些思考重新加以整理，使其系統化。本書就是這一勞動成果的結晶。

　　由於筆者教學工作繁重，家裡還有老人和孩子需要照顧，所以本書能夠付諸出版實屬不易。此時，最想說的就是感謝。首先，感謝我的父母、老公和兒子，謝謝你們的支持、鼓勵和陪伴。尤其是我的老公，他一直在鼓勵和鞭策我完成本書的寫作。如果沒有他的及時提醒和鼓勵，估計難以完成本書的初稿。其次，感謝學校領導、學院領導和同事們給予我的幫助。你們的鼓勵和支持給我增添了極大的動力。

國家圖書館出版品預行編目（CIP）資料

唐詩英譯研究 / 趙娟 編著. -- 第一版.
-- 臺北市：崧博出版：崧燁文化發行, 2019.05
　　面；　公分
POD版

ISBN 978-957-735-828-8(平裝)

1.英語 2.翻譯 3.唐詩

805.1　　　　　　　　　　　　　　108006276

書　　名：唐詩英譯研究
作　　者：趙娟 編著
發 行 人：黃振庭
出 版 者：崧博出版事業有限公司
發 行 者：崧燁文化事業有限公司
E - m a i l：sonbookservice@gmail.com
粉絲頁：　　　　　網址：
地　　址：台北市中正區重慶南路一段六十一號八樓 815 室
8F.-815, No.61, Sec. 1, Chongqing S. Rd., Zhongzheng Dist., Taipei City 100, Taiwan (R.O.C.)
電　　話：(02)2370-3310 傳　真：(02) 2370-3210
總 經 銷：紅螞蟻圖書有限公司
地　　址：台北市內湖區舊宗路二段 121 巷 19 號
電　　話:02-2795-3656 傳真:02-2795-4100　　網址：
印　　刷：京峯彩色印刷有限公司（京峰數位）

本書版權為西南財經大學出版社所有授權崧博出版事業股份有限公司獨家發行電子書及繁體書繁體字版。若有其他相關權利及授權需求請與本公司聯繫。

定　　價：350 元
發行日期：2019 年 05 月第一版
◎ 本書以 POD 印製發行